PRAISE FOR
OUR LOVE WILL DEVOUR US

"A terrifying, twisted roller coaster of a book. From the first page to the last, R. L. Meza's gripping debut novel affirms a rising star in horror."

—Noelle W. Ihli, author of *Ask for Andrea*

"Genuinely terrifying, Meza's isolated world pulls you in and keeps you turning pages. *Our Love Will Devour Us* is a stunning exploration of family, trauma, and sacrifice. It left a scar on my heart that'll never vanish."

—Steph Nelson, author of *The Vein*

"R.L. Meza tells a heart-wrenching (and stomach-wrenching) drama of family, monsters, and the depths we trawl for our loved ones, both past and present. *Our Love Will Devour Us* asks the reader one simple question: Is love always enough?"

—Drew Huff, author of *Free Burn*

OUR LOVE WILL DEVOUR US

Copy edited by Marissa van Uden
Book Design and Layout by Rob Carroll
Cover Design by Rob Carroll

ISBN 978-1-958598-17-7 (paperback)
ISBN 978-1-958598-32-0 (ebook)
ISBN 978-1-958598-33-1 (audiobook)

darkmatter-ink.com

First Dark Matter INK paperback edition May 2023.

Copy Edited by Marissa van Uden
Book Design and Layout by Rob Carroll
Cover Design by Rob Carroll

ISBN 978-1-958598-17-7 (paperback)
ISBN 978-1-958598-32-0 (eBook)
ISBN 978-1-958598-35-1 (audiobook)

darkmatter-ink.com

Our Love Will Devour Us

R. L. Meza

DARK MATTER INK

OUR LOVE
WILL DEVOUR US

R. L. MEZA

For Dre, my light in the dark.

DEBORAH

IT WAS BACK again, the only tree on her land that wouldn't put down roots. Deborah sat forward in her rocking chair, pen scratching in her journal, eyes fixed on the section of forest framed by her bedroom window. Beyond the white expanse of snow blanketing the clearing, a looming wall of red pines hemmed the cabin in, swaying as the wind howled through the trees. When the wind lapsed, the trees fell still.

All but one.

Deborah's pen moved lower on the page, sketching the tree's new position. She didn't own a camera, had never bothered to buy another after her daughter ran away from home, taking Henry's Nikon with her. It was probably gathering dust in a pawnshop somewhere—a disgrace to her husband's memory. With an arthritic fist, Deborah clutched the musty quilt draped over her shoulders, pulling it tighter to stave off the shivering fit that always arose when she thought of Henry. Her other hand continued sketching, clamped around the pen despite the pain in her gnarled joints. The scritch-scratching reminded her of something trying to get out.

Or in.

Someone was whispering her name. Deborah cocked her head, listening as the wind whistled through the cracks in the logs. Cold air nibbled at her ankles. Closing her eyes, she muttered a prayer under her breath. When she returned her gaze to the window, the tree was closer—in the clearing now.

Standing alone.

Deborah documented the changes, scowling. The record was for her, to aid her failing mind. She had nothing to prove, not to her nosy neighbor, Evelyn, and certainly not to the doctor Evelyn had dragged out to examine her. Armed with a prescription pad, the hack had poked and prodded Deborah with his frigid stethoscope, tutting about the dangers of living off the grid at her age. He'd smiled as he spoke—not to Deborah but to Evelyn—about advanced stages and care homes.

But Deborah had lived alone for decades. She didn't need the doctor's advice or his medication. She had her faith. God would protect her, show her the way. And if God saw fit to lead Deborah into the forest, to wake her in the small hours of the night with the icy waters of the stream flowing past her knees, that was God's business. Who was she to question His plan? The pills only dulled her senses, closing Deborah's ears to His message. Her mind was sharper without the doctor's prescription.

Without the pills, Deborah noticed things.

Like the tree.

She squinted through the frosted windowpane. The tree was a pale, blurry brushstroke, barely distinguishable from the snowy backdrop of the clearing. When she blinked, it shuddered like a mirage, leaping closer.

Deborah flipped to the next page. Her hand was cramping, unable to keep up. The tree was moving faster than usual. Like it was desperate to close the distance between them.

Eager to reach her.

The intensity of her focus wavered as fatigue took hold, tugging her eyelids down like window shades. The pen's scratching slowed. Her head bobbed, then sank.

And then the well opened up below, a hungry black mouth swallowing her alive and whole, and she was plummeting down, down, down—

The pen struck the floorboards and Deborah woke, gasping. Anxiety squeezed a clammy fist around her chest. She clawed at the rocking chair's armrests, spilling the journal from her lap. Inhaling shaky breaths, she stared up at the knots in the ceiling and waited for her racing pulse to slow, to resume its thready limping.

She couldn't recall the last time she'd managed to drift off at a reasonable hour. Every night, the insomnia moved her bedtime back further, withholding rest, until she gave up, resigned to waiting for dawn.

On the nights when she did sleep, Henry always woke her.

Deborah rose unsteadily, shaking her head. A cup of tea would calm her nerves. Grimacing as her hips creaked out their usual complaints, she retrieved the journal from the floor. She stood up, laid the pen across the journal's leather cover, and patted it, as if to reassure it—and the tree standing just outside her window—that she would return.

Not bothering with the lights, Deborah made her way into the kitchen. Fifty-three years she'd lived in the cabin; she could navigate it blind.

The floorboards were quiet underfoot, not squeaking and cracking like she was accustomed to. She sighed. She was losing too much weight. She was never hungry, and so she forgot to eat. The groceries from Evelyn's weekly deliveries sat untouched, moldering, until the smell prompted Deborah to dispose of everything. But she was an adult. If she was hungry, she would remember to eat. And if she sometimes forgot? Well, then that was a problem with her appetite, not her memory.

Deborah returned to the bedroom with her cup of tea, switched on the bedside lamp, and glared at the pen lying on the floor—the pen she'd placed atop the journal. She was sure.

Although…things had been moving around on her as of late. Only yesterday, she'd found her slippers out past the stream. Her glasses strayed from room to room, hourly. And she kept losing teeth. But she no longer wasted time searching. It was a small cabin. Her missing items always turned up—in the shower, the freezer, the basement—eventually.

The leather strap was another matter. On the night after Henry's death, and every night since, Deborah had found it laid across her pillow. She could never say how it got there, or when. The leather was worn smooth from use. The initials *FJT* engraved on the handle did not belong to Henry or to any member of their combined families.

But years of trials and tribulations had taught Deborah to recognize the strap as a tool, a gift from the Lord. And so, she had used it, as He instructed, in the battle for her daughter's soul. After *she*—Deborah wouldn't speak, wouldn't even *think* her daughter's name—had succumbed to the temptations of the Devil, the strap had become an unbearable reminder of Deborah's failure. It was the punishment she deserved for believing her daughter's lies. For letting her out of the basement, to run off into the night.

Deborah glanced over her shoulder. The strap had been moved from under the bed back onto her pillow.

As she stooped, groping for the pen, Deborah's eyes drifted up to the window. Startled, she cried out. Hot tea sloshed over the rim of the cup, scalding her hand.

Something stared back at her through the glass. Eyes flashed like green mirrors, reflecting the light from the lamp. A pale flutter of movement tapped against the pane—too solid to be snow, too thin to be human.

Cowering, Deborah shielded her eyes with a quaking hand. When she finally mustered the courage to peek between her fingers, it was only the tree outside. Standing close enough for Deborah to make out the network of faint blue veins running beneath its smooth, skin-like bark.

November exhaled, breathing winter into the cabin. Skeletal branches scritched across the window, a sound not unlike the scratching of Deborah's pen. A patch of fog expanded across the glass.

Deborah frowned. She wiped the glass with her fingertips, but no lines appeared in the fog. It was on the other side of the pane. The cloud diminished, shrinking.

And then a new cloud appeared, near the top of the frame. As if whatever was breathing on the window had grown weary of crouching to peek inside. Deborah shuddered. She yanked the curtains closed. She would not worry about the thing outside the window, the tree that looked less like a tree with each passing night.

She returned the pen to her journal, slapped it hard against the cover. She placed both inside the cookie tin on her nightstand and secured the lid, so they would not wander off.

She sipped her tea, made a face, and spit the tepid liquid back into her cup. A clinking sound gave her pause. Deborah dipped a finger into the tea and fished a tooth out. She added it to the cookie tin with the others, then wiggled the few remaining teeth in her gums, pondering as she probed the empty sockets between with her tongue.

No, she would not worry or call the doctor.

She would pray.

Deborah knelt before her bed. Hands clasped, she bowed her head and prayed for God to reveal his plan.

When her devotion was proven, Deborah rose from her aching knees and climbed into bed.

Listening to the squeal of branches on glass, she waited for Henry to come.

HE NEVER SPOKE, not when he was in her room. Not when he was seated at the foot of her bed. Not when he was crawling up over her, springs squeaking as his weight folded the mattress in two, with Deborah cradled at the center—wide awake, unable to move.

He did not utter a sound. Not when he was perched on her chest, crushing the air from her lungs, a sensation like drowning, but colder. Heavier.

Like an avalanche, burying her alive.

"Henry," she croaked. "You're hurting me."

But Henry said nothing. Green fire flashed in his lidless eyes, writhing like the aurora borealis in a starless sky. Licking outwards to illuminate gaunt cheekbones, the exposed hollows of his nasal cavity, the gaping, yawning, drooling mouth that was not Henry's, couldn't be.

"You're dead," Deborah whispered, expending the last of her breath. As if it would make a difference, reminding her husband that she'd already laid him to rest—more than thirty years prior—over a hundred miles away from where he now crouched.

Owl-like, Henry tilted his head. His ear ticked past his shoulder, his collarbone, vertebrae popping as his chin took the place of his forehead.

And yet, Henry's inverted grin said, lips peeling back from teeth like porcupine quills.

And yet, and yet...

Here I am.

Most nights, Deborah waited for the paralysis to subside. Once she was certain Henry was gone, she would creep from her bed to close and lock the front door, though Henry never needed a key to get in. When the door was locked, she would fall to the floor and pray until the light of dawn pushed the shadows back into the corners.

Waiting for the next visit, and the one after that.

Over time, Deborah had begun to doubt. She wondered whether God had abandoned her. For hours, she prayed but the Lord, like Henry, never spoke aloud. The silence was deafening.

She had never felt so alone.

But on this night, Henry took Deborah's paralysis with him. As he lumbered down the hall, she collected the tin from her nightstand and padded barefoot after him. Fumbling with her necklace, Deborah pinched the gold crucifix between her fingers. The tiny nub of her crucified savior bit into the pad of her thumb. She was awake.

This was real, not another nightmare.

And she was so very tired of waiting.

At the front door, Henry turned—a pale, twisted tree filling the frame. He crooked a finger, beckoning for her to follow.

And so she did.

Wearing only her nightgown, Deborah cradled the tin against her chest and followed Henry out into the cold. A single trail of footprints marked their passage through the snow.

Looking back, Deborah smiled.

It seemed the Lord was carrying her after all.

CLAIRE

IF THE DOOR was locked, she would leave.

Claire approached the cabin at a slant, flexing her hands to release the nervous energy building in her chest. The cabin seemed smaller somehow, as if the harsh Minnesota winters had whittled it down in her absence. The squat structure with its slanted roof and weathered shingles appeared almost harmless now—hardly the fearsome trap she had escaped from as a teenager.

Without her mother, the cabin was little more than a box of logs waiting to be emptied and sold. Claire breathed out, hard, and climbed the four steps to the porch in a rush—

My.

Mother.

Is.

Gone.

—gripped the knob and turned.

It was locked.

Claire put her back to the door and slid into a crouch. Her dark hair fell in a wavy curtain to cover her face. Tears spilled down her cheeks. The warmth of home had never felt so far away.

She'd lied to herself: the door was locked, but she couldn't leave.

The gallery was failing; she hadn't finished a painting in two years. Emma was working extra shifts at the hospital to support their family of four. On the rare nights when their schedules collided, they avoided each other. When they did speak, they fought.

Sighing, Claire leaned her head back. The oppressive silence of the forest was just as she recalled. No cheerful bird song to distract from the shadows creeping into her mind to darken her thoughts. Nothing but the sound of the wind blowing through the trees, the cold promise of bad memories seeking her out. She almost wished she'd relented and let Emma come along, if only so she wouldn't have to face her childhood trauma alone. But then she remembered the promises she'd made at their last appointment with the marriage counselor—to quit drinking, open up about her feelings, share her past—and she was grateful Emma wouldn't be there to supervise. Prying with questions. Watching, waiting for her to backslide.

Claire rose, determined. She had come here with a purpose: Selling the cabin would help alleviate their financial stress. Once the past was behind her, she would share a few stories with Emma—the ones with their teeth pulled by time—to satisfy her wife's need to understand.

More importantly, she would sober up here in isolation, where her family wouldn't be punished by the symptoms of her withdrawal.

She brushed at her eyes and checked the time. Their neighbor Evelyn was due to arrive with the keys at noon. Anxiety tightened its hold. Claire stamped her feet, trying to chase the blood flow back to her frozen toes. She was forty-one-years old—not the frightened, shrinking girl who had fled from her mother's cabin twenty-five years before but a grown woman with children of her own.

She could do this.

Alone.

JUST BEFORE NOON, a faded green truck pulled into the clearing and parked outside the cabin next to Claire's shiny white pickup truck. The hearty old driver climbing down from the cab selected her footing with the deliberate care of a woman who has passed the threshold of sixty with both hips intact. Eyeing Claire's truck, she whistled and said, "She's a beauty. Yours?"

Claire shook her head. "A rental."

"Ah, of course." The woman smiled, crinkling the crow's feet around her steel gray eyes. She peered up through thick-lensed glasses and extended a hand. "You must be Claire. I'm so sorry about your mother, dear. Truly awful, her wandering off the way she did."

Claire shook her hand, momentarily speechless.

Evelyn bobbed her head as if Claire had spoken, wiry silver curls bouncing about her round, lined face. She unlocked the front door and stepped inside.

"Let's get some light in here, brighten up this cave," Evelyn said, pulling the curtains back from the pair of windows facing the clearing. "Ah, much better."

Claire remained anchored to the porch, paralyzed by the sight of the living room.

"What's wrong," Evelyn asked.

"Nothing, I—I just…" Claire stammered, embarrassed. Heat flared in her cheeks. "You're sure she's gone? My mother?"

Evelyn's expression softened. "It's been a year with no sign, no word. We're persistent around these parts. We don't give up searching if there's any hope…"

"But they never found her body."

Evelyn smiled, sadly. "Come inside, dear."

She reached out a hand and Claire took it. She felt like a child as Evelyn led her over the threshold.

Once inside, her fears seemed silly. It was obvious the cabin was abandoned. Cobwebs shrouded the furniture. A thick layer of dust covered every visible surface. Walls constructed from stacked red pine logs swallowed the light from the windows. Poorly insulated cracks bred shadows. Insects scuttled into hiding as Claire's boots thumped over the worn floorboards.

"Are you cold? Evelyn asked as she bent to examine the woodstove positioned between the living room and the kitchen. "I can get a fire going."

"No," Claire said. "Thank you."

She was sweating—a combination of nerves and withdrawal. Her moist palm smeared a clean stripe through the faded green brocade of the couch facing the front windows.

To the left of the couch, her father's antique record player stood on a corner table with a collection of records housed in plastic crates underneath. There was no television. A Bible lay open on the coffee table. Claire closed it without looking. The book thumped shut, dispersing dust in a swirling cloud.

Evelyn sneezed. "This place could use a good cleaning."

"My mother, she'd never let it get like this," Claire said. "Not if she was in her right mind."

"I tried, dear. Truly, I did. But your mother was stubborn as hell. When Doc diagnosed her with dementia, she chased him out with a broom. She wouldn't even consider moving to a care home. But…" Evelyn blinked up at the ceiling. "I should have tried harder. I know that. Instead of enabling her, bringing her groceries, gas for the generator. But if I'd cut her off, she would have just gone without."

Claire stared into the framed picture above the couch, studying the image of *The Last Supper* as if she might discover something new. But they were the same faces that had hung over her for sixteen years. Everything was exactly the same. It felt like a horrible injustice, that this place had persisted so effortlessly while her life in California was falling into ruin.

Claire drifted past the woodstove and the hall, moving into the kitchen. To her right, the heavy oak dining table her father had carved by hand stood with two accompanying chairs beneath a window looking out onto the porch. The refrigerator, sink, and stove stood like ancient relics on her left, separated by two shared countertops. The basement door, set in the kitchen floor, lay flush against the far wall; her eyes glanced off it, repelled. She directed her gaze to the window directly above instead: the view of the shed at the clearing's edge.

"I'm glad you got my emails," Evelyn said. "I'd have reached out sooner, but it took a while to find you under the new last name."

"I got married," Claire murmured.

"Oh? Who's the lucky guy?"

"Gal," Claire said. "Emma Brooks, my wife."

"Even better," Evelyn said. She tossed the keys on the dining table and turned to the refrigerator. The door released a sucking sigh as she pulled it open. Evelyn fell back, grimacing. "Ough, we'll have to leave the door open, let this sucker air out. How long are you staying?"

"Just as long as it takes to clean this place up. We're hoping to sell as soon as possible."

The basement door was pulling at Claire's focus like a flaming car wreck in her peripheral. Her eyes kept straying to the slot—a narrow twelve-by-three-inch opening with a swinging metal flap—and the keyhole above the doorknob. She could almost hear the deadbolt thudding home.

"Is the basement locked?" Claire asked.

"Oh, yes. But give me just a minute—"

"No, that's okay." Claire snatched the keys from the table before Evelyn could reach them. "I'm going to look through the bedrooms."

Frowning, Evelyn tilted her head. Claire shied away from her scrutiny, feigning interest in the assortment of cleaning supplies and linens behind the rolling closet door in the hall.

Evelyn trailed along behind her, saying, "I'm sure you remember the well's around back. The pump is a bit rusty but work it long enough and the tanks will fill. You'll have plenty of running water for dishes, a shower…"

Claire leaned into the cramped bathroom at the end of the hall. The door swung inward, just missing the toilet on the left to bang against the corner of the tiny counter with its yellowed sink on the right. She approached the clawfoot tub crammed against the back wall and pulled aside the mold-speckled curtain. The shower attachment was bent, the porcelain lining of the tub stained.

"How Deb managed to get in and out of that monster without a railing, I will never understand," Evelyn said. "Just be careful you don't slip and crack your head open."

Claire backed out of the bathroom and into the hall. She could keep going, rewind her way into the truck, drive back to the airport.

Her childhood bedroom waited to the right, her mother's bedroom to the left. Pushing her fists into her coat pockets, Claire went left.

The walls of the master bedroom were bare. The queen-sized bed with its four-post bed frame was positioned opposite the door, in the lefthand corner, so that even lying down, her mother could look straight into the bedroom across the hall. Claire prodded the chair pulled up to the window, watched it rock in the dim light filtering through the flower-print curtains. The quilt piled in the seat still held the vague shape of her mother's shoulders.

"Still no landline here, of course," Evelyn said, "and no Wi-Fi. If you need to make a call, you'll have to go down the road, nine miles or so, to the One Stop."

"Thanks," Claire mumbled, distracted by the contents of her mother's closet: more bedding, several modest dresses on wire hangers, boxes overflowing with paperwork and old photographs taken by Claire's father. The only three photos deemed worthy of framing stood in tarnished frames atop the nightstand beside the bed. Claire didn't need to look to know she wasn't in them.

The door to Claire's bedroom stood open. That there was a door at all was unexpected; shortly after Claire's twelfth birthday, her mother had removed it from its hinges and stowed it in the basement. Later, Claire had used the door as a mattress—a slight reprieve from the basement's cold concrete floor. Her mother must have hauled it back up.

Opposite the door, a white metal bed frame set lengthwise against the wall supported a twin mattress. Claire recalled lying awake at night, staring at the window past the foot of the bed to avoid her mother's beady, watchful eyes. The full-length mirror was gone. Her mother had smashed it to pieces before locking Claire in the basement for the first time.

Claire didn't need to search the dresser in the corner to know there was nothing of value inside. She'd taken everything that mattered when she ran away from home. With her father's camera slung around her neck and a crumpled twenty-dollar bill in her pocket, she'd fled without looking back.

As she stepped inside her childhood bedroom, her eyes fixed on the leather strap lying at the center of the mattress. She stiffened, as time seemed to collapse. Her vision narrowed to a pinprick. The room was suddenly far too warm for all the layers she had on, stifling.

Suffocating.

She was dimly aware of Evelyn sidling past her. Gesturing at the eastern wall, Evelyn said, "My place is about a mile that way if you cut straight through the forest. But I'd advise sticking to the road so you don't get lost, even though it's closer to a mile and a half that way. Just look for the mailbox. And be sure to bundle up if you're walking."

Claire managed to nod, but the strap demanded her attention. She needed to touch it, to prove it was real.

As Evelyn continued talking, Claire approached the mattress.

Even after years of lashings, the strap seemed longer than she remembered—and thicker. As if the four stitched layers of leather had expanded over time. Claire's heart skip-thumped.

Then, her anger took control. She seized the leather strap and marched through the cabin with it held at arm's length, the way she might handle a venomous snake. She carried it outside, all the way to the tree line, where she hurled it into the forest, watched it spin end over end, strike a branch, and disappear.

A low whistle spun her around.

"Good arm," Evelyn said. Leaning against the porch railing, she removed a flask from the inside pocket of her coat, took a long draft, and offered it to Claire with her eyebrows raised. "You look like you could use it."

Without hesitation, Claire tipped the flask to her lips. The whiskey burned her throat. Heat blossomed in her stomach. She swallowed, coughing. "Sorry, I'm—"

Evelyn raised her hands, palms out.

Claire sniffed and nodded her thanks. She would contend with the guilt of breaking her promise to Emma—*already*—when she could breathe again. Later.

Always later.

"Come on," Evelyn said. "We're out here now. Might as well give you a refresher course on the generator."

AFTER THEY FINISHED in the shed, Evelyn showed Claire the wood stacked behind it, covered with a blue tarp to keep it dry. "There should be enough here to get you through the rest of winter, though I doubt you'll be here that long. The woodstove's been cleaned, so you don't have to worry about burning the place down—unless you really want to."

Claire managed a weak smile. The long-dreaded home-coming had sapped her energy, so when Evelyn offered to bring dinner, Claire surprised herself by accepting. She didn't want to be alone on her first night at the cabin.

"You can get a few groceries at the One Stop, but you'll be paying tourist prices," Evelyn said, snorting. "Highway robbery. You write up a list of the stuff you can't find there, and I'll pick it up on my Friday run to Zup's."

"No," Claire protested, "I couldn't ask you to do that."

"You're not asking; I'm telling. The drive's an hour long each way, so I only make it once a week. No sense in both of us being miserable."

Only after Evelyn's truck had rumbled back down the drive-way out of sight did Claire allow herself to crumble onto the porch steps. She lowered her head into her hands, breathing in the smell of the pines, the lingering odor of liquor on her breath, and wept.

When she had nothing left but congested gasps to offer the surrounding trees, she straightened and walked to the rental truck. Blasting the heater, she tuned the radio through hissing static until she found an oldies station.

As she followed the road, passing Evelyn's mailbox on the left, Claire rehearsed her impending phone call to Emma: careful optimism, a light tone—maybe a joke. She didn't want Emma to worry. Worried Emma asked a lot of questions.

The One Stop slid into view through the trees, a boxy log structure announcing its purpose with large wooden letters fastened to a shingled roof. Claire tightened her grip on the steering wheel. She considered driving on—back to the highway, the airport, the warmth and safety of California.

Instead, she pulled into the gravel parking lot. If she was lucky, Lily and Silas would be home when she called. Thinking of her children strengthened her resolve. She squared her shoulders, forced a smile. Whatever it took, she would get through this—for her family.

No more running.

EMMA

EMMA SLID OUT of her Prius with her cell phone pinned between ear and shoulder, turning sideways to avoid bumping into Claire's Volvo. The station wagon had been moved; the thirty-degree angle between the front bumpers suggested that the person responsible had not been driving long, which could only mean…

"Lily!" Emma hollered, thumping her elbow against the door separating the garage from the kitchen. The straps of her reusable shopping bags were cutting off her circulation. Her hands were otherwise occupied with juggling her purse, lunch bag, and a hardback novel. As the voicemail from Claire ended, Emma shouted her daughter's name again.

The door swung open. Lily's face appeared in the gap. Her cheeks were flushed, her hazel eyes wide and questioning beneath the nest of long dark curls gathered in a messy bun atop her head. Stray hairs floated about her temples. Steam billowed from the pot on the stove behind her.

"Oh, hey—" Lily's easy grin spread. "Here, let me get that."

As Lily's nimble fingers unburdened her arms, Emma breathed in the scent of herbs, garlic, and mushrooms. Her stomach grumbled in anticipation, even as she groaned aloud.

"Shi—oot," Emma said. "It was my night to make dinner, wasn't it?"

"Late *again*," Lily said, clicking her tongue. Her socks spun on the linoleum, long legs returning her to the stove in an elegant glide. "Good thing I heard about the accident on the radio."

"Yeah, well, accident aside, we were short-staffed again. Both Trish and Julie called in sick. There was no one else, or I would have been home hours ago." Emma sank into a chair at the kitchen table and removed the pins holding back her short blond hair. She narrowed her eyes. "The radio…You wouldn't be talking about the *car* radio, right?"

The spoon-on-skillet stirring sounds stopped for half a beat, then resumed.

"Because a learner's permit requires an adult to be present," Emma said, "and as much as I appreciate you picking up the slack with dinner—"

"You need a learner's permit to *drive* the car." Lily pointed with her wooden spoon. "Not to listen to the radio."

Tomato sauce dripped from the spoon's end, and Lily disappeared below the level of the kitchen counter with a dish towel in hand. She reappeared, straightening to her full height to stretch her spine. Emma would never get used to craning her neck to look up at her daughter. A blink, and Lily had gone from six years old to six feet tall.

"That kind of thinking won't keep you from getting pulled over," Emma said, "or prevent some idiot drunk driver from blowing through a red light. I know Mom lets you go to the store and back sometimes, and I hate playing bad cop, but—"

"There's a message from Silas's school."

Irritated by the knot of trepidation forming in her stomach, Emma approached the machine. She was forty-three, far too old for the sickening stomach flips that accompanied any brush with authority. But the girl inside her—the goody two-shoes who had moved from hall monitor to summer camp leader to sober driver—quailed at the possibility of a reprimand. Being a stickler for the rules had carried Emma safely and successfully through nursing school and into a profession where her discipline and (here she could see Claire rolling her eyes) *anal retentiveness* were actually appreciated. Necessary, even.

And Silas wasn't the type of kid to screw up; he was the type the screw-ups ganged up on. Emma knew; she'd been that kid once. She played the message. Listening to Silas's principal drone on about an altercation between several of the boys, Emma wondered when the man would come to terms with the reality that suspension alone was not a viable solution. If anything, Silas would get it worse when the bullies returned from their mandatory vacations.

When Lily's name was mentioned, Emma's eyes popped open. She hadn't realized she'd been drifting off, asleep on her feet and still wearing her scrubs. The principal concluded his message by requesting that Emma contact him after the winter break to set up a meeting.

She shook her head in disbelief. "You..." Emma leaned on the counter just as Lily pushed a plate of spaghetti under her nose. Saliva flooded her mouth, but she ignored her growling stomach. "You *assaulted* a child, Lily?"

"Assaulted?" Lily rolled her eyes, a near-perfect replica of Claire. She deposited two plates piled high with spaghetti on the kitchen table, then returned for the garlic bread, scrubbing her mouth with the back of one hand. Emma realized she was trying—and failing—to keep from smiling.

"What part of what I said is funny to you?" Emma snapped.

"It's not funny, I—" Lily glanced down the hall at Silas's bedroom door, then lowered her voice. "You want to do this now? Dinner's getting cold."

Emma flared her nostrils and tried her best to burn holes through Lily with her eyes.

Lily sighed. "Okay, just...can you please not bring it up to Silas, at least not tonight? It took forever to get him to stop crying after I picked him up—"

"You *what*?"

Lily pressed the air down with her hands. "Shh. I know, I know. Silas was texting me—Don't look at me like that; you *said* his phone was for emergencies. Well, this was an emergency. He'd already tried to get ahold of you at the hospital."

Lily checked the hallway again for signs of movement. "The other boys were picking on him and...they made him eat a, uh, dog turd they found on the soccer field. He wanted to come home. I couldn't just leave him there. So I walked home, got the car."

"You're only sixteen. They just let you drive off with him?" Emma pulled her hands back along her jaw to knot her fingers behind her aching neck. "What the hell were they thinking?"

"Probably that I look a bit older than sixteen with Mom's sunglasses on. The way I marched in there, they didn't have a lot of time for questions." Lily sighed. "Memma, I really am sorry. I went five under the speed limit there and back. If there had been any other way…"

"Don't you 'Memma' me," Emma said, scowling despite the tug of nostalgia she felt at Lily's use of the affectation, a blend of "Mom" and "Emma" that Lily had mashed together as a baby, then later passed along to her younger brother. Claire and Emma were so rarely in the same room anymore that their children's need to distinguish between them verbally had been rendered almost obsolete.

Emma massaged her temples, exhaled slowly through her nostrils. As her anger deflated, guilt and a vague, familiar sadness seeped in to replace it. She was tempted to let the subject drop, but…"That doesn't explain the thing with the kid. The principal said you—"

"When I got there, one of the boys who'd been messing with Silas was still hanging around, calling him names. The teacher was too busy watching the other kids to notice him tossing rocks and bits of garbage at Silas. And Silas wasn't doing anything to stop him, just sitting there on the front steps, crying. Then, the little asshole—"

"Lily."

"The little *a-hole* squished a piece of chewing gum into Silas's hair, right as I was walking up. I guess I just kind of…lost it." She shrugged. "I picked him up by the shoulders and carried him through the front doors, hung his jacket up on one of those hooks they have in the entryway. He just happened to still be inside it—the jacket, I mean."

Emma tried to summon a reprimand and couldn't. "But he was only, what, seven or eight years old? Lily, his parents could sue."

Lily's lips twitched into a smile. "I wish you could have seen it. He was kicking his short little legs, screaming bloody murder as all the kids came back from recess."

Claire would know what to say. Emma envied the ease with which her wife interacted with their children, the trust between them. The kids told Claire everything, and were forgiven everything, while Emma was left to dole out punishment. It wasn't fair, but she couldn't blame Claire for being the favorite parent. "So…there's probably a message from your school on the machine too, then?"

"Probably. There goes the dream of perfect attendance."

"That's not the point, Lily."

"It was just the last two periods, math and history. And I'm a week ahead in both."

From down the hall, Emma heard Silas's snot-choked voice call out, "Memma?"

She shot Lily a look—*we're not done talking about this*—then called back, "Dinner's ready, Si. Come and get it."

Silas padded into the kitchen on bare feet, pushing up his glasses. He threw his arms around Emma's waist with an intensity that knocked her off-balance and mumbled into her stomach, "I need a haircut."

Emma combed his hair back from his face. It hung to the middle of his back, golden and lustrous, except for a patch near the crown of his head that stood on end. Where Lily had hacked away the chewing gum, Emma realized.

"It's barely noticeable," Emma said. She licked her fingers and tried to smooth the errant patch down, but it sprang back up.

"I still need a haircut, though," Silas said. When Emma lifted his chin to get a better look at him, his brown eyes were shining with tears. "Alicia says my long hair makes me look like a girl."

Lily pulled a chair out from the dining table and dropped into it, muttering, "Well, Alicia is a little see-you-next-Tuesday."

"Lily, did you already take your insulin?" Emma asked.

"Yep. Right before you got home."

Silas wrinkled his nose at his plate. "I thought it was Memma's turn to cook."

"What makes you think I didn't?"

A sly smile spread across Silas's face. "Because it stinks."

"Like you can smell anything with your nose full of snot. Blow it, would you? I'm trying to eat over here." Lily tossed a napkin across the table to Emma.

Silas took the napkin from Emma. More and more, he insisted on doing things himself. Blowing until his nose honked, Silas watched Lily chase the noodles hanging from her fork. "You're supposed to use a spoon, Lily. Memma, she forgot the spoons!"

"I'll get them," Emma said. She returned in time to catch Lily flinging a noodle across the table at her brother. "Hey, no food fights inside the house."

"It's not a fight," Lily said, wiping her orange-stained lips with a napkin. "It's an exchange. He was just about to hand one back across the table. Isn't that right, Si?"

Cheeks bulging, Silas opened his mouth to reply, but Emma shot him a pointed look. Silas chewed, swallowed and said, "Ugh, you can have all of it."

"That gross, huh?" Emma suppressed laughter with a bite of her own, then grimaced. "Is this sauce from a can?"

Lily threw up her hands. "Couple of foodies, you two. You've been watching too many cooking shows."

"Mom makes the sauce from scratch," Silas said. "It takes *hours*, but you can't rush a good sauce."

"Well, your mom is an excellent cook," said Emma. "I just front the money for groceries. And your sister here covered for me, since I was running late, so I think we both owe her a thank you."

"More like 'no thank you.'" Silas stuck his tongue out at Lily.

"How's Mom?" Lily asked. "Did she call yet?"

"She did, but I missed it. And before you ask, no, I can't call her back. There's no landline at the cabin."

"She's alive, though? Sounded all right?"

"Yeah."

Lily's eyes flicked up from her plate to scan Emma's face. Searching for evidence to the contrary, perhaps. "What's the plan for winter break? Will Mom be back by then?"

"Winter break is...?" Emma muffled a yawn with the back of her hand.

"The next two weeks," Lily prompted. "Starting after this weekend."

Emma reached for her cell phone. "Today is...Tuesday?"

"All day."

"I'll call your schools in the morning, let them know that I'm taking you out early for a family trip."

"Are you?"

Emma took a bite of spaghetti, chewing slowly to buy time to think. She didn't want to admit that between the heated fight she'd had with Claire the night before and the extra hours of overtime, she had completely forgotten about winter break. With the false cheer of Claire's voicemail still ringing in her ears—*This place needs a lot more work than I was expecting, but I should be able to get it done. I'll need to stay longer than planned, though.*—Emma was faced with the possibility that Claire might not be home for Christmas.

That this could prove to be the first in a long line of split holidays hurt Emma's heart. They'd been circling the idea of a trial separation for the last year. But it was too soon. She had meant to try harder to fix things, to work on their marriage, but the time had slipped through her fingers.

Lily kicked her under the table, repeating the question.

"Maybe. I'm not sure yet," Emma said.

"Oh!" Silas interrupted, leaning across the table to point his fork at Lily. "Do you exist in real life or are you made up?"

"Yes or no questions only," Lily said. "And I think you mean *fictional.*"

Silas said, "Fine. Are you *fictional*?"

Lily's eyes slid from Emma to Silas. "Yes."

Relieved, Emma sat back in her chair. Lily and Silas's perpetual game of Twenty Questions had been cropping up mid-conversation with increasing frequency over the last six months. Emma suspected it was their way of coping with the inexplicable tension that had crept into their daily lives.

"How's the homework situation?" Emma asked.

"All done with mine." Lily pushed back from the table and gathered their plates, rumpling Silas's hair. "I'll help with yours. But first you need to shower."

"It's *your* stinky food," Silas said, hooking his fingers around the last word to form air quotes. Emma wondered where he'd picked that up from—another development she'd missed during her long hours at the hospital.

While Emma washed the dishes, Claire's voicemail played on a constant loop through her mind. Underneath all the forced, high-pitched optimism, her wife had sounded rattled.

On impulse, Emma dried her hands and dialed the hospital's number. A plan was forming in her mind. Twenty minutes and three short conversations later, Emma checked in on Lily and Silas, then pulled her laptop from its case and climbed into bed. Keying in her password, she couldn't help but imagine Claire drinking herself to sleep, despite the promises she'd made during their counseling session.

Emma played the message again, listening to Claire navigate the one-sided conversation like a tight-rope walker. But there was a tremor in her voice right before she said, "I love you," and ended the call. An echo of the young woman who had clawed her way out of vivid nightmares—sweat-drenched, screaming, and often swinging—nearly every night for the first year they'd lived together. Emma had been there, by her side, to hold her until she stopped shaking.

But now Claire was alone, isolated at the source of the childhood trauma she refused to discuss. Emma would have given anything to be with her, to lend the support that Claire had once drunk up like water in the desert; the same support that she now resented, rejecting Emma at every opportunity.

"So how are things, really?" Lily was watching her from the bedroom doorway.

Emma groped for a believable response and settled for what she hoped was a casual shrug.

"You could talk to me about it, you know," Lily said. "If you wanted."

But she couldn't, not without forcing a wedge between Lily and Claire, or between herself and Lily. Against her better judgement, she asked, "Has your mom mentioned anything to you?"

"She let slip that you were in marriage counseling a while back. But," she hurried to add, "it was an accident. You know Mom."

"Right." Emma didn't need to ask if Claire had been drinking at the time; it would have taken a crowbar to loosen her lips, otherwise. She chose her next words carefully. "Things... could be better. But we're working on it. How's your blood sugar?"

Lily leaned her head back, sighing. "Fine. I told you I'd let you know if there were any problems."

"And you—"

"*Yes*, I took my insulin. You don't need to ask three times a day."

"I'm sorry. Lately it feels like everything is flying past me. Thanks for tonight, by the way. Dinner, taking care of Si."

Lily bowed, then sidled over to sit at the foot of Emma's bed. Folding her coltish legs beneath her, she said, "Maybe you could talk to Mom about homeschooling again. He's so small for his age, and he doesn't have any friends."

"You know how she feels about homeschooling."

"Just because she had a bad experience doesn't mean it's the wrong choice for everyone. And it's what Silas wants."

"We *both* feel like Silas will be better off in the future if he doesn't run from his problems," Emma said. "He'll make friends, eventually. Once Mom's back, we're going to talk with the other kids' parents—"

"You know that won't work."

"I know that I'm his mother, and yours. You're just going to have to trust me on this."

"Whatever. It just seems like you and Mom have a lot going on. Maybe you're not seeing the whole picture." Looking up at the ceiling, Lily said, "Just tell me this: are you actually trying to make it work, like, for real, or are you just holding things together for me and Silas?"

Emma's mouth fell open. Were they that transparent? All the tiptoeing around, trying to hide the conflict in their marriage, seemed pointless if Lily could read their situation so easily. And if Lily had noticed their relationship failing, how long before Silas started asking the same questions?

"I love your mother more than I ever have, or ever will love another person in this world," Emma said, "except for you and your brother."

Lily nodded. Her gaze drifted to the laptop. "Working?"

"No, I've been thinking about that trip. I already called in a few favors at work, so I have some time off."

"Uh-huh..." Lily's expression was guarded. "So, you thought we'd fly out to Minnesota and surprise Mom?"

"I'm worried about her."

Lily tugged her hair loose from its messy bun and twisted a strand around her finger.

"You think it's a mistake," Emma said.

"I think..."—Lily took a deep breath—"Mom needs space. Especially if she's trying to quit drinking. Yes, she told me. And you just showing up, it might be kind of, like, an invasion of privacy? That's all I'm saying."

From the next room: "Lily! Are you old?

"What's old?" Lily shouted back.

"Over...twenty-five?"

"I must be ancient," Emma said.

"Yep." Lily winked at Emma. "I'd better go unplug him. The light's off, but he's probably under the blanket with his phone. Just...think about what I said, okay?"

Emma tucked Lily's hair behind her ear and kissed her forehead. "When did you grow up?"

Lily smiled. "Love you."

"Love *you*. Close the door behind you, please."

Emma lay back into the pillows with a groan. Finally released from her daughter's scrutiny, her mouth twisted as a tangle of emotions surfaced. She put on her headphones and called up the playlist of songs Claire had put together on her phone, insisting that Emma's selection of music was *cringeworthy*. Smiling as their favorite Paul Simon song flooded her ears, she closed her eyes, and tried to breathe.

It could be a nice surprise: a Minnesota holiday. They could do their shopping tomorrow, fly out on Thursday. Emma mentally listed off the various items they would need to pack, unaware—or unwilling to admit—that she was no longer thinking in hypotheticals.

And anyway, she'd already bought the plane tickets. They were on special, and nonrefundable. Decided, Emma smiled. It would be a nice surprise.

CLAIRE

CLAIRE WORKED A splinter out of her finger and glared into the woodstove. The sun was sinking fast below the treetops, taking the heat from the cabin with it. She had the makings of a fire but no way to light it. She'd searched everywhere and couldn't find a single match.

An approaching rumble signaled Evelyn's arrival.

A door slammed outside, and a voice called out, "Room service!"

Frustrated, Claire went to greet her neighbor. At the sound of nails clicking on wood, she froze. But it was too late—the door was already open, and a massive black shape surged through the gap. Claire shrank back against the wall, drawing her arms up as fear cinched her windpipe closed. She couldn't force enough air from her lungs to scream.

"Oscar!" Evelyn shouted, jostling the plastic bags looped over her arms as she entered. The foil-covered dish balanced atop the cardboard box in her hands emitted a fragrant puff of steam as Evelyn made her way toward the kitchen. The dog padded after her. "Sorry about him. It's walk-o'clock and I forgot. Way too smart for his own good, that one. I hope you don't mind that I brought—"

Evelyn turned to find the living room empty and paused. Claire had retreated to the porch the instant the dog went into the kitchen. She hadn't been aware of moving; her feet had fled on instinct. She was trembling, but not from the cold.

"I'm sorry," Evelyn said. "I really should have asked first."

Claire tried to respond, managed a feeble whistle of air.

"You're scared of dogs."

Claire nodded. "I—I had a bad experience when I was younger."

"I can take him home." Evelyn forked her fingers between her lips and whistled. "I really should have asked. I can't tell you how sorry I am."

"No...it's okay. I'm okay. I just wasn't expecting it, is all."

The large black dog padded into the living room and sat down beside Evelyn. He cocked his head, tail sweeping the dusty floorboards. Hooking a paw into his scruff, the dog scratched at the red collar around his neck. His pointed ears—one was half-missing—flattened against his skull, lips stretching back into a canine grin as the collar completed three circuits, tags jingling.

"Don't be rude, Oscar," Evelyn said. "Say hello to Claire."

Evelyn chuckled as Oscar raised his forepaw to claw at the air. For her part, Claire tried her best to smile. But the dog's shiny dark eyes were fixed on her, watching as she inched back over the threshold into the living room.

"You're sure it's okay he's here?" Evelyn asked.

"It's fine." Claire smiled again, hoping it was more convincing this time. "What happened to his ear?"

"Oh, this?" Evelyn fondled Oscar's left ear. "There's this young bull that crosses my property from time to time—"

"A bull?"

"A male moose. Ever seen one?"

Claire shook her head. "No, but then I've never seen much of anything around here. It's always been quiet."

"Anyway," Evelyn continued, looking pointedly at Oscar, "*somebody* got too big for his britches, tried to argue territory. It could have been a hell of a lot worse, but Oscar's a fast son-of-a-bitch. Lucky, too. He won't be trying that again. Will you?" She cooed at the dog as she gripped him by the muzzle and shook his head *no*.

Claire still felt uneasy, but at least she could breathe evenly now; it was an improvement compared to the terror that had liquified her insides upon the dog's arrival. Oscar seemed friendly enough.

She reached out a hand and was relieved to find it was trembling only slightly. Oscar stretched his neck to sniff her fingers. The cold touch of his nose was followed by a warm pass of his tongue. Claire flinched, and then their introduction was concluded. Oscar turned his attention to the dish on the kitchen table.

"We'd better dig in before he does," Evelyn said, opening the kitchen cabinets. "Just two of everything, huh?"

"We never had guests." Claire accepted a plate heaped high with meatloaf and roasted potatoes. Her stomach grumbled eagerly.

Evelyn eased into a chair, adjusting her heavy blue snow coat around her. She tucked back the curls winging up from beneath the ear flaps of her fur-lined leather hat and then repositioned the cigarette balanced over her ear. When she was finally settled, she loaded her fork with a hefty bite. Between mouthfuls, she said, "Tell me more about the dog that bit you."

"How do you know it bit me?"

Evelyn shrugged.

"It was my neighbor's dog," Claire said, rubbing her left arm, "a mix of some kind—huge. He went after this stray cat I used to feed, and I got caught between them. I guess…in a way, I'm sort of glad it happened?"

Evelyn raised her eyebrows. "Oh?"

"I just—I mean, I don't know if I would have met my wife, otherwise."

"Did the cat get away?"

Claire laughed; had their roles been reversed, she would've asked the same question. "She did get away, fortunately. We both did. I took her with me when I moved in with Emma."

Working her sleeve up over her forearm, Claire revealed the network of scars where the dog had torn her open, wrist to elbow.

Evelyn's eyes bulged. She swallowed, then said, "Pardon my French, but that's got to be *the* worst fucking dog bite I've ever seen, and I was sheriff for thirty years. That right there calls for something stronger than water."

Evelyn rooted through one of the plastic shopping bags and retrieved a bottle. She poured two fingers of whiskey into a glass, then handed it to Claire.

As they toasted, clinking their glasses together, Claire thought again of the promise she'd made to Emma. But she could still quit drinking tomorrow. The end result would be the same, and her wife would never know—her wife who couldn't even be bothered to pick up the phone.

Claire had made sure to call two hours after Emma's shift had ended, but there had been no answer. Was she already building a new life in Claire's absence, filling the space between them with friends—maybe even lovers? Claire thought of the stale scent of cigarettes on Emma's dirty scrubs, the cheap plastic lighters she kept finding in the washing machine. Knowing that Emma also had secrets made it a little easier for Claire to drain her glass.

Evelyn smacked her lips in satisfaction and poured them another drink. "So how does meeting your wife factor in? I hope you don't mind all the questions. Don't get much company, way out here."

Claire swallowed the liquor back. "Emma was working as a scribe for one of the doctors in the emergency room. Scribes, they—"

"Take things down in the charts, spare the rest of the staff from the doctor's chicken scratch."

"Exactly." Claire's head was just beginning to buzz, but the details of the day weren't fuzzy enough yet for her to fully relax. She motioned to the bottle, and Evelyn pushed it across the table. Claire filled her glass halfway. "I was pretty freaked out, bleeding all over the place. I'd already fainted once. They had to flush the wounds, stitch me up. Just the sight of all that blood..." She pinched the bridge of her nose, squinting as the memory triggered her nausea. "Anyway, Emma saw that I was about to pass out, so she distracted me. She held my hand the whole time, telling these really awful dad jokes—corny puns, you know. But it worked.

"After we'd been together a few years, she told me I was the reason she'd decided to go into nursing instead of becoming a doctor. She wanted to be more hands on with patients, more involved. But that's Emma: always trying to fix everyone."

Claire sniffed, rubbed the corners of her eyes. She let her hand fall, and a cold nose grazed her palm. Tentatively, she stroked the top of the dog's head.

When Oscar angled his muzzle toward Claire's abandoned plate, Evelyn said, "If you find yourself unable to resist his charms, you can give him a bit of meatloaf—just a *tiny* bit, though. The Lab in him would be perfectly happy living his best life as a big fat potato, but his shepherd hips won't hold the weight."

Claire offered Oscar a small chunk of meatloaf, pinched between her fingertips. But when his lips parted to reveal pointed white teeth, she jumped, dropping the meat on the floor. Oscar snatched up the morsel, then stared hopefully at Evelyn.

"No more, you glutton," Evelyn said, lurching to her feet with a grunt.

As Claire collected their dishes and carried them to the sink, Evelyn riffled through the plastic bags on the counter. "I brought you a few things, Claire. Some canned goods, bandages, and Betadine—in case of emergency—and a gallon of clean drinking water. I'm guessing you didn't make it out to the well to pump?"

Claire stopped twisting the sink handle to no effect and lowered their plates.

Evelyn spared her the indignity of a response. "It's been a long day. Do it tomorrow morning, early, and you can thaw out in the shower after. Oh, and you'll be needing these."

Evelyn shook a box of matches and jerked her head at the woodstove. Claire realized, with dismay, that she was a terrible hostess. Her guest was still bundled up in her winter clothing. "I'm sorry," she said. "You must be freezing. I tried to start a fire earlier, but I couldn't find the matches."

Evelyn threw her head back and laughed. "I've lived my whole life here, dear. I could wear a thong bikini in the middle of winter without shivering. Besides, I like to have a smoke after dinner. No sense in taking everything off just to put it all back on again."

Evelyn knelt before the stove and struck a match. The fire crackled to life.

"There's another bottle of whiskey in there for you, too," Evelyn said. "Call it a house-warming gift. Anything you don't use, just pile it up with the junk you want tossed, and I'll have Andrew haul everything off to the dump when you're finished."

"Thank you, Evelyn, for everything. Really."

"Well, if you feel like humoring an old woman, there's a project I've been working on that I'd like to talk to you about. I'm a bit of a self-appointed historian—keeps me busy in my retirement—and I've been putting together a more comprehensive history for the lesser-known parts of St. Louis County. Trying to, I mean. There are a lot of gaps. Back then, an overturned canoe was enough to wash out decades of history.

"One site of particular interest is on your mother's prop—your property, I mean. I don't know if you ever went out there as a kid, but about two miles downstream there's an abandoned boarding school by the lake. It's been there since the late 1800s. One of those awful places meant to integrate the indigenous children." Evelyn grimaced, spat. "A rather disgusting part of our history, if you ask me. Those poor kids…Well, I'd like to finish my work out there—with your permission, of course. I could take you out there and tell you some of what I've learned about the place."

Oscar shot between them, barking furiously as he leapt at the window above the basement door.

"What the hell's gotten into you?" Evelyn bellowed. To Claire, she said, "Turn the light off, would you? I can't see a damn thing out there."

Claire flicked the switch. The fire in the woodstove throbbed orange and cast light through the living room, but it barely reached the kitchen. As Claire waited for her eyes to adjust, her other senses searched for input, like fingers combing through black sand.

"Did Deborah have a rifle," Evelyn hissed, "a weapon of any kind?"

"I don't…" Claire struggled to remember. "After my father passed, she got rid of our rifles. Why? What is it?"

"Probably just an animal," Evelyn muttered. "They like to try their luck with the garbage bins sometimes."

Have you seen a single living thing since you got here, Claire Bear? She shook her head, hard, as if the action might prevent her mother's voice from burrowing into her mind again after so many years of silence.

Oscar stopped barking. He pressed his nose to the window, his dark eyes locked on the shed.

The utter absence of noise made Claire long for the comfort of the city she called home. Gone were the sounds of traffic, the murmur of human voices. There were no wailing sirens, no distant television chatter or music, only the muffled quiet of a forest blanketed in snow. Even the nighttime hooting of an owl would have been a relief—proof of life outside the cabin, at least. But she couldn't remember ever hearing an owl as a girl.

Apparently satisfied that the threat had passed, Oscar trotted over to the sink, put his paws up on the counter, and dipped his long muzzle into one of the plastic shopping bags.

Evelyn's shoulders relaxed. Her hand left the hunting knife snapped to her belt, and she said, "You can turn the light back on."

When Evelyn turned away from the window, she looked twenty years older. Her complexion was pallid; the ruddy flush brought on by the whiskey had evaporated.

"Did you see something out there?" Claire whispered, feeling foolish for being afraid to raise her voice.

Frowning, Evelyn fumbled the ear flap of her hat aside to touch the cigarette perched over her ear, then seemed to reconsider; she settled for a slug of whiskey instead. The bottle was half empty already. Claire couldn't remember drinking so much, just the two of them.

Ah, but there's plenty you don't remember, Claire Bear.

Her mother's dry laughter echoed inside her head.

Just ask your wife.

"I haven't been sleeping," Evelyn said. "My mind's not what it used to be."

Evelyn collapsed onto the couch in the living room. Oscar hopped up beside her, turned four tight circles, then curled into a ball at her feet. Evelyn removed her glasses and sighed. "Sorry about that; I get a bit jumpy after dark. Still, you ought to have a rifle around, staying way out here on your own. It's common sense."

"Do I *need* a rifle?" Claire eyed the windows with caution, wringing her fingers.

Evelyn put her glasses back on and squinted up at Claire. "Better to have and not need, I always say. I have a spare I'll bring you when I come for your grocery list on Friday." She slapped Oscar's rump. "Come on, lazybones. We'd better hit the road, let this fine lady get her beauty sleep."

"Maybe you should spend the night on the couch."

You just don't want to sleep alone, the sly voice in the back of Claire's head intoned. *Not here, Claire Bear. Not when I might be watching.*

"Nonsense, it's not far. And hey, I'm sorry about him going off like that." Evelyn cocked an eyebrow at the dog. "Always puts me on edge. I can't imagine how you must've felt, what with…" She motioned to Claire's bite scars. "I really should've left him at home. I'm sorry, truly."

Claire waved off the apology. She was trying to invent an excuse to convince Evelyn to stay, anything but the childish whimper—*please don't leave me*—rising in her throat.

Evelyn patted Claire's cheek. "We're the last two cabins at the end of a long dirt road. Don't you worry. I don't imagine Highway Patrol's out there waiting to nail me with a DUI. Worst I can do is crash into a tree or a snowbank."

"That really doesn't make me feel any better about letting you drive. You could get stuck and freeze—"

Evelyn laughed. "I'm going to walk in a straight line to my truck. I promise you, if I can't, then I'll spend the night."

"I'll hold you to it."

Evelyn winked. "Come. Witness."

True to her word, Evelyn's passage through the snow was steady and unerring. She turned a circle midway, arms thrown out like a grinning showman.

After her truck had rattled away down the driveway, Claire turned to face the cabin. She'd left the door open without thinking. The cabin was losing heat.

A rectangle of light from the kitchen window shone onto the snow near the cabin's eastern wall. There was something lying there—a long, slender object. Claire's heart fluttered against her ribs. Recalling how Oscar had barked at the shed, she crept along the side of the cabin with her back to the weathered logs, keeping the shed in her view. The object was the leather strap she'd hurled into the trees, back when the sun had been shining. A line of tracks angled to and from the forest, vanishing beyond the shed. Claire knelt to inspect them. The surrounding snow was knee-deep, but the tracks were soft, no deeper than the tip of her finger. And yet, their outline was distinct: human footprints.

Bare.

She picked up the strap and followed the tracks to the shed. Peering around the side, she called out, "Mom?"

She shook her head; she was being ridiculous, making something out of nothing. But when she tried to explain away the prints to herself, she couldn't. Bare footprints, right outside the window where Oscar had been barking. Evelyn hadn't removed her boots, and even if she had, why would she walk around in the snow barefoot?

Claire scanned the trees, wondering if she was being watched. Someone had been out here spooking the dog. Someone had returned the strap.

But who?

Not me, Claire Bear. Her mother snickered. *I'm supposed to be dead, remember?*

Claire let her anger fill her, felt it burn out the chill of her unanswered questions. How dare someone peek into her windows, or try to scare her by bringing back a piece of her past she needed to be rid of? Bad enough she was stuck in the cabin alone for the night.

"Mom!" she shouted.

But, of course, no one answered.

Not aloud, anyway.

I'm gone, Claire Bear. You're jumping at shadows.

You can't run from your demons forever.

"Try me," Claire growled. She stomped over to the heavy metal box against the shed wall that housed the outdoor garbage bins, threw back the lid, and shoved the leather strap inside.

Invigorated by her display of courage, she kicked through the tracks, destroying them as she made her way back to the cabin.

She closed the front door behind her—slowly, as if to prove she wasn't retreating—and locked it. Then she proceeded to draw the curtains over every window, making a point to avoid the view outside. By the time she was finished, she had almost convinced herself the incident with the strap had been blown out of proportion by her imagination, warped by the stress of spending her first night in the place she dreaded most in the world. Not to mention the alcohol she had no business drinking.

Evelyn had mentioned that someone named Andrew would take the unwanted items from the cabin to the dump. Perhaps he'd stopped by earlier to check out the property and had found the strap, leaving it outside so he wouldn't interrupt her visit with Evelyn. Hell, he might tromp around barefoot in the snow all the time, for all she knew. Claire nodded to herself, chasing this idea with a swallow of liquid courage from the whiskey bottle. She could ask Evelyn about it when she saw her next. Until then, there was no sense in worrying. Whoever it was had clearly come and gone. If she found fresh tracks in the morning, then there would be cause for alarm.

Let it go. Go to sleep. Everything's locked up tight.

You're just drunk and scared of sleeping alone.

It was probably nothing.

Only later, after she had swallowed a sleeping pill, did her thoughts wander back to the tracks in the snow. Her mind rolled the memory around like a sharp stone, trying to smooth away the worrisome edges. But the facts kept catching, pulling her back from sleep: tracks outside the cabin; the forest was not as lifeless as it seemed.

She was not alone.

Not just tracks. The whisper rustled like snakeskin through the folds of Claire's brain.

Footprints, Claire Bear.

Footprints.

LILY

"LOOK, SI," LILY said, breathing through a bout of nausea brought on by her mother's erratic driving. "We found the One Stop. It does exist. Now, let me out so I can throw up."

"Hang on, we're almost to the cabin," Emma said. "We're supposed to turn right past the One Stop and go up a dirt road, but—" She slammed on the brakes, jerking their seatbelts tight. The compact blue SUV skidded to a stop sideways in the middle of the road. She cursed under her breath. "Sorry, guys. You know, if the rental place had just given me chains like I asked—"

Lily and Silas groaned in unison. The absurdity of voiding the rental agreement with the use of chains was a mantra they'd listened to her repeat several times already.

Ignoring their pained expressions, Emma said, "I don't even *see* a road, do you?"

"We could ask at the One Stop," Lily suggested. The flight had left her feeling sore and irritable. Her stomach flopped as she wiped sweat from her brow. "I could really use the fresh air."

Glancing over, Emma said, "Have you checked your blood sugar since—"

"Yessss," Silas answered for Lily. "And I'm starving to death. If you care. Plus, I need to pee. Bad. Like, really bad. Can we pull over now? Please?"

"Okay, but let's make it quick. I want to surprise Mom while there's still enough light out for pictures."

"And you're sure about this? Surprising her, I mean." Lily nibbled at the frayed edge of her thumbnail. Anxiety squirmed in her chest. Combined with the carsickness, it was making her miserable.

Emma's lips pursed. "You've made your position more than clear."

"Ooh, scary voice," Silas whispered. "Careful, Lily."

Lily settled for a wordless exit from the SUV. The chain of bells dangling from the door jingled against the glass as they entered.

"Excuse me, where's the bathroom?" Silas asked.

The bored-looking teenager behind the register stared down at her cell phone, ignoring him. Silas looked to Lily for help.

"Excuse me," Lily said. "My brother needs to use your bathroom."

With a surly glance in Lily's direction, the cashier snapped her gum between her teeth then jabbed a finger at the handwritten sign on the counter: *Bathroom for Customers ONLY!!!*

"Wow. Three exclamation points? Seems a bit much, but okay." Lily tossed a pack of gum on the counter and fumbled a five-dollar bill out of her pocket.

Without breaking her dead-eyed stare from her screen, the cashier pointed to a dark hallway next to the refrigerator units lining the back wall.

"*Hey.*" Lily slapped a hand on the counter, felt a tug of satisfaction as the girl's head whipped up. "My change?"

The cashier smirked, mouth puckered into a lipstick-greased knot. She passed Lily's change back, then returned to her phone.

As Lily followed Silas to the bathroom, the bells jingled again. Emma entered and headed directly to the counter. She began trying to coax information from the cashier. "The road that turns right past the shop, it leads up to 1712 Grange?"

Lily browsed through the aisles of snacks. She considered a ginger ale, to settle her stomach, but she didn't want to listen to her mother gripe about the sugar. She grabbed a cold water instead, along with a box of over-priced crackers.

When Silas emerged from the bathroom, she asked, "Did you wash your hands?"

"Nope!" He rushed her and wiped his splayed fingers down the front of her shirt. To the cashier, he piped, "You're out of paper towels."

"Go pick out something to snack on," Lily said.

Emma was still struggling to get the cashier's attention. "Are you the one I talked to on the phone yesterday? I left a message for my wife, Claire. She's staying nearby. Blue eyes and freckles, dark hair to here." She cut a hand at her collar bone. "Has she come in today?"

"She might have," the cashier said, smiling at something on her phone. "But lots of people come through here. I don't remember all their faces."

Lily cast a look at the empty parking lot and said, "Right. Well, it helps if you actually look at the faces when they're talking to you."

The cashier rolled her eyes up to meet Emma's. "What's she look like again?"

Emma repeated the description.

"Nope. Haven't seen her."

Defeated, Emma paid for their snacks, dropped the change in the tip jar, and said, "Come on, you two. Let's go."

As Emma hurried out the door, Lily waited for Silas, who was dawdling and looking longingly at a display of party decorations near the counter. "You want a real tip?" she asked the cashier.

When the girl looked up, Lily mimicked her sarcastic not-smile from earlier. "Pick a different shade of lipstick next time. Your mouth looks like a second asshole."

The girl scoffed. "Take your dipshit brother and go. You don't want to keep your *moms* waiting."

A colorful plastic package whizzed past the cashier. She glared at Silas. "Did you just throw—"

"I'm not a dipshit," he said. "And your eyeshadow makes you look like a clown. Clowns like balloons, right?"

He grabbed another package of balloons from the rack and tossed them at the girl, then darted toward the door, cackling. "Run, Lily!"

The girl flipped Lily off. But Lily was laughing too hard to return the sentiment; she'd needed an outlet for the tension that had been building steadily inside her, and Silas had delivered. God, she loved him.

The drive up the winding dirt road felt even longer than their highway crawl. The road was unplowed. A thin layer of dirt-flecked snow shushed under their tires and disguised the numerous ruts and potholes. Lily stared through the windshield, worrying her thumbnail with her teeth.

"Quit that." Emma swatted Lily's arm, then returned her hand to the steering wheel immediately, as if the snow was just waiting for a lapse in her ten o'clock, two o'clock death-grip to wrestle control of the rental away.

Pines crowded inward along the one-lane track. Stands of quaking aspen reached bare skeletal branches across the strip of pale sky above.

At the end of this road lay a fight, Lily was sure of it. Things had been uncomfortable for the last year, but in recent weeks her mothers had been avoiding each other like repelling magnets. Not touching, not talking—unless you counted their "secret" meetings with the marriage counselor. And now Emma was traveling the well-worn track toward collision, invading Claire's privacy with the blind optimism that this time would be different.

Lily sank lower in her seat and hugged her knees. She would spend the whole trip trying to keep Silas out of the middle while she played peacemaker alone, filling the uncomfortable silences with banter, buffering the cutting remarks. If she'd learned anything over the last year, it was that she couldn't take sides. The knowledge made her feel more weary than sad.

"Lily," Silas said, "are you tall?"

"I really don't feel like playing right now, Si."

Emma braked, lurching around another turn in painfully slow increments. Lily's stomach turned a cartwheel.

"You remembered your insulin?" Emma asked.

Lily sighed. "What's tall to you, Si?"

"Taller than…Memma?"

"That's a very low bar. You're, what, like, four feet tall?"

"Five-*one*," Emma said. The SUV shuddered to a stop in front of a mailbox. She scanned the numbers on the side, then frowned. "Not it. But we're getting warmer."

"Speak for yourself." Lily's toes were numb in her sneakers. Her new boots were tucked away in her suitcase with the other cold weather accessories they'd purchased during their whirlwind shopping trip the day before.

Silas kicked the back of her seat.

"Yes," Lily said, "I'm tall."

Silas hummed and asked, "Are you still alive today?"

"Unfortunately," Lily muttered. She swallowed back her nausea and rested her forehead against the window. The cold helped a little.

"Here it is," Emma chirped, smiling so wide her cheeks trembled.

Lily eyed the mailbox sticking up from the snow. Its flag was missing, and if the dented metal and chipped paint were a preview of the cabin at the end of the driveway, then their stay would be even more uncomfortable than she'd anticipated. She wasn't picky, but Memma's idea of sleeping rough was a hotel that didn't provide breakfast. And Memma was not one to suffer in silence.

As the SUV pulled into the clearing, Emma made a sound crossed between "ick" and "ugh," frowning at the cabin as if the dingy wood box had spit in her face. Lily stifled a groan. Oh, yes. There would be a fight. One that would probably bring the dilapidated shack crashing down on their heads. If she was lucky.

"It's, uh, rustic," Emma said, pasting on a new smile. She pulled in beside a white truck and parked. "What do you think?"

It looks like the kind of place where teens get drunk and topless before an axe murderer slashes them to pieces, she wanted to say. The porch steps were sagging, the windows dull, the log exterior faded. She couldn't imagine growing up somewhere like this, so far from other people. It was as if the cabin had been dropped into the middle of nowhere specifically so the world could forget about it. "I think it looks nice. Just needs a little work, is all."

Silas unclicked his seatbelt and wiggled over the backseat, pedaling his legs. He reappeared with the strap of Lily's camera bag twisted around his arm.

"Careful with that," Lily said.

"Sorry." Silas grinned as Lily untangled his arm. "Get a picture of Mom's face when she sees us. She'll be so excited."

"That's right, she *will* be," Emma said, voice steadily climbing toward the shrill octave she usually reserved for holiday get-togethers with extended family. "We're going to have a white Christmas this year. Hot cocoa and a snowman, the works."

Lily pulled the Nikon DSLR camera she'd saved for two years to buy from its bag, switched it on, and removed the lens cap just as a pale oval appeared at the window to the left of the front door.

The door opened, and Claire stepped out.

Silas was already racing toward the porch, shouting, "Surprise, surprise!"

Lily watched through the viewfinder as Silas clamored up the porch steps and threw his arms around their mother's waist. Save for the *click* of the camera, and the soft creaks and groans of trees moving in the wind, the clearing was silent.

"Surprise!" Silas craned his neck to look up at Claire. She blinked rapidly, as if she was finally coming awake, and tucked Silas's hair behind his ears. Real happiness warmed her expression. Authentic joy.

Click.

Lily trailed after Silas, holding her camera up before her like a shield. Claire's sharp blue eyes darted up to look directly into the lens. Then her gaze fell on Emma, and her expression hardened. "What are you doing here, Em?"

"We didn't want you to spend Christmas alone," Silas said, echoing the excuse Emma had repeated over and over during their shopping spree. "Are you surprised?"

"I am." Claire planted a kiss on Silas's forehead. *Click.* "Why don't you and Lily start bringing your stuff inside?"

Their mothers were ten feet apart, staring. *Click.*

"You could have called first," Claire said.

Emma's smile faltered. "I did. All day yesterday. I even left a message for you."

Silas pulled Lily away toward the SUV, puffing like a draft horse, and the rest of their exchange was lost beneath the volume of his excited babbling.

Amused, Lily said, "Let me put my camera away and I'll help you."

"I can get my own suitcase," Silas insisted. His overburdened antics broke the tension, earning laughter from their mothers.

"See?" Emma said, passing Lily on her way to the trunk. "Everything's fine."

Lily tightened her hold on her suitcase and climbed the steps to the porch. Pushing the door shut behind her with her toe, she asked, "Where should I put this?"

"Ah, I haven't had much time to clean up. I wasn't expecting..." Claire trailed off, watching Silas barrel down the short hall and back. Lily dropped her bag beside the door.

"Is this it?" Silas asked.

Claire spread her hands and said, "This is it."

"You really grew up here? It's so...small." He ran a hand over the coffee table, wrinkling his nose. "And dirty."

"Rude, Si." Lily steered her brother back down the hall. "Show me around."

"This is it," Silas repeated, baffled.

"Well, which rooms are ours?"

"Room." Silas held up a finger.

"I'll fight you for it," Lily said, pulling the hood of his coat over his head. "Loser sleeps outside?"

"Mom," Silas howled.

"You can stay in my old room," Claire said. "It's on the right."

"Dibs on the bed," Silas crowed.

While Silas jumped on the mattress, Lily eyed the bare log walls. She grazed the woodgrain with her fingers. There were no holes or scraps of tape—nothing to indicate their mother's bedroom had ever been decorated.

"Ease up on the bed, Si," Lily warned, "or we'll both be stuck on the floor."

Wringing her hands outside the bedroom, Claire said, "Silas, let your sister have the bed."

"We could share," Silas offered.

"If Mom can find some blankets, I'll build you a tent," Lily said. "It'll be fun, like camping."

Silas rolled his eyes. "You don't build a tent; you *pitch* it."

Lily smacked him with the bed's only pillow.

From out in the hall, Emma said, "This is nice, isn't it?"

Claire's pained expression suggested otherwise. Her eyes were red-rimmed and puffy, as if she'd been crying or missing sleep—maybe both.

Clinging to Emma's sweater, Silas said, "Lily's going to pitch a tent for me."

Claire tousled his hair. "Guess that's my cue to go find blankets," she said, and disappeared down the hall.

Lily headed back to the living room to retrieve her suitcase. On her way, a loud thud from the kitchen startled her. She turned and saw a glass object rolling across the countertop—a bottle. *Of course.* She felt her heart sink with disappointment as she watched her mother stow the contraband in the cabinet above the refrigerator.

"Everything okay?" Lily asked.

Claire threw a wild glance over her shoulder. "Fine," she said, closing the cabinet. "Just cleaning up a bit."

"Did you find the blankets?"

"I'm working on it."

Recognizing the terse, petulant tone that betrayed her mother's poorly disguised hangover, Lily decided to leave her suitcase packed, in case there was a midnight drive to the airport waiting in their future.

Silas shuttled the shiny wrapped packages from their suitcases to the living room and left them piled in the corner. As Claire squeezed into the bedroom with an armload of blankets, he followed her, complaining, "There's no tree."

"Look outside," Lily said. "There's literally nothing *but* trees."

Casting a hopeful look in Claire's direction, Emma said, "Maybe we can cut our own?"

Claire nodded. "Maybe. Hey, do you want the tour before I try to figure out dinner?"

"The tour?" Silas pushed up his glasses, looking around. "Is there another cabin in the back?"

"I'll work out dinner while you show them around," Lily said.

Claire smiled at her. "Thanks."

While Claire detailed the sparse amenities of off-grid living, Lily listened from the kitchen as Emma's enthusiasm waned, then soured. When one of her comments earned a snapped rebuttal, Lily called out, "Silas! Come help me!"

Silas appeared beside her, looking worried. Claire stalked past and slammed the front door behind her. A moment later, Emma came in, sniffling. The mascara rimming her brown eyes was smudged, as if she'd been crying.

"What's down here?" Silas knelt on a door set in the kitchen floor against the far wall and tugged on the knob. "It's locked."

Emma blew her nose, then said, "A basement, maybe? I'm sure there's a key around—ah!" She plucked the keys from a rusted hook screwed into the wall above the basement door. "Here we go."

"There's some canned food in these bags," Lily said.

But Emma was too busy testing keys in the lock to respond.

Silas stopped bouncing around the door and turned toward Lily. He tapped his skinny wrist. Nodding her thanks, Lily said, "I'm going to use the bathroom. Yell if you find any buried treasure."

She was in the bathroom, returning her glucose meter to its black zipper case, when a fist pounded on the door. She opened it to find Silas, out of breath, pale. Lily hugged him to her.

"What happened?" she asked.

"Mom's mad," Silas whispered. "We just wanted to see the basement."

"Are you still hungry?"

Silas shook his head.

"Yeah, me neither."

"But you took your insulin. You have to eat something."

Lily sighed; he was right.

A metallic clanking sound issued from the kitchen. "Dinner!"

Silas looked up at Lily. She shrugged. "Your guess is as good as mine."

They approached the kitchen with caution.

"Dinner's going to be cold because I can't get the stove to work," Emma said, spooning something out of a can. "Lily, did you take your—"

"Yes," Silas and Lily replied in unison.

As they took their seats across from each other at the dining table, Emma deposited their plates and directed her gaze out the window. "Some view," she said.

Lily couldn't tell from her tone if the remark was sarcastic. Dusk had stripped the details from the trees surrounding the clearing, reducing the picturesque scene to a dim wall of shadows.

"That porch is a deathtrap," Emma muttered, then returned her attention to their plates. "Well, what are you waiting for? Dig in."

"I can barely reach," Silas said, stretching his arms up to demonstrate. The kitchen table was too high for him to eat comfortably.

"So sit on your feet." Emma moved to the cabinets and began opening and closing them, searching for something.

Lily tensed, waiting for her to open the cabinet above the fridge and discover the bottle, but the search ended when Emma located a spray cleaner and a sponge beneath the sink. As she often did when she and Claire were fighting, she started scrubbing.

"Where's Mom?" Silas asked. "Isn't she going to eat?"

Lily kicked him gently under the table and shook her head. Silas took the hint. He poked the cold cheese draped over his beans and made a face.

Lily's stale tortilla cracked between her fingers, spilling out black beans. Unwilling to make matters worse by complaining, she lowered her head to eat, but the smell of bleach from the spray cleaner was spoiling the meal, along with Emma's constant grumbling as she speculated over what Claire had been up to, since she sure as hell wasn't cleaning.

When Lily and Silas were finished, Emma spirited their plates away to the sink. Before they could evacuate the table, however, Claire stomped into the kitchen, cutting past Emma to rattle the basement door. Satisfied that it was still locked, she positioned herself in the corner between the table and the window. Without looking at Emma, she said, "Winter break doesn't start until Monday. Why did you pull them out early?"

Did something happen? That's what she was really asking. Lily shot a look at her brother, hunkering lower to hide behind his long hair, and interjected, "I have something I wanted to ask you both. You know the photography class I'm taking?"

Claire nodded.

Lily took a deep breath and plunged forward. "Well, Ms. Evers is offering a field trip to Yosemite National Park this summer. It's a really big deal, and I was hoping—"

"How much is it going to cost?" Emma asked.

"A couple hundred," Lily admitted. "But food and gas and lodging are included."

"Lodging? You mean tents. You'd be camping."

"Yeah, but it's only for two weeks. And it's supposed to be really great experience—especially with all the wildlife, the scenery."

"I don't know," said Emma.

Claire smiled at Lily. "We'll make it work."

"I think we need to talk about it first, don't you? Claire, she's never been away from home for more than a weekend, and with her condition—"

"Well, you have my full support," Claire said.

Emma bumped past Lily's chair and left the kitchen.

"Sorry," Lily mumbled. "Probably wasn't the best timing, but I'm supposed to get back to Ms. Evers before the end of the month."

"It's not you," Claire said. "This whole thing was…"

"A surprise?" Silas offered.

"Exactly. But I'm happy you're here." Claire took Silas by the chin, tilting his face up to kiss his nose. "And whatever happened at school, we'll talk about it when you're ready, okay?"

Hoping to salvage the evening, Lily asked, "Can we do something together before bedtime? I brought a pack of cards in my suitcase. If we scare up some loose change, we could finally teach Silas how to play poker."

Teaching Silas new things was one of the few activities their parents still enjoyed together. But Claire grimaced. "I don't think so. My head's killing me. Rain check?"

"Lily," Silas whined, "can I read my new comics now?"

"Sure. Let's say goodnight to Memma first, though."

"Thanks," Claire whispered. She kissed Lily on the forehead, then collapsed into a chair at the kitchen table.

After a quick goodnight to Emma, Lily steered Silas into their bedroom for the night. She was grateful she'd thought to buy him comics at the airport; aside from what they'd brought with them, there was nothing in the cabin to entertain children. The record player might work, but it was out in the living room. At Silas's urging, she used the bed frame, blankets, and suitcases to erect a makeshift tent. With a flashlight clamped between his teeth, Silas army-crawled beneath the drooping blankets.

"How is it?" Lily asked.

His small hand stuck out, gave her a thumbs up, then felt around for the comic book he'd left on the floor.

"Okay if I turn the light off?"

"Yep!" He clicked his flashlight on.

"Lights out by nine," Lily said, putting her earbuds in.

She was just starting to drift off when the mattress shook. Silas whispered, "Are you awake?"

"I am now," Lily groaned, checking the time. "But you shouldn't be."

"I can't sleep. They're still *discussing.*"

"Here." Lily passed her earbuds to Silas with her phone. "Better?"

"Yes. I like this song." Silas exhaled. "Thanks."

Sometime later, Silas shook Lily awake again. He stood beside her but was facing the window, one hand locked on her shoulder, the other holding a flashlight. The sweat from his palm had already soaked through her shirt, and the beam of his flashlight, trained on the floor, trembled.

"Silas? Are you okay?"

An unpleasant smell permeated the bedroom, strangely familiar.

"Turn the light on," Lily said.

"No!" he whispered, and his hands fluttered, urging her to stay still. His glasses were crooked, his hair rumpled. He stared down at the flashlight in horror and clicked it off. "No, she'll see us."

"Who will see us?" Lily dragged her hands over her face and sat up. She recognized the smell now.

"The old lady—she was watching us through the window. When I shined my flashlight on her...her eyes glowed. I got scared and—"

"It's okay, Si," Lily said. "I'll clean it up. But I'll have to turn the light on."

"Don't tell Memma, please?" He didn't want to go back to the child counselor. Lily didn't blame him; having to explain his bed-wetting to a complete stranger had to be humiliating.

She got up and switched on the light. Silas squealed. He dove into his tent and peeked out at her, gathering the sheets at his chin.

Lily approached the window, but the light made it impossible to see anything beyond the reflection of their bedroom. "See?" she said. "There's nothing there. It must have been an animal—a raccoon or something." She whipped the dirty curtains closed.

"No, it was a lady."

Lily crouched to Silas's level. "You said her eyes glowed?"

Silas nodded.

"That's called eyeshine. There's a membrane that reflects light back, so it looks like the eyes are glowing. But only animals have it. People don't. There. Mystery solved."

While Silas changed into clean pajamas, Lily pulled the wet bedding out of his tent and padded barefoot toward the front of the cabin. She walked slowly, allowing her eyes adjust to the darkness.

Someone was slumped over the kitchen table.

"Mom?" Lily whispered.

"Hey, what are you doing up?" Claire sat up and took in the bundle of blankets and pajamas in Lily's arms. "Again? I really thought he was past this."

"Don't say anything to Memma, okay? I promised him."

"She won't hear it from me. There's a washer and dryer in the basement—or there used to be."

"You don't know?"

"I haven't…been down there yet."

Lily waited. "So, are you going to unlock the door?"

"I guess Silas probably told you about earlier."

Lily shrugged.

"I'll explain it to both of you, someday."

When you're older. Lily stared at the floorboards to keep from rolling her eyes. She wanted to go back to bed, not start a fight.

"Anyway, I pumped earlier, so there should be enough water for a load," Claire said. The keys jingled as she struggled to unlock the door; her hands were shaking. She leaned the door back against the wall, took a step away. A steep wooden staircase descended into the darkness below, bordered by the shared kitchen-basement wall on the left and a rickety-looking railing to the right.

"You can stay up here," Lily said, pretending not to notice her mother's erratic breathing. "I'll take it down. Is there a light?"

"The switch is at the bottom," Claire said, apologetically. She turned the kitchen light on. A yellow rectangle of light spilled down part of the basement wall to the left of the stairs, illuminating only the uppermost steps. The stairs below seemed even darker by comparison.

"If I die, tell Silas his secret died with me," Lily muttered.

As she started down the stairs, she kept close to the wall, not trusting the railing to her right. The steps creaked and sighed underfoot with a slight tremor.

At the bottom of the stairs, she felt for a switch and flipped it. A single bare bulb flickered to life, illuminating a rectangular room with concrete walls. In the lower right-hand corner of the far wall, underneath the porch, the concrete had cracked open and was crumbling. Her gaze panned right, passing over the sagging wooden shelves stocked with dusty cans and jars that lined the wall adjacent, and she turned around to find the washer and dryer tucked against the rear wall of the basement. Except for the fridge and stove overhead, Lily had never seen a more ancient pair of appliances.

She stuffed the laundry into the washer, tossed in a scoop of dry detergent, and started the wash cycle. As she moved back toward the stairs, something glinted in the crumbling wall under the porch. When she tilted her head, the shiny object amid the scarred concrete sparkled again. Curious, she crossed the room to inspect the irregularity.

She shivered. The temperature had dropped dramatically as she moved under the porch. Near the corner, the crumbling concrete bowed inward. Cold emanated from the wall, sinking deep into her bones. Dirt pressed through a gap and had tumbled out to form a small pile on the floor.

She squinted at a shattered glass jar mixed in with the dirt on the floor, then moved aside to let the light strike the wall, so she could locate the sparkling object again.

There.

A shard of glass embedded in the dirt between the loose concrete. Almost as if someone had broken the jar and used the piece to dig. Lily wiggled the shard free and examined the gouged earth. There were furrows dragged through the gap, spaced like claw marks. Her hand floated up, fingers fitting into the grooves as if she'd dug them herself. Something rough scraped the pad of her middle finger. Lily felt around, located the tiny object, and pried it loose. She angled the object toward the light.

It was a fingernail.

"Everything okay?" A hissed whisper.

Lily jumped. She had forgotten her mother was waiting upstairs. She considered mentioning the fingernail, then recalled her mother's aversion to the basement. Was the fingernail somehow related? If so, the last thing Lily wanted to do was bring up a touchy subject while her mother was nursing a secret hangover.

She could keep the disturbing little discovery to ask her about it later, but the idea of taking the fingernail with her felt wrong. Where would she put it? Why would she want to keep it anyway? She'd never work up the courage to ask her mother about it, so why bother?

After tucking the fingernail and the glass shard into the pile of dirt at the base of the wall, Lily returned to the kitchen. She climbed the stairs two at a time, wiping her hands clean on her pajamas before she reached the top.

Maybe some things were best left buried.

LATER, LILY LAY awake listening to Silas's soft snoring. Sleep wouldn't come. She couldn't stop thinking about her mother's reaction to the basement, and the fingernail she'd found embedded in the wall. Sighing in frustration, she got up, went to the window, and parted the curtains.

Between the tree line and the cabin, a trail of pockmarks wove through the moonlit snow. Lily pressed her forehead to the glass, following the tracks to where they ended, just below the bedroom window. There were smudges on the pane. Frowning, Lily fogged the glass and wiped at the marks. But the smudges remained.

She traced the smudges, seeing a hint of what almost looked like a forehead, cheeks, and chin. At the center, a grayish patch with brown-stained edges sparkled with frost.

A face?

Lily pulled the curtains shut. She was back in bed, blankets pulled up over her nose, before she remembered to breathe again. It couldn't be a human face; Silas had seen its eyes glow. And why would someone be looking in at them, way out in the middle of nowhere?

It was an animal.

When Lily finally drifted off, she dreamed of animals with flat-pressed human faces, burrowing with ragged fingernails into the basement.

EMMA

EMMA WOKE UP to an empty bed. She sneezed once, twice, watching through watery eyes as dust motes swirled in the morning light. The beginnings of a headache pulsed in her skull. Yawning, she pulled her bathrobe on, stuffed her feet into her house shoes. The pressure in her sinuses was worse now that she was standing. She couldn't breathe through her nose. A hot shower would set her right.

She shuffled into the bathroom, sneezed again, groaning, and buried her runny nose in a wad of toilet paper. Then she twisted the faucet handles on the tub.

Nothing.

She could not imagine why anyone would choose to live off the grid.

There was a light knock on the bathroom door. She opened it to find Claire waiting in the hall with a steaming cup of tea. She wore the tentative smile reserved for their awkward, post-fight encounters—the closest she would ever come to an apology. A part of Emma hated that sad, crooked smile. But she was freezing, determined to make amends.

"Thanks," Emma said and sipped at the tea.

"The shower should be ready in a few minutes. Lily's out back, working the pump."

"And Silas?" From outside, Emma heard a loud *thwack*, followed by a peal of laughter.

"Lily taught him how to chop wood."

"Does Lily know how to chop wood?"

Claire smiled; this time it was genuine. Warmth spread across her delicate features like sunlight spilling over a valley. Emma felt love sink its familiar hooks into the meat of her heart, and she closed the distance between them, slipping her arms around Claire's waist to kiss her.

"I have something for you," she told her. She went back to the bedroom to collect the paper bag. "Here. Sorry I didn't have a chance to wrap it."

Claire slid the small drawing pad out of its bag. Her lips pressed into a thin line.

Emma's heart sank. "You don't like it?"

"No, that's not…It's nice. Thanks. I just…You know I can't work."

Emma held her tongue.

"I know, I *can* work, but it's just not…" Claire exhaled and ran a hand through her hair, rolling her eyes up to search the ceiling. "The inspiration's not there. The drive, motivation, whatever you want to call it."

She headed for the kitchen, and Emma followed her. "Well, maybe if you just tried—"

"Like I haven't been trying?" Claire opened a cabinet. She removed a pot and banged it down onto the stove. "Six days a week, I'm at the gallery, Em. I can't make them come in."

"That's not what I'm…Look, forget the gallery. Forget *selling* your work. You never used to care about that."

"I didn't *used to* have two kids and a mortgage, or a wife working herself to death to support us." There were dark circles under Claire's eyes. Her lids were puffy, her corneas bloodshot. She looked hungover. Claire crossed her arms. "What, Emma? What is it now?"

Lily and Silas burst into the cabin.

"Close the door behind you," Claire called out.

Lily knelt before the woodstove and motioned for Silas to deposit his armload of chopped wood. She added fuel to the stove, then grabbed the matchbox.

"I want to start the fire," Silas whined.

"No way." Lily said. "And don't give me that look. You know why not."

"The shower should work now," Claire said to Emma.

Lowering her voice suggestively, Emma replied, "We could shower together. Conserve water."

"I'll get breakfast going." Claire turned back to the stove.

The shower was too brief and tepid to clear Emma's sinuses, and it did nothing to remove the sting of Claire's reaction to her gift. She combed her dripping blonde hair back and sighed. Her headache was getting worse.

When she leaned out to reach for a towel, her feet slipped on the wet porcelain and her legs squirted out from under her. She clutched at the curtain as she fell. The metal rings rattled as the mold-speckled plastic tore, and the tub elicited a loud hollow *bong* as her knee connected.

As she rose shakily, the door cracked open.

"Everything okay in there?" Claire asked.

"Yeah, the curtain got the worst of it."

Claire poked her head in. "What the hell happened?"

"I'm fine, by the way." Emma snatched a stiff towel from the rack and dried her face. Even with her sinuses clogged, she could smell the mildew.

She shouldered past Claire, trembling from the shock of the fall and the cold and the frustration that had only seemed to worsen as the morning went on. She didn't want Claire to see the effect this place was having on her. She couldn't bear to have her poor attitude thrown in her face again—more evidence that the trip had been a mistake.

When she finished dressing, she crossed the hall and tapped her nails on the door frame of Lily and Silas's room, asking, "Did you eat breakfast yet?"

"Yeah, Mom made some instant oatmeal." Lily was perched on the edge of the bed, brushing her hair. "Silas ate too."

"Where is he?"

Through the wall, Silas shouted, "What happened to the shower curtain?"

"I fell," Emma shouted back. "Tried to take it down with me."

Lily winced. "Are you okay?"

"I'll live."

They both tensed as the hiss of shower spray filtered in from the next room.

"I'd better get in there before he floods the cabin," Lily said. "Silas, throw a towel on. I'm coming in."

"The towels *stink*."

"He's not lying," Emma said. "Hey, Lily?"

"Yeah?"

"Thanks."

Lily tilted her head. "For what?"

"For not..." Emma blinked back tears. "You were right, before—about this being a bad idea. Thanks for not rubbing it in."

Lily grinned. "I'm sure I'll get around to it, eventually."

The growl of an approaching engine disturbed the early morning silence. Claire emerged from the kitchen and exited through the front door. Emma went to the front windows to peer out as a faded green truck pulled into the clearing. A stout woman bundled in a thick coat climbed out. Claire waved to her from the porch.

Lily came up from behind, rested her chin atop Emma's head.

"Stop that." Emma ducked. "You know I hate that."

"Short people problems," Lily said. "Who's that?"

"Ask your mother. Did you take your—"

"Yes, I took my insulin."

A black dog leaped out of the truck and bounded toward Claire. Her arms came up, but she didn't recoil or scream. After a moment's hesitation, she surprised Emma by reaching out to scratch the dog behind its ear.

Their visitor called out, "Good morning!"

"Good morning," Claire said. "It's good to see you again. Both of you."

The dog barked in response.

"Is that a dog?" Silas ran into the living room, jostling Emma as he pressed his nose to the window. He squealed and rushed to pull the door open.

The black dog turned toward the cabin, cocking its head, before it shot up the steps and through the door, bowling Silas over. He released an ear-piercing shriek of delight. The dog spun excited circles around him, tail thumping his face, knocking his glasses off. The cord connecting the earpieces prevented the glasses from falling. They swung around his neck until he fumbled them back into place. Silas hated the cord, but Emma had insisted he wear it after breaking not one but two pairs in the same month. She stiffened as he hugged the big dog's neck.

"Don't worry, Oscar's harmless," the owner said as she stepped inside. She stuck out a gloved hand. "I'm Evelyn. You must be the missus."

"Emma." She shook Evelyn's hand.

Silas giggled, rolling on the floor as the dog licked his face.

"Silas, introduce yourself," Emma said.

"You just did."

Lily smiled at Evelyn. "I'm Lily. Hi."

"Aren't you just the prettiest thing?" Evelyn gasped, leaning back. "And so *tall*. If I was your height, I'd be damn near unstoppable."

As Claire shut the front door, Evelyn said to her, "I didn't know your family was coming."

"That makes two of us. Sorry, I didn't have a chance to make that list yet."

"Oh, forget the groceries. That can wait for tomorrow. Let me take you all on a tour out to the lake. It's early yet. We can all drive down to the One Stop for sandwiches after." Evelyn's gray eyes sparkled. "What do you say?"

"I say yes!" Silas tossed one of his gloves across the living room and clapped when Oscar retrieved it.

"He'll say yes to anything if there's a dog involved," Lily said.

While Emma didn't love the idea of tromping through the snow in the cold, spending the day inside the dark, dusty confines of the cabin was even less appealing. Maybe the fresh air would help clear her sinuses. Forcing a smile, she said, "Claire? What do you think?"

Claire shrugged. "Sounds like fun to me. Lily, you could bring your camera along."

"And I can bring my new drawing pad," Silas said. He darted down the hall and returned with the drawing pad Emma had given Claire.

Wounded, Emma donned her new snow gear and helped Lily and Silas gather their things. They joined Claire and Evelyn on the porch. The older woman was smoking. Emma must have made a face, because Evelyn quickly stamped the cigarette out and tucked the butt into her pocket.

"I'll ask Andrew if he came by the next time I see him," Evelyn said to Claire, squeezing her arm. "It was probably just him, trying to get a quick look at the place. I mentioned you might need a handyman. He would've parked out on the road and walked in so he wouldn't disturb us. Likes to keep to himself, but he's harmless. The barefoot thing is a bit odd, though."

"Barefoot?" Emma glanced between them, lost. "Who's Andrew?"

Claire's face tightened. "A guy from town. He's going to help us take all the junk inside to the dump."

"Oh!" Evelyn said, "I almost forgot. Before we go…"

She tromped through the snow to her truck, pulled the door open, and removed a rifle from the cab. Emma felt a stab of alarm. Images of gunshot victims she'd treated paraded through her mind—accidents and ill intent, all amounting to the same ends. Her arm flew up instinctively, pushing Lily and Silas behind her.

"Relax, Em," Claire said. "Evelyn was a sheriff for thirty years. She knows how to handle a rifle."

"We're going to a lake. Why do we need a rifle?"

Evelyn grinned. "Better safe than sorry. "I'll leave her with you, after the tour."

"Sounds great, thanks," Claire said. "Though it's been a long time since I've fired a gun. I might need a refresher course."

Emma gaped. "A refresher course? You've never fired a gun."

"I started hunting with my father when I was Silas's age. We shot empty cans, mostly. Target practice."

"Cool," Silas said. "Can I try it?"

"No!" Emma snapped, making Lily jump. She hadn't intended to shout, but her son's excitement, and the sight of his hand reaching toward the rifle…

"Em—"

"*No*, Claire. Absolutely not. Thank you, Evelyn, but I'm not comfortable having a gun in the cabin with the children."

Claire and Emma stared at each other across the porch.

Cutting between them, Lily said, "Shall we?"

Evelyn smiled and slung the rifle's strap over her shoulder. "Follow me."

"To the lake!" Silas crowed.

As Evelyn led them through the forest behind the cabin, Silas trailed close behind with a barrage of questions. He pointed at the ranks of trees, and Evelyn said, "Those are Norway pines. Your granddad built your cabin out of these. That's why the logs are reddish in color."

Silas opened his drawing pad. Lily nudged him, slipping a pen into his hand. He sketched a pine, then asked, "What's the scientific name?"

"*Pinus resinosa*," said Evelyn, grinning. "Seems we have a scientist in our midst. That's good. Every expedition needs a scientist."

Evelyn spelled it out for him, then laughed as Silas tugged her onward by the sleeve of her coat. "These up ahead are white spruce. *Pinus strobus*."

Silas held out his drawing pad while Evelyn printed the name. "The bark's different," he said. "It's gray."

"Smart boy. Now, look at this tree here. Red or white?"

Silas rolled his eyes. "Neither, duh."

"Duh, indeed." Evelyn rolled flat, needle-like leaves between her fingers and held them out to Silas. "Smell that? Balsam fir. *Abies balsamea*."

"They look more like Christmas trees," Silas said.

When he reached out to poke the blistered bark, Evelyn pulled his hand back. "Careful. Those blisters are filled with resin. Get it on you, and you'll stick to everything."

"Where are all the animals?" Lily asked, surveying the surrounding forest through her camera's viewfinder.

"It's winter," Emma said, "most of the animals are probably hibernating."

"Even the birds?" Lily scanned the trees.

"They migrate, don't they?"

"There aren't any animals around here." Claire said. "Never have been."

Emma looked at her in surprise. It was the first time she'd spoken since leaving the cabin.

"That's weird," Silas said. "How come?"

Claire shrugged. "You'd have to ask them."

"That's a handsome Nikon you've got there," Evelyn said. "Bought it yourself, didn't you?"

Lily blushed. "How'd you know?"

"I'm good at reading people. And you, my dear, have 'hard worker' written all over you."

"Yeah, I worked my ass—ets off," Lily said, glancing at Silas, then Emma.

Emma smiled. *Nice save.*

Pulling Claire closer to show that there were no hard feelings after last night's discussion, Emma said, "Lily's going to be taking a field trip to Yosemite with her photography class this summer."

Lily beamed at her.

"Yosemite's beautiful. You're going to love it," Evelyn said. As Silas chased Oscar down the sloping bank to the stream below, she added, "You'll want to keep an eye on him around the stream. The water level's up a lot higher than usual this time of year. She's deep—and fast. We'll need to walk further downstream before we can cross."

"Silas, stay back," Emma shouted. She let go of Claire to quicken her pace.

Silas was kneeling beside the stream. Wiggling his hand from his glove, he reached out to touch the water rushing past.

"Hey." Emma yanked him up by the hood of his red snow coat. "I told you to leave it alone."

"Okay, sorry." Silas pushed up his glasses with a dripping hand and stood. He squinted at a narrow log laid across the stream. "Is that the bridge?"

"No, Evelyn says we need to go downstream. We can't cross here."

"Well, somebody did." Silas pointed to a line of footprints trailing down the bank to their left. The trail descended to a narrow log laid across the icy stream and reappeared on the opposite side, weaving off into the trees.

As the rest of their party joined them, Emma asked, "Do we have any other neighbors?"

At the sight of the footprints, Claire froze.

Evelyn knelt to inspect the tracks. "That's strange," she said. "Were any of you out here earlier?"

Emma shot a questioning look at Lily and Silas; they shook their heads.

Claire's jaw clenched. "No, we haven't left the cabin."

"Well, there shouldn't be anyone else around," Evelyn said. "Good thing we brought Matilda for protection."

"Matilda?" Silas tilted his head. Evelyn patted the rifle and he laughed.

"Huh." Lily set her boot beside one of the prints. "Who walks around barefoot in the snow?"

Evelyn rose and dusted snow off her knee. "I was just wondering that myself. Claire, you said the tracks you found near the shed were barefoot."

"Near the shed?" Emma felt a twinge of anxiety. "When was this? Are we safe here?"

"We're *fine*, Em." Claire scuffed at one of the prints with her boot. "The first night I stayed here, I found some tracks outside the cabin. But it was just Evelyn's handyman."

"Probably," Evelyn added. "Though these prints seem a bit small...and I can't for the life of me explain why he'd be walking around way out here without boots on."

"Ugh," Silas groaned. "Who cares? He probably froze his stupid feet off and went home. Can we go now? Please? I want to see the lake before *my* feet freeze."

"There's another log crossing about half a mile downstream," Evelyn said. "Much safer."

Emma stared at the footprints, concerned. If there was a stranger moving around the property, maybe they shouldn't be staying here. The person could be dangerous.

Claire had turned a sickly shade of green. As Emma racked her brain for an explanation, a possibility dawned on her. Evelyn was right; the tracks seemed too small to belong to a man, but a woman…

"You don't think…" She reached for Claire. "I mean, it would be a miracle after all this time, but…Claire, do you think it could it be her?"

"No." Claire shrugged Emma's hand off.

"But—"

"Just leave it, Em. It's not my mom; she's gone." Claire jerked her head at Evelyn. "Can we talk?"

They moved off together, downstream, following Lily and Silas. He was chasing the dog, while his sister tried to keep them both on course. With a high-pitched shriek, Silas tripped and fell facedown in the snow. The dog circled him, barking. It was chaos.

Emma shoved her hands into her pockets and trudged along behind Claire and Evelyn, maintaining enough distance to avoid being accused of eavesdropping on whatever they were discussing in a low murmur. From the way Claire had hustled on ahead with the neighbor, Emma had sensed she wasn't welcome to join their conversation, but maybe she was just being overly sensitive. Probably. She sighed and hugged herself.

Lily traversed the log crossing first, long legs carrying her over the frost-rimed wood. Emma crossed last. Claire waited for her, took her hand, and helped her step down to solid ground. Emma's heart leaped. Claire finally seemed to be warming up to her presence. Maybe there was still a chance to turn this mess into the memorable family vacation she'd envisioned. On impulse, she hooked a hand behind Claire's neck and pulled her in for a kiss.

"Memma," Silas whined. "Come on."

"You should be glad your mothers love each other," Evelyn said to him. "A lot of kids aren't so lucky."

Lily grimaced. When she caught Emma watching, she flashed a smile that didn't touch her eyes.

It seemed they weren't the only ones headed for the lake. Emma didn't mention the reappearance of the barefooted tracks. She didn't want to risk another turn in Claire's mood, not while they were actually getting along for a change.

"Are we there yet?" Silas asked. He clung to Oscar's collar as the dog towed him through the snow.

"Look there, Si." Emma pointed ahead to where the trees opened up to a lakeside.

The remains of six buildings poked up through the snow near the shore. Four log structures formed a rectangle, their empty doorways facing inward. On the outskirts, a ruined pair of shacks was being slowly reclaimed by the undergrowth.

"White Hook Lake," Evelyn said.

Emma saw it now, how the flat expanse of powder-dusted ice curved like a hook around the shore.

"What's all this?" Lily asked, aiming her camera at the buildings.

"The boarding school," Evelyn replied. "Indigenous children were brought here to receive instruction."

Silas's brow wrinkled. "What kind of instruction?"

While Claire and Emma fumbled for an explanation, Lily said, "How to be White 101."

"Assimilation," Emma explained. "There were schools like this all over the country. The government thought it would make the children more 'civilized' if they separated them from their families. They'd force the kids to leave their homes and march them off to boarding schools far away, where they'd cut off their hair and make them learn English, and try to make them more—"

"White," Lily said. "These places did a lot of harm."

Evelyn nodded somberly. "The students received their lessons in the schoolhouse." She pointed to the longest building. It was bordered on three sides by water, and its roof was partially collapsed, open to the sky above. Debris cluttered the interior.

"And over here"—she motioned to the long, squat box standing to the left—"is the bunkhouse where the children slept."

"No windows?" Silas squinted through the door into the gloom. "How come there aren't any beds?"

"Bunks had to be built from scratch. You had to cut down the trees, split the logs, fit everything together. It took time and money. According to his private journals, Father—their instructor and keeper—was more concerned with teaching. Comfort wasn't a priority."

"It was for whoever lived in this one," Lily murmured, peering into the dilapidated cabin to the right of the schoolhouse. "Is this where Father stayed?"

"Yes. With his daughter, Grace." Evelyn turned to face the building opposite the schoolhouse. "It's hard to tell now, but this used to be a cookhouse: a combination dining hall, kitchen, and storeroom."

Lily circled the cookhouse, angling her camera at the two outlying shacks. "What about these?"

"Before Father came along and repurposed everything, this was a settlement built by hunters and trappers, and visitors still passed through. Traders and the like. Father would rent the shacks out in exchange for supplies."

"So, what happened?" Emma asked. "The school closed down?"

Bored with their conversation, Silas pursued Oscar across the clearing. Evelyn waited until he was out of earshot, then said, "Father believed he was betrayed, and indeed, someone had reported abuse and other misdeeds to the government. But there were also rumors of unpaid debts, misuse of funding, which may have contributed to their closing. Other schools were opening up—less remote, easier to monitor."

Lily whispered something to Claire, then headed off into the trees.

"Where is she going?" Emma asked.

"To test her blood sugar."

"Why does she need to wander off?"

"Privacy."

Emma frowned. "She used to let me prick her finger and run the tests, and now she has to take a hike to get away from us?"

"You know Lily." Claire shrugged. "She doesn't want to seem weak."

"She told you that?"

Claire removed her beanie and ran her fingers through her hair. "Yeah."

"So why couldn't she tell me?"

"Because you don't listen, Em. You're so set on helping—on *fixing*."

"Well, I'm sorry for—"

Evelyn coughed. Emma flushed, embarrassed; she'd forgotten Evelyn was within earshot.

"Hey!" Lily shouted from the trees. "There's something back here!"

Oscar darted into the forest with Silas close behind him.

"Woah!" Silas called out a moment later. "You have to see this. Hurry!"

Evelyn linked an arm through Emma's and powered them both forward.

They emerged through the trees to find the edge of a large pit gouged into the earth. Lily was kneeling at the bottom, clearing snow and duff from low heaps of bones. She held up a partial skull to show them. "What was this, you think? A wolf?"

"Could be," Evelyn said. "Back when this place was first built, the men who stayed here snared and shot and skinned everything that moved. Anything that couldn't be sold, they tossed into this pit. Then they set up traps and hunting blinds to kill the predators and scavengers drawn by the carcasses. After a while, it was like the animals could smell the place was tainted. They knew better than to come around—even the birds. Does greed have a smell?"

"Murder does," Emma said, as Oscar paced the rim of the pit, whining softly.

Evelyn led them down into the pit. She made kissing sounds at the dog and called his name, but he wouldn't descend into the pit with them. His black coat stood up in a stiff ridge along his spine. His behavior was making Emma uneasy.

They shouldn't be here. What kind of mother was she, letting her kids dig through bones crawling with germs? She closed her eyes and forced herself to breathe. She needed to wash her hands, really scrub them red and raw.

"We should start heading back," she said.

"No-ooo," Silas whined, glaring at her through glasses flecked with snow.

"Yes. That attitude right there, the stink eye you're giving me? That's the hunger. If we skip lunch to dig through dirty old bones all day, you'll be a monster by dinner time."

Claire picked Silas up from behind, shaking him. "He's a little monster already."

"Put me down!" Silas screeched. But Claire held him fast while Lily pelted his exposed stomach with snowballs. "Stop it, Lily! It's going down my pants, you jerk. Stop!"

Watching them together, Emma felt like an outsider—the only one incapable of loosening up enough to enjoy the moment.

Claire swung Silas into a snow drift, then kicked him gently in the rear, saying, "Move, soldier."

"This is child abuse," Lily said, grinning.

"I won't tell if you don't."

They climbed from the pit in single file, following Silas back toward the clearing. He hurried on ahead, leaving clear tracks in the snow.

"Someone else is here," he cried out from the clearing ahead, and Emma ran to catch up with him. She broke through the trees just in time to see his red coat disappearing inside the ruined building to the right of the schoolhouse, the one Evelyn had designated as Father's cabin.

"Silas!" Emma followed his trail up to the doorway, where a second pair of prints joined his smaller ones. Both sets of tracks funneled inside. "Silas, get out of there. It's not safe."

She ducked into the decaying building, half-expecting a stranger to leap at her from the shadows. Scraps of broken furniture littered the floor, half-buried in the snow that had fallen through the cracked open roof to form a pile at the center of the single room. Silas turned away from the snow pile, grinning. "Look, Memma."

He held a gold pocket watch in his outstretched hand. A leather strap dangled by his side.

"See the initials?" Silas turned the strap and the watch to show her the letters engraved into each. "They match."

"FJT," Emma read. "Very cool. But let's look at them outside, okay?"

A metallic object caught Emma's eye: on the far side of the snow pile sat a blue and silver tin, the kind that usually held shortbread cookies. She had the urge to retrieve it, then thought better of it. Silas would linger to watch what she was doing, and the image of her lifting the tin only to have the building cave in on them was just plausible enough to turn her toward the door.

Guiding Silas back out into the sunlight, Emma asked, "Evelyn, what were Father's initials?"

"FJT, according to the records," Evelyn said. "Though, to everyone but the government, he was just *Father*." She shuffled over to inspect Silas's finds. "Oh, these are beautiful, my boy. Don't know how I could've missed them. Be careful around these buildings, though. You're lucky you didn't get hurt, poking around in there."

"I wasn't poking around. They were sitting in the middle of the room, right on top of the snow. I just picked them up. Lily, come look!"

Lily looped her camera strap around her neck and crossed from the tree line. When she arrived, Silas thrust the watch out for her to admire, but wouldn't let her hold it.

Claire, the last to join them, stopped short and barked, "Where did you find that?"

Silas's smile faltered. "The watch?"

Claire grabbed the strap from Silas's hand. "*This*. Were you digging through the garbage?"

"Claire, he found it in there with the watch." Emma gestured to the doorway at her back.

Silas's lower lip quivered. "They were just lying in the snow."

Claire loomed over him. "In the snow or on top of it? Did you dig?"

"No, I already told Evelyn—They were right there. All I did was grab them."

"Jesus, Claire, would you ease up? What's the matter with you?" Emma steered Silas out of her path as Claire headed for Father's cabin. Tears flowed down Silas's cheeks. She handed him a tissue. "Are you okay?"

He sniffed. "Yeah."

"She didn't mean to get mad at you. She's probably just hungry too." Emma tried to return his focus to the watch. "That's a neat treasure you found, huh?"

Silas cast a tearful glance at Father's cabin and shrugged. Claire exited, holding the tin Emma had spotted earlier. The tin rattled.

Claire paused a few feet away and cracked the lid. The blood drained from her face.

"What is that?" Emma moved closer. She glimpsed leather and yellowed pages as Claire moved the lid aside to open the book stored within. Claire's face hardened.

"It's nothing." Claire said, closing the tin. "Let's go."

As Emma turned with the kids to begin the walk back to their cabin, she overheard Evelyn muttering to Claire, "Isn't that the strap you threw into the trees when you first got here?"

Claire nodded.

"Then how…?"

"I have no fucking idea."

"Lunchtime, Silas," Lily chirped, giving her brother a friendly push toward the trees. "Lead the way. Oscar's waiting."

Silas brightened as he caught sight of the dog romping along the lakeshore. "Come on, Oscar. We're going home!"

If only, Emma thought.

BY THE TIME they got back to their cabin, Emma's headache had returned, and she needed a nap. She chose to stay behind while the rest of her family went to get lunch with their neighbor.

"We'll follow you down to the One Stop," Claire said to Evelyn. "That way you don't have to bring us back here before driving all the way to the grocery store."

She whistled at Lily and Silas, who were thumbing through the records in the corner of the living room. "Kids, go hop in the truck. We'll be out in a minute."

Emma jotted down a quick list of essentials for Evelyn and thanked her for the tour.

"Ah, of course," Evelyn said. "It's good we went today. Over the next few weeks, there'll be some nasty storms rolling through. Unless you want to be stuck here through New Year's, you might consider packing up soon."

"I'm not going anywhere until this place is ready to sell," Claire said. She tossed the strap into the cabinet above the refrigerator, then slid the tin in after it. "I don't want to have to come back."

After the family had gone, Emma waited a full hour before the pull of curiosity overcame her determination to respect Claire's privacy.

"Oh, screw it," she said, getting out of bed. *Just a quick look.*

She pushed a chair over to the fridge and reached around for the blue and silver tin. Instead, her fingertips brushed glass.

She withdrew a bottle of whiskey. It was a quarter empty.

You don't know that it's hers.

She scratched a faint line into the label with her thumbnail and returned the bottle to its hiding place, then picked up the tin.

She cracked the lid open and peeked inside. A scuffed leather journal.

A collection of teeth—a dozen or more—roots crusted with old, dried blood.

She quickly replaced the lid. Once everything was back where she'd found it, she climbed down and ran the tap until it was steaming. She lathered her hands with soap, thrust them under the hot water, and scrubbed her skin raw.

But she couldn't wash the contents of the tin from her mind. And there was something else disturbing her. Though she checked the locks and drew the curtains over every window to shut the forest out, she could not rid herself of the sensation crawling over her skin, raising the fine hairs at the back of her neck.

The feeling of being watched.

GRACE

1893

GRACE IS NOT her name. Her true name belongs to a language she cannot speak or understand, lost with her mother. Father says her mother died in childbirth, but Grace doesn't know how this is possible. Because she remembers her mother's hands. She remembers tracing her mother's lined palms with tiny fingertips, exploring the calluses, like rough islands rising up from the soft brown warmth of her skin. The smooth backs of fingers stroking her cheek as she drifted off to sleep.

And she remembers her mother's voice, resonating. Songs sung in the language of Grace's lost name, swelling her little chest to bursting as her infant tongue babbled, eager to join in. Laughter, like birds taking flight.

Grace remembers running, then being carried. Ragged breath, stars shining in the night sky. Branches reaching through the blurred darkness to scratch and pull. She remembers being squeezed to her mother's breast so tight it hurt. Her mother's heartbeat, pounding, as if it meant to shake the world apart, drowning out the wind, the shouting. And then the drumbeat slowed. The arms loosened their hold. And where the snow touched her mother, it changed color.

Black in the moonlight, spreading.

Father says he named her for the grace of God. He smiles when he tells her this, like he's bestowing a gift, lines creasing his face like old cracked leather. As if God's grace should make her feel warm and loved. But it feels like a lie. It feels like standing alone in a cold shadow while Father nods and smiles and spreads his hands to show the pale-faced government men that change is possible. There is hope for the heathens infesting the land that the Good Lord has entrusted his faithful servants to cleanse.

Savages.

"Half-breeds," like Grace.

The words sting the soft meat between her ears like angry wasps. Grace lowers her head as Father gestures at her shorn hair. He spins a finger, and she turns.

The modest dress she wears is stiff and new; it itches, but Grace doesn't dare scratch. *Like an animal.* She's a lady, Father insists, swearing by his handiwork. Grace will be twelve years old in a week's time, no longer a child. Her dress was not made for running through the forest and climbing trees. It's for kneeling—a demonstration. Father snaps his fingers in front of Grace's nose to remind her. She sinks to her knees, hands folded in prayer.

The courthouse is stifling, windows shutting out the fresh air. The government men shift in their chairs. Grace is the focus of their attention, yet their eyes refuse to land on her.

Father's worn Bible opens between her hands, eager to spill its words into listening ears. Grace lets the pages flutter past Father's marker. She's supposed to read aloud, convince these men to fund Father's boarding school. She's meant to be an example—a shining product of faith and education—a stone smoothed by hours, days, weeks of relentless tumbling. All that remains of the child from her memories has been polished away.

But Grace still carries a few rough edges. She hides them deep. She can feel them now as she grinds her teeth to keep from screaming at these smug men. She can see the doubt in their eyes. To the government men, she's nothing more than a trained beast being paraded around in human clothing. A curiosity.

But can she read?

Is she "civilized"?

Grace flips to the passage of her choosing, finger gliding through vengeance and hellfire as her lips produce their coveted words. When she's finished, there's only the sound of her breathing, bellows stoking the fire in her chest. The men applaud, clap Father on the back. They shake his hand, congratulating themselves on their noble charitable intentions.

But Father's eyes are hard, promising the leather strap.

Grace bites the inside of her cheek to keep from smiling. Because Father doesn't know: years of beatings have turned strap to strop, honing her hidden edges. Deep inside, she's razor sharp. And it's only a matter of time before Father bites down too hard.

FATHER DRESSES GRACE differently when they visit the band of Chippewa near Lake Vermilion. A costume, that's what Father calls the soft deerskin leathers that remind Grace of her mother's touch. The leathers are new, purchased from a reservation they passed through on their long pilgrimage north; a glance is all it takes to see they've never been worn.

Her hair is just long enough to braid, but Father's fingers are clumsy and unpracticed. And no one ever taught Grace how to do it herself. So she listens to Father grumble, trying not to cry out as he yanks on her scalp. The braids are sloppy, unconvincing. She repositions the feathers when he isn't looking.

Visiting the reservations is worse than the performance in the courthouse. The government men were easy to read, disdain written on their faces as clearly as the words printed on Father's Bible pages. But after days spent listening to Father's speeches—short, simple words uttered to a translator—Grace finally recognizes the emotion flickering in the eyes of their audience.

Pity.

They don't see what's being offered; they see what has been taken from her. Though they wear the same skin, Grace cannot speak their language. She cannot join them in song. She does not share their fires, their god. Grace stands before them with her crooked braids, wearing leathers that have never tasted sap or rainwater, embarrassed. She isn't fooling anyone.

These people just want to be left alone.

With the white men, Father nodded. On the reservation, he shakes his head. Belittling, condescending. Can't they see how low they live? Don't they want better for their children? He holds Grace out to them like a key—*See? My daughter was just like you, once.*

Still, it doesn't matter in the end. The opportunity Father presents them, the civilized life he's offering their children, is not a choice.

It's a trick.

They send their children—twenty-one boys, ages five to fourteen—to be fed and clothed and taught. To be stripped and tumbled smooth, like Grace.

Remade.

THE JOURNEY TO White Hook Lake is arduous. The settlements along the way are few and far between, but they stop at every one so Father can read scripture and accept donations. While everyone is assembled, Grace fulfills her secondary purpose: she creeps between the vacant houses, gathering valuables. Father says she's doing God's work by setting these people free from their worldly attachments, that greed is the Devil's poison. And yet, Father seems to value his expensive pocket watch more than his Bible. He's always holding it, polishing and caressing the gold, long after the Bible has been stowed away and forgotten. Stealing makes Grace sick to her stomach, but she has no choice. Not if she wants to eat.

Naabek understands. He shares Grace's burden, eyes shadowed as he boosts her up through open windows, whistling low between his teeth to warn her when the assembly has ended. Naabek is the oldest of the boys, the tallest. Father calls him Dog, but Grace would never; Naabek is her best friend. Her only friend in the world. She practices his true name until it fits her tongue. She wants to keep it for him, as if remembering his name will soothe the pain of losing her own.

Naabek is teaching her to speak Anishinaabemowin. Grace doesn't know if it's the language of her childhood, but when she sounds the words out under his patient guidance, she can almost hear her mother's voice. As she learns, the words fill her. She no longer feels quite so hollow.

They move on before the light of day reveals the empty spaces left in Father's wake. Grace bears the weight of her deeds on knees bruised from hours spent kneeling, begging God for forgiveness. Most days, she feels like a glove Father wears to keep from getting his hands dirty. She wonders if he'll toss her aside when she's no longer useful.

She wonders if he's really her father.

ONLY NINETEEN BOYS reach the shores of White Hook Lake.

The youngest succumbs to illness one week after they leave behind the last settlement. Naabek carries the boy, the one he calls Nishiime, sacrificing his own meager rations until the child hangs limp in his arms. Father denies Nishiime a proper burial. When he cannot drag Naabek from the body, Father beats him for his disobedience, then turns the wrath of his strap to the younger boys.

That night, Grace wakes to find Naabek's blanket empty. Certain her friend has abandoned her, she huddles beside Father's sleeping form, sobbing. But a part of her is glad Naabek fled. She knows what awaits the boys at the boarding school. She prays Naabek makes it home.

But Naabek returns before dawn, dirt under his nails, fingertips scraped raw from clawing at the earth. He withdraws a lump of charcoal from his pouch and blackens his forehead, then Grace's. While the other boys sleep, he moves around the fire, smudging each of their foreheads in turn.

All but one. Father wakes before Naabek is finished. He forces the boys to wash in a nearby creek, holds each of them under until they breathe the water in: a baptism. He holds Grace under the longest.

The next night, Naabek begs her to help him stay awake. Shadows lick at his somber face as he stares into the fire, feeding the flames. But the heat tugs at their eyelids. They drift off to sleep. And in the morning, Aandeg is gone.

Grace screams as Father makes an example of Naabek for corrupting his flock and inspiring Aandeg to run. Later, while she splints her friend's broken arm with branches and strips torn from her dress, Naabek whispers a warning: should the dead boy, Nishiime, return, Grace must not go with him. No matter how much he might beg and plead.

No matter how lonely he must seem.

Grace promises. And when the rustle of small feet pauses beside her blanket in the night, she keeps her eyes tightly shut. *Nishiime.*

Only later does Grace recall the word's meaning. *Little brother.*

THE BOARDING SCHOOL is nothing like the elaborate descriptions Father sold to the government men. But it's exactly as Grace remembers it. She doesn't know what Father did with the money he was given, but it didn't go into the shoddy log structures standing in the clearing. Except for Father's cabin and the schoolhouse with the well inside, all of the buildings are old, remnants of an abandoned settlement.

There's no money in the gaps the wind whistles through, invading the unfurnished rooms. No money in the dirt floors. No beds in the bunkhouse. Nineteen boys crammed inside a long box without windows. Barely enough room to breathe. Each of them receives one threadbare blanket, crawling with tiny insects, spread out on the cold hard ground. Father says it's the kind of living they're used to.

Father orders the boys to strip. Their breath fogs the air as he sets fire to their leathers and the rest of the belongings they brought from home. Naked, shivering, the boys crowd close to the flames for warmth. Father shaves their heads. He beats the boys who cry, and so the others endure the ministrations of his dull blade in silence. Their heads, bare and nicked and bleeding, are bowed. Their shoulders tremble. They stare at the ground. Before Father will hand out their new clothes, they must scoop up their hair and feed it to the fire. The school uniforms are all one size.

When the boys are dressed, Father gives each of them a number, calling it out with a physical trait to help him remember. Frowning, Grace dutifully records the information in Father's ledger. It's been weeks since they left the reservations behind, yet Father is still unable to distinguish between his students.

One—big nose.

Two—lip scar.

Three—rabbit teeth.

Father lines up the boys in a row. He teaches them to march. He leads them into the schoolhouse, where there are no desks and the only books are tattered Bibles with moldy pages. There aren't enough to go around. Father claims it will teach the boys to share, just as they must learn to share the table in the cookhouse. The long benches are designed to seat only ten, but all the students must take their meals at the same time. After Father finishes his evening sermon, the boys stand or sit, hunched over bowls of gruel, chasing every last drop with a chunk of stale bread. No one complains. There is only one meal a day; they cannot risk losing it.

Grace finds some of the government money in the cabin she shares with Father. Here are the beds, the table and chairs, the rugs and blankets and other basic comforts denied to the students. Father's cabin even has windows, two small squares fitted with real glass instead of oiled paper, to let the light inside. Father keeps the key to the storeroom door on his person. Though there is enough food for everyone, he refuses to share more than the bare minimum.

Grace doesn't understand why there is a well inside the schoolhouse.

Father will not tell her.

BEYOND THE CLEARING lies a pit, a monument to waste. Grace sneaks away to join Naabek, and they try to count the animal remains lying at the bottom by picking out the skulls among the discarded bones. She wonders whether the meat was devoured or left to rot once the valuable hides were stripped. Visions of slaughter poison her dreams.

Trappers still pass through from time to time, rough men who reek of blood and sweat and damp furs. Father permits them to stay in the outlying shacks. He sits awake with them, late into the night, drinking and laughing.

On the nights when Father is too drunk to stumble back to their cabin, Grace reads from the journal he keeps tucked away in the chest at the foot of his bed. When she's finished, she understands why Father keeps the book hidden. The journal is a record of bad investments, failed mining ventures and unpaid loans. Gambling debts. Names and numbers that make her head swim.

Grace remembers the towns they passed through on their long journey to Minnesota, always rushing and looking over their shoulders. But never so hurried that Father couldn't afford to stay a night or two. Sending Grace out into the darkness with her nimble fingers, while he followed the siren's song of diamonds and spades, clubs and hearts, into the warmly lit saloons.

Grace has never been good with numbers. But she doesn't need to subtract to know there's nothing left of the money from the government men.

Less than zero.

THE NIGHTS ARE growing short and cold. As autumn shifts toward winter, Number Four, the boy named Miskwaadesi, runs off. He doesn't make it far. Two days later, Father brings him back.

Then Grace learns what the well is for.

CLAIRE

CLAIRE'S EARS STRAINED at the silence. Just after midnight, Emma had slipped out of bed and had not returned. Knowing she was elsewhere in the cabin, unsupervised—probably snooping—made it impossible for Claire to sleep. She listened for the cracking of floorboards underfoot, the creak of a chair, the thump of a drawer or cabinet—any sound that might hint at Emma's whereabouts. When no sounds came, she slipped out of bed and crept down the hallway.

She found Emma on the couch, hunkered over a book and nibbling her thumbnail ragged.

Not just a book, Claire realized, but her mother's journal.

"Oh—" Emma straightened, slapped the journal shut. "I'm sorry. I wasn't—I didn't mean to pry."

Claire stared at the open tin on the coffee table. "You didn't mean to pry..."

"I was—"

Claire snatched the journal from her, slammed it into the tin, and stomped into the kitchen. She glared at the chair Emma had pulled up to the refrigerator, shoved the tin deep into the cabinet, then leaned on the counter, head down, fingers digging into her temples. She waited for the hurt at Emma's betrayal to harden into rage. She couldn't even scream like she needed to, not with their children sleeping just down the hall.

"I want you to leave," Claire said. "Tomorrow. Take Lily and Silas and go home."

"What am I supposed to tell them?" Emma's lower lip quivered.

"I don't care."

"I would have understood, you know." Emma blinked, tears spilling over. "It was awful, what she did to you, but it wasn't your fault. You could have told—"

"Did it occur to you that I would have told you, eventually, if you had waited? If you'd let me come to you?" Claire shook her head, disgusted.

"I just don't see why—"

"I'm not doing this with you, Em. I don't want you here. I never did."

"But—"

"Go to bed."

"Twenty years we've been together," Emma whispered, "and you might as well be a stranger. I don't understand why you can't open up to me."

"Can't and won't are different things, Em. It's never enough for you. You want to feel needed all the time, but the truth is, you need me more than I need you." As the words left her mouth, Claire wished she could take them back, never mind if it was true. There was a sense of something having been torn irreparably in two. A pregnant silence filled the space between them.

Emma stood and wiped her eyes. "Okay. First thing in the morning, we'll be out of your hair."

"Em…"

"No, you're right. Enough is enough."

The cold finality in her voice filled Claire with regret. She saw a future of separate houses, custody battles. But it was too late to reopen the conversation; Emma had already left her behind, was closing the bedroom door between them. Shutting Claire out.

You wanted space, Claire Bear. You've got it.

"Shut up," Claire hissed under her breath. She paced the kitchen floor, restless. The bottle in the cabinet pulled at her. The urge to forget was impossible to resist.

She removed the tin and the whiskey from the cabinet, ignoring the rattle of enamel on metal. She did not want to speculate about why her mother had taken to collecting teeth in her old age. She didn't want to explore her mother's poisonous mind. But if reading the journal could provide evidence of Deborah Schilling's mental decline, then it was worth a try. Claire needed to know for certain her mother was not coming back. That she could not possibly have survived, living alone in the forest all this time.

Because of the strap? Her mother's tittering descended into a snarl. *But you've earned it, Claire Bear. All your life, you've earned it.*

It's your inheritance.

If her mother wasn't responsible for moving the strap around the property, shoving it in Claire's face repeatedly as if taunting her, then who was? No one else but her mother could know about the object's significance.

She supposed her neighbor could have left it on the bed for her to find, but Evelyn's confusion over the strap's presence at the boarding school had felt wholly genuine. And the idea that her handyman, Andrew, could have moved the strap seemed less likely after Evelyn's comment about the size of the footprints.

But the footprints had to belong to someone.

Her thoughts returned stubbornly to her mother. She tried to picture Deborah Schilling as an old woman, shriveled and feral, crouching in the ruins of the boarding school and scribbling in her journal. She imagined this gaunt woman, now a stranger, wobbling through the trees, trying to find food, saw her struggling to chew with toothless gums. Except there was nothing to eat in the area—no fish in the lake, even. Claire and her father had tried countless times to catch something, but always returned empty-handed. She supposed it was possible to live off of plants, but for how long?

And the tracks. They had been laid out in a steady, even line. Not the trail of an elderly woman hobbling on cold-sensitive bones. If her mother was still out there, her bare feet would be blackened clubs.

Claire's rage flared. More than the idea of her mother taunting her with the strap, she hated not having a logical explanation, someone else to blame. She hated games. She almost wished her mother would show herself, if only so Claire could confront her and unleash the fury that had poisoned her life. Perhaps the later entries in the journal would provide some insight. If the footprints at the boarding school did belong to Deborah, if she had left the strap and the watch and the tin with the journal for them to find, then maybe the reason was scrawled within the journal's pages.

With night pressing in on the cabin, it was becoming all too easy to imagine her mother as a malicious presence, roaming the property with eager intent, waiting to snatch up the strap she had wielded against her daughter to teach her one final lesson. One last punishment for running away as a girl and leaving Deborah to face her dementia alone.

Claire reached into the cabinet to touch the strap; it was right where she'd left it. Her mother would have to come inside if she wanted to move it again.

She settled down on the couch and stared at the bottle, willing herself not to open it. As the light gleamed on the label, she noticed a faint line scratched into it. Someone had marked the level of the whiskey inside.

Not someone—your lovely wife.

Claire tugged the cork free and tried to flush her mother's voice from her skull with a long pull from the bottle. The whiskey burned down her throat, assuaging her guilt. It wasn't the first time Emma had marked one of her bottles. Claire would just add water at the end of the night to bring the level back up. But it bothered her that Emma had not mentioned the whiskey when they were arguing; it meant she was storing ammunition for later, when the time came to prove Claire hadn't changed, that she would continue to break her promises, choosing liquor over her family.

Emma wasn't wrong. Claire *had* promised.

Just like she'd promised never to drink again after picking up Silas from a failed slumber party in the middle of the night, certain—right up until the moment she'd flattened their mailbox with the Volvo—that she was sober enough to drive. Emma had been waiting inside with the empty bottle in hand. She'd ripped Silas away, screaming. It should have ended then, three months ago.

Claire had stopped counting the bottles she'd drained since.

Seeking a distraction from her failure, Claire thumbed through the journal. The earliest entry was dated two years after her parents had married and purchased the property where her father had built the cabin. Her mother's journal was a record of hardship, from the severe post-postpartum she'd suffered after Claire's birth to the death of her husband and the difficulties of raising their daughter alone. The good memories were few and far between.

Claire turned pages until she found the dates corresponding with her early adolescence. Shaky lines appeared amid Deborah Schilling's formerly neat cursive—signs of her growing distress. Here was her interpretation of the damning secrets she'd found hidden in a shoe box under her twelve-year-old daughter's bed: a collection of love letters to a classmate. Claire had never sent them; she'd known she was invisible to Jenny. But that hadn't stopped her from dressing up for the middle school dance.

Claire shuddered, recalling how she'd been caught slow-dancing alone in front of the mirror, confessing her love to Jenny as she practiced kissing her hand. The straps of her dress had burned her shoulders as her mother tore it off. After that first night in the basement, Claire had sworn to never reveal her true feelings to anyone, ever again.

Deborah Schilling had pulled her daughter from school the next day. Claire never got to say goodbye to her friends. No one made the long drive out to check on her.

Claire smoothed the page Emma had wrinkled when she'd closed the journal, then poured more whiskey over the shame and indignation roiling in her gut. The way she'd been treated by her mother was humiliating. Emma wouldn't be able to resist addressing it for long.

But Emma was leaving.

The idea that Claire might return home to find half of everything they owned gone, along with her wife and kids, didn't bother her as much as it should. But that was probably just the alcohol, working like it was supposed to.

Claire reached for the whiskey bottle, shivering as she listened to the wind bully the cabin. The fire in the woodstove had died down to a dull orange glow while she was reading. Grateful for an excuse to abandon the journal, she got up and added more fuel to the fire, smiling at the hatchet-scored lengths of wood Silas had split. The fire's crackling warmth was comforting.

She took another drink. The liquor went down like water. At the rate she was going, it would be damn near impossible to bring the level up to Emma's line without altering the whiskey's color. *Screw it.*

Two could play Emma's game. She would never admit to marking the label. When the whiskey was gone, Claire would throw the empty bottle into the bins outside. Let Emma dig through the trash, if she wanted to catch her so badly.

She continued reading. It was strange, experiencing this unguarded side of her mother. Deborah Schilling had never been shy about voicing her disapproval, but here were the things she hadn't said aloud to her daughter. Venomous words, biting. Claire did not look away. She drank her medicine and kept turning pages. Maybe she deserved to hurt this way, for breaking her promises.

When she reached her mother's account of Henry's first visit, Claire raised her eyebrows and reread the entry. Here it was: the first sign of dementia. Claire's father had been dead for decades prior, and yet after this point, his name was repeated through the journal with increasing frequency. For years, Claire realized, as she read on. Her mother had become convinced her resurrected husband was somewhere on the property. She'd even ventured out to the boarding school in search of him, but had returned with only a journal she'd found in the ruins, written by someone named Grace.

Claire scowled at the name, trying to recall where she'd heard it before. But the alcohol made her memory fuzzy. She moved on, skimming as her mother rambled on about savages and God and discipline. Grace soon became the "Devil child." Claire immediately sympathized with the girl. How many times while sitting in the dark basement had she listened to her mother spit those same words at her through the kitchen floor? Deborah concluded the entry by stating that she refused to finish the Devil child's journal and let those evil images into her mind. She wrote that she'd put the cursed journal "where it belongs, with the other one."

Intrigued, Claire glanced around. Where would her mother put a "Devil child's" journal? The woodstove, maybe. She could definitely see her mother burning anything she considered evil. But what was this "other one"?

The quality of Deborah Schilling's handwriting deteriorated further as the years passed. Words collapsed and slanted illegibly off the page, disintegrating into scribbles and violent, jagged scrawls. She seemed to believe something had followed her back from the boarding school. Claire raised the journal and turned it, scrutinizing her mother's chicken scratch. A tree had followed her? Christ, she should've been put in a nursing home.

Rust colored specks dotted the pages where Deborah noted that her teeth had begun falling out. She hadn't questioned her declining health, just discounted everything as "God's plan." Though she did begin to beseech God for guidance. Claire imagined the extra hours of prayer bruising her mother's knees. She tried to feel sorry for her, but a part of her hoped her mother had suffered.

Finally, Claire reached pages covered in drawings that captured what her mother's ailing mind could not put into words. The margins of the last few entries were cluttered with them. She had never seen her mother doodle so much as a heart or spiral. Confused, Claire flipped through the rest of the journal. Images stretched across the remaining pages, bleeding over the edges. Scratched deep into the paper.

A slender tree, replicated again and again, as seen from the window in her mother's bedroom. Moving closer.

Right outside.

Okay, that's enough crazy for one night.

Claire slapped the journal shut, no closer to determining whether her mother was dead or not, but with a much clearer understanding of what her mental state had been like in her final years. She checked her watch; it was after three in the morning, and the bottle was two-thirds empty. She'd been putting off her swelling bladder for hours. She stuffed the liquor bottle between the couch cushions and stood, swaying as the blood rushed to her head.

She stumbled down the hall to the bathroom. After she'd finished relieving herself, she brushed her teeth, took a sleeping pill, and returned to the couch. She reclined with the journal and tried to read, but the medication was already taking effect, muddling her thoughts and blurring her vision. She needed a nightcap, one last drink from the bottle. The liquor went down like water. As the heat from the woodstove lulled her to sleep, she struggled to keep her eyes open, certain she was forgetting...

something...

She shivers beneath a starless sky. Branches brush her arms, needles prickling her bare skin. Cold sears the soles of her feet. The wind wails—a child's cry—chilling the warmth between her naked thighs.

Blind and groping, she wades through the darkness—falls, crawling. The snow crunches beneath her, an icy crust that scrapes the skin from her knees and elbows.

An orange sliver of light appears overhead. She reaches for it with slippery palms. Whispers leak through the trees. Branches stir, a sound like the thin papery rustle of pages being turned. Other lines of light emerge above, distant and devoid of warmth, joining the first to form a rectangle.

The outline of a door.

The ground beneath her gulps the snow greedily, until only the hard concrete floor of the basement remains. The walls close in, shelves crowding her from all sides. Tin cans pummel her head and shoulders. Jars shatter, splashing her with noxious fluid.

A shadow moves in the corner, darker than the surrounding black.

Rank breath tickles the hairs on her arms as she reaches out, no longer caring who or what she shares the cramped space with, so long as it means she isn't alone.

Her fingertips brush frozen flesh.

She wants to scream, to flee in terror, but there isn't enough space to fill her lungs. She can't move. She's trapped, pinned—

Eyes like twin black holes open in the darkness. Something cold and wet presses against her hand. A void yawns open, breathing into her palm.

Teeth snap shut on her fingers, shaking her arm, dragging her over concrete, snow, ice—

Claire screamed as her eyes flew open. Blinded by the white light of early morning, she lashed out with her fist. Her cold knuckles connected with an audible crunch. There was no pain, only a rush of triumph—it was the creature that had broken, not her hand.

And then the fog of terror dissipated.

Reality rushed in.

She wasn't in the basement; she was on the couch, pushed back into the cushions with her fists balled up.

Emma backed away, hands cupping her nose. Blood leaked between her fingers. Her eyes were wide, shiny with pain and confusion.

As Claire struggled to her feet, Emma flinched.

The bottle thudded to the floor, rolling to a stop between them.

"You promised," Emma said. Blood trickled down her wrist, staining the sleeve of her sweater red. The sight made Claire's head spin, but she couldn't afford to faint; she needed to apologize, explain.

"Em, I—It was—" Claire stammered. "I didn't mean to—"

"I met someone." Emma's words struck Claire like a slap.

"What?" She was certain she'd misheard, but with Emma's nose pouring blood, Claire couldn't look her in the face. There were bandages in the bags Evelyn had brought. Claire moved toward the kitchen.

Emma took a step back.

"What—" Claire's tongue wouldn't coordinate with her sluggish brain. She was still drunk, she realized, needed to sleep it off. But there wasn't time. She swallowed, a dry click. "Em, I was having a nightmare. It was an accident. I would never hurt you on purpose."

"You can't even apologize." Anger replaced the fear in Emma's tone. "Didn't you hear what I said? I met someone, Claire. Someone else. Someone who isn't you."

Claire felt the couch rise up beneath her. "Did you fuck her?"

Emma's mouth dropped open. "Really? All the questions you could've have asked—who is she, are you leaving me—*that's* what matters to you?"

"No, I—"

"Do you honestly think I would do that to you, to our family? It's not about sex, Claire—and never mind that you haven't touched me in months. It's about you and me, drifting apart. I don't recognize you anymore."

Claire wanted to cross the distance between them, but her head was spinning, her stomach roiling. Every time she moved, Emma took another step back.

Not looking at Claire but past her, Emma said, "You were so broken when we first met, so afraid. All I wanted to do was take your pain away. When you woke up screaming, I held you. When you cried, telling me how ugly and worthless you were, I stayed. Even when you tried to chase me away.

"But at some point"—Emma wiped her tears, smearing blood over her cheeks—"you just decided you didn't need me anymore. We'd spent all this time building something real, and then you put a wall around it, with me on the outside. You shut me out. I touch you and you move away. I joke and you get angry."

"We've been working on it," Claire said. "We're going to counseling and—"

"*I'm* working on it, Claire. *I am.* I made the appointments; I showed up on time when you forgot. But you? You just keep drinking yourself into a stupor. You blame it on work, complain you haven't finished a painting in years. But every time I drive by the gallery, it's closed."

"You've been checking up on me?" *Spying.*

"You promised me, Claire. After everything we've been through, a promise should mean something. Do you know how it feels, having to rehash entire arguments for you because you can't remember what you said or did the night before? Is it fair that I have to relive your mistakes in order to make you understand why I'm hurt, that I have to experience it *twice* just so you can mumble some half-assed non-apology before you do it all over again?"

Guilt crushed Claire into the couch, burying her in self-loathing. Still, a part of her railed against Emma's claims, unable to stop, even if she was making things worse by retaliating. "I'm sorry, Em, *so sorry*, that I didn't want to go on using you as a crutch. I needed some independence, to prove to myself…You were my first—the only person I've ever been close with. It's always been 'us.' I never had a chance to figure out who *I* was.

"But this compassion of yours—the empathy you pride yourself on having?—it's suffocating. You're relentless. You just keep pushing and pushing. Did you ever stop to think that maybe you need me to be broken? I mean, without something to fix, what purpose do you have?"

"You're still drunk." Emma's tone was flat, emotionless; it scared Claire in ways Emma's anger could not.

"Who is she then, this someone who isn't me?"

Emma sighed. "Someone who doesn't see compassion as a character flaw."

"What is her *name*?"

"Lenore. We work together at the hospital. We've gone to dinner a few times, but we haven't…done anything. We just talk."

"What do you talk about?" Claire tried to remember if Emma had ever mentioned a Lenore. She wondered if the woman was younger than her, prettier, whether she had children of her own.

"Everything. That's the point. Lenore actually *talks* to me."

There was one question left for Claire to ask—the one she should have asked first, because it was the most important—but Emma's confession had skewered her. She felt hollow, wasted.

"I tried to convince myself you could change," Emma said. "I stuffed my feelings down and came on this trip, thinking that after you put your mother's memory to rest, we'd find some kind of peace out here. That you'd finally have room in your heart for something besides anger. But I was wrong." For the first time since the start of their argument, Emma's eyes met Claire's. "I can't do this anymore."

"You're leaving me?"

Emma nodded.

"I need you to say it."

"I'm leaving you."

Between the wind howling outside the cabin and the blood rushing in Claire's ears, there was another sound, steady and mechanical.

Ticking.

It was coming from the antique pocket watch cradled in Silas's palm. He stood in the hall, wide awake and dressed for the snow in his red coat, brown eyes darting like harried birds between the bloody hand cupped over Emma's nose and the bottle of liquor on the floor.

The floorboards creaked deeper in the cabin, startling Silas to action. He bolted toward the door, dodging Emma as she tried to catch him. The door banged open.

Claire and Emma gaped as the door slammed shut. Footsteps thumped across the porch.

"See?" Emma shouted, "*This* is why I'm leaving. Look at what you're doing to him, to both of our children."

"Oh, sure. This is all *my* fault. You're the one who wants a divorce. If I had my way—"

"Stop it—both of you! Just stop!" Lily screamed, storming through the living room. She pulled on her coat, stuffed gloves into her pockets, then grabbed Silas's socks and boots from beside the door.

"Wait," Emma said. "We'll come with you."

"No, you've done enough," Lily snapped. Her hazel eyes blazed with fury as she pointed at each of her mothers in turn. "Stay here and work your shit out. I'll bring him back."

Lily rushed out into the cold.

"We should go after them," Emma said. "What if they get lost?"

"I really don't think your helicopter parenting is the solution here, Em."

"Screw you," Emma spat. She tilted her head back, wincing. "After I'm done setting my nose, I'm packing our things. We're leaving."

"We?" Claire hated that she had to question whether that word still included her.

Emma headed down the hallway.

"What do you want me to do?" Claire called after her. "I'll do whatever you want, just tell me."

But Emma didn't answer. She closed the bathroom door behind her.

Claire folded inward on the couch, pressed a pillow to her face, and screamed—an inarticulate outpouring of shame and rage and sorrow. A wretched cry that only she could hear.

When Emma finally emerged from the bathroom with a bandage taped across the bridge of her nose, she went straight to the bedroom and closed the door.

Claire turned over, buried her face in the cushions. Hours passed while she dozed.

She woke to find Emma peering out into the clearing through the front windows. The snow was falling in thick, heavy drifts, blowing sideways through the forest. Wind rocked the cabin.

Claire stood and moved unsteadily toward the window. The pillow wrinkles spread across Emma's cheek suggested she'd been sleeping, too. There was no sign of footprints beyond the porch. The clearing had been transformed. Their rental vehicles were barely visible through the roaring sheets of white.

Emma's breath fogged the glass as her lips moved. She was so congested, Claire had to ask her to repeat what she'd said.

Emma turned, forehead creased with worry.

"Lily and Silas aren't back yet?"

LILY

THE WIND PELTED Lily with snowflakes, pushing her sideways and whipping her hair about her face. It was freezing out, but she hardly felt it. Inside, she was boiling, furious with her mothers for choosing the middle of nowhere to host their final showdown.

Silas was crouched behind the shed. His hand was cupped around something, shielding it from the wind. Without looking up, he said, "Leave me alone, Lily."

"Si—"

"Go away."

The expression of misery on his flushed, tear-streaked face was like a knife in Lily's heart. But the raw pain in his voice hurt even more. She understood his anger; she was supposed to be his shield, and she'd failed him. Silas returned his attention to the cheap plastic lighter closed in his fist. A flame sprang to life; the wind snatched it away. Lily shifted her position to block the wind, saying, "If that's what you really want, then okay. But you're going to put your boots and gloves on before I go."

Silas shook his head, stuffed his hands into his armpits. He could be so stubborn. She nudged his bare foot with her boot. "You don't want to end up like those guys on Everest, do you?"

"I don't care."

She knelt beside him, pinched one of his pink toes. "This little piggy got frostbite."

"I don't have any socks."

Lily removed a pair of socks from her coat pocket with a magician's flourish.

Silas eyed her remaining pockets. "I didn't have breakfast, either."

"Join the club." She had rushed out without taking her morning insulin injection, and her kit was back in the room.

Once she calmed Silas down, they would go back—no harm done. Before he could ask, Lily added, "Yes, Memma. I took my insulin."

At the mention of their mother, Silas scowled. "Do you think it's true?" Snowflakes collected on his glasses as he searched her face for answers.

Lily didn't need to ask what he meant. She plucked the glasses off his nose, careful to avoid hooking Silas's ears with the cord that connected the earpieces, and busied herself cleaning the lenses. She did not want to have this conversation, not with the counselor her parents kept pushing her to see and certainly not with her little brother. If what they'd overheard was true, she couldn't see a future where their parents were still together.

When she remained silent, Silas asked, "What if they get a divorce?"

"You'll still have me—always."

"You promise?"

"Yeah, you're stuck with me for life." She pulled him to his feet and dusted the snow off his clothes.

Silas put his glasses back on and peeked around the side of the shed. "I'm not ready to go back yet."

"If you light the shed on fire as a distraction, I'll get the keys. We could run away to Mexico for Christmas. Should we take the truck or the SUV?"

Silas choked out a laugh. "Can we just go for a walk?"

"Sure." She turned her face up to the darkening clouds. "But just to the stream and back."

He took Lily's hand and led her into the forest. The wind was picking up, stirring the trees. Looking up at their swaying tops made her head spin—or maybe it was her blood sugar making her feel dizzy. She slowed to stop. She needed a minute to breathe and let her nausea pass. Silas let go of her hand. He looked ahead to the stream, visible through the trees. Their walk was almost at an end, then she could go back to the cabin, take her insulin and rest.

"Hey, do you still have that watch with you?" she asked.

"Yeah." Silas dug a gloved hand into his pocket. The watch leapt free, spinning on its chain. "The time's set right and everything."

Lily snagged the watch, flipped the cover open. "Did you mess with it—try to fix it somehow?"

Silas frowned. "No."

"Then how—" Searching her pocket for her phone, Lily swore. "What?"

"Nothing. I forgot my phone. I was going to compare the times."

"I told you it's right. I checked it."

"How'd you get it working again?"

"Grandma fixed it." A snowflake landed on Silas's nose. Crossing his eyes, he tried to reach it with his tongue. "She wants me to come find her."

"Grandma...Do you mean Nana?"

"Nana?" Silas wrinkled his nose. "No."

A sound reached Lily's ears—there and gone, riding the wind. "Did you hear that?" she asked.

Silas cupped his hands behind his ears. He grinned. "I hear her. Let's go."

"Her? Si—" Lily tripped on a root buried under the snow and sprawled as Silas raced from the tree line, down the bank toward the stream. "Silas, wait! Wait for me!"

Her head felt light and airy, disconnected. They needed to get back to the cabin. She could hear Memma's voice in the back of her mind, admonishing her for forgetting her insulin. She struggled to her feet.

Silas was shouting something. She had to catch up with him.

The snow fell thicker, fat flakes blowing like sheets flapping on a laundry line. Lily caught a glimpse of red nearing the narrow log laid across the stream.

"Grandma," Silas hollered. The wind carried his cry to her ears, but the word didn't make any sense.

He held his arms out to the side as he took his first step onto the log. He took another tottering step, just as the log shifted. His boot slipped. Windmilling his arms, he fought to regain his balance.

Lily screamed his name as the log rolled and he plunged through the layer of snow-dusted ice into the stream. And then she was running down the bank, cold air clawing at her lungs.

Silas thrashed, flailing his arms as the current sucked him downstream. The water rolled him over, held him under. He came up, spluttering. His feeble doggie paddle strokes were no match for the current.

Lily sprinted after him, boots skidding on the stream bank. The water washed over the pale moon of her brother's face. She glanced up at the log crossing ahead. "Silas! Grab onto the bridge!"

A wet log from the crossing struck Silas in the back of the head, and the stream swept him under again. She kept running, trying desperately to keep up with the shape of his body under the water.

When he resurfaced again, facedown, the crossing was far behind them. They were approaching the lake now. The distance had flown by, stealing away breath and strength and time. Lily screamed for their mothers, for help. Anyone.

But they were alone.

The cold wiped her mind clean, squeezing the breath from her lungs. She saw a flash of red in the water and lunged in after it. The stream drank her up greedily. Wrapping her arms around Silas, she tried to find purchase on the streambed to stand, tried to keep his head above water. But the stones were too slippery, and debris snagged her boots, dragging her under. She slapped at a snowy bank with her other hand, but it slipped away. The current spun her around, disorienting her.

She inhaled water, coughed. Her limbs were stiff, numb. She was losing her hold on Silas. Her sodden clothes and boots weighed her down like heavy anchors.

Where the stream emptied into the lake, the bottom dropped away and Lily sank, pulling Silas down with her. Dim light filtered through the ice, granting visibility for a few feet before the lake bottom descended into darkness. She kicked hard, trying to push them back toward the shore.

Her frozen fingers lost hold of Silas. He floated beyond her reach, limp. Sinking.

She swam to the thin ceiling of ice above them, beat at it with her fists to clear it, and broke through into the light of day. She filled her lungs, dove back under. Silas's red coat was fading from sight below. Lily swam toward it. Untied laces drifted like skinny water snakes. Her fingers closed around his boot, pulled him up.

Lily surfaced through the hole in the ice, gasping. The boot was empty. He'd slipped out of it somehow as she swam. She tossed it onto the ice and descended again in a pillar of bubbles. She was running out of time.

Against every instinct, Lily inverted herself, pushing her head deeper, further from the light above.

She had him. Arm locked around his chest, she set her sights on the surface.

But her energy was gone. Hope wouldn't be enough to save them; she needed something stronger to fuel her efforts. She thought of her little brother, lying pale and motionless in a child-sized casket. Of funerals and sympathy cards, flowers and casseroles—a parade of mourners with cheap, factory-bought condolences. She thought of the remaining pages in Silas's drawing pad, how they would stay blank, forever unfinished...

And she thought, *No.*

She kicked her legs, screaming the last of her air out into the water.

Her head bumped against ice, causing her to bite down on her tongue hard. Blood spilled into her mouth. But she had broken through.

Swallowing water, spitting blood, she smashed the surface ice in her path as she stroked with one arm toward the shore.

The distance was too great.

She closed her eyes, tried to focus on her legs; she wasn't sure they were moving. Water flooded her nostrils. And then her boots struck thick muck, sticking. She hauled Silas out of the water and collapsed onto the bank, panting and crawling. The gradual incline felt like a sheer wall.

Silas's lips were blue, his eyelids half-open. Thanks to Memma's cord, his glasses had survived the current.

But he wasn't breathing. As she reached out to turn him onto his side and unblock his airways, her hand seemed to take an eternity to reach him. She positioned her hands on his chest, began pumping. Pinching his nose, she lowered her mouth to his and filled his lungs with her breath.

Silas lay still, not breathing. She resumed pumping.

"Please," she whispered. "Please."

Again, she inhaled. And, as she breathed into her brother, emptying her lungs, she felt her consciousness slip away.

WHEN LILY CAME to, she couldn't feel her body. She thought she was dead until, groaning, she managed to turn her head and saw only snow beside her.

Silas was gone.

She sat up, shivering violently. The shape of her brother's prone body was outlined in the snow; she hadn't imagined pulling him from the water.

"Silas?" Her voice came out a breathless squeak, leaked through chattering teeth.

A narrow trench led away from the patch of disturbed snow where she'd pumped his chest, breathing into his mouth. But everything past that was a blank. Crawling on hands and knees, she followed the trench up from the shore. There were footprints on both sides, almost as if...

Someone dragged him away.

"Mom? Memma?" Lily coughed. She rose on wobbling legs and loosed all her desperation in a scream: "Help! Someone, please help me!"

The wind tore through her drenched clothes, shoving. If she fell, she wouldn't have the strength to get back up again. She plodded forward, shielding her eyes with dripping gloves as snowflakes pelted her face.

The tracks led her into the clearing.

To the schoolhouse.

Lily hesitated in the doorway.

"Lily!" Silas called out to her from a great distance.

As black spots riddled her vision, she clung to the door-frame for support.

"Lily! Help me!"

She ducked her head, shuffling into the splintered ruins, toward the partially collapsed roof. The snowflakes descending through the gap above had layered everything with pure, unblemished white, but a stone slab at the far end of the building was swept clean, as if someone had moved it recently. She reached the slab, and found stones like molars ringing a gaping hole in the ground. The tracks led to the edge of the hole, then vanished.

Lily was crawling again, though she couldn't remember falling. The hole breathed dank air into her face. Silas's voice echoed up from below. It was a well, she realized, as she clung to the ring of stones. There was another smell, sickly sweet.

Wiry hands gripped Lily's ankles like manacles and levered her forward as a weight slammed into her from behind. Her hands slipped over cold stone, out into the black void beyond—

and then she was falling,

plummeting

down

down.

EMMA

"YOU SHOULD HAVE gone after them," Emma said to the empty cabin. She paced between the windows, waiting for a squad car to pull into the clearing, waiting for Evelyn and Claire to emerge from the forest behind the shed. Waiting for her children to return.

Waiting.

You should have gone after them.

She pulled on her coat, zipped it up, folded her knit beanie down over her ears, and worked her hands into her gloves. There was nothing left on the coat rack beside the door. The vacant hooks curved up toward the ceiling, reminding Emma she was alone.

The storm rendered the landscape in muted shades of gray, charcoal smudges of shadow deepening, spreading as the minutes passed. She could barely make out the tracks Claire and Evelyn had left. Lily and Silas's footprints were gone, erased by the wind-whipped snow that had been falling for hours. Emma checked her watch. Fifteen more minutes, and then she would leave a note on the door and go out to search for her missing children.

And what if they come back while you're gone?

She needed to maintain the fire burning in the woodstove, keep the cabin warm, explain the situation when the authorities arrived, convince them to mount a search. She checked her watch again; almost 4:30 p.m. and still no squad car.

She went outside, determined to refill the water tanks and replenish their wood supply before the worst of the storm arrived.

The wind cut through her coat like a frozen knife. The gusts bent the trees, threatening to tear away their branches and snap their trunks. Flurries spun across the clearing like wayward ghosts. Her hair lashed her cheeks, blinding her.

Emma worked the handle of the pump.

She checked her watch. Five more minutes. The cold was suffocating. And her children had been out in this weather for hours.
You should have gone after them.

But she hadn't. Tired of being the helicopter parent, of having
her concerns labeled as overexaggerating and paranoia, Emma
had ignored her instincts.

And look what happened. It was the same internal voice that
had woken Emma every night after Lily was born, dragging
her into the nursery to check her baby's breathing. Look away
from the playground for a second, and Silas would be snatched
by a stranger. Lose sight of Lily at the public swimming pool,
and she would surely drown. A moment was all it took.

Emma frowned.

She stopped pumping. The voice nagged, insisting she was
forgetting…

Emma's eyes snapped open wide. She ran for the cabin, not
pausing to acknowledge the headlights cutting through the
swirling snow in the clearing. Not bothering to close the front
door behind her.

In the children's bedroom, she yanked drawers open, tossed
clothes to the floor, clawed at the blankets on Lily's bed. Both
children had left their cell phones behind.

A faint knock. "Ma'am?" someone called from the front of
the cabin.

She flipped Lily's pillow over, picked up the small black
zipper case with trembling hands, and fell to her knees.

"Ma'am, we're coming inside…"

She unzipped the case. Lily kept a small notebook inside where
she jotted down the dosage for her insulin and the time adminis-
tered. Emma's finger slid to a stop at the final entry penned.

Her miserable wail brought the deputies running.

DEPUTY BERRY LOWERED his pen to his notebook.
"You said the children left the cabin early this morning. And
you waited…three hours before going out to look for them?"

At least three, Emma thought. *And then we wasted more time searching for them ourselves, before Evelyn showed up with the groceries. And then she had to go pick up her dog to help with the search, and I had to drive all the way to the One Stop to call for help while Claire stayed behind to keep looking. And now we've waited hours for you to show up. All that time lost...*

She looked up at the tall, broad-shouldered deputy, but couldn't quite meet his eyes. "My wife and I were sleeping. We didn't know they were still outside."

"Sleeping." The other deputy, a stout woman with close-cut blonde hair, tapped the side of her nose. "What happened to your face?"

Caught off-guard, Emma said, "I slipped on some ice this morning, out by the well. I was being careless." *So, this is where we are now? Lying for Claire after she hit you?* "It was an accident," she added.

"Was this before or after the kids went missing?"

"After."

The woman straightened. "But you said you didn't bother searching until *after* you woke up from your nap. That would've been in the afternoon, correct?"

"Didn't bother?" Emma's hands clenched Lily's black zipper case. "Listen, Deputy..."

"Ryerson," the woman supplied.

"Whatever. We don't have time for this." She showed her Lily's kit. "My daughter needs her insulin; without it, her blood sugar will keep rising. They don't have any food with them. Her body will start shutting down, if it hasn't already—"

"Emma, was your wife alone with the children before they went missing?" Ryerson's voice was steady, calming. Wasting more precious time. Behind her, Berry's pen jotted something in the notepad.

"No," Emma said, impatiently. "We were both in the cabin. Lily and Silas were outside."

"Do you have any reason to believe she might have done something to harm—"

"Absolutely not. No. Never."

"Emma, what happened to your nose?"

"I already told you: it was an accident."

"You slipped on some ice," Ryerson said.

"Yes."

"Is there any reason you can think of, anything that might have motivated the children to run away?"

Emma laughed in disbelief. "This is ridiculous! No, I don't think our children are stupid enough to run away *on foot* in the middle of fucking nowhere. They're out there somewhere, right now, lost and alone in the dark. The temperature's dropping. You need to call this in now."

"We already have, ma'am. The search and rescue team is on their way and will be here any minute. They're bringing dogs." Ryerson crossed her arms. "We don't drag ass when it comes to lost kids and storms."

"But *we* should be out there searching instead of standing around talking."

"Listen, ma'am," Berry said.

"No, *you* listen," Emma snapped. "It took *hours* for you to show up, the search team still isn't here, and now you're trying to—"

Ryerson held up a hand. "It's a two-hour drive from the station. We came as fast as we could. Let's go back to these footprints you saw…you said the person seemed to have bare feet?"

Emma paled. The children never would have run away. But what if they'd been taken?

"Have you seen anyone aside from your neighbor and family near the cabin—anyone at all?"

"No," she said. "Just the footprints."

"Berry," Ryerson said, "why don't you conduct a preliminary search of the clearing while we finish up here? See if you can't scare up the neighbor and the other Mrs. Brooks while you're at it."

"Sure thing." Berry tucked away his notepad, pulled his hat lower, and moved toward the door.

"Keep your radio close," Ryerson added. "It's getting nasty out there. We don't want to lose you too."

As the door closed behind him, Emma said, "We should be out there with him. Please, we need all the eyes we can get."

"We've got every radio station for miles broadcasting a call for volunteers to meet us here at first light. The search and rescue team should arrive soon. If we haven't found your children by—"

The front door banged open, and Evelyn and Deputy Berry hauled Claire into the living room, panting and cursing. As Ryerson rushed to assist them, Emma stared into the static blur beyond the door, not daring to breathe. But no one else stumbled in from the cold behind them.

You should have gone after them.

Oscar bolted in through the doorway and circled Evelyn, whining low in his throat.

Claire was soaking wet, shivering, one hand clamped around a small boot. The boot dripped onto the floor. Wet...

Emma felt her stomach drop. "Oh god," she whispered. She dropped Lily's zipper case and lunged at Claire.

"Where did you find that?" She clutched fistfuls of Claire's frigid wet coat, shaking her wife. "Where are they, Claire? What happened?"

An unintelligible moan passed between Claire's chattering teeth. Her purple-tinged lips pinched around words that refused to form. Her face was bright red from the cold. She blinked as Emma shook her harder, but her eyes remained dull and distant and she trembled uncontrollably. "Please, Claire. Tell me where you found the boot. We have to know where to look."

"The lake," Evelyn said. "That's where I found Claire, anyway, thrashing around in the icy water. She didn't want to leave. Barely managed to get her out and back here."

"The boot was at the lake?" Emma let go of Claire and took a step back. "I have to go there, now. Oh god, if they fell in. If they..."

She couldn't bring herself to say the word aloud, but she could read it in the eyes of the deputies. *Drowned.*

She wanted to run outside, keep running until she reached the lake, to scream for her children and find them herself. But

Claire was hypothermic, unresponsive. She needed to warm her as quickly as possible.

A quiet calm spilled through Emma. Here was a problem she could solve, an ailment to treat. She could make sure Claire was safe before leaving her with these strangers. "We have to get her out of these wet clothes. Ryerson, get a chair from the kitchen and put it near the woodstove."

Emma hurried down the hall to the master bedroom and ripped the comforter off the bed. She grabbed a towel from the bathroom. When she returned, Ryerson had positioned a chair by the woodstove. Claire was standing on her own now, using the back of the chair for support. Emma began stripping off her coat. "Ryerson, can you get her boots off? Evelyn, I need you to boil some water for tea."

One glance at Evelyn, and Emma felt sorry for barking the order. The woman was slumped against the wall, her face ashen, breathing labored.

"Berry," Ryerson said, "help the old woman out, would you? My hands are full."

"Old woman!" Evelyn croaked.

Berry approached and reached out for her arm, but she slapped at his hand, waved him off. "I can make the fucking tea myself, thank you very much. C'mon, Oscar."

Emma peeled off Claire's wet clothes, already rimed with a stiff layer of frost. She bundled the comforter around Claire and eased her down into the chair.

Claire grabbed Emma's wrist with bright red fingers. "I have...to go back."

"After we warm you up." She wrapped the towel around Claire's wet hair, then took her hands and breathed onto them, rubbing. "Where did you find his boot, Claire? Where *exactly*?"

"Out...on the ice."

"On the ice?" Emma's hands tightened around Claire's. "Not *in* the lake?"

"The ice..." Claire squeezed her eyes shut and forced the rest out. "The ice was broken...up. The boot was...on the ice, but when I tried to reach it—"

"Why would his boot be off? Claire, were there any footprints? Like the ones we saw near the lake?"

"I looked everywhere, but I didn't see anything." Claire's eyes wandered toward Evelyn. "Do you think…Could my mother still be alive? Could she have taken them?"

Ryerson said, "Do you have something of hers we can give the search dogs? Something from each of your kids too."

"The quilt," Claire said. "On the rocking chair."

Emma went down the hall to the master bedroom, retrieved the quilt, and ducked into the children's room to grab two pairs of dirty socks.

When she returned, she passed the bundle to Ryerson. Letting go of the socks was nearly impossible. She'd lost so much already.

"I'm so sorry, Em," Claire whispered as Emma rejoined her by the woodstove. "This is all my fault."

Yes, the voice in Emma's head agreed. *It is.*

"Please," Claire said, "I have to go back out there."

Ryerson jerked her chin at Berry. They moved toward the door.

The teapot whistled from the kitchen, and Evelyn took it off the stove.

Emma's patience was fraying. Her muscles thrummed with tension, urging her to move, to act—to go bring their children back. She eyed the door blocked by the deputies. *Get Claire warm, stabilized, and then go. GO.*

Evelyn returned from the kitchen and thrust a mug of hot tea into Claire's hands. "Drink this."

"Stay with her, Evelyn." Emma shot toward the door, prepared to claw her way past the deputies if they tried to stop her. The dog followed, as if he was the only one in the room who grasped the urgency of the situation.

Ryerson stepped sideways, closing ranks with Berry. "It would be better if you stayed, Emma."

"Like hell," Emma snarled. "I've been to the lake. I'll take you right there. Evelyn's in no condition to escort—"

A hand fell on Emma's shoulder. Evelyn's husky voice came from just behind her: "Evelyn's fine, now that she's had a minute to catch her breath. You've only been out there once, and never in weather like this."

Emma whirled on her. "I'll manage. My children need me."

"So does your wife."

"She'll be fine here, next to the fire."

Evelyn raised her eyebrows. "And you trust her not to come running after us the second we leave?"

Emma fumbled for an argument. Behind Evelyn, Claire leaned forward in her chair, trying to stand.

Stay down. Stay here, like I had to. Stay here and wait, wait, wait.

This is all your fault.

"I can't just sit around doing nothing. Please," Emma begged.

But, she realized, *nothing* was exactly what she would be doing, because Evelyn was right: she knew the property better, and someone needed to be here to keep Claire from running back out into the cold.

You should have gone after them.

After they left, Emma watched the flashlight beams flickering in the snow-spun darkness beyond the living room windows. She turned and looked into Claire's eyes, and saw the thought reflected there too.

They waited together. When Emma went to stand beside the chair, Claire wrapped her arms around her. Neither of them spoke. The wind howled. Snowflakes ticked against the glass like tapping fingernails.

Eventually, when Claire had stopped shivering, they moved to the couch. Claire lay with her head in Emma's lap, holding her down.

Holding her back.

"I'm so sorry," Claire whispered. "For earlier, for everything."

"I know."

"Please don't…"

Emma stared at the black zipper case, still lying on the floor where she'd dropped it. She counted the hours they'd lost. Too many. Tears rolled down her cheeks.

"Please don't leave me, Em."

"Later," Emma said. "We'll talk about it after Lily and Silas are home. We'll all talk about it together."

After the search and rescue team pulled into the clearing, they conferred quickly with Claire and Emma before proceeding out to the lake. Emma watched their lights move off through the trees, wishing she was among them. Just before dawn, headlights stabbed at the front windows. Emma shook Claire awake.

The first of the local volunteers had arrived.

LILY

LILY DRIFTED BACK to consciousness one sense at a time. Someone was sobbing, inhaling hitching breaths between pitiful whimpers. Panic stretched its fingers through her chest. She forced her eyes open, blinking, but the darkness remained unchanged.

A copper-flavored slick coated her throbbing tongue, draining down the back of her throat. Pain lanced through her skull. She tried to wiggle her toes, but she couldn't feel them. Fear gripped her, accompanied by the certainty that she was paralyzed.

She gritted her teeth and tried to move, felt her legs shift and heard a splash. Relieved, she drew in a shaky breath. She wasn't paralyzed; her boots were just soaked and her toes were just numb.

The back of her head was pressing into what felt like a wall. She reached a hand back, gloved fingers fumbling. Wet hair clung to her cheeks. Strange shapes jabbed into her back and thighs—an unsteady bed of hard angles and knobs.

There was movement beneath her other arm. A small hand grasped her wrist.

"Silas?" Lily pushed herself upright, feeling her way up his arm to find him in the darkness. She hugged him to her chest. "Are you all right? Say something."

Silas gasped. "I'm okay. My arm really hurts, though."

"Sorry." She released him from the hug but kept one arm curled around his back so she wouldn't lose him again. "Can you move it?"

"Not really. It hurts." He squirmed against her. "Your breath smells funny."

"Thanks a lot."

"No, I mean…" The rest was lost beneath the volume of his chattering teeth.

Lily unzipped her coat, meaning to enfold him, but her coat was drenched too. Frigid water swirled around her elbows. Silas buried his face in her armpit, mumbling.

"What?" When he didn't respond, she shook him. "Hey, I know it's cold, but you have to stay awake."

"Your breath smells fruity." Silas paused. "Did you take your insulin?"

"You sound like Memma," Lily said, feigning irritation to mask the worry in her tone. Her brother was shivering so violently she could barely understand him, and yet he was only worried about her.

"So you did take it?"

"Yeah." Lily squinted up into the impenetrable black surrounding them. "How long have we been down here?"

"Hang on." Silas moved beside her, digging into his coat.

Eight hours. Lily remembered Memma's lecture very clearly; she'd heard it at least a thousand times over since she was diagnosed at age twelve. Without insulin, her blood sugar would rise unchecked until diabetic ketoacidosis set in. Eight hours, and then...

As her mind ran through a list of symptoms, Lily made an effort to control her breathing. She was just a little rattled, hyperventilating. Judging from the shivering spasms, she was probably hypothermic. She needed to urinate badly, but that was to be expected, considering she hadn't used the bathroom before leaving the cabin. A concussion would explain her nausea. And of course her muscles were aching; she'd just survived falling down a well.

You didn't fall. You were pushed.

Silas must be imagining the fruity breath...

Someone was tugging on her arm. Silas sounded scared; he was repeating something, but Lily couldn't focus on the words. Her head felt like it was being split in half. Like something was hatching from her skull.

"Lily, wake up." Silas pounded her chest with his fists. His teeth clicked like castanets in the dark. He was freezing; they both were.

Coughing, Lily sat up.

"I can't check the time with my arm all messed up."

"I'll help you. Give me the lighter." As he pushed a round object into her hand, Lily said, "Or the watch, I guess."

A flame leapt up to Lily's right. Holding the lighter near the open face of the pocket watch, Silas said, "I don't know what time we fell down here. I don't know when to start from. I can't...think. I'm too cold."

Lily was nodding off again, the watch slipping from her hand. Silas goaded her back to consciousness. She swallowed with a dry click, distantly aware that she was no longer shivering. She felt warm, peaceful. Lily knew this should bother her, but she couldn't seem to muster the strength to do anything about it.

"How long was I out?" she mumbled.

"I don't know. I couldn't wake you up. I was about to go to sleep too...I'm so tired."

Lily shook her head. "Ow. Okay, so...if we woke up this morning sometime before nine..."

Her stomach knotted. The flame vanished as she shoved Silas off her lap and scrambled to her feet to distance herself from him. She dry-heaved, an awful raw sound that reverberated off the well's rounded walls.

Silas sloshed around behind her. "Lily? Where are you?"

"Stay back." Lily choked the words out. She didn't want him to see how bad she must look or else he'd worry. "Don't use the lighter. I'm...peeing."

It was the best excuse she could come up with. And it wasn't a lie; she'd lost control of her bladder while trying to move away from Silas. She already needed to pee again.

Eight hours.

"Did you bring your insulin?" Silas asked.

"Here, take the watch back. Keep it safe so it doesn't get pee on it," she said, hoping the change in subject would throw him off. "Who would put a well here?"

"Huh?" Silas located her in the darkness. His trembling hand took the watch.

"Inside, I mean." Lily lowered herself into a sitting position. "Who puts a well *inside* a schoolhouse? And where's the opening?"

"She covered it," Silas whispered.

It took a moment for his answer to sink in. Lily's head jerked up. "She?"

"Grandma. She pushed…something over the top to cover it, after…"

"She pushed me in." Scraps of memory fluttered through Lily's pounding head like shredded photographs.

"I'm sorry I followed her," Silas said, voice breaking. "I just thought…if I could bring her back, it would make Mom happy again. And then maybe we could cut down a stupid tree for Christmas, and Memma wouldn't make us leave—"

Silas cried out in pain as Lily embraced him. "Sorry," she said, loosening her hold. "I'm so sorry. I forgot."

"It's okay. Don't let go."

"I won't. How's your arm holding up?"

"It's not so bad." Silas shifted beside her. "I can move it a little now. Maybe it's not broken. I don't know. I can't really feel anything; I'm so cold."

"You need to stand up, stay out of the water as much as you can."

"You're not standing."

"I…" *Can't.* Lily sighed. "How did you know it was Grandma's voice, Si? We've never met her."

Silas honked back snot. Lily pictured Memma holding a tissue to his nose and saying "blow" while Silas scowled, because he was much too old for…

"Lily?"

"Yeah."

"You're falling asleep again."

Lily opened her eyes wide, rubbed her wet gloves on her cheeks. "Sorry, go ahead."

"I was…telling you how Grandma…fixed my watch."

"When?" Lily shuddered. Her muscles were aching, taking turns so that no part of her was without pain.

"In my dream…when Grandma came back to our…to our bedroom window." Silas's voice faded as he slumped. She straightened her arm to keep him from sliding down into the water, then bit back a scream as her joints flared in protest.

"Sorry, the bottom's…hard to stand on," Silas said. He was shaking harder, forcing the words out in fragments. "Stuff… keeps…shifting around."

She heard the lighter click, click. The flame illuminated the water's murky surface.

"There's something under…here…" he said.

A pale rounded shape crested the surface, balanced on the arch of Silas's foot.

"What happened to your boot?" Lily asked. She knew she should know, but she couldn't concentrate for more than a few seconds before her focus fizzled out. Silas's legs jittered as another shivering fit stole through him.

As the object tumbled from his foot, empty sockets rolled toward her. She glimpsed a nasal cavity and tiny teeth before the small skull sank beneath the water.

Silas swore, then ducked his head sheepishly. His eyes slid sideways to meet Lily's. "Sorry for cussing."

"I won't tell if you don't," she said, handing him her boot. "Put this on."

"What…was it?" Silas squinted at the ripples left behind by the skull.

"Just more animal bones, like we found in the pit." But between the flickering light and the fuzziness of her memory, she wasn't sure. The teeth had not been pointed, like most animals'. They had been tiny and *flat*. She nudged the boot in his hand. "Put it on. It'll keep your foot from freezing off."

"What about *your* foot?"

"We'll take turns."

The light went out.

"Shit," Silas said. "I can't…do the lighter and the boot… at the same time. I can't stop…shaking and my stupid arm won't…work!"

Lily uttered a muffled whimper into the shoulder of her coat.

"You…okay?" Silas asked.

No. She coughed. "I'm fine. Some spit went down the wrong pipe."

"Gross." He huffed as the lighter clicked again.

"Get the boot on first, then worry about the lighter."

"But the water's just going to fill it up."

"Better than you impaling your foot on all this crap at the bottom." She felt him wiggling beside her, heard something plop into the water. "Was that the boot?"

"Yeah."

"Tell me you didn't lose it."

"Nope, it's on." He resumed fiddling with the lighter, rasping the flint.

Lily kicked out with her remaining boot, trying to put as much distance as possible between them and the skull. She didn't want to think about the other sinister shapes poking into her from below. Those thin curved pieces that could be ribs pressing into her calf. The hard knobs with pointed protrusions, strung out in a line, beneath her thigh. A spine? Something sharp was digging into her backside. Her hand moved of its own accord. She leaned forward and retrieved the object from behind her.

The shape of the lower jaw was unmistakable. Many of the teeth were missing, but even with her gloves on, she could feel the square molars and a narrow pair of front incisors. The jaw was too large to belong to the skull Silas had exposed. "Silas." She tried to keep her voice even. If her brother learned what lay beneath them, he'd have nightmares for the rest of his life. "Give me the lighter. I'll get it working again."

He passed it to her without argument. When she finally got the lighter to ignite, Lily directed it at the wall behind them, searching for a way to escape.

"Tell me about the dream you had," she said.

Silas craned his neck to look up at the short section of wall illuminated by the lighter's flickering orange glow. "Grandma was…at the window again," he said. "Her mouth was moving… funny, like in those movies Mom watches. You know…the ones where their lips…don't match the words?"

Lily nodded, thinking about how Silas had already been up and dressed before she woke up that morning, how his pajamas had been wadded up in the corner, wet and cold. But not with urine—there had been no smell.

"Did you go outside last night?" Lily asked.

"In the dream, yeah. Grandma wanted...to see the watch. It was weird, though. I knew Mom...that she'd been drinking, even before...before her and Memma started fighting, because when I snuck outside in my dream, Mom was...asleep with the bottle...on the couch."

"So you dreamed Grandma fixed the watch, and in the morning it was actually working?"

"She must have fixed it...but I don't know how. She just sort of...put it in...her mouth, sucking on it with the chain wiggling between her lips. I would've laughed, except...it was kind of scary. Every time...I shined my light on her face... her eyes would flash. And the noises she was making...

"When she told me...to come find her, it was like a message playing through a speaker. She kept...saying it over and over... but her lips couldn't get it right. And then she grabbed my arms and...she shook me." Silas pulled his sleeve up. "See? I tried to pull away, but she dug her nails in." Lily moved the lighter closer.

She examined the scratches on his forearm. "If Grandma hurt you, then why did you follow her?"

"I had to. She said...I owed her for fixing the watch...She told me if I didn't come...find her, she'd take you instead and I wouldn't...I'd never get you back. I'm sorry, Lily. If I'd known it would be both of us..."

The lighter's flame vanished.

"Hey." Lily reeled her brother in and blindly brushed his hair back. "I can't tell if you're crying, but if you are, knock it off. This wasn't your fault. If Mom and Memma hadn't been fighting—"

"But I'm the one who told Memma."

"What?"

"Before you...woke up. Grandma said I had to wait until morning, then tell Memma...what I saw in my dream. About Mom...and the bottle. She said it would distract them so I could sneak out. I thought...if I brought Grandma back with

me, then they'd be so relieved to see her they'd stop...fighting.
We could all spend Christmas together. I didn't mean to—"

"Enough. Just breathe with me, okay? There you go. In through
your nose...and out through your mouth." She pressed a hand
to Silas's chest, waited until his heart stopped smacking against
her palm, then said, "Mom and Memma have been messed up
for a while now, and *none* of that is your fault. And my being
here? That's not your fault, either. I'm always going to run after
you—I have to. If you want to blame anyone, blame the bitch
who clawed up your—hey, what are you doing?"

"Taking my coat off. It's getting too warm in here."

"*Stop.*" Lily pulled Silas's hand away and zipped his coat up.
She hadn't meant to snap at him. He was right: it was too warm.

Because we're dying.

Lily fought to maintain focus. The heat was a lie—a physiological
trick. She'd watched enough mountain-climbing documentaries
with her mothers to recognize the signs of severe hypothermia.
They'd been freezing for so long, the muscles responsible for con-
stricting blood flow to keep the warmth at their cores were giving
out. Blood was rushing to their extremities.

We're out of time.

Panting, she said, "You have...to leave it on...Got it? It's...
too cold."

"It's *not* cold, though."

"Please...trust me."

"Lily, why are you breathing like that?" Silas's voice was distant, as if he'd tumbled down a second well without her and
was calling up from below.

"Twenty," Lily coughed out. "It's your turn for Twenty
Questions. Pick a good one. Something that'll take me a while."

"Okay...let me think."

The grinding of stone on stone dragged Lily to her feet. Silas
clung to her arm. There was light above—a thin gray crescent.
Slowly, the crescent widened into a full circle.

The well was uncovered.

Lily opened her mouth to scream, but Silas cut her off, yanking on her coat sleeve and hissing like he was afraid of being

heard. She cursed, was about to grab him and cuff him, hard, but the shock of her own irrational fury stayed her hand. This was unlike her—she'd never struck Silas in anger. She was just tired, hungry.

Terrified.

"Be quiet," Silas whispered. "It's Grandma."

She couldn't understand why he was trying to continue their conversation from earlier when help was so near. Besides, he was supposed to keep the answer to himself while she asked her twenty questions. By telling her straight away, he was spoiling the game.

"*Lily,*" Silas whined. "Please, we have to hide."

Lily blinked up at the light, unable to organize her thoughts. What was she…What had she been about to…

Silas splashed beside her, trying to drag her down out of sight. The water barely came up to her chest. To be fully submerged, hidden, she'd have to lie flat. She drew in a deep lungful of air, tinged with the sickly sweet odor of her breath, and lay back on the bed of bones.

The last thing she saw before the water closed over her upturned face was a rail-thin silhouette stretched across the round gray window above like a slitted pupil.

Like a hook caught in the well's open mouth.

GRACE

1893–1894

WINTER.

Hungry eyes watch Father as he performs the morning count. Since he put Miskwaadesi down in the well, no one has attempted to run. The boy's pleas haunted the schoolhouse for days; they were not letters or numbers but a lesson all the same.

White Hook. The students whisper the name. Father believes it is the frozen lake they fear. He tries to rid them of this foolish superstition with long soaks in the icy water. But Grace understands what Father does not. It was Father who dragged the boys from the safety of their homes, who smiled as they thrashed and twisted before he brought his boot heel down. Stripping their names away like skins. Gutting their language and traditions.

Reduced to lonely numbers on a strange shore, the boys whisper the name of the thing they long to escape. Because they will not speak the true name for what Father is. To speak the name would give it power. And so they call him White Hook instead.

A stomach growls. The supplies have not come, but Father is not concerned. He assures them the Lord will provide. A shivering sea of blankets ripples outward as he paces through the bunkhouse. They do not want to touch him.

Father asks for a volunteer to accompany him on a hunting trip. The boys cast furtive glances at Naabek, who shakes his head when Father's back is turned. The warning is clear. No one volunteers.

The hunt will not be successful. The animals smell the corruption in Father. They avoid the poisoned earth of the boarding school on instinct. Paw prints stop at the perimeter, angling abruptly around. Flocks of birds part to either side as if the air is polluted, an invisible bubble with Grace trapped at its center. The sense of corruption coating her skin, seeping into her pores, is a weight she can't shake off. Like being buried alive. Suffocating.

Father catches the boys off-guard. He removes his prized pocket watch and declares they have one minute to decide who will join the hunt, or he will choose for them. The watch swings on its gold chain, ticking the seconds out.

No one speaks.

No one moves.

When their time is up, Father plucks Diindiisi from their midst, then bars the door from the outside. The bunkhouse is a narrow box without windows—a coffin, if Father fails to return. He takes the rifle, the last of the food. Locking Grace inside the cabin they share, Father swears his time away will be brief. God will guide him. He has faith.

But Father has no ammunition. If he did, Grace would have found it. She would have shot him through the head while he slept, to silence the formless demon language leaking from beneath the warm, thick blankets of his bed. She can see the ugly thing uncoiling inside Father, testing the limits of his skin. His true nature is emerging, greed and hate made flesh, infecting everything he touches with fear.

Cruelty incarnate.

Night after night, Grace has watched Father feed their dwindling stores into his gullet, devouring their rations without chewing—a bottomless pit. And still, his skin clings to his ribs. Winter has whittled Father's students down to thin frozen sticks, but he wants for nothing. The floor beneath his bed is littered with bones.

After sunset on the first day, Father returns from the hunt. The sack he carries bulges at odd angles. The Lord has provided.

But Grace has been awake since Father left. She's been listening for the crunch of boots on snow, signaling his return. And she hasn't heard a single rifle shot. Not one.

The Lord giveth, and he taketh away. Father has returned alone. Grace peers through the cracks in the cabin door, but Diindiisi does not follow him into the clearing. Father disappears into the cookhouse. Hours pass.

When Grace finally lays hands on the meat from the sack, only scraps remain for their watery stew. Ragged-edged morsels. Father knows how to butcher an animal, so why does the meat appear torn in some places and, in others, chewed?

No one asks about Diindiisi.

Father spreads his hands magnanimously over the steaming bowls, assuring the boys that they will not be punished for their friend's betrayal. His cadaverous audience nods in acceptance, too weak to hold their own heads up. Too hungry for questions.

Diindiisi must have tried to run. They will hear him tomorrow, calling up from the well.

The boys bow their heads as Father thanks God for sending the doe. He tells them how she lay down by the creek, patiently waiting for the shot that would pierce her heart: God's gift, a willing sacrifice. The boys' gaunt faces are shadowed with doubt; they've seen Father practice with the rifle. He misses every shot.

Naabek's eyes meet Grace's across the table. She shakes her head—subtle, barely a twitch—and Naabek lowers his bowl. The other boys follow his example.

Frowning, Father surveys the students gathered in the cookhouse. His mouth forms the shape of a puckered scar. Knuckles throbbing white, his hands flex as if he means to tear his old leather Bible in half.

Ungrateful. Father spits the word, a feral snarl. He places the Bible on the table and reaches for the leather strap. Naabek stands, already removing his clothes for the beating. But Father's hand moves past the strap to his knife, the dull blade still crusted with blood.

Grace is terrified, uncertain. If she is wrong—if the meat in their bowls is venison—then Naabek's sacrifice will be for nothing. Worse, the harm Father inflicts on her best friend will be her fault. She has no plan. There's no time to think. Grace raises her bowl and tips it to her lips. The smell floods her mouth with saliva. Warm broth washes over her tongue, spilling bits of meat between her teeth. Father watches, rapt.

Grace collapses. Her head strikes the floor, eyes rolled up to whites. She spews meat into the dirt, thrashing. Broth dribbles from her open mouth. Her body is a riot of movement, flailing arms and jerking legs. She thinks of witches and demons and the evil thing playing pretend in Father's skin. She arches her spine. She releases an inhuman roar. She can play pretend, too.

It's not an elegant solution, but her act is convincing enough. Father is beside her at once. The cookhouse empties behind him. Naabek hovers in the doorway, refusing to abandon her. As Grace twitches a signal with her fingers, his expression shifts from worry to wonder. His smile flickers, then dies. Naabek turns to follow the other boys out into the night.

Grace goes limp. She pretends she is boneless, unfeeling, as Father tries to massage life back into her limbs. He's murmuring prayers. A sliver of fear tickles Grace's heart. Father's voice has changed. His touch has gone hard. The hands clamped around her shoulders squeeze. Long cold fingers dig into her back, nails gouging her spine.

Fluid trickles hot over Grace's neck. She opens her eyes. Father's head is cocked against his left shoulder, tilted like an owl's at an impossible angle. Thick, steaming ropes of drool hang from his bared teeth. His eyes catch the lantern light, flashing green. Grace screams.

Father shakes his head slowly, running his hands over his face as if he's forgotten what he looks like. His fingers are bending in all the wrong places. A pungent smell roils off him, climbing into Grace's nostrils. Black spots plague her vision like wheeling vultures.

Bending low over Grace, Father hushes her frightened whimpering. He gathers her into his arms and carries her back to their cabin. She can count Father's ribs through his shirt, and yet his gut bulges beneath her, shifting as though something is stirring within. He has to stoop to fit through the door.

When Father is asleep, Grace sneaks into the schoolhouse. Naabek is waiting. Together, they push and pull at the stone slab until a narrow crescent of darkness appears. They whisper down into the well's black mouth.

But Diindiisi does not answer.

SPRING.

The supplies arrive weeks later than expected. The trader rides into the clearing, swaying in his saddle. Grace recognizes him immediately: one of Father's drinking partners. His supply bags hang deflated. Considering how poorly the man gambles, it's a miracle he has anything left. His eyes are rimmed red. He greets Father with a gap-toothed smile, his breath a yellow cloud of sick. Between excuses, he spits sticky strings of chewing tobacco.

Father is not concerned with the meager quantities. There are only five mouths left to feed. While Father uncorks a bottle of whiskey and ushers their visitor into one of the shacks, Grace unpacks the supplies, eyeing the locked box in the corner of the storeroom as she stocks the shelves—the shelf. There's even less here than she expected. Enough to feed Father and his drunkard friend for a week, maybe two.

And for the boys? For Grace?

Father intrudes. He's laughing, drunk before noon. He turns the key in the lock of his private box in the corner, pulls forth a length of graying meat, then slams the lid shut. He tells Grace they're going south, back to the reservations, to replenish their stock. The drunkard friend will stay and watch the younger boys.

Grace's stomach clenches. The truth drags her down to the floor. It's all she can do to keep from screaming.

More boys. Another winter.

Father orders Grace to write letters, one from each boy— even the dead ones. Especially the dead ones. Simple words, each in a slightly different hand, to show the boys' progress to the government men. Father needs more funding. He wants to expand.

When she refuses, Father takes the strap to the boys. He leaves her no choice. She scrawls lies onto wrinkled scraps of paper. As a reward, Father begins feeding Naabek again. The beatings cease. Only later does she realize it's because Naabek is coming with them.

Father ensures the journey's success with threats. Every night, he sits with Naabek by the campfire, reminding him to remain silent. There will be no passing of secret messages, no warnings whispered to the families they will visit. If Naabek disobeys, Father will cut out his tongue. What happens to one happens to all at the boarding school. Would Naabek sacrifice his remaining friends for strangers?

Father explains the course of events that will unfold, with or without Naabek's interference. If the families refuse to send their children, the government will withhold vital supplies from the reservations, and the children will be taken by force. There are other boarding schools in Minnesota. If the young ones are not sent to White Hook Lake, they will be sent somewhere else—somewhere worse, perhaps. The thought that there could be other creatures like Father, other schools, has never occurred to Grace. She wonders how far this civilizing effort will spread before someone recognizes it for what it is:

A culling.

Grace writes her own letter. She keeps it hidden. And when Father delivers the letters addressed to the government men, Grace slips her anonymous warning into the bundle.

They tour the reservations. Families approach Grace, asking about the welfare of their children. She cannot meet their eyes. When she looks into their desperate faces, she sees their little dead boys looking back. Father has stolen their futures, and she cannot even tell them. She must pretend she cannot understand their pleas. If Father learns she can speak their language, he will cut Grace off from her friends. Isolate her.

The idea of existing alone in that cold winter limbo, with only Father to talk to, scrapes away at the sharp edges Grace keeps hidden within. They are not so deep as they once were. She hates Father with every fiber of her being. Because of him, her friends will never receive a proper burial. Their families will never know what happened. They will mourn unanswered questions, grieving for their vanished children. But they will never find closure.

The children assemble in a line behind Father. The line grows as they travel. But Father is not pleased. Other boarding schools are forming, plucking students from every reservation within reach.

Competition, Father snarls, pouring himself another drink. His hand dips into the stained sack beside him. Glaring into the flames of the campfire, he gnaws on a strip of meat. Yellow-white shapes wriggle in his beard. The smoke does not diminish the rancid odor.

Though his ammunition pouch is full again and the wildlife plenty, Father does not hunt. He ignores the goods sold in the settlements they pass through, refusing the meat offered by passing traders. He feeds only from the stained sack he has carried all the way from White Hook Lake. When the sack is emptied, one of the new students runs away.

And the sack is full again.

Naabek does not cry out when Father takes his tongue. His warning has spared the lives of his cousins. His uncle will spread the word to other reservations: If you must give up your young ones, do not send them to White Hook Lake.

When Father is sound asleep, gorged on meat, Grace steals the knife from his belt. She could open his throat into the dirt, send the children running back to their homes, but Father left his friend with instructions. Should he fail to return to the school by summer's end, the drunkard can dispose of the remaining students however he pleases before moving on.

Grace moves to the fire instead. She heats the knife in the flames. Cradling Naabek's head in her lap, she presses the glowing blade to the end of his tongue. He squeezes her hand, grinding the bones together. She takes as much of his pain as she can. When it's over, they rest their foreheads together. Their journey back to White Hook Lake begins in the morning. The worst is still to come, but for now the fire is warm, the breeze is cool and clean.

They have each other.

Father stirs. Grace moves back to the wrong side of the fire. Naabek smiles at her through the flames. She smiles back as their fingers flutter, scattering silent shadows over the sleeping children. They've never needed words to communicate.

A plan is forming between them. Grace doesn't dare record it in her journal. If Father found the leather book she keeps secreted in her bedroll, it would be the end of them.

She writes a single word instead:

Hope.

FATHER STARES AT the return correspondence from the government men. He crumples the letter in his fist. The funds have been secured, but there are conditions. They are sending a second teacher—an outsider—who will report back on the students' progress and their living conditions.

A spy, Father insists, trembling with rage. *As if I cannot be trusted to do God's work alone.*

Grace bites the inside of her cheek to keep from smiling. Changes are coming. The new teacher will be their salvation.

Father drives them toward the lake at a breakneck pace. The boarding school is vacant. There is no sign of the drunkard or his wards. Father sweeps the bones from under his bed, moves the locked box out of the storeroom and into his cabin.

The new teacher, Mr. Schaefer, arrives too late. He stows his possessions in one of the unoccupied shacks, unaware that he is moving into a graveyard. But he has his suspicions. He also has questions.

Father wears a grim expression as he speaks of hard winters, unruly boys, runaways.

All of them? Mr. Schaefer cranes his neck to look up at Father. *All of them, gone?*

Back to their families. Father shakes his head, the humble shepherd of a wayward flock. *If they made it that far. The winters are harsh, the land unforgiving. These children require a firm hand, but I am only one man. It's good that you are here.*

Mr. Schaefer wears his emotions for everyone to see. The mask he wears now is disbelief. But he will need evidence to move the government men to action. Absent are the threadbare blankets and the bloodstains. The boys and girls are fresh-faced, unscarred. Father explains the well inside the schoolhouse with a laugh and a shrug, piling new schoolbooks atop the stone slab. *It was here before. We built around it.*

But the wildflowers picked by the children to welcome their new teacher cannot erase the smell wafting up from the depths of the well; the stone slab cannot contain it. Mr. Schaefer keeps a handkerchief pressed to his nose. A permanent frown creases his brow. He distributes books to the students seated cross-legged on the floor, shaking his head. Do they not smell it?

Grace writes Mr. Schaefer a letter. She folds it into a tiny square, moist from the sweat of her palm, and slides it under the door of the shack. She thought he was smarter, this man, but autumn is already approaching its end. Winter is waiting for them with long-fingered hands.

Time is running out.

The days are shrinking. The nights are swelling, drinking up the light. Eyeshine flashes from the shadows. Something tree-thin and ice cold is stalking the new teacher's path. The barefoot prints it leaves atop the first layers of snow-fall are feather-light, quickly erased by the wind. Gone by morning. Had Father not devoured it, Naabek's tongue could have warned of what's to come. But it falls to Grace to speed Mr. Schaefer's lessons along.

TWO LETTERS ARRIVE with the supply delivery. One is as wrinkled and yellowed as the drunkard who sent it, the other crisp and official. The first letter sends Father into a rage. Grace huddles under her blankets while he storms through the cabin, hurling anything that isn't nailed down. It's been months since the last runaway, and Father is getting weaker. Since Mr. Schaefer's arrival, the well has not been opened once.

Father towers over Grace's bed like a lightning-stuck tree, hollowed out. The pocket watch ticks in the silence as he strokes the gold case with his thumb. His tongue whispers over the backs of his teeth, murmuring its demon language. Grace would flee if she could, but she senses this would be the worst possible move—the excuse Father is looking for. He wants her to run. He wants to sink his teeth into her softest parts to drag her back. She doesn't need to guess. The whispering tongue tells her so, every night.

All night long.

The first letter lies crumpled on the floor, discarded—another debt of sorts. The drunkard is not the friend Father believed him to be, just another open hand. He wants Father to buy his silence. Grace doesn't need to see the number to know Father can't afford the price.

Father unfolds the second letter. He reads it aloud, choking the words out. And then he goes very quiet. He does not breathe. He lies down on the floor, still as a corpse, with the pages clasped to his chest like a funeral bouquet.

The sun rises. Father does not. He stares, unblinking at the roof above.

Until a fist comes rapping on the cabin's door, a voice inquiring after the second letter—the one that was not addressed to Father. Then, Father stands up all at once. His eyes are fixed on the door like twin burning suns. Even in his weakened state, he could break through the flimsy barrier in a second. Grace longs to scream at Mr. Schaefer to go away. But then Father's liquid black eyes will remember her and come searching.

Instead, she watches from under her bed as Father's mouth opens like a needle-rimmed crater. He crumples the pages of the letter, one by one. He stuffs them between his teeth. The fist knocks again as Father chews. Muffled by paper, something snaps; Father spits his last human molar onto the floor. He yanks the door open.

Mr. Schaefer—the traitorous *meddler*—falls back from the shadow looming in the doorway. The inquiring voice quavers, uncertain. The topic shifts to Grace, and whether she'll be attending that day's lessons. Grace crawls out from under the bed and rushes out. Father's nails snag her bedclothes, then lose hold as she slips past Mr. Schaefer. She is free, for now, wading through fresh snow toward the schoolhouse.

During that day's lessons, under the shelter of Mr. Schaefer's watchful eyes and amid the comfort of warm bodies like her own, Grace summons the courage to write another letter. When the time comes for the students to leave the schoolhouse, her nimble hands sneak the folded paper into Mr. Schaefer's coat. Grace's letter is the scream she could not let out.

Father knows about Mr. Schaefer's correspondence with the government men. There will be no more funding. They are closing the boarding school at White Hook Lake; other schools are being constructed, newer with better management. Closer. Easier to watch. The students at White Hook will be transferred south with Mr. Schaefer. But he must leave now—*now*—while the weather allows. Before Father decides what to do next, how to handle his latest failure.

That night, Grace creeps from her bed with a new note. She is certain her message did not get through, because Mr. Schaefer has not packed his bags or prepared the students for their departure. Father's bed is empty. Grace hasn't seen him all day. The thought of bumping into him in the dark freezes her in place. She cracks the door open. Someone is inside the schoolhouse. Light shines between the gaps in the logs.

Grace moves between the bare islands of earth showing through the thin layer of snow, careful not to leave footprints. When she hears the low grinding of stone on stone, she realizes her mistake; she never should have mentioned the well in her letter. But now it's too late. A shadow is detaching from the tree line, drawn by the noise.

Father crosses the clearing with long fluid strides. Grace can feel the cold rolling off his naked gray flesh as he passes her by—there and gone. Inside.

Mr. Schaefer cries out, a startled shout that fades quickly into silence, as if Father has thrown him a great distance.

Or dropped him, like a stone.

The light goes out. Grace flies back to the cabin, leaping between bare patches, ducking through the door and diving into bed. Only now that she's beneath her blankets, Grace is more frightened than she's ever been.

Because the note is missing. The reason she crawled from her bed, the last desperate warning—*GO NOW*—is not in the folds of her bed clothes. It's not in her blankets, or on the floor. And the new students are only just learning to read and write. Those two damning words could only be hers.

Outside.

But Father is already stooping, coming through the door. His right hand is closed into a fist. His face is hard.

The next morning, Father gathers the students in the schoolhouse, arranging them in a circle around the well's open mouth. He leads them in prayer, raising his voice to be heard. The children are silent, their heads bowed, eyes squeezed shut like Father's fist. But Grace cannot force her eyes closed. Not with Father staring at her—*into her*—like he knows. As the voice of her former teacher echoes up from below, Father smiles at Grace like they're sharing a secret. His right hand blooms open. Skeletal fingers peel back to reveal the scrap of folded paper cradled in his palm.

Father pokes Grace's letter between his lips.

He takes two of her fingers as punishment.

CLAIRE

WHITE HOOK LAKE curled like a crooked finger, beckoning to the search party that had formed on the shore. Claire pulled her coat tighter around her. Over the restless murmur of conversation and rising wind, Ryerson shouted, "Everyone, listen up! We've got a storm moving in and two missing children. The oldest, Lily, needs her medication. Time is short! We need to move quickly."

A helicopter passed overhead. The search and rescue officers from the forest service were already combing both sides of the lake with trained German shepherds. Divers had been in the water since first light, searching the lake bottom. Watching the deputies organize and dispatch dozens of volunteers to established search-grids, Claire felt a flicker of hope. She was relieved to see that hope reflected in Emma's eyes. Since the deputies had returned empty-handed the night before, Emma had been unresponsive. But in the light of day, it seemed certain their children would be found. Claire clung to that certainty; it was the only way she could avoid shutting down.

Hours passed as Claire and Emma searched their assigned grids with the help of Evelyn and Oscar. They shouted for the children, slogging through the layers of fresh snow. Listening for a return cry, a call for help.

Just as they finished with the grid closest to the boarding school, Claire heard a shout. Deputy Berry approached through the trees and waved them over. Dogs barked in the distance.

"What?" Emma rushed toward him, pulling ahead of Claire and Evelyn. "Did they find something? What is it?"

"The dogs found something inside the schoolhouse. A slab, covered by debris." Berry rubbed his mouth. "We think it's a well. We thought you would—"

Emma brushed past him.

"—want to be present," he finished.

But Emma was gone, running toward the schoolhouse. Claire called out for her to wait, but her boots kicked up rooster-tails of snow in her wake.

Berry turned and jerked his chin at Emma's back. "If you'll just come with me..."

He shoved his hands into his coat pockets and headed after Emma.

"You said the well was *inside* the schoolhouse?" Claire said, hurrying to match his stride. "That doesn't make any sense."

Berry grunted. "I'm just as baffled as you are, ma'am."

As the structures came into view through the trees, Oscar streaked ahead.

"When I searched here last night," Evelyn said, "Oscar wouldn't quit whining. Kept acting all squirrelly. I had to tie him to a tree while we looked through the ruins. He chewed right through the lead. Figured there must be something worth finding but..."

"He doesn't seem to have a problem now," Claire said.

Evelyn shrugged. "Must've been the wind making him nervous. Spooked the hell out of me, the way it was whistling through the cracks and holes in everything. We checked all the buildings twice." She shook her head. "After the winds we had last night, I can't believe they're still standing."

"Search and rescue already brought the dogs through here last night, and then again first thing this morning," Berry said, scowling at the remains of the boarding school. "We figured it made sense to start close to where the boot was found, but they got nothing. Brought the dogs back for another pass about, oh, twenty minutes ago, and they went nuts." He spat. "Something's off about this place."

He led them toward the open door of the schoolhouse. An officer stood outside with a pair of German shepherds. Claire hurried past them, careful to keep Berry between her and the dogs.

Emma was already inside with Ryerson and members of the search and rescue team, standing near a well with a climbing rope descending into it.

Ryerson moved aside to make room for them. "Stand back and let the team work," she cautioned.

Claire joined Emma and took her hands. They held fast to each other, staring into the darkness, listening to the hollow scuff of boots on a wall, the creak of the rope and harness. Light glanced off the stones rimming the opening as a male voice shouted from below: "Still a ways to go."

Minutes passed, and then a cry echoed up the well's stone throat. "I'm at the bottom."

Splashing sounds emanated up the shaft. "I found something..."

The words lit up, electric in Claire's mind. Emma's hands squeezed hers. She listened for her children's voices...The rush of relief was replaced by a crushing sense of dread.

"What is it?" Emma shouted. "What did you find?"

When he failed to answer, Claire and Emma crowded close to the well's edge, ignoring Ryerson's warning.

"Christ!" The officer's voice was stricken. "I'm coming back up."

Claire blanched, swayed, and felt a large hand hook under her armpit to prevent her from collapsing. She turned, blinking up at Berry's stern expression.

"Lily!" Emma screamed, lunging forward. "Silas?"

Ryerson dragged her back from the well's edge.

"What did you find down there? Answer me, damn you!"

Claire hurried over and folded Emma into her arms. "Just wait. He's coming up." But there was a reason he hadn't answered Emma's question.

Claire's dread curdled into a grim certainty.

Moments later, the headlamp crested the well's rim. The officer's face and hands were covered in dark smudges—*ash?*

His companions helped him climb from the well and began taking the items he'd cradled under his arm: Silas's red coat and snow pants, a wrinkled sock, a pair of gloves...and something else: a small skull, missing its lower jaw.

Child-sized.

No. Oh, no. Please...

The officer held it out to Berry, who rushed forward, shaking out an evidence bag.

Emma shrieked and launched herself at the men. Claire grabbed her around the waist, pulling her back, but Emma had the sleeve of the red coat. It waved between Emma and the search officer like a warning flag.

"Emma, it's not him," Claire shouted. "It can't be. Tell her, Ryerson! That skull is too old!"

Claire knew she was whining, pleading. She didn't care. Just seeing that skull bundled in with Silas's clothes was enough to let her fear consume all reason. If someone didn't back up her theory soon, she was going to lose her tentative grasp on reality.

Emma clutched at the red coat, sobbing, until Ryerson said, "She's right, Emma. It's not your son. Please, try to calm down."

"Hey," a man yelled from outside. "The dogs've got something here!"

Claire and Evelyn each took one of Emma's arms, and together they followed Ryerson back outside.

Behind the cookhouse, the German shepherds were circling the trunk of a tall red pine, barking.

"What is it?" Claire asked. "What are they barking at?"

Emma's blank eyes traveled up the trunk of the pine, arresting on the highest branches. Her fingers dug into Claire's arm.

About seventy feet above the ground, a small boot dangled from its laces.

"It's Silas's," Emma whispered.

Claire leaned back, unable to rip her eyes away from the boot despite the rush of vertigo.

Evelyn elbowed the search and rescue officer, asking, "How do you figure that boy's boot got way the hell up there?"

"Your guess is as good as mine." The officer gestured at the bare trunk and shook his head. "That's thirty feet up to the lowest branches. There's no way a kid could climb that. I probably couldn't even *throw* it that high if I tried..."

The dogs circled out to a radius of fifty feet, then seventy-five. Claire and Emma followed, stumbling as they held each other tight. They watched from the rim of the pit as the dogs descended into the collection of bones coating the bottom. The officers stepped cautiously around the pit's perimeter to avoid trampling the remains while the dogs searched. The deputies remained above with their evidence bags held at the ready.

Claire looked around for Evelyn. The older woman had hung back with Oscar a short distance from the pit. The dog whined, loping in half-circles, but he wouldn't come close enough to Evelyn for her to grab his collar.

"How?" Emma kept asking, needling Claire for an explanation. "How did his boot get up in that tree? How is that possible?"

"I don't know." She thought about the absence of Lily's clothes. There had been no sign yet that she'd been with Silas. Was she still in the lake, floating somewhere under—

Stop it. Don't.

But she couldn't help herself. She pulled Emma along to where the deputies waited. "Ryerson, have the divers found anything at all in the lake yet?"

The deputy shook her head. "Not yet. But they're almost finished. We should know if they found anything soon."

Claire stared up at the thick blanket of clouds overhead. She'd lost all concept of time during the search. When she checked her watch, she was surprised to find it was nearing one o'clock in the afternoon.

"What about the footprints?" Emma asked.

Ryerson said, "We haven't found anything to indicate the children were abducted, but we aren't discounting the possibility. Everyone in the county—hell, the whole state—is on alert."

"More human bones mixed in with this lot," one of the officers called up to the deputies. "Some kind of dumping ground?"

Berry and Ryerson descended for a closer look.

The dogs finished sniffing through the remains and continued up the opposite side of the pit.

A dog handler called out, "They're not picking up anything else here. We're expanding the search area." He followed the German shepherds as they trotted off through the trees.

Claire's gaze drifted over the bones strewn through the disturbed snow. Her family had explored this pit—this mass grave—with no idea that they were walking over human remains. Berry was right about this place being off—wrong. She felt sick to her stomach.

Responsible.

This is all your fault, Claire Bear. Her mother's voice chortled. *They were yours to love and protect...*

And now...

"They're gone," Claire whispered.

THE STORM REGAINED its fury, bringing darkness down early. The search party retreated to Claire's cabin, hands linked to arms and shoulders as they trudged through the whiteout, heads bent, faces burnt red by wind and cold. Discouraged. They had searched every hollow, crevice, and blowdown for miles.

Claire's legs were cramping from hours of slogging through the snow. Emma would probably tell her she was dehydrated, if Emma was speaking; she hadn't said a word since Berry called off the search—a temporary measure, he assured them. Claire knew it was the right decision for the safety of the rescuers, but she still resented the deputy for making it.

She couldn't blame the volunteers for not continuing the search tonight. Despite their cherry-red noses and heavy-lidded eyes, she knew that every man and woman in the party would still be out looking if the weather hadn't taken such a nasty turn. She bid them farewell and thanked them for trying.

Now, the clearing was almost empty except for the deputy's vehicle and Evelyn's truck. The heavy snowfall was already filling the tire tracks of the departed vehicles. Any clues they might have missed were being buried deeper by the hour.

"It's not over," Claire said, guiding Emma through the open door. "They'll be back as soon as the storm lifts. We just have to wait it out."

Emma was too weary to put up a fight. Claire averted her eyes from the shiny packages piled—and forgotten—in the corner where they might have put the Christmas tree, if the children were still with them. If Emma had not decided to leave her.

Because you broke your promise.

Don't pretend this isn't your fault, Claire Bear. You know what you did.

What you lost.

"I'll bring more of those paper cups up from the One Stop in the morning," Evelyn said, adding fuel to the woodstove. "And more coffee. Storm like this? We're going to need all the heat we can get."

The deputies stood near the front door, conversing quietly. Ryerson cleared her throat and said, "Brooks family, could we have a word?"

As they joined the deputies, Claire's attention was drawn sideways to the front windows. Ryerson began by offering promises and reassurances, but her voice became a background murmur as Claire stared out through the windows. Hoping for a last-minute miracle. The world beyond was a muddled landscape of black and gray, stirred into a frenzy by the wind buffeting the exterior walls. The cabin groaned; it felt as if the storm was trying to pry it up from the ground. She couldn't stop searching. Even now, trapped inside, she squinted at the snow whirling through the clearing, waiting for a flash of lime green, a flicker of red. She couldn't bear to imagine her children wandering through that unforgiving landscape alone in the dark. And if what Emma had said about Lily's blood sugar was right…

"No one is giving up on your children," Berry said. "I swear. We will continue to search for as long as it takes, even if that means I'm still driving up here after the thaw."

Ryerson nudged Berry from behind, and he clapped his mouth shut. His brows twitched, knitting together as they all considered the meaning behind his words.

"We'll be back first thing in the morning to expand the search," Ryerson said. "I'll commission a plow to clear the road again. If history's shown us anything, there will be an even bigger turnout of volunteers tomorrow. We're not giving up."

"Thank you," Emma mumbled.

"For everything," Claire added. "I wish we could do more."

Ryerson patted her shoulder. "Rest, gather your strength for tomorrow. We'll see you at first light."

The way Berry removed his snow hat to press it to his chest, face solemn as he drew in a deep breath, reminded Claire of the deputy who had delivered the news of her father's death. But then, Claire had already known her father was dead; she had witnessed it, after all.

Their children were a different story. Berry didn't—*couldn't*—know.

"You'll need to remain inside until the storm has passed," he said. The concern in his eyes conveyed the unspoken part of his message: *or we'll be searching for more bodies.*

The doubt in the faces of the deputies was infectious, spreading through piteous glances, slumped shoulders, downturned mouths. Claire shook her head, disgusted. Was she really so quick to give up hope?

She said goodbye to the deputies and Evelyn, then shut the door behind them, pushing her back against it as her knees went weak. Emptied of people, the cabin felt massive, hollow, without their children.

She curled into a ball on the floor, knees pressed to her chest, hands knitting in her hair. She listened as the squad car's engine faded into the distance. Without lifting her head, she waited for Emma's hands to descend on her, offering comfort and warmth. She was unwilling to call out and betray her weakness—the gut-wrenching need that reeked of hypocrisy after what she'd said to Emma during their fight. But Emma did not come. Why would she? By insisting that her attention was unwanted, unneeded, Claire had driven her off.

There was a thump in the kitchen followed by the *clink* of glass on glass.

Claire pushed herself up from the floor. The heat from the woodstove had driven the cold from her limbs and taken with it the last of her energy reserves. She stumbled through the living room.

Emma was seated at the kitchen table with the unfinished bottle of liquor that had rolled between them; it felt like a lifetime ago, that argument, like a hangover Claire couldn't shake. Emma nudged the glass aside, took a long swallow directly from the bottle, then held it out. "Go ahead, Claire Bear. I know you want to."

To hear her mother's old nickname for her resurrected from the past, voiced with the same sing-song disdain, sent Claire reeling to the sink. She splashed water on her face, struggling to breathe. Emma had been reading her mother's journal; she hadn't plucked the name out of thin air. She was just trying to be hurtful, and that was good—yes, better than Emma announcing, dead-eyed, that she was leaving. Because if Emma was trying to get a reaction, it meant she still felt something.

So Claire went against the instincts that had only ever led her wrong. She absorbed the blow, remained silent.

"I wanted you to quit for the family. But..." Emma took another long drink. Breathing the burn out, she wagged the bottle at Claire.

It would be so easy to accept. Claire pulled the other chair out, dropped into it, and shook her head.

"I wanted to go after them," Emma said.

"I know. I should have let you." Claire lowered her head into her hands. She felt a touch on her wrist, cold fingertips pressing in.

"I don't blame you, Claire."

Claire kept her gaze fixed on the wood grain of the kitchen table. "I do."

"No," Emma said, "it's my fault—all of this. I'm the one who brought them here without asking. And I'm the one who couldn't keep my voice down when we were fighting. After Silas woke me up...I should have known he'd be listening. I was just so angry. I should have listened to my instincts and gone after them. I should have..." She turned her purse upside down, dumped its contents onto the table.

Looking up, Claire asked, "What's wrong?"

"I can't find my fucking lighter," she mumbled around the cigarette pinched between her lips.

Claire plucked the cigarette from her lips and crossed to the stove. She ignited the burner—on the first try, a small mercy—then passed the cigarette back.

As Emma took a long drag, Claire studied her face, the features Emma dismissed as plain. Her understated beauty had been altered overnight, leaving behind a stranger with a bandaged nose, sunken eyes nested in bruised sockets, a pale grim cut of a mouth. Creases lined Emma's once-radiant skin.

I did this to her.

Claire tried to recall the last time she'd made Emma smile—*really* smile. The effect was transformative, like watching the petals of a flower unfurl to greet the sun. She wondered if she would ever see that smile again.

Emma caught Claire looking and, mistaking her expression for one of disapproval, perhaps, she ashed her cigarette into the glass and stared at the burning cherry. "It's stupid, I know. Petty. You ragged on me for months to quit when we first got together. And I wanted us to be a long-term thing, so I did. I only started back up because of the fight we had, after you drove drunk to pick up Silas—you know, when you spent the night in a motel?"

Claire nodded.

"I guess I just…needed a way to get back at you, to make you feel, I don't know, less important than a substance. It's how you've made me feel every day for the last three years." Emma laughed bitterly. "I tried to let you down, and you didn't even notice."

"Oh, I noticed," Claire said, leaning back in her chair. "The kids, too. I've been fielding complaints about the smell on your clothes, making up excuses. It's no big secret, Em. Where do you think your lighters keep running off to?"

Emma raised her eyebrows.

"Yeah. Lily's confiscated at least three of them from Silas. I got a call from the school a couple of weeks ago."

"What? I didn't know…"

"Because you're never home, Em. You've been putting in so many hours at the hospital—"

"Not because I want to. We're up to our necks in unpaid bills. We're drowning, Claire. And I won't take another loan from my parents. Maybe if we sold this place *and* the gallery—"

"I know," Claire put her hands up in surrender, backing away from the conversational pitfall they always circled back to when they argued: their finances, the lack thereof. "The truth is—and I'm sorry to say it, here and now of all places—but a part of me feels better when you're not around. It's exhausting, trying to hold us together for Lily and Silas. And I know I don't try hard enough. I'm just going through the motions, looking forward to the end of the day when I don't have to drive anywhere, talk to anyone. Or explain to Silas in a hundred different ways that we're fine, like it's normal for parents to go days without speaking to each other.

"I'm there, but I'm not. I'm just waiting to sit back alone, have a drink or two, and then before I know it, the whole bottle is gone. I tell myself it's meant to unblock me, help me paint without that awful fucking anxiety shaking me up. But really, I just want to be numb. To not care.

"Because I miss you, Em. And then, when you're with me, all I can think about is getting away again. Trying to find some relief from the tension. Because whatever's wrong with us, I can't ever seem to fix it. I always make it worse."

Emma sniffed, wiping her eyes.

"I'd give anything to have those moments back," Claire said. "All those hours I floated through, just waiting to get drunk. I should have…"

"We both should have done a lot of things." Emma produced another cigarette, lighting it off the first. She inhaled, then deflated, saying, "We really fucked things up, didn't we?"

"Yeah. Hey, no judgement here, but you might want to slow down with the—"

Emma lurched to her feet, hand clamped over her mouth, and she rushed to the sink. Claire tossed her cigarette in a glass, then moved to hold Emma's hair back as she retched.

"I can't remember when we ate last," Emma moaned between dry heaves. She ran the tap, rinsed her mouth, spit. Head still hanging in the sink, she said, "I want to go back out. I need to."

"I know. Me too."

Emma wiped her mouth and straightened. Determination flared in her eyes. "So, let's go. Screw the deputies. We can still find them, just us."

Claire glanced out the kitchen window at the blurry white void obscuring the shed. Another gust of wind shoved the cabin, shaking the logs, rattling the glass in the windows. "The storm's even worse than last night, Em. If something happens to us, if we don't make it back, and the rescuers find Lily and Silas tomorrow..." She trailed off, letting her piece the rest together.

Emma's face fell. Her eyes drifted out of focus. "Fine."

"Em..."

"I said fine," she snapped. "Just...leave me alone."

Claire backed away and went to the bathroom. After she finished relieving herself, she undressed, left everything in a pile on the floor. Wearing only a loose undershirt and a pair of black cotton panties, she went to the children's room. She left the light off. If she had to look at the empty bed, Silas's vacant tent, the pain would tear her in two. Claire navigated the room in the dark, riffling through Lily's suitcase to pull on a pair of the absurd and endearing socks she collected. She bundled Lily's blanket to her chest, breathed in the smell of her lavender lotion.

Lily's camera was on the dresser. She picked it up and took it over to Silas's makeshift tent, cradling it under her arm as she crawled inside. She gathered his toys and comics around her, clutched a plastic robot to her chest. As the skewering pain of sorrow and regret ran her through, she sobbed into Silas's pillow. She didn't notice when Emma turned the light on.

Gentle pressure on her back, rubbing slow circles, brought Claire back to herself. Emma's lips touched her neck.

"I'm sorry for snapping at you," Emma whispered. "I'm just...I feel so fucking helpless."

The whiskey lingering on her breath was overpowered by another smell, warm and thick and familiar. Claire rolled toward her. Steam wafted up from the mug in Emma's hand as she rattled the spoon and said, "You need to eat."

"What about you?" Claire sat up, careful to keep her head ducked so she wouldn't disturb the roof of Silas's tent.

Emma shook her head. "Not hungry."

"Neither am I." Her stomach growled.

Emma raised her eyebrows. "Share it with me?"

After the day they'd had, it didn't seem possible to complete a task as simple and mundane as eating. But they passed the mug between them as the wind rocked the cabin, siphoning away the heat from the woodstove. The tomato soup was tasteless on Claire's tongue, but her stomach didn't reject it like she'd expected.

"They must be so hungry," Emma said, grimacing at the mug. When they were both done, she set it outside the tent, unfinished.

Claire lifted Lily's camera, eager for a distraction from the guilt turning her stomach. She lay back down on her side, and Emma curled up behind her, one arm encircling her waist. Claire could feel the press of Emma's breasts against her back, the round softness of her belly, the strong thighs, knees fitting in behind hers as if they were two interlocking pieces. It was the closest they'd been in years.

Emma's words replayed in her mind: *Someone else. Someone who isn't you.*

Claire scrolled through Lily's recent photographs, eyes fixed on the digital screen. She felt cheated; with the exception of a few selfies, Lily wasn't in most of the photos because she'd been behind the camera. The images of their family were incomplete without her.

One shot was of Silas, smiling at the camera. Claire let herself drift off into that smile, briefly entertaining the idea of getting him a dog after they returned to California. But if Emma followed through with the divorce, Claire would be stuck taking care of the dog alone for half the time when the kids were staying with Emma. Silas would never want to leave the dog. It would just be another source of pain, something else to be taken from him.

"She has such a natural talent," Emma whispered. "I wish I had her eye. Half the photos on my phone have my thumb in it."

The next series of shots was devoted to the pit. Lily had angled the camera to capture the depth and scale with Silas crouched at the center, the sides sloping upwards to meet the trunks of the pines bordering the bowl-shaped depression.

"Huh," Emma said, reaching up to touch the screen. "Is it just me, or does that tree move a little between frames?"

Claire scanned the blurred background, the rim of the pit and the trees occupying the upper third of the frame. It took her several seconds to find the strange angles lurking three or four trees deep, an aberration she had mistaken for a skeletal pine, stripped of all but two of its branches. But, unlike the other pines, its branches bore no leaves. Its trunk grew thinner toward the middle, bowed while the others stood straight. She clicked ahead to the next photo, then back again, repeating the exchange.

A distant crash made them both jump. Emma was trembling. Claire stroked her arm and pulled her closer, saying, "It's just the wind, knocking a tree down. They're cut far enough back from the cabin. We're safe here."

"I want to go home," Emma murmured.

"Me too."

They lay there together, sheltered inside the tent their daughter had built for their son, listening to the wind wail, to the cabin's ominous creaks and groans.

Waiting for the light of morning to call them back into the storm.

EMMA

THE SUN ROSE.

The search party swelled until the clearing was packed with vehicles, the forest crowded with seeking eyes, the snow trampled with prints layered back and forth between the cabin and the stream, the stream and the lake, the lake and the ruins of the boarding school.

The sun set.

The sun rose.

They moved beyond the established grids, extending their efforts for miles in every direction. They slid into gulches, crawled through blowdowns, waded through icy water. With the image of the boy's boot still fresh in their minds, the members of the search party invented scenarios that compelled them to investigate even the most unlikely of places. Anything seemed possible.

The sun set.

The sun rose.

The search party dwindled down to the locals, those who could still afford to take time off from work to wade through the snow for hours, shouting the names of children they'd never met—children it seemed they never would meet.

The snow fell.

The wind picked up.

The sun set.

And then the deputies urged Emma and Claire to sit down.

"You're giving up?" Claire said. "It's only been a few days."

"Weeks," Ryerson corrected, softly.

Emma blinked. That couldn't be right. Staring at the presents piled in the corner of the living room, she said, "We were going to cut down a tree. Christmas is…"

"Yesterday," Evelyn murmured.

Berry rubbed the back of his neck and coughed. Ryerson tugged at a string unraveling on the sleeve of her coat.

Emma looked between them, trying to understand. But her ears were shut against their gentle explanations, their feeble attempts at sympathy. Her tongue lay limp behind her teeth like so much useless meat.

Evelyn said, "There's a blizzard coming—"

And Emma laughed. Even as their heads turned toward her, eyes widening in surprise, she couldn't seem to stop. Tears blurred her somber-faced messengers of death into runny watercolor portraits. Claire was pulling, trying to cradle her. But Emma was up and moving before she could catch hold.

Emma seized an armful of shiny packages, marched out to the porch, and threw the gifts out into the snow. When a box fell short, she bent to retrieve it, slipped, landed hard. Helping hands fell upon her like vultures. Emma thrashed. Desperate to escape, she ran for the trees.

Emma blinked. She was back on the couch, a mug of coffee in her hands. Ryerson was saying something about reevaluating their options after the incoming blizzard had passed. Berry was wiping his eyes. Offering consolation, measly scraps of hope.

Evelyn ushered the deputies out. The last of their search party disintegrated into the driving snow.

Now Evelyn was trying to convince her they'd been searching for two weeks. It couldn't be true. No one could go fourteen days without eating, without sleep; Emma was living proof.

But Evelyn was shaking her head.

No.

Emma was just coming home from work. They hadn't left California yet. The kitchen was warm with the comforting smell of Lily's cooking. But the hall beyond was dark, the rooms empty.

Silent.

"Em?"

Old pine logs whirled past as she choked on dust, the antique odor of neglect. This place was not her home.

A familiar face—Claire. She was holding a glass of water. Emma swallowed the pill she offered without asking what it was or where it had come from.

Emma blinked. She was lying on the couch. Half-asleep, she listened to the hushed conversation unfolding in the kitchen. Evelyn was whispering about the remains recovered from the pit and the well: two adults and nineteen children—maybe more; they were still sorting. All the skeletons reassembled thus far were more than a century old, unidentified.

Except one. They surmised that Deborah Schilling must have been confused, disoriented when she fell into the well and became trapped. But as to how the well came to be covered again, following the accident? No one had answers, only guesses.

A wet nose burrowed into Emma's palm. When she patted the couch, Oscar leaped up beside her and curled into a ball against her stomach. Eyes closed, she worked her fingers through his black coat. She tried to match her breathing to his, and drifted off.

Claire woke her with a plate of food. Oscar sniffed at the hot meal with interest, but Emma couldn't muster the energy to sit upright.

"Are you okay?" Emma mumbled, feeling sleepy. "About your mother, I mean."

Claire set the plate on the coffee table and sucked her lower lip in, chewing. After a long moment, she said, "Yes and no. A part of me is glad she's dead. Is that terrible?"

Emma shook her head.

"But then I wonder, now that we know for sure that she's gone…"

As Claire trailed off, Emma noticed her pallid complexion, the circles under her eyes, the way she kept flinching and hugging herself. It seemed she was more affected by the truth about her mother than she'd let on. But that was Claire, always stuffing things inside. Drowning the pain with alcohol. Emma was surprised she couldn't smell liquor on her breath.

"If my mother is dead, then who left those footprints behind? And if she wasn't responsible for taking the children, then how did Silas's clothes get in the well with her remains?"

Emma rubbed her eyes but found it difficult to speak. She thought she muttered something about not knowing, but there was a disconnect between her mind and her tongue. Her gut rumbled in the silence.

Claire guided a loaded fork toward her mouth. Eager to be left alone again, Emma chewed. Swallowed. She repeated these mechanical acts until her stomach cramped, then burrowed back under the blanket.

The wind woke her next. Emma surfaced as Claire pushed the front door closed. Beyond the front windows, Evelyn was wading out into the snow. Emma glanced down at Oscar, still lying beside her.

"Evelyn said he could stay with us for the night." Claire released a watery sigh. "Having him around helps a little, right?"

Emma scooted forward on the couch so Claire could squeeze in behind her. Oscar moved down to curl up at their feet. The flames in the woodstove crackled. The wind rocked the cabin. Claire hummed a song in her ear—Paul Simon. The cheery tune was incongruous with the storm raging outside, the abandoned search, the gaping hole that Lily and Silas had left behind. But in that moment, it was exactly what Emma needed to hear.

"I love you, Betty," Claire said.

And Emma whispered, "I love you, Al."

A LOUD CRASH jolted them upright. Oscar jumped down from the couch and scrabbled at the door, barking. An alarm blared outside.

"What was that?" Emma said.

"I don't know." Claire extricated herself from the couch and went to the window, cupping her hands around her eyes. "It sounded like a tree fell on one of the rentals, but I can't make out anything past the porch."

Claire retrieved their keys from the kitchen. She clicked one key fob, then the other. The alarm fell silent. She swore. "It was the truck. Does your SUV have four-wheel drive?"

"Why?" Emma's mind felt sluggish, her reactions delayed. "What was in that pill you gave me?"

"In case we need to leave," Claire said.

Emma frowned. "I thought we were staying until we find Lily and Silas."

"Yeah, but if there's an emergency?"

"I think it's…all-wheel?" Emma licked her lips. Her mouth was so dry. "Claire, that pill you gave me—"

Claire swore again. Her eyes narrowed. Nose pressed to the pane, she said, "I can't see anything moving."

Oscar stopped snuffling at the crack under the door and went to lay beside the woodstove. His loss of interest dispelled the tension in Emma's muscles. She said, "We'll worry about the damage in the morning."

"There's no way I'm falling back to sleep now."

"Come on." Emma rose from the couch and took her hand. They moved down the hall toward the children's bedroom.

"You lie down," Claire said. "I'll be right back."

Emma crawled into Silas's tent and poked her head out. Claire returned seconds later with her mother's journal tucked under her arm.

"Here, a little light reading to pass the time." She handed it to Emma before crawling inside the tent to join her.

Stunned, Emma said, "Are you sure?"

Claire nudged the journal, pushing it closer. The tent's side billowed inward. Oscar poked his nose between the blankets, head cocked, as if seeking permission to enter. They waved him in.

Long after Claire had dozed off, snoring softly with her arm around Oscar's neck, Emma lay awake reading, learning every terrible detail about her wife's childhood. She wept as she read. Because she finally understood. She regretted pushing when she should have waited, should have let Claire come to her.

But if Claire could change by sharing her most private secrets, then Emma could change, too. She squeezed Claire's shoulder, whispered, "Hey."

"Hmm?" Claire cracked an eye open and mumbled, "Done already?"

"No, I just…I wanted to tell you I'm sorry."

Claire yawned. "For what?"

"Before…" Emma searched for the right words, then plunged ahead without them. "There is no one else. What I said that morning when we were fighting, I was just trying to hurt you. It was wrong, and I'm so—"

Claire kissed her then, pulling Emma into an embrace that melded two into one. Her heartbeat lulled Emma to sleep.

WHEN EMMA OPENED her eyes again the blizzard was assaulting the cabin from all sides. Careful not to disturb Claire and Oscar, she tiptoed into the living room, drawn to the front windows by curiosity and the grim, gray storm light of morning. She looked outside, then quickly donned her coat over her pajamas and did not pause to exchange her house shoes for boots.

Because she could make out shapes in the clearing.

Something massive was lying out by the crumpled front end of Claire's rental truck. The red stain spreading outward from the wreckage was the only color in the blizzard-spun world, an errant paint stroke marring the unblemished white canvas of the storm.

But…no.

Emma hurried through the snow, wind tearing at her coat. Now she could see more color: a swatch of lime green just behind the truck's rear tire.

A glove.

CLAIRE

"CLAIRE!"

Oscar stirred, kicking Claire in the gut as he rocketed out through the tent opening. She sat up, groaned. "What?"

"Claire!" Emma's voice came from outside; she sounded agitated. There was no elation in her cry, nothing to indicate their situation had changed for the better overnight. A tired resignation settled over Claire.

What now?

"Claire!"

"I'm coming!" Claire stumbled out of the room, pulling her bathrobe closed against the icy gust of wind that greeted her in the hall. The front door stood open, framing the hectic flurry of snowflakes in the clearing beyond where Emma stood with her back to the cabin. Erratic pits and trenches marked her path from the porch to the truck.

Claire reached for her boots but then saw Emma's still lined up beside them. Concerned, she stuffed her feet into her boots without lacing them and pulled her coat on. Claire matched her footsteps to Emma's in order to hasten her progress through the snow. She halted near the truck.

A moose had collided with the truck on the passenger side. The impact had twisted the animal's neck and punched in the window and quarter panel. The wind scattered fresh powder over the crust of frozen blood matting the moose's brown hide. Broken glass littered the truck's interior, sparkling in the drifts piled on the seats, the center console, and the floor, and the front tire was flat. Claire stared at the massive antler lodged in the wheel well, shaking her head in disbelief. She reached out, wrapped her hand around the smooth arch of the antler and pulled. There was no give, not even a wiggle.

The moose's eye was open, glazed over with ice. Oscar sniffed the animal's hindquarters and pawed at its leg, knocking away snow to reveal the torn hide beneath: rent flesh, a glimpse of bone. A slippery ribbon of fear stirred in Claire's stomach.

Something must have been chasing the moose—hunting it—though she couldn't imagine a predator capable of inspiring such a blind panic in an animal this size. What would cause a moose to charge through a blizzard in the dead of night fast enough to break its neck when it slammed into the truck? A bear? A pack of wolves?

Emma came running from the other side of the truck. Ignoring the accident, she held something out to Claire. At the sight of Lily's bloodstained glove, Claire's breathing stopped.

"I f-found it out here, in the s-s-snow," Emma said, teeth chattering, red nose dripping onto blue lips.

Claire curled an arm around her shoulders and tried to pull her toward the cabin. "You're freezing. We need to get you inside."

"No," Emma protested. Her eyes shone fever-bright. "Look, someone left this here for us to find. Claire, j-just stop for a minute and *look*." She pointed, her finger jittering as another spasm of shivers seized her.

Claire squinted at the snow, confused.

"Someone left Lily's glove here," Emma insisted. She yanked on Claire's coat, pulled her closer, jabbing a finger at the fading tracks leading up to the truck.

"Shit," Claire breathed. The tracks must have been made recently or the snow would have covered them.

Emma turned toward the forest. Her house shoes were soaking up melted snow, and her hands were exposed. She could barely stand, she was shaking so hard. She took a step toward the tree line.

Pulling her back, Claire said, "Em, take the glove and go inside."

"I want to see where those tracks lead."

"Let me go. I've got my boots on. You need to go inside and get warm." She turned Emma toward the cabin and added, "Evelyn's supposed to swing by soon to pick up Oscar. If I'm not back before she gets here, then you both can come after me, okay?"

When Claire took a few steps away from her, Emma moved to follow.

"Emma, for fuck's sake—" Claire bit back her anger, took a deep breath. Emma was only trying to help. "*Please*, just take the dog inside and wait."

Emma rewarded her request with a glare. She stomped off toward the cabin without further resistance, towing Oscar along behind her.

The footprints were similar to the ones she'd found near the cabin before—larger, yet still shallow. She could almost imagine the person who'd made them had been walking atop the snow instead of through it. The outline of bare feet was unmistakable. Claire tensed, heart racing, as she rose and followed the trail past the porch.

The tracks paused beneath the kitchen window. Their shape was muddled, as though the visitor had shuffled their feet while peering through the glass. The snow was marred beneath the next window as well, and every window thereafter, the same prints circling the cabin. Her skin broke out in gooseflesh. Their visitor had tried to look in on them while they slept, but the curtains were drawn tight. So why had they paused at each window anyway?

She considered retreating inside and locking the door, but the image of Lily's glove kept her going. Whoever had left the trail might know where her missing children were. The tracks circled the cabin twice before exiting the way they'd come, through the trees behind the rental truck.

Claire continued through the trees until the footprints vanished at the base of a red pine. Cursing, she circled outward. The snow was falling heavier now, roused into flurries by the wind, erasing the trail even within the shelter of the forest. She stared at the place where the tracks had ended. The front half of one bare foot was outlined where snow met bark. "What the hell?"

Had their visitor left the ground for the trees?

She craned her neck, but the wind had knocked all the snow from the swaying branches. It was impossible to determine whether someone had climbed it. She couldn't imagine how anyone could have shimmied up the bare trunk to reach the lowest hanging branches anyway.

A powerful gust of wind bent the trees sideways, causing them to pop and groan as their branches churned. Claire looked down at her boots until her head stopped spinning. Defeated, she headed back toward the cabin.

Emma greeted her at the door, ushering her inside and asking, "What did you find? Anything?"

Claire shook her head. "A little ways in, the trail just...stopped."

"What do you mean it just stopped?"

"I mean, the tracks went up to the base of a tree and just..." She moved her hands, trying and failing to pull a better explanation out of thin air. "They went right up to the trunk and disappeared."

"Did you look up?"

"Of course I did," Claire snapped.

Emma scowled, her lips pursed into a rosebud of fierce concentration, her eyes boring into the distance.

"I'm sorry," Claire said. "I get that you want answers, but I don't have them. I'm just as lost as you are, Em."

"Who would do something like this, leave Lily's glove for us?" Emma clutched the glove to her chest, chewing her lip. "The person who left those tracks was barefoot, just like whoever was running around on your mother's property when we took the tour to the lake...Maybe someone really did take Lily and Silas. Maybe that's why we haven't found them. But then...why leave the glove instead of a ransom note? Who could be that cruel?"

Claire shuddered, haunted by visions of a faceless abductor spiriting their children away beyond the reach of their search efforts. She rubbed her temples. Her exhausted mind kept looping back to the tracks in the snow. "The dogs would've picked up a scent, some kind of evidence."

"They missed the well the first time. And the boot in the tree." Emma worried the fabric of Lily's glove. "There's blood here. What if someone hurt her?"

"We can't know that, Em. She could have just as easily hurt herself somehow." Claire hated this conversation, hated arguing over their daughter's fate, whether she was being held captive or buried under the snow somewhere, yet to be discovered.

Emma sat on the couch, blinking, as if struggling to organize her thoughts.

Claire sank into the couch at the opposite end. "Thank fuck you drew the curtains." She lowered her head into her hands, running her fingers through her hair. "Whoever left the glove was trying to look in through the windows.

"We should call the sheriff's office. We're not safe here. I can feel it. They'll want to know about the glove. Maybe they can bring the dogs back and try again."

"Do you think the SUV will make it through this storm to the One Stop?"

Growling out her frustration, Emma rose and moved through the cabin, checking locks and curtains while Oscar followed. When she returned, bumping into the dog as he crossed her path, Emma asked, "Does Evelyn have a phone?"

"I doubt it. She's the one who told me I'd have to drive to the One Stop."

"What time is she supposed to come for Oscar?"

"Before noon. I'm sure she'd give us a ride."

Emma checked her watch. "The blood on the glove...If Lily's out there and hurt, she might be confused. Silas too. Should I go out and shout for them for a while? If they're nearby, lost in the storm..."

Claire stood and closed the distance between them, hugging Emma and stroking her hair. "The kids didn't leave those prints. They were too big to be Lily's."

Emma buried her face in Claire's chest. "I'm starting to wish I'd let you keep that rifle Evelyn tried to give us."

At the mention of his owner's name, Oscar whined. His nails clicked on the floorboards as he trotted from room to room.

"I feel bad," Emma said. "Evelyn didn't leave us anything to feed him."

"Where the hell is she? I'm getting worried."

Oscar settled down in front of the door. Head on his paws, he whimpered.

"I know..." Emma knelt beside the dog and ran her hand down his back. "She'll be here soon."

Thinking of the size of those prints, the way they'd vanished, Claire said, "A rifle would be nice."

"Do you really know how to shoot?" Emma sounded doubtful.

"Yeah, but like I told you, it was mostly just target practice with cans. Harmless stuff. I went hunting with my dad a few times as a kid—not that there was anything to hunt. There weren't many animals around, even then. But I was so little, I guess I didn't notice. Or maybe I forgot."

"I can't picture you hunting."

"Well, that was before..."

"Before?" Then, perhaps remembering what she'd read in the journal, Emma said, "Oh."

"It happened out near the boarding school. We kept pushing out farther, searching for tracks, scat, any sign of wildlife." Claire cleared her throat and stared up at the ceiling, willing her eyes to remain dry; she was too exhausted to cry. "Coroner said it was a heart attack."

"But no official report was going to convince your mom it wasn't your fault."

Claire nodded, suddenly glad she'd given Emma permission to read her mother's journal. Because it meant she didn't need to evade or explain, didn't have to say those awful words aloud. "I wasn't paying attention—too busy trying to find a rabbit or a deer—and I got turned around. I didn't even realize he wasn't behind me until I heard him fire six shots. He'd fallen. By the time I found him, he was gasping, breathing his last, and mumbling about something he'd seen in the trees. But I was just a kid—no one would listen. Never mind that his eyes were so wide, they were bulging out of his head. And those six shots...there was no blood, no proof he'd hit anything."

Claire hung her head. History just kept repeating itself, stealing her loved ones without explanation. The wind drove snowflakes against the front window, ticking rhythmically like the pocket watch Silas had been holding the last time she'd seen him.

"Will you come lie down with me while we wait?" Emma asked. "I'm so tired."

Claire followed her to the children's bedroom. They lay down in the bed that had been Lily's for a short time. When Emma began to cry, shaking the twin mattress, Claire wrapped her arms around her and closed her eyes, trying to absorb some of her misery, to bear the burden for them both. As Emma's breathing slowed, Claire shed her own tears in silence.

When Emma turned in her sleep, releasing fretful moans, Claire slid her arm free and sat up against the headboard. Staring at the curtains drawn over the bedroom window, her eyelids drooped. Her chin nodded down to touch her chest. And then she jerked awake, her heart rate quickening as her mind tried to process the image blurred by her fluttering eyelids.

Someone's at the window.

A rail-thin shadow stood behind the curtain, stretching from the bottom of the frame to the top. The sound that had woken her came again: a dull, muffled thud. The glass rattled in its frame.

Claire moved toward the window. Now was her chance to see who had left the glove behind.

A rumbling growl made her jump. Oscar crouched low in the doorway, hackles bristling, his black eyes fixed on the window. His lips peeled back, revealing pink gums and sharp teeth. Ears laid flat, chest almost brushing the floorboards, he inched closer to the window. Claire shied away and climbed onto the bed.

Emma sat up, mumbling, "What is it? Is Evelyn...Is Oscar growling?"

She scrubbed her eyes with her hands, looked over at the window, then pressed back against the headboard, kicking the blanket off the bed as she hissed, "Claire, what the *fuck*? Who is that?"

But Claire couldn't respond. She was stuck. The dog was angled like a black dagger at the window.

Slowly, Emma swung her legs off the bed and crept to the window's left side. She reached out, then retracted her hand, casting a look of uncertainty at Claire. "Should I open it?"

Claire nodded.

Emma parted the curtains slightly, exposing a sliver of window. Then, she yanked both curtains aside and darted back toward the bed. Oscar released a confused, garbled sound—half yelp, half whimper—his nails skittering on the floorboards as he propelled himself backwards, away from the pale silhouette lurking outside.

Only the lower third of the figure's tangled, bushy head was visible, sagging above its emaciated chest. Ribs pushed out in stark white lines behind pale breasts. A distended stomach bumped against the glass. Skeletal arms tapered down like melted wax.

The figure leaned closer, its face a gruesome mask of blood caked over gray-blue flesh. Hazel eyes stared in at them, unblinking.

Devoid of life.

"Claire, oh my god..." Emma whispered.

Lily had come home to them at last.

EMMA

EMMA FLOUNDERED THROUGH the snow, desperate to touch her daughter—to prove she was more than a grief-conjured specter. The sight of her frozen flesh filled Emma with confusion and despair. She shouted her name, but Lily did not turn. Her gaze remained fixed on the window. She stood naked atop the snow as if she weighed nothing at all, tangled dark hair whipping in the wind.

Claire reached her first. She stretched a hand up to touch Lily's cheek, but her fingers fell short. Lily loomed over her like a figure plucked from a surrealist painting, elongated limbs drooping from her emaciated torso, skin pulled taut like blood-streaked silk over starkly delineated bones. Her distended stomach pushed out from between the sharp angles of her hips and ribs, laced with stretch marks and pulsing blue-black veins.

"Lily?" Emma pulled on Lily's wrist, and cold seared her palm.

But Lily did not stir; she did not shiver or speak. She might have been a statue carved from ice, left outside their cabin as the cruelest of jokes. Emma couldn't even be certain she was breathing. She reached up, up—*Christ, she's so tall*—and pressed a hand to Lily's chest, feeling for signs of life, searching her face as she said, "Honey, it's Memma. Can you hear me? Where's your brother? Where's Silas?"

Claire turned to Emma, wide-eyed and helpless. "What's wrong with her, Em? Why isn't she saying anything?"

Emma took a deep breath, felt her mind still in preparation for the challenge at hand. The buzzing hive of questions in her mind quieted. There would be time for questions later, but for now…

"We have to get her inside," Emma said.

Lily did not resist, yet she was nearly impossible to move.

"What is this, Em?" Claire asked, looking down at Lily's frostbitten feet, visible on the mound of snow she stood on.

"We need to get her moving."

Together, pushing and pulling, they managed to tug her into motion. As she walked, her feet broke through the snow layer and sank down to their level. Emma grunted. Claire swore. When Lily was healthy, she had weighed one hundred and twenty pounds. The effort required to support her now suggested she had *gained* weight in her absence—an observation that was incongruous with her wasted form.

By the time they shuffled through the door with Lily between them, Emma and Claire were gasping for breath. When they ducked out from under her arms, Lily remained frozen in place in front of the couch, back bowed, shoulders hunched, arms extended over the shapes of their absent shoulders. Emma probed Lily's wrists and throat, saying, "We have to get her to a hospital—now, Claire. I…I can't find her pulse."

At the sound of loud scratching, Claire's head turned toward the hall. Seconds later, Oscar shot into the living room and skidded to a stop at Lily's feet. He circled her bare legs, whining.

Shooing him away, Claire said, "Where the hell is Evelyn?"

"We don't have time to wait," Emma said. "Get the keys, warm up the SUV."

"I don't know if we'll even be able to get down—"

"We'll just have to risk it. And yell for Silas as loud as you can. If she made it back, maybe he's close by."

Claire nodded. "I'll circle the cabin." She donned her coat and hat, then pushed through the door with Oscar on her heels.

"Tell me if this hurts, okay?" Emma said to Lily, as she gently searched her scalp and face for the source of the bleeding.

Outside, the engine started, followed by a string of curses. Claire burst back into the living room and stalked into the kitchen. Slamming drawers and cabinets, she rummaged through the contents and then stomped back out with an ice scraper.

Emma's exam failed to locate any wounds. The blood was still tacky in places, but it wasn't Lily's.

Puzzled, she retrieved Lily's black zipper case from the dining table in the kitchen. She removed a sterile lancet from its packaging and pricked the outer edge of Lily's finger, just above the line where the color shifted from purple-blue to pink.

Nothing.

Emma moved the lancet up to the meat of Lily's palm. Blood beaded from the puncture, wicking up the test strip. The glucose meter beeped.

Normal.

Baffled, Emma pricked Lily a second time and received the same result. She sat the kit aside, determined to try again later.

She ran into the children's bedroom and threw open Lily's suitcase, looking for something to dress her in. She returned to the living room with the spare snow clothes she'd purchased for Lily before the trip. But they looked far too small. She held up each item against Lily's large frame and shook her head.

She could hear Claire outside, screaming their son's name.

Please find him. Please.

Emma rushed into the master bedroom and gathered an armload of clothes from Claire's suitcase instead, including an oversized bathrobe. But every item was too small, too tight. Somehow, Lily had outgrown her mother.

Claire's pajamas were thick and warm; more importantly, they were loose. She had to lean into each of Lily's legs in turn, in order to shift her weight enough to slip the pants over her feet. The waistband wouldn't extend out far enough to accommodate her belly, so Emma knotted the strings at Lily's hips. It almost seemed like she was pregnant, but that wasn't possible. Emma had seen Lily's stomach when they'd tried on clothes for this trip, and it had been flat. She remembered thinking Lily was getting too thin. If this size belly was a pregnancy, she'd be at least…six, seven months along. Parasites made more sense. Lily was vegan, but if she was starving and desperate, she might have consumed something that infected her with worms.

Though neither pregnancy nor parasites accounted for the change in her height. Lily's ankles stuck out from beneath the hems of the pajama pants, defying explanation.

Dressing her in the matching top was another challenge entirely. Emma stood on the couch to slip it over Lily's head. Wrestling with each of her daughter's leaden limbs, she finally managed to get her dressed, though the hem of the top bunched up beneath her breasts.

"Lily, do you know where Silas is?" Emma asked as she worked. She sharpened her tone. "*Lily*, look at me. Was he with you? What happened?"

Lily didn't answer. Emma worked her arms into the bathrobe, but she was unable to draw it fully closed. She settled for knotting the tie over her distended stomach. The stretchy wool socks were the only item of clothes that fit her properly. Emma tried not to let the inexplicable change in Lily's size distract her. She needed to concentrate. Their son was still missing.

The door banged open, and Claire said, "Are you ready?"

"Almost. Can you grab my boots?"

Claire lifted the pair of boots beside the door and brought them over as Emma knelt at Lily's feet. She could tell at a glance that they were too small. She gestured at Claire's boots. "Put your foot alongside hers."

Claire obliged, and Emma swore. "Okay, we'll just have to use garbage bags for now."

"Em, what the fuck is going on? Why doesn't anything fit her? What—"

"Later," Emma snapped. "I need two garbage bags, and some tape."

Emma hopped onto the couch, pulled a beanie low over Lily's ears, then dropped to the floor to help with her feet.

After the tape was secured around Lily's calves, Emma threw her own snow coat over Lily's shoulders to keep her dry. She quickly donned the snow boots that hadn't fit her daughter. "Okay. Let's go."

As they shuffled through the door with Lily between them, Claire asked, "What about Silas? We can't both leave. What if he comes back while we're gone?"

"We'll leave the cabin unlocked. You can come back after we call the ambulance from the One Stop, and I'll ride with Lily to the hospital." Emma's tone was level and assertive, betraying none of the uncertainty rampaging through her system, and for that she was grateful. Because Claire was wild-eyed, visibly shaking. Emma needed her to focus.

Beyond the porch, the SUV's headlights poked feebly at the blinding snowfall. They waded through the snow and folded Lily's stiff, lanky body into the backseat. Emma crawled in after her.

As Claire slid in behind the steering wheel, a black shape streaked toward the SUV.

"Shit," Claire said. "Oscar."

"Leave him. Evelyn will show up, eventually."

"But he'll be stuck outside."

"Then bring him, Claire. For fuck's sake—"

"Okay!"

"We need to go, *now*."

Oscar leaped in through Claire's open door. He squeezed past the steering wheel into the passenger seat and poked his head over the center console to sniff at Lily. His ears flattened, then flicked upright.

Pointing at his snow-flecked muzzle, Emma said, "Growl once and you're out."

Oscar sneezed and shook his shaggy black coat. He turned and tucked his tail around his hindquarters as Claire guided the SUV down the driveway onto the road. The wipers slashed futilely at the snow that covered the windshield. Claire leaned over the steering wheel, eyes narrowed. The SUV lurched forward as she accelerated, sliding to the right.

"Careful," Emma warned.

"Do you want to give this a try?" Claire's face was a bloodless mask. Pumping the brakes and wrestling with the steering wheel, she managed to steer the SUV away from the incline sloping downward to the trees below. They shot down the road toward the next curve, fishtailing as Claire braked. The SUV shuddered to an abrupt stop. Claire stomped on the gas. The tires spun. Oscar turned in his seat, whining.

"Are we stuck?" Emma asked.

Claire's lips pressed into a thin white line as she shifted the rental between reverse and drive, rocking the SUV. The tires gained traction. They were moving again. Emma scooted closer to Lily and buckled their seatbelts. The heat blasted through the vents on the highest setting, spreading warmth into the back seat. Emma allowed herself to hope.

They were going to make it.

The front bumper struck something submerged in the snow. Claire jerked the wheel. The SUV slewed sideways, trees and road spinning past the windows. Emma cried out in alarm. The tires bumped down into the ditch to the right, and the SUV tipped. Screaming, Emma clung to Lily as the rental rolled down the hill. They slammed sidelong into the trees.

The blood was rushing to Emma's head, the seatbelt cutting into her hips.

Claire hung upside down in the front seat. Oscar squirmed over to her, licking Claire's cheeks. Groaning, she said, "Em… are you okay?"

"We're…" Emma winced as she turned her head toward Lily.

Lily's neck was cocked, her cheek lying flush with the roof of the SUV, eyes open and staring at Emma through a curtain of hair. She blinked. Emma inhaled a whistling breath, relieved.

"Emma?" Claire tugged on her seatbelt, panicking.

"We're okay." Emma braced a hand against the roof and un-buckled her belt. "But the door's blocked on Lily's side. We'll have to pull her out through mine."

Carefully, Emma cradled Lily's head and shoulders as she released her seatbelt. She grabbed the fallen coat and beanie from the floor, then proceeded to drag Lily through the open door.

"Watch the glass," Claire said, reaching in from behind to help.

"What did we hit?"

"A branch or something? I don't know. It startled me and—I'm so sorry, Em. I just reacted." Claire kicked the SUV's crumpled frame. "Shit. What the hell are we going to do now?"

"We'll have to go back," Emma said. She couldn't wrap her head around the idea that the meager distance they'd managed to cover would be erased. But what choice did they have? "We can follow the tire tracks to the cabin while you go to Evelyn's. Once you have her truck, come get us, and we'll go from there. Claire? Hey—"

Emma hooked a hand behind Claire's neck and pushed their foreheads together. Nose to nose, they breathed. Two, three...

"Yeah," Claire said. "Okay. I can do this."

"We can do this."

Snowflakes pelted them from all sides as they struggled up the embankment with Lily between them. Once they reached the road, Emma checked Lily over for injuries, murmuring reassurances. But Lily appeared unfazed by the accident. She stared blankly into the trees.

Emma stretched on tiptoes to pull the beanie snugly over Lily's head. They rearranged Emma's coat over Lily's shoulders, flipping the hood over the beanie to help prevent the coat from sliding off.

"Here." Claire shrugged out of her coat, ignoring Emma's protests. "Just take the damn thing, please? You're freezing."

"And you're not?"

"I got us into this mess. It's the least I can do." She held the coat while Emma worked her arms into the sleeves. Oscar bounded down the road toward Evelyn's. He turned, barking.

"Yeah, yeah," Claire shouted. "I'm coming!"

But Emma caught her by the wrist, pulling her back. She pressed her lips to Claire's and whispered, "I love you."

Claire hugged her tightly. "Love you too."

"Be safe, okay? And hurry."

Claire nodded. "I'll see you soon."

As Claire followed Oscar down the road, Emma and Lily stumbled in the opposite direction. The wind at their backs felt like a gift, a subtle but much-needed push to keep Emma moving despite Lily's daunting weight. Her shoulder ached, back muscles screaming. They followed the SUV's tire tracks back toward the cabin.

Emma's pace slowed and she panted with the effort. They covered the remaining distance to the cabin inches at a time. She'd never felt so cold. The air burned her lungs and throat. The *tak-a-tak* racket issuing from her teeth was constant. Lily's weight was immense, pulling her off-balance.

Emma paused before the porch to gather her strength for the final push up the steps. Her legs were trembling, and she could hardly lift her boots. She hauled Lily up onto the porch, crying out with exertion at each step, and dragged them both over the threshold into the living room.

Emma led Lily to the couch, then pressed a hand to her daughter's bloated stomach, urging her to sit, but Lily resisted.

Something moved under Emma's palm.

She recoiled, and then chastised herself; she was a nurse, not some skittish aide working her first shift. As she parted the bathrobe to check Lily's stomach, Emma shook her head. She was exhausted and had probably imagined it. Claire would return soon. Lily could remain standing until then.

You just don't want to touch her again.

Emma rubbed Lily's back to prove her inner voice wrong, murmuring, "Mom will be back soon. Any minute now. We just have to wait."

Emma paced before the front windows, restless. She longed to warm her daughter, but if there was any chance of them getting stuck in the cold again before reaching the hospital, then rewarming Lily's tissues too early would only cause further damage. She retrieved a digital thermometer from the bathroom, poked it between Lily's chapped lips, and proceeded to search the cabin for first aid supplies. She found what she needed in the kitchen. One of the plastic bags Evelyn had brought them—piled, forgotten, near the basement door—contained a bottle of Betadine, several packages of gauze, and sterile bandages.

The thermometer beeped.

The reading in the small plastic window decided her: *LO.* Emma could wait no longer.

She ran a lukewarm bath, led Lily into the bathroom, and undressed her, frowning as she examined her daughter's extremities. Her symptoms didn't make sense. The tips of her fingers and toes were cyanotic, the ugly shade of purple-blue indicative of Grade Two frostbite, but the discoloration shouldn't have been visible until at least twenty-four hours *after* rewarming. The discoloration suggested she'd already spent some time rewarming her frozen flesh elsewhere.

Something didn't add up, but Emma pushed her questions aside. Lily needed her undivided attention.

Ignoring the complaints from her strained muscles, Emma kicked off her shoes and climbed into the tub. With an exhausting amount of pulling and pleading, she helped Lily lift one leg over the side, then pulled and rocked her daughter forward until she was tilting into the tub. She threw her arms around Lily, scrabbling at her emaciated back to hold her, trying to keep her feet from slipping. They stood like that for several seconds, with Lily's other leg dangling limp out of the tub behind her. Emma's back muscles screamed.

"Please, Lily..." she groaned through gritted teeth. "Help me. Just a little. Please. I can't do this without you."

She felt a nearly imperceptible shift in Lily's weight.

"There you go, yes..."

Lily reeled her leg in and settled her frostbitten foot on the bottom of the tub.

"Okay, honey, I just need you to bend your knees now and sit down, nice and easy."

She pushed the back of one knee to demonstrate. "Please, honey?"

Her knees bent. Lily folded into the tub.

"Oh, thank god," Emma breathed. Once Lily was seated, she reached into the water to straighten her legs. "Good, honey. Thank you."

She hoped Lily would be more responsive when the bath was over, otherwise she'd never get her out.

Working as quickly as possible, she poured water over Lily's filthy hair, then washed her face until the white patches on her cheeks, nose and forehead turned pink. Rotating between Lily's hands and feet, Emma gently swirled her extremities until they were no longer hard.

When the flesh had softened, flushing red, she drained the tub and cleaned Lily's frostbitten parts, stifling the panic that nipped at her nerves. Whether Lily would lose parts of herself was no longer a matter of *if*, but *how much*. She would never walk the same again or be able to cut her own food without the aid of prosthetics.

A muffled scraping sound interrupted Emma's ruminations: Lily was grinding her teeth.

"Lily, stop that." Emma gripped her daughter's chin. But Lily's skull slid sideways above her fingers. A thin runnel of saliva dripped from her pinched lips. "Lily, please. Stop."

The grinding continued.

Emma gathered Lily's wet hair into a towel and helped her stand. She was relieved to find the bath had improved her daughter's responsiveness. Lily followed her basic commands as she coaxed her out of the tub. Emma patted her tender flesh dry. Lily moaned softly.

"I know…I'm sorry," Emma said.

She guided her out to the living room, left her standing by the woodstove while she retrieved a dry pair of pajamas from Lily's suitcase in the bedroom. The fire in the woodstove was dying down. Shivering, Emma fed the flames with the last of the wood stacked beside the stove, the pieces she'd been saving because Silas had split them.

Once the fire was roaring again, heat swelling to fill the living room, Emma moved a chair in from the kitchen and urged her daughter to sit. Lily complied with sluggish movements. The chair creaked as she settled onto the seat.

After rubbing antibiotic ointment over Lily's face and extremities, Emma wrapped her frostbitten parts in thick bandages.

When Lily's hands and feet were swaddled, she worked the fleece pajama top on, then the bottoms. The elastic waistband strained as she pulled the pants up all the way. She guided Lily over to the couch and stood back, trying to determine if she was forgetting anything.

Now that Lily's injuries were treated, Emma felt her sense of urgency abate from screaming alarms to a background roar. Her mind returned to Lily's shocking growth spurt. The pajamas had been a gift from Emma's mother. That Nana could never get the sizes right was a running joke in their family. She insisted that she bought everything oversized on purpose, because the children grew too much between visits. Emma stared at Nana's pajamas, speechless.

Fatigue clouded her thoughts. She needed to sit down, but not on the couch…not near Lily. She backed away, legs folding beneath her, and sank to the floor.

Without being prompted, Lily mimicked her action and sat on the couch. The hems of her pajama pants dangled around her calves. The sleeve cuffs ended just below the elbows.

Lily's jaw slid back and forth, grating. Crunching. Her stomach growled.

Emma jumped at the sound, suddenly ashamed. Here she was, worrying over pajama sizes, when her daughter hadn't eaten a solid meal in weeks. She returned her attention to Lily's zipper case. A third test confirmed the blood-glucose meter must be defective; there was no possible way Lily's blood sugar levels were normal. Emma chewed her lip, uncertain.

She drew up the minimum dose of insulin—just enough to get Lily by until they could get a more accurate reading at the hospital—injected her, and then helped her lie down on the couch, cushioning her head with a pillow.

Despite the sweltering heat from the woodstove, Lily's skin remained cold to the touch. Emma layered blankets over her, then took her temperature again.

LO.

Cursing, she checked her watch. Nothing in this godforsaken place was working properly. Where was Claire? They had to get to a hospital.

She went to the window and scanned the clearing and the road beyond for headlights, but there was only the white static of the storm. Her back was turned when a heavy thud spun Emma around. Lily had fallen between the couch and the coffee table and begun to seize. Her bandaged extremities jittered, drumming the floorboards. Emma pulled the coffee table aside and shifted Lily's head to her lap. Her daughter's eyes were rolled back to whites. Saliva leaked between her bared teeth.

"I'm sorry," Emma whispered, overwhelmed with guilt. This was her fault. But what was more likely, that the reader had malfunctioned three times consecutively, or that Lily's time spent starving in the forest had cured her diabetes?

"Breathe," Emma murmured. "It will pass. Just breathe. I'm so sorry, Lily. I'm here with you. I'll never let you go again, I promise."

When Lily went limp, Emma eased her head down onto a pillow. She did not possess the strength to lift her alone, so she made her as comfortable as possible on the floor.

Sidestepping into the kitchen, she kept one eye on Lily's still form while she felt for the knob on the stove. She needed to boil water to make tea, to warm Lily from the inside out. But the burner refused to ignite. The pilot light had probably gone out again, and Claire was the only one who knew how to fix it. Swearing, Emma kicked the stove. She limped back to the living room.

And froze.

Lily was gone. The blankets were strung out across the living room. The front door stood open.

"Lily!" Emma flew down the porch steps, hands cupped around her mouth as she screamed her daughter's name into the storm. "Lily, where are you? Lily! Silas?"

Maybe she'd run back into the cold to bring home her brother.

Hope buoyed Emma, lending her energy. Through the wind-driven snow, she caught a glimpse of blue and plowed toward it. The outline of Claire's rental truck came into view, the hulking carcass of the moose, and...

Lily was crouched atop the moose, head lowered between her shoulders. Her hair had tumbled loose from the towel, covering her eyes, but her mouth was still visible, pressed to the moose's haunches. Her jaw worked, gnawing at the animal's frozen hide.

Emma's stomach twisted in revulsion. She tugged on Lily's elbow, but her daughter shook her off with ease. Emma stumbled back as Lily crawled higher, attacking the moose's hide from different angles. But her blunted teeth couldn't tear through.

Defeated, Lily slumped. When Emma pulled on her again, she did not resist. For the third time that day, Emma led a dead-eyed statue in from the cold.

She spent the next hour changing her soaked bandages. As she worked, Emma rambled on about the things they would do once they were back in California—about summer and Lily's upcoming trip to Yosemite. She needed to believe that her daughter had a future; she needed Lily to believe it too.

But she also needed to know what had happened to Silas. Ugly scenarios plagued her imagination. Lily never would have left him behind. Not if he was still…

It felt like a betrayal to Lily, to receive the gift of her return with an open hand demanding more. But if Lily had made it back—the child they'd least expected to survive—didn't that mean it was possible, even probable, that Silas had defied the odds too?

"Lily, I'm sorry to ask again, but if you know where Silas is…" Emma took her daughter by the chin. "Look at me, Lily. Please? I just need you to tell me if he's okay. Tell me where he is."

Lily shuddered. Her damaged hands lay limp in her lap, a harsh reminder that if Claire didn't return soon, she could lose both her hands and feet. The cyanosis had progressed to Grade Three frostbite at an alarming rate. Emma reapplied ointment, hunting within the archives of her nursing experience for anything that would explain the accelerated deterioration, the discoloration creeping further up toward Lily's wrists and ankles by the hour. Securing the bandages, Emma bundled Lily up on the couch.

Lily's stomach growled again. Emma backed into the kitchen, determined not to let Lily out of her sight for a second. They had never bothered to put Evelyn's groceries away. She fumbled a can of soup out from one of the shopping bags and felt around through the drawers for a can opener. But when she tried to open the can without looking, the lid stuck. As she wrenched the lid free, the serrated edge bit deep into her thumb.

"Shit," Emma hissed. And then, remembering the pilot light was still out: "*Shit.*"

She drifted back into the living room with a bowl of cold soup in hand and sat it atop the woodstove. When the soup was lukewarm, she approached Lily and rattled the spoon against the bowl.

Lily's nostrils flared. Her hazel eyes widened, alighting with interest, as she raised her head. Emma held the soup out to her, but the pain from her injured thumb made it hard to hold the bowl steady. Soup sloshed onto the blanket between them. As Lily stared down at the mess, Emma switched the bowl to her good hand and moved it beneath her daughter's nose. But Lily had lost interest now. Her head sagged back onto the pillow.

Emma set the bowl on the coffee table in case Lily changed her mind and sat on the floor beside it to bandage her bloody thumb. Lily watched through slitted eyes. Short brown hairs still clung to the seeping cracks in her lips. Her stomach rumbled again.

Distancing herself from her feral daughter, Emma moved to the front door and sat with her back pressed against it, guarding the cabin's only exit. The hours passed.

Emma waited.

But Claire did not return.

CLAIRE

THE RIFLE CRACKED, and pain seared Claire's left shoulder. Oscar thrashed, slipping through her fingers like oil. He ran toward the door of Evelyn's cabin. Another shot whizzed past him. Claire ducked down, shielding her head with her arms. She inhaled a deep, shuddering breath and shrieked, "Evelyn, it's me! It's Claire! Stop shooting!"

The rifle cracked once more, then fell silent. Claire waited. If she didn't move soon, she would no longer have the option. The idea of unfolding her leaden limbs, letting the storm strip away the meager heat she was guarding at her core, made her want to give in to the bone-deep exhaustion. She closed her eyes and counted off the seconds in her head.

A cold nose prodded her neck. Claire forced her eyes open as Oscar pushed his muzzle beneath her chin. When she tried to curl back into herself, the dog jerked his head upward, clacking Claire's teeth shut on her tongue. The pain startled her awake. She reached for Oscar, and the agony of her wounded shoulder brought her back the rest of the way.

She moaned, grabbing the dog's collar. He bore her weight until she was back on her feet and then led her toward the cabin, whining. She staggered after him and up the porch steps. They entered through the yawning maw of the splintered door frame. Claire braced against the wall inside to catch her breath, taking in the chaotic ruin of Evelyn's living room.

"Evelyn," Claire called out. "I'm here with Oscar."

Glass from the shattered front window crunched under her boots. Oscar hopped nimbly over the broken shards and vanished down the hall.

There was no fire burning in the woodstove. It was as cold inside as it was out. The wind whipped the curtains on their rod, scattering snowflakes from the door to the overturned recliner chair against the back wall.

Hugging her injured arm against her body, Claire picked her way through the destruction. Dim light filtered through the windows, rendering Evelyn's sparse collection of damaged furniture in grayscale. The walls were riddled with holes. Claire craned her neck to follow the arc of a stain—dark, almost black—up the wall to the ceiling. She stumbled over the folds of an area rug, and the twisted footrest of the recliner broke her fall. The chair's cushions had been torn open. Stuffing mingled with the snow accumulating on the floor. The cracked case of an old television leaned against the woodstove, spewing electronic innards into the hall.

Claire was afraid to call out again. Evelyn had not responded before, and whatever was responsible for the damage could still be inside—hiding, perhaps. Listening.

She inched down the hall as quietly as possible, approaching the only open door at the end. The carpet runner squelched under her boots. It was becoming increasingly difficult for her to pretend the drag marks she was following—the scuffs and smears and splashes painting the hall—were spills. Ink or coffee or…

A soft rustle came from the open bedroom door, and she whispered, "Oscar?"

Blackout curtains obscured any light from the window, but a pair of dark eyes glinted from down near the floor. Claire stared into the room until the shadows coalesced into the shape of a figure slumped against the bed.

She flipped the wall switch. Light flooded the bedroom, and Evelyn gasped. She sat on the floor against the bed, her head tilted back, gray eyes blinking up a distant point beyond the ceiling. She wasn't wearing her glasses. Oscar lay across her lap. He lowered his head and whimpered, a disconsolate cry. One of Evelyn's wrinkled hands clung to the rifle; the other pressed a wadded-up blanket to her neck. Below the knee, her left leg was shredded. Bone winked through tattered strips of calf muscle.

Her eyes rolled down to meet Claire's, and she smiled with pink-stained teeth. Claire clung to the doorframe as her vision blurred.

Evelyn tried to wave Claire's concern away, and the blanket tumbled from her hand. With a wet, sucking sigh, the wound in her neck gaped open. "Oh..." Evelyn said, probing the ragged edges of her neck wound as if she was discovering it for the first time.

The room spun around Claire, the floor suddenly unsteady beneath legs turned to jelly.

Oscar burrowed his nose into the crook of Evelyn's elbow, and she released her hold on the rifle to pat his head. "I guess... it doesn't look so good, huh?" she asked Claire.

Claire shook her head—shook all over. She tried to breathe, gagged. The air was heavy with the scent of blood. When Oscar shifted, a base human odor wafted up from Evelyn's lap.

Poor Evelyn. Against every instinct, with the gorge rising up in her throat, Claire dropped to her knees beside them.

If Emma had been the one to find Evelyn, then perhaps she could have done something. But Claire was useless. She couldn't even look at Evelyn without feeling like she was going to faint, or vomit—maybe both. Probably both. She couldn't breathe. The air tasted...

A hand alighted on the back of her head, stroking gently. Evelyn petted her head with the same slow and soothing rhythm she'd just used for Oscar; even on the brink of death, she was using her remaining strength to comfort them.

Claire picked a clean spot on Evelyn's shirt to focus on while she balled up the blanket and pressed it to the woman's neck.

"We need to get you help," Claire said. "Do you have a phone?"

Evelyn shook her head.

"The truck, then. Where are the keys?"

"I don't..." Evelyn frowned, licked her lips. "Lost them...I..."

She clawed weakly at her snow coat, struggling to work one shoulder free. "You—you'll need..."

Claire realized what she was trying to do and said, "No, keep it on. I'll find your keys, get you down to the One Stop—"

Evelyn laughed, wincing. "I won't…make it."

Evelyn was determined to remove the coat, with or without her help, and Claire couldn't hold the pressure on her neck with her moving around. So they stripped her coat off together, one arm at a time.

Claire donned the coat and zipped it up. Evelyn fumbled with the leather sheath on her belt, unsnapping it. She held out her hunting knife in a trembling hand and kept trying to speak. "You have…to go…" Her eyes searched the room. "Have to…"

"Evelyn, please—"

Evelyn's red palm silenced her. "Lily…"

Claire looked away. "We found her! Evelyn, she's safe! But now we need your truck. I'm going to get you out of here. I just need you to hold the blanket, okay? Try to rest while I find the keys."

Evelyn coughed, and something shook loose inside her. Groaning, she pushed the rifle at Claire. "Not…going anywhere."

Evelyn feebly scraped loose ammunition up from the floor and piled it back into its box.

Claire made a show of adding the knife and the box to her coat. Slinging the rifle strap over her shoulder, she said, "Okay, just…hold tight while I—"

"Take Oscar?" Evelyn pleaded.

"We will," Claire said. Tears spilled over her cheeks. "You and I will take him together."

But Evelyn shook her head. She groped at the breast pocket of her shirt. Claire helped her work the pack of cigarettes free. Evelyn poked a cigarette between her bloodless lips and pointed toward the lighter on the nightstand.

When Claire turned back, Evelyn's chin was resting on her chest, the cigarette dangling from her lower lip. Oscar whined and slathered Evelyn's cheeks with kisses, but her eyes remained closed. With her gored neck concealed, she almost looked peaceful—might have been sleeping. Her limp hand slid from Oscar's back.

Oscar raised his head and howled.

Breathless, Claire pressed her fingers to Evelyn's wrist to feel for a pulse. She blinked through the tears and wrapped a hand around the dog's collar. He fought her, legs splayed, as she wrestled him out into the hall. But after she'd shut the bedroom door behind them, he ceased struggling. He hung his head, whimpering.

"I'm sorry," Claire said. She hugged him around the neck, buried her face in his coat. "She wants you to go. We have to go."

She repeated the words until the strength returned to her legs. Using the rifle for support, she stood. She made it into the living room before the pain from her shoulder cut through the shock of Evelyn's death, bowing her forward.

The truck.

Claire peered through the shattered front window at the truck parked alongside the cabin. Had the doors been open when she'd passed it? She couldn't recall. She'd been a little preoccupied. Claire laughed, a jittery, humorless sound that made Oscar jump. She was losing it. Even the dog could see it. Oscar edged away from her toward the door.

Claire followed, picking up Evelyn's fur-lined leather cap from the floor as she passed.

Losing it and looting a dead woman in the process.

Never mind that Evelyn would have insisted she take the hat, same as she'd insisted Claire take everything else. From that first day at the cabin, Evelyn had done nothing but give. Claire tried to clear her throat, but the lump there persisted, swelling.

"Ready?" Claire glanced at Oscar. He whined in response. "Yeah, me neither."

They stepped out into the storm.

There was blood on the driver's side door, and more blood on the seat, the steering wheel. The keys weren't in the ignition. Claire checked all of the pockets of Evelyn's coat, hoping the old woman had been wrong about losing the keys, but she found nothing. She kicked at the snow between the truck and the cabin, stirring up pink stains as she walked back and forth, searching. Still nothing. The snow was falling too fast, the wind blowing, already erasing the gouges her boots had left behind.

The keys could be anywhere.

She returned to the truck and climbed in from the passenger side to avoid the blood. A flash of green under the glove box caught her eye. Leaning, she plucked the item from the floor mat. It was Lily's missing glove—the one that hadn't made it home with its match.

The wind slammed the door on the driver's side shut, startling her. Claire cried out. There was a strand of long dark hair adhered to the frozen blood on the dash. Evelyn's hair was gray. But Lily's…

Desperate to get back to her wife and daughter, she tore the truck apart searching for the keys. If Evelyn had been confused…if she had been injured, then maybe…maybe…

Claire beat her fists against the dashboard, screaming out her frustration.

She would have to walk back. And they were still stranded, no closer to getting help for Lily.

Claire shouted for Oscar, and he came running from behind the cabin. He watched, wind tousling his fur, as Claire climbed down from the truck. She took hold of his collar again, and took a moment to orient herself, before leading him in the direction of her mother's cabin. They left the clearing for the forest, weaving between the trees. Her shoulder was on fire. She focused on lifting her knees, planting one boot in front of the other.

After ten minutes spent slogging alongside the dog, she jerked him to a halt. Stunned, she reached out to touch the tented fabric of Lily's coat, snagged on a fallen branch sticking up from the snow. The coat was no longer the lime green color that matched Lily's gloves but the deep red-brown of Evelyn's savaged leg, her opened throat.

Another quarter mile, and Oscar's nose led them to Lily's pants.

Then, a shirt.

A sock.
Thermal leggings.
Underwear.
A sports bra.

They followed the trail of clothing, strewn across the mile of forest between the two cabins. But Lily's coat was the only article of clothing Claire could reach.

Everything else was in the trees.

GRACE

1894

GRACE SHARES A cabin with a monster. It watches her while she pretends to sleep, motionless as a statue when she peeks, moving with fast bursts of speed when her eyes are closed. But she doesn't need to see its spindly limbs carry it across the floor and up the wall to the ceiling. She can listen to the snakeskin whisper of taut gray flesh over splintered logs. She can mark its position by smell alone.

It drips down like spilled ink, crushing her chest. She hears the grin splitting its face in half—the wet, sucking release as its mouth drops open wide. It laughs, rattling long teeth like porcupine quills. An evil spirit. A waking nightmare that clings to her every step.

If ever it was a person, the last pathetic shreds of humanity have been nibbled away by Father's corruption. What remains is cold and thin and wicked sharp. A greedy thing. White Hook caught them, and it means to keep them. To devour them.

It's saving Grace for last.

This winter is worse than the first. Brutal storms tear at the shoddy buildings. The cold works icy fingers into their uniforms, claiming the children one by one. The survivors hobble through the snow like dead-eyed specters, hollowed out by hunger: a parade of bloodless fingers, ears, and noses, stumbling on blackened toes. They are dying in pieces.

A new lesson replaces the reading and writing, a cycle round as the well's open mouth. White Hook chooses a student. And while the others watch, mute, the chosen student is fed three meals a day: meat, from the locked box in Father's cabin. Fed to bursting. If the student refuses to eat, he is beaten. He is taken to the well, tied with a rope, and lowered into the darkness where the other boys have gone before, where all the fed children end up, whether or not they cooperate. The other students must gather around and bear witness for however many days it takes for the cries to fall silent. Only then does White Hook unlock the schoolhouse door to let them out.

To choose another.

And then, one night, Grace wakes to a hand clapped over her mouth. Naabek nods at the filthy bed in the corner. The moonlight spilling through the cabin's windows illuminates a nest of stiff blankets and crumbled earth, bristling with leaf litter. The bed is empty. She follows him out into the night, careful to place her feet where he has already stepped. His passage is soundless. His hand is warm around hers, firm but gentle. Determination burns fiercely in his eyes.

Together, they watch through a sliver between the logs of the schoolhouse as a shadow boils up from the well, a demon surfacing from hell with a small limb clamped in its jaws. The creature tears a fresh piece from the limp form draped over the well's rim. It casts a handful of broken bones back into the darkness it crawled from. The bones splash, joining countless others at the bottom.

Grace knows what must be done.

The government men aren't coming to save them. White Hook forged a letter from their former teacher, confirming his plans to bring the children south at winter's end when the worst of the snow has melted and the roads are passable. But the end of winter is months from now. How much more time will pass before the government men discover the lie and realize the children never arrived? How many weeks, months, until they send someone north to White Hook Lake to inquire after the missing students? All those miles to travel—would they even bother?

No.

Grace knows these men. Relieved of their commitment, they would be only too glad to turn their heads and forget. They have no obligation to civilize the missing. The erased.

Are there official records, Grace wonders, of the students' names and the tribes they were taken from? Their families will know. They will remember Grace, the "civilized" child at her father's elbow: the bait who lured their young ones away. She owes it to them to bring their children back. As many as she can.

And so, Grace and Naabek move forward with their plan. Once the monster is bedded down with its belly engorged, Grace moves to the cabin's windows, pulling back the flimsy curtains to let the moonlight in. Then, she creeps over to the monster's nest.

Not daring to breathe, she lifts the pair of keys tied around White Hook's neck. When she tugs the cord out from under its misshapen head, the monster stirs. A yellowed claw scratches the ragged hole that was once a nose, raking bits of flesh back from bone. White Hook smacks its lips. A bruised tongue snakes over the dried gore painting its chin. The sight of it revolts her, but she cannot look away. She remains stuck in place, caught by the idea that if she looks long and hard enough at the crea-ture's moonlit face, she might be able to find traces of the man it used to be. She searches her memory for Father's face, but the image runs like melted wax, becoming the thing lying in the bed. Perhaps the man she knew was nothing more than a mask, a costume worn by the monster within. White Hook's sunken eyelids flutter. With a rumbling belch, it rolls toward the wall.

Grace moves to the chest at the foot of the bed. Since their return from the south, White Hook has kept the chest locked, with the new pouch of ammunition stored inside—unused, now that it no longer bothers with the pretense of hunting. She turns the key, cracks the lid, and removes the pouch.

She takes the rifle with her. While Naabek stands guard out-side the cookhouse, she waits for her eyes to adjust; she did not bring a lamp. She's afraid White Hook might wake to find her missing. The light would betray her location. Grace unlocks the storeroom door to reveal stocked shelves.

The container of kerosene sloshes in her arms, nearly full. They've spent the winter living by the light of the moon. White Hook cannot abide the sight of an open flame; its eyes are attuned to the dark. Its gray flesh has no memory of warmth.

They are forbidden to build fires, even for heat. Grace no longer cooks. They never eat. And the chosen student who is permitted to feed must consume everything as White Hook does: raw and cold.

But no more.

Once the kerosene is secreted away inside their former teacher's shack, wrapped in blankets and stuffed into a wooden chest, Grace sneaks back to the cookhouse. Naabek follows her in. Working together, they move the bulk of the food supplies out of the storeroom.

Snowflakes drift down from above as they cross the clearing. At the northern end of the bone pit, beneath a massive pine, they shift the blanket of bones aside to reveal a hole gouged in the hard, frozen earth. The sight of it makes Grace's fingers ache and burn with the memory of the night before—the hours spent digging, using bones for shovels.

They bury the supplies, replace the cover of bones, and then eliminate their tracks as best they can, using branches like brooms. The clouds open up as if gutted, spilling fat snowflakes in thick white curtains. Grace whispers a prayer of thanks to anyone or anything that might be listening.

They leave the branches at the tree line. It does not matter if White Hook sees the prints in the clearing, so long as it cannot follow their trail beyond. All that remains is to return to the cookhouse and lock the storeroom door.

But White Hook is waiting for them inside.

One long-fingered hand grips Naabek's skull, cracking it against the wall. The other hand reaches toward Grace, beckoning for the keys.

Grace's eyes dart to Naabek, lying in a crumpled heap on the floor. His eyelids are fluttering. A dark puddle forms beneath his shorn scalp, but there's no gray mixed in with the red. The rise and fall of his chest gives her hope. She needs to distract White Hook, draw it away from Naabek. She flees through the open door. Fingers knot in her hair, dragging her back, and then forward.

Toward the schoolhouse.

The well.

Grace fights only enough to slow the creature down, but she does not break free.

Naabek is back on his feet, propped against the doorframe. As White Hook tows Grace across the clearing, Naabek's hand dips into the leather sack he brought back from the south. He shoves its contents into his mouth in fistfuls, chewing, swallowing. The sight breaks Grace's heart.

She doesn't feel the leather strap whipping her legs until she cannot stand. She does not resist when White Hook pins her left hand on the stone slab beside the well. She's trying to count the seconds between this moment and the one that will bring Naabek through the door behind White Hook. She's hoping she can remain strong, or Naabek's sacrifice will be for nothing.

White Hook pries her left hand open. It rakes a long claw across the backs of her remaining fingers, splitting open the skin above the knuckles of her hand. She screams as her blood stains the stone slab. It slices again, taking its time, drawing the seconds out between each pass, carving a trough through bone and severing tendons and ligaments. Then it grips her wrist, lifts her hand to its mouth, and chases her dangling fingers with its tongue. It severs the last strips of skin with its teeth, swallowing the bites without chewing, and Grace screams in pain.

In rage.

It wasn't supposed to happen this way.

The rifle's muzzle flashes.

White Hook spins, blood bubbling between its lips, spattering the walls as it laughs. Naabek stands in the doorway. Roaring, the monster falls on Naabek before he can fire again, enveloping him in roiling shadow. It drags Naabek through the school-house, and over the edge of the well, plunging in.

Down.

Grace turns, already running out the door and toward the teacher's shack. Leaving her best friend behind. Her hatred for White Hook drives her on, searing her insides.

Everything is going according to plan.

SAVE FOR THE gentle slosh of the kerosene, Grace's passage through the schoolhouse is silent. She listens as White Hook consumes its last meal. A cough echoes up from the well, followed by a splattering rush of fluids. She smiles.

The feast is at its end. The meat has been devoured, but the stuffing isn't settling; it's spreading. The handfuls of dried water hemlock that Naabek ingested are working through him, a final gift to White Hook. Repayment for the beatings, for Naabek's tongue and Grace's fingers. For all the lost little ones.

From the corner of her eye, she can almost see Naabek standing beside her, smiling with her. She feels him lending her strength. The cold stone vibrates beneath her palm, as if the well itself is seizing, hacking and choking as the poison spreads from gut to blood, from heart to brain. She hopes it hurts.

She prays it's agonizing.

Grace tips the can over the well's edge. Kerosene gurgles through the spout, spilling over earth and rock. Trickling down. When the can is almost empty, she dips a torn strip of cloth inside and leaves the dripping end trailing. She strikes flint against iron. Flames kiss her fingertips.

Grace lets the can, the remaining fuel, and the fire fall.

White Hook screams. Grace squints into the flames, but she does not shrink away.

The time for shrinking is over.

Creator, destroyer, she stands over her private portal to hell and raises the rifle. Training the barrel on the charred monstrosity writhing like a slitted pupil in the well's flaming iris, Grace fires until the howling ceases and the ammunition is exhausted. Until a small hand finds hers, pulling her back from the pillar of smoke.

The fire has died, but when Grace closes her eyes, the inferno—the hate scalding her insides—is still very much alive. Afterimages obscure the faces of the children gathered behind her. Together, they push the stone slab over the well, sealing its mouth shut, and then Grace leads them out into the cold.

They're leaving tonight—now. White Hook Lake won't hold them prisoner for a moment longer. Grace is a burning torch, leading the children south. Winter will not stop her. The cold cannot touch her. She no longer fears the dark.

She's taking them home, every last one.

She writes one final journal entry, hastily scrawled. She will leave it behind, not only as evidence of the atrocities committed but also as a warning to those who might come after.

LILY

THE HUNGER PULSES low and red.

The wind worms icy fingers through the cracks between the logs, prying. Cold sinks its hooks into the walls. The schoolhouse shudders. A voice is crying out from the depths of the well, begging for release.

Not yet.

Gritted teeth.

Grinding, the stone slab slides back into place. The throat is closed.

Patience.

Faith.

But the nights are long.

Empty.

Endless.

Hell on Earth.

The Lord speaks. The wind carries His words through the darkness, spelling His will out in the clouds, the snow. Other voices filter through…

Two women, speaking in hushed tones. One is comforting, the other pained. But there are no women in this place, only the girl. *He* hesitates. The scent of blood draws *Him* out.

Where there should be a frozen lake, there is a hall instead. At the end, a door.

"You're lucky it only grazed you…I know, just try to breathe."

"Evelyn's gone."

"Where?"

"No, Em, she's *gone*. Dead. Something attacked her."

"Are you serious?"

He licks his lips. The boy in the well can wait.

"But you said there weren't any animals around. And now we've got a moose stuck in our truck and—what, a wolf? A bear?"

"I don't know, Em. I didn't get a good look at the bites."

"I'm surprised you didn't faint."

"Thanks."

"I didn't mean—"

"I know. I'm sorry, I just—ow!"

"Almost done. Hold still."

His chin is slick with saliva. Nails scratch wood, a subtle push.

"And...done."

Hinges squeak. The women turn, wide-eyed, to face *Him*.

"Lily?"

Teeth crunch into muscle. Blood sheets over Lily's chin.

Hot.

Crimson.

"Jesus Christ, Em—her tongue."

"Help me with her!"

The taste is exquisite.

Ecstasy.

Heaven.

Lily smiles.

He drinks it in.

EMMA

"I NEED GAUZE." Emma was trying to force Lily's mouth open to inspect her bleeding tongue. But her jaws were clamped shut, her lips pressed together like the seam of a scar, curling upwards at the corners to form a wistful smile. She swallowed the contents of her flooded mouth with loud, greedy gulps. The dining chair creaked beneath her weight.

"Is she..." Claire's frost-nipped face turned from pink to a sickly shade of green. "Is she drinking—"

"The gauze, Claire. In the bathroom."

When Claire returned to the kitchen, Emma plucked the gauze from her hand and nodded at the unoccupied chair. "Sit."

"I can help..." Glancing over at Lily, Claire pressed a fist to her mouth. Her chest hitched. "Just...give me a minute."

"Sit down, before you end up on the floor—and stop looking. You're torturing yourself."

Once Emma managed to pry Lily's teeth apart, her jaw fell open as if a hidden catch had been released. The bite was bad, but Emma had seen far worse. Lily wouldn't need stitches, and that was a relief, because having her fingers in Lily's mouth made Emma nervous. She couldn't stop thinking about the moose, the way Lily's teeth had raked the frozen hide again and again, seeking a way in...

Emma clamped the gauze down on Lily's tongue, willing her hands to be still, firm. She couldn't let Claire see her unraveling, or their problems would be doubled.

"Thank you, Em." Cold fingers squeezed Emma's wrist, then released.

"For what?" The bleeding was slowing. Emma applied more gauze.

"You know...for patching me up, taking care of Lily. I feel so useless."

Emma tried to smile. But then the image of Lily gnawing on the carcass resurfaced.

"What?" Claire asked. "What's wrong?"

"Nothing. You're not supposed to be looking over here, remember?"

Claire leaned back in her chair, closed her eyes. "How is she?"

"Better. The bleeding has almost stopped."

"Has she eaten?" Claire peeked between her eyelids. "How's her blood sugar?"

"I'll find her something to eat right now," Emma said. The memory of Lily's seizure filled her with guilt. If Claire found out, she would question every one of Emma's decisions moving forward. And the last thing Emma needed was more doubt.

"Em, she's not...I mean, she couldn't be pregnant, right? Because it looks like—"

"No, her belly couldn't grow that fast," Emma said. "She was only missing for two weeks, not months. It could be parasites— worms or something—but I'd have to check her stool to know for sure, and she hasn't used the bathroom yet."

Staring into the refrigerator, Emma sighed. Instead of cleaning out the old food to make room for Evelyn's latest delivery, Claire had shoved everything to the back. A rotten stench permeated the refrigerator. Emma dug through the cluttered shelves, where old groceries mixed with the new. When she found the source of the odor—bottom shelf, back corner—grief sank its hooks into her heart, rending wounds that hadn't even begun to heal.

Emma collapsed. An acorn squash tumbled from the fridge and rolled across the kitchen, and a produce bag filled with sludgy greens fell into her lap. She gazed blankly at an opened block of moldy cheese lying on the floor. She should be weeping. But the sorrow of the previous weeks had wrung her dry.

"What is it?" Claire asked. Despite her injured shoulder, she hauled Emma up from the floor and hugged her from behind. "What's wrong?"

More questions she couldn't answer. Emma laughed—an awful, inhuman croak. Everything was wrong, had been for weeks. The tears were coming now. Crumpling inward, Emma said, "Silas left the cap off the milk again."

"Okay," Claire whispered as she ran her fingers through Emma's hair. "It's okay, I've got you."

Emma relaxed into her arms. It felt good to be held, supported, when she was too drained by grief to stand on her own. Sniffling, she said, "I think something's wrong with Lily. Beyond the regular...When I tested her blood sugar earlier, it was normal."

"What does that mean?"

"I have no idea. It shouldn't be possible."

"I found one of Lily's gloves in Evelyn's truck," Claire whispered. She sounded scared. "I'm worried—"

"We don't have to talk about it right now," Emma said, turning to cup Claire's face in her hands. "You need to rest. And you really should eat something."

"Lily, too."

Emma sighed. "Yeah, I tried. But the soup was cold. I couldn't get the stove to work."

"The pilot light—"

"I know *why* it wasn't working."

"Easy..."

"Sorry."

"Sounds like you're hungry, too."

"Shut up." Emma smiled and wiped her nose on her sleeve. "If you fix the stove, I'll make us something to eat."

"I'll do you one better and show you how to fix it yourself."

Emma watched Claire reignite the pilot light, then they gathered up the groceries scattered across the floor. It felt strange, the two of them working together—like relearning a skill that had once come naturally to them both.

Like progress.

Emma read the label on a package wrapped in butcher paper and asked, "How's steak sound for dinner?"

"Are you asking me or Oscar?" Claire nodded at the dog, whose tail thumped the chair leg. "Because if you have to choose, then the steak goes to him—no contest. I never would've made it back without him."

Emma hefted the meat. "Feels like Evelyn bought the whole cow. I'm sure there's enough for both of you."

"Well, if we run out, there's always plenty of moose in the truck."

Emma stiffened. "Claire, when you were gone, Lily—"

"Oh..." Claire leaned against the stove and pinched the bridge of her nose, blinking. "Sorry, I just got lightheaded there for a second."

Emma pressed a hand into the small of her back. "I can take it from here. Go sit down, please."

"I'm good—I'm fine now."

"*Sit.*"

Oscar dropped his haunches neatly to the floor. Head cocked, he watched them with bright black eyes. Emma said, "He listens better than you do."

"Well, maybe Evelyn's a better trainer than you are," Claire fired back.

And then their light-hearted banter dissolved into a heavy silence as they both remembered what Claire had found at Evelyn's.

Claire dropped into a chair and scratched Oscar behind the ears. "What are we going to do with him...after?"

Emma went to Lily's side, tucked her dark hair back, and began applying more ointment to her frostbitten ears. "If Oscar saved your life, then I guess he's part of the family now."

"Silas will be thrilled," Claire said. "He loves this dog."

There it was—what Emma needed to hear most—delivered by Claire like a precious gift: Silas, in present tense. Alive. A future with their son in it.

Lily's jaw dropped open, and the gauze tumbled from her mouth. But before Emma could examine her tongue, her teeth clacked shut. With her chapped, flaking lips pressed into a hard line, Lily's jaw shifted side to side.

Claire said, "What's that sound?"

"She's grinding her teeth again."

"Again? Can you make her stop?"

"I'm open to suggestions." The sound was maddening, worse than nails on a chalk board. Emma took Lily by the chin and said, "Lily, stop. Please. I'll make you something to eat. What sounds good?"

Moose? Emma's stomach flipped.

The grinding continued, relentless.

Emma heated a pot of soup and a cast-iron pan on the stove. With her back turned, she could almost pretend she hadn't seen Lily's knees touching the underside of the table.

"Lily, I'm making you tomato soup," Emma said. The forced cheer in her tone made her sick. She was falling apart, not fooling anyone.

"Maybe…" Claire trailed off. Emma turned to find her nibbling at her thumbnail—a nervous habit that was so distinctly *Lily* in nature that it hurt Emma's heart to watch.

"Maybe what?" Emma prompted.

"I mean, she's been out there all this time. Maybe she needs something a little more substantial than soup?"

"The steak? But…she's vegan." Emma needed to believe that something—*please, just one thing*—about Lily had not been changed by her time away. The girl in the chair didn't feel like their daughter. She was a mute stranger, impossibly distant. She had torn into the moose's hide like it was—"No, I know. Don't say it. I hear how ridiculous it sounds. But her tongue's swollen. The soup will be easier for her to eat."

The butcher paper rustled as Emma unfolded it and transferred two steaks to a plate. A loud knocking made her jump, and Claire yelped in surprise. Oscar's nails skittered over the floorboards as he backed into the living room.

"Her knees," Claire explained, eyeing Lily warily. "She jumped a little, moved the table."

Lily's spine was ramrod straight. Even seated, she was taller than Emma standing. Her bandaged feet were flat on the floor, knees elevating the table. The tube of ointment was slowly sliding down the table toward Claire.

The grinding sound intensified, underscored by a rumble like thunder from Lily's distended belly. Oscar whined softly.

Trembling, Emma turned back to the stove and moved one of the steaks to the cast-iron pan. She didn't like having her back to Lily. She didn't like that she didn't like having her back to Lily. The steak hissed, sizzling.

"Em..." Claire whispered. "Emma."

Emma glanced over her shoulder and froze. Lily's eyes had come alive. They burned like hot coals in her hollowed sockets. Her lips were moving as if she was trying to form words. Until that moment, Emma hadn't realized how desperately she longed to hear her daughter's voice.

But Lily's jaw only drooped, exposing her tongue's clotted wound. A runnel of pink saliva leaked over her lip.

Claire reached across the table with a napkin and wiped it away, saying, "Hang on, Lily. Dinner's almost ready."

Emma flipped the steak.

Wood squalled over wood and the table legs dropped with a heavy *thunk*. Emma spun around as the kitchen chair clattered to the floor, but Lily was gone. Claire's blue eyes were impossibly wide, her mouth agape, as she stared at Emma—no, past Emma...

A thick musky odor filled Emma's nostrils. She turned, smacked into Lily upraised arm, and cried out. Claire was beside her in an instant, switching off the burner, as Lily towered over them with the raw steak clutched in her hand. Juices seeped from the force of her grip, staining her bandages. Her lips curled back from her teeth.

"Lily, honey...your soup is ready." Emma's heart hammered, smashing all coherent thought to pieces. She reached for the steak in Lily's hand.

Lily's teeth snapped shut on empty air as Claire pulled Emma back, stepping between them. Emma uttered a strangled sound—half scream, half sob. Lily had tried to bite her. And her teeth were still bared, as if she meant to try again.

Lily evaluated the raw meat in her bandaged fist with fever-bright eyes, angling her head like a hawk contemplating the best way to dismember its prey. Her head darted forward. She ripped a chunk from the steak and swallowed without chewing. Pink juice dribbled down her chin. Another chunk disappeared between her teeth.

"She's going to choke," Emma said, "or get sick. It's raw. We have to stop her."

The very notion of reaching for the steak again—of risking those jaws snapping shut on her fingers—was paralyzing. But when Claire grabbed Lily's wrist, Lily did not attempt to bite; her compliance stuck like an arrow in Emma's chest. Lily had lunged at Emma like a feral dog, yet when Claire was involved, Lily did what she asked without conflict. Claire had always been better with the kids, a natural.

But Emma? Everyone pushed her away.

Stop it. Could you be any more selfish? Claire's just doing what you asked her to. And if Lily's not putting up a fight, it's not because she likes Claire better. It's because...

She's choking.

Lily's eyes bulged. Her chest hitched, unable to draw breath. Emma could almost make out the shape of the meat blocking her windpipe. But Lily wasn't pawing at her neck with her bandaged hands; she was staring at the floor, dead-eyed once again.

Emma moved quickly. She turned Lily toward the sink, reached up and around to knot her hands at the base of Lily's sternum, and compressed.

Nothing.

Again.

Lily was going limp.

Again.

Emma couldn't hold her weight much longer. She was losing her.

Please, please...

A lump of meat flew from Lily's mouth and landed in the sink. Beneath the band of Emma's arms, Lily's stomach contracted. A gout of dark ichor and undigested meat spilled into the sink, splashing up the stainless-steel sides. Claire flinched back from the smell. Emma stayed through sheer force of will, but the reek was unlike anything she'd ever experienced.

Claire gagged. "I'm...ough...Sorry, Em. I'm gonna—"

"Go," Emma said as Claire rushed for the bathroom, hand clapped over her mouth. "I've got this. I've got you, Lily. Shh, I'm here. It's okay."

Emma ran the tap until the sink was cleared, though the smell did not diminish in strength. She wet a dishtowel and mopped the sweat from Lily's forehead. Then, cracking the window above the table open, she gulped at the clean frigid air.

"I found the thermometer," Claire said. Shirt pulled up over her nose, she poked the thermometer between Lily's lips.

"She doesn't have a fever," Emma said. The thermometer beeped: *LO*.

"We could test her blood sugar again, just to be—"

"*No*," Emma snapped. "Just…help me get her onto the couch. She needs to be near the stove."

After they finished tucking Lily in on the couch, Emma tried to apologize, but Claire waved her off. "You know what you're doing. I shouldn't have questioned you."

Emma caught her by the wrist and took her hand. "Still, I shouldn't have snapped at you. You were only trying to help. Maybe…I don't know…if we just apologized more often, instead of trying to shrug things off…"

With a tired smile, Claire said, "You're starting to sound like our shrink."

"Marriage counselor. And I mean it, Claire. I'm sorry."

Claire nodded. "Okay. Accepted."

She released Emma's hand and moved toward the kitchen.

"Where are you going?" Emma hated the fearful whine in her tone. When had she become so needy?

"To feed the dog."

"Come back when you're done? I don't want…"

To be alone with her.

Claire paused in the doorway to the kitchen. An unreadable emotion played over her delicate features. Emma felt compelled to explain her unease. But she didn't need to.

"I know," Claire whispered. "I'm scared, too."

The confession caught Emma off-guard. It was unlike Claire to open up about her feelings without being prompted. Emma uttered a brittle laugh and said, "What kind of mother am I? Scared of my own daughter."

Braced for judgement, she sneaked a look at Claire.

"The same kind I am, apparently." Claire shook her head and sighed. "I'll be right back. Keep an eye on her."

Emma stared at the rifle she'd leaned in the corner after dragging Claire in out of the storm. The rifle should have made her feel safer, but it was just another grim reminder of the danger still lurking outside. What if the animal that had attacked Evelyn was still around? There was only a mile of forest separating the two cabins.

She listened to the sounds of the dog feeding in the next room and shuddered, thinking of the raw steak sliding in thick lumps down Lily's throat. Claire's footsteps drifted down the hall toward the bedrooms, then returned.

"Do you want to be Big Spoon or Little Spoon?" Claire asked. She was holding an armload of blankets and pillows.

Emma stifled a sob. The question was like a long-lost friend, one she thought she'd never hear from again.

"Things must be really bad," Emma mumbled, burying her face in a pillow so Claire wouldn't see her cry. "You haven't asked me that in years."

"Little Spoon it is." Claire snuggled up behind her. She was holding her breath, preparing to say something Emma didn't want to hear. So Emma said it first: "You're leaving in the morning."

"I have to. I'll walk down to the One Stop, call an ambulance."

There was no point in arguing; there was no other choice. Lily needed a doctor.

"You'll take the rifle?"

"I will."

"Because whatever attacked Evelyn, it could still—"

"I can't think about that right now, Em. You didn't see her. It was…awful. Another reason we can't stay here. And if we don't get Lily to a hospital soon—"

"I know. Her frostbite…I didn't want to mention it before, when she was awake, but the cyanosis is spreading fast—way too fast. They might have to…She could lose her hands and feet, Claire, but she doesn't seem affected by it. I just don't understand. She shouldn't be capable of standing, much less walking. But you saw how she moved in the kitchen, how she's bending her fingers and toes like it's nothing. She's been missing for weeks, yet she somehow manages to *gain* weight?"

"And she's taller," Claire interjected.

Emma rolled over. Nose to nose with Claire, she whispered, "I feel like such a coward for saying this, but I don't want to be alone with her."

Claire kissed her forehead. "And I don't want to leave you two alone, but it's the only way. I need you to take care of her while I'm gone, Em. Can you do that for me?"

"Of course." Emma pressed her ear to Claire's chest, listening to her heartbeat. She said, "This feels…weird."

"Weird doesn't come close to touching it."

"No, not that. I mean…us, actually talking like this."

"Yeah, there could be a book in it for our shrink. We'll have to tell her all about it when we get back."

"Back." The word felt foreign on Emma's tongue. They'd been trapped in their snowy limbo for so long that leaving had become a distant concept. A fantasy.

"Home," Claire said. "We *are* going home. All of us. You, me, Lily…and Silas. I promise. Lily knows where he is, and once she's feeling better, she'll start talking again. With her help, we'll find him."

Alive? Emma bit back the question. It wouldn't do either of them any good to think like that, not with Claire going back out in the morning.

"Okay," Emma whispered. "Home. Together."

They slept fitfully as the wind buffeted the cabin's walls. The pine logs groaned and popped around them, refusing to fall. And then the wind died down. The ticking of snowflakes against glass diminished. For the first time in days, their world fell silent. Exhaustion overtook them, and they slipped away completely.

Until the alarm sounded in the morning.

And they found the couch empty.

"YOU SEARCHED THE bedrooms?" Emma shouted.

The basement door was still locked. She tore open the hall-closet door: nothing but cleaning supplies and linens.

"Both bedrooms. Twice," Claire shouted back. She sounded out of breath.

Emma understood the feeling. Her chest had been locked in a vise since they first discovered Lily was missing.

Again.

Again, again...

"Under the beds?"

"*Yes*, Emma. Christ, I'm not fucking blind!" Claire stormed through the cabin and forked her fingers between her lips, whistling. "Oscar's gone too. Shit!"

You should have told Claire about before, when Lily went after the moose. You should have sat up, watching her...

Emma rubbed her hands over her face, but she couldn't dispel the negative thoughts. She couldn't focus with Claire raging through the living room, throwing pillows and blankets.

"I can't believe this. I can't believe we lost her *again*." Claire stalked toward the door.

"Where are you going?"

"Lily knows where Evelyn's cabin is. Maybe she went back."

"Back?"

"I found her glove at Evelyn's, in the truck."

"Lily was *at Evelyn's*?"

"I told you." Claire pivoted, nostrils flaring. "Last night."

"You didn't."

"I *did*." Claire was donning her snow gear, but she was flustered, putting things on out of order. Her gloved fingers fumbled at her knotted laces.

"Give me that." Emma untied the knot and handed the boot back.

Claire exhaled a heated cloud. The fire in the woodstove had gone cold; the cabin was freezing. Emma considered lighting another fire, but without Lily there didn't seem to be any point.

As Claire jammed her foot into her boot, Emma said, "I'm going out, too."

"No, you need to stay here, in case—"

"No, Claire. I'm sick of waiting. And there are other places she could've gone. Maybe she went back to the lake to look for Silas."

Claire's head whipped up. "You think so?"

Emma pulled on her knit cap, then handed Evelyn's hat to Claire. "I have no idea, but it's a start. It's something. And I can't just stay here. I should have told you…"

"What?"

"Lily left once before—yesterday, while you were gone. I found her in the clearing, and she was…chewing on the moose. Trying to eat it."

"To eat—" Claire gagged. "Oh, shit. *Shit.*"

"It's my fault she's gone," Emma said, working her gloves on. "If I'd told you, we could have been better prepared."

"Let's go," Claire said. There was no blame in her eyes, only determination. "We'll have to split up. If you get lost—"

"I won't. I've been out there a hundred times now."

"Whatever got Evelyn could still be out there. You should take the rifle."

"No, I'd just end up shooting myself in the foot. You're going to Evelyn's; you take it."

Before they parted ways, Emma and Claire circled the cabin in ever-widening circles, shouting their daughter's name. But there were no footprints, no sign of which direction she might have headed.

They reunited at the shed. Emma was already winded, feeling the pain of the previous day's hike through the snow with Lily. The forest beckoned, the trees laden with snow. Without the wind tearing at her clothes, it was almost peaceful.

"I left the front door unlocked in case she comes back while we're gone," Emma said.

"We'll meet back here at noon?" Claire kissed Emma's lips, her nose. She pressed their foreheads together. "I love you. Be careful."

Emma nodded. "You too."

They separated, making their way through the trees without looking behind them.

CLAIRE

EVELYN'S BODY HAD been moved. Only her boots were visible, protruding into the scene framed by the open bedroom door, as if she'd been dragged away from the bed. *That door should not be open,* Claire thought. She distinctly remembered closing it before she left. But something had opened it again. Some*one* had turned the knob.

A pitiful whine echoed from the room.

"Oscar?" Claire whispered. She edged closer, clutching the rifle. "Lily?"

She did not want to go into the bedroom.

"Lily, are you here?"

Another soft whine from the black dog quaking in the corner beyond the bed. Oscar inched forward, tongue lapping nervously at his muzzle. White crescents flashed as his bulging eyes darted toward Evelyn's body. He growled, a low rumble tapering to a high-pitched whine. Claire patted her legs to urge him on. "Come here, Oscar. Come on."

Oscar tensed his hindquarters and launched himself through the doorway. He bounded past Claire, then spun like a black tornado, twisting around her legs, jumping up at her. She hesitated, unsure if she should touch him with his hackles raised. The familiar old fear was back, insisting that frightened dogs bit without thinking; he could be dangerous. But when he pawed at her chest, she did not push him off. He was trembling, just as scared as she was.

"You did it," Claire whispered, wrapping her arms around him. "Good boy. You did it."

Oscar pushed off her chest and trotted to the end of the hall. Claire longed to follow him, but she couldn't leave until she was certain Lily wasn't hiding in the bedroom.

"Stay." Oscar sat, cocking his head as Claire pointed and said, "We're in this together now. You'd better not leave me."

He barked once, loud and sharp, then lay down, resting his muzzle on his paws.

Claire nodded. "Good...Okay, I'll be right back."

Make it quick—in and out.

She entered the bedroom.

The abattoir.

And then she was in Evelyn's kitchen, vomit trailing from her lips as she ripped the cabinets open. A bottle of whiskey in her hands.

Stripped flesh.

She yanked her gloves off to uncork it. Tipped the bottle back.

Torn muscle.

Claire swallowed, gasped.

Bone exposed and winking.

Gnawed.

But she couldn't flush the red, wet images out.

Mutilated.

Vivid snapshots flashed through her mind. Claire lowered the bottle. Coughing—*ragged tissue, yellow gobbets of fat*—she gagged and pressed a hand to her mouth, willing the whiskey to stay down. Sour heat burned her throat. Oscar sat beside her, panting. She fondled his torn ear and said, "You could have warned me, you know. I mean...what could have done that? A pack of wolves?"

Claire wiped her mouth. "I'm talking to a dog."

Oscar tilted his head and whined.

"Well, we aren't going to find her by sitting here feeling sorry for ourselves." She set the bottle down and looked around. A welcome numbness was spreading through her. Riding a wave of liquid courage, she moved through the rest of the cabin, searching for Lily before she lost her nerve. But Lily wasn't in Evelyn's cabin.

She could be anywhere.

Frustrated, Claire spat. Melancholy stole through her, exacerbated by the liquor. Emma would smell it on her breath. There was a fight waiting on the horizon; Claire couldn't put it off forever. She led Oscar into the forest, back toward her mother's cabin.

Back. Not home.

THE DOOR TO the cabin was open when she returned. The narrow gap that greeted Claire as she climbed the porch steps was just wide enough to permit Oscar to slip inside. She shouldered the rifle. There were bloody fingerprints on the doorknob; animals didn't leave fingerprints.

"Emma? Lily?"

A small frightened part of her wondered if she had died when Evelyn shot her, if she was now reliving the same series of events as punishment for breaking her promises, for hurting Emma.

For losing their children.

But if Emma hadn't brought them here in the first place, then Lily and Silas would be at home in California. Emma's the one who couldn't resist barging in. To help, to help—sure. Emma's always helping.

Claire shook her head. That was the alcohol talking. She didn't want to be that woman anymore: bitter and resentful. *That* woman had split her family into pieces, driving her children out into the cold. That selfish version of herself was drunk again, despite all her promises, wasting time on the porch because she was afraid of what she might find inside.

Enough.

She should be searching for whoever left the door open. Claire unslung the rifle and went inside, making her way toward the hall. Without the snow and the uneven ground to blame for her faltering, the weave in her step was impossible to ignore. The woodstove was still dark. Claire's breath plumed in ghostly clouds.

At the end of the hall, Oscar lay with his nose wedged under the door to the children's bedroom, snuffling as if he meant to suck all the air out of the room. The knob was smeared with red. Claire turned it, and Oscar pushed through. He leaped onto the bed, wiggling into Lily's lap. A pile of soiled bandages tumbled to the floor. But Lily paid the dog no mind.

The sight of her daughter's bare hands and feet turned Claire's insides to liquid. She felt the rifle slide from her arms, heard it hit the floor. The flesh of Lily's ankles was a mottled purple-blue, the feet below blackened and hard.

Dead.

"Lily?" Claire withdrew her hand from Lily's toes, uncertain how she'd come to be kneeling beside the bed. Lily's pajamas were soaked. The blood smeared on her face chilled Claire. She moved closer, searching for the wounds. "Honey, are you hurt? Where have you been? We've been looking everywhere—"

Lily scooted away from Claire and jerked her legs up, folding them beneath her. Held in the cyanotic cage of her over-long fingers, the camera looked like a child's toy. She frowned, lips pursed in concentration, as she turned the camera around to face her, fumbling at the buttons. Her mouth dropped open, and an odor of decay roiled up from her throat. Even seated on the floor, the pungent smell found Claire, as if it was too heavy to rise like normal heat, too thick to dissipate. Claire's eyes watered. Her stomach lurched, but she was determined not to let her revulsion show. She didn't want Lily to feel embarrassed.

The camera flashed.

Lily held the camera up to her face, as if she was trying to snap a close-up selfie, and opened her mouth wide, tongue protruding. The camera flashed again. Lily tipped her head back until the dark, tangled spill of her hair brushed the mattress. She angled the lens at her tongue, pressed her black finger down. The camera flashed, flashed.

Afterimages danced like bright windows in Claire's vision. Oscar peered over the edge of the bed at her, tail thumping the mattress. He seemed calm—happy, even. When he jumped down to the floor, Lily's head turned to follow the movement.

Her eyes landed on Claire. She licked her lips.

"Mom?"

Lily lowered the camera to the bed, releasing it. Her ruined hands drifted up to tuck ratty lengths of hair behind her ears, then stopped as she held them out before her, staring. She did not scream or cry. She blinked once—slowly, as if she'd been sedated—and said again, "Mom?"

"Yes, yes." Claire crushed Lily to her chest. "I'm here. It's me, I'm here, Lily. Yes."

"Memma?"

"She's out looking for you. We woke up, and you were…We didn't know where you were. Lily, where did you go?"

Lily pushed back, surveying the room. Her eyes fell on Silas's blanket tent, and her face crumbled.

"We've been looking for Silas, too. If you know where he is—"

Lily moaned, folding into herself. Her blackened fingers yanked on her tongue, as if by pinning it in place she could manipulate the muscle to form the words she needed.

Claire didn't want to push. She could feel Lily's heart pounding, the panicked rise and fall of her ribs. *I can't even get my arms around her anymore.* But she needed to know, desperately. "Lily, what happened to Silas?"

Lily managed a heart-wrenching whine.

"Please, try to remember."

"With…me," Lily said.

"He's not, honey." Claire didn't want to say the words aloud, watch the hope drain from her daughter's face. But pretending wouldn't bring her son home. "You made it back, but Silas… he's still out there. Anything you can tell us—"

"Can't," Lily groaned. Her hand came up, smacked her temple. "With…me."

"Lily, stop." Claire wrestled her hand down. *Christ, she's strong.*

"With…me." Lily twisted out of Claire's arms. Her eyes roved wildly around the bedroom, and then she dove for Silas's blanket tent. It collapsed beneath her. She clawed at the blankets, fingers like charred sticks opening and closing on nothing. Tears spilled over her gaunt cheeks. "With…"

Lily gripped her head in her blackened hands and howled.

The cry shattered her lucidity like glass. Gravity pulled her limp body to the floor. She rolled onto her back as Claire and Oscar bracketed her motionless body. Claire stroked her face, clearing the matted hair from her forehead. Her skin felt rough, tacky. Claire lay beside her and stared up at the ceiling with her daughter, whispering, "I'm sorry. We don't have to talk about him anymore. I'm sorry. Let's talk about something else—anything you want."

Lily's breath ghosted the air, a rotten fog. Her eyes narrowed to slits. She clapped her hands over her ears and growled. The guttural rumble vibrated through Claire's bones, but she did not shrink away. However, Oscar backed toward the door. Ears flattened, he returned the growl.

"Claire?" Emma's voice came from down the hall, tentative.

"In here!" Claire rubbed Lily's arms, shook her. She willed Lily's eyes to clear. For Emma to have missed their daughter's brief moment of lucidity would be too cruel.

Just a spark, please. Just one more word.

Emma pushed past Oscar and dropped to the floor beside Claire, lifting Lily's arms and searching her scalp, behind her neck, beneath her clothes. Watching Emma's fluttering hands was making Claire's head ache. "What are you looking for?"

"All this blood…" Emma pulled down Lily's pajama pants, working them off over her feet. "It has to be coming from somewhere. She's injured. I'm trying to find…"

Emma trailed off as she noticed the rifle lying on the floor. She looked over at Claire, sharply, her face twisting into a scowl. "Would you put that thing somewhere else before one of us gets shot?"

Claire bit back a retort. She wasn't an idiot; the safety was on. If she hadn't soaked her brain in alcohol beforehand, she'd have put the rifle down somewhere more responsible. But the damage to Lily's hands and feet had caught her off-guard. And the blood…Even now, she could hardly bear to look at the gore cracking and flaking on their daughter's face. Her pajamas, the bandages she'd removed, were covered in it.

She picked up the rifle and carried it out to the living room to deposit it in the corner beside the front door. She was tempted to remain there, to keep her distance from Emma to prevent her from smelling the liquor on her breath, but Lily needed her. And she owed it to Emma to help if she could. Before she could change her mind, Claire hurried down the hall and into the bedroom to confess. "I've been drinking," she said, kneeling beside her wife. "At Evelyn's."

Without looking away from Lily, Emma said, "I need the pajamas from my suitcase in the bedroom."

"Did you hear—"

"And clean bandages. From the bathroom." When Claire failed to move, Emma's expression softened. She touched Claire's arm. "It can wait. We'll talk about it later."

Claire stood, feeling strangely unmoored. She had expected anger, disappointment. Hurt. But the tenderness in Emma's touch was somehow worse; understanding was a gift she did not deserve.

Anxiety fluttered in her stomach as she gathered the supplies Emma had requested.

A thought skittered through the back of her weary mind, seeking a way out into the light. Begging for a connection to be made. It had been buried down deep, with the memories from Evelyn's cabin—

She stopped short in the hall.

The blood on Lily's clothes, her face.

Evelyn's ravaged body.

Lily wouldn't...

Numb, unable to finish the thought, she returned with the supplies Emma had requested. She helped Emma dress Lily in clean pajamas, held their daughter's hands and feet up as Emma swaddled her extremities in bandages. Lily bore their administrations without blinking or moving. Without making a sound.

"I don't understand," Claire said. "She was speaking before."

Emma stiffened. "What? When?"

"Before you came back. It was only for a few minutes."

"Before I came back." Emma's lips pressed into a thin white line.

"I'm so sorry, Em. I did everything I could to try and keep her talking."

An inscrutable emotion flickered across Emma's face. "Let's get her into bed. Grab her legs."

Claire hoisted Lily's legs while Emma hooked her hands under Lily's armpits. Together, they managed to get her into bed. But she didn't fit. Her bandaged legs dangled over the metal bed frame, feet brushing the floor.

She's still growing.

When Oscar crept forward to sniff at Lily's bandaged foot, Emma pushed him away. She finished cleaning the last of the blood from Lily's face as Claire tucked the blanket in around their daughter's legs.

Without Emma's directions to distract her, Claire's mind worried at the facts she'd been trying to ignore. Like how Lily's stomach wasn't growling anymore, and how it was rounder than ever.

She looked eight-months pregnant now, though like Emma had said, there was no way a pregnancy could grow this fast.

And they hadn't fed her.

Almost two miles, roundtrip, through the snow.

When she'd first come back to them, Lily had been covered in blood. Blood that was not her own.

The glove.

Her glove and hair were in Evelyn's truck…

Her clothes were scattered between the two cabins. But there were no footprints.

Do you really believe she could cross that distance in such a short amount of time and not leave any footprints?

Emma had said Lily's frostbite was abnormal. Regardless of the necrotic color of her feet, she obviously had no difficulty walking. And the way Lily's fingers had operated the camera…

They didn't seem stiff and dead at all.

"Are you coming?" Emma had switched the hall light on and was beckoning to her. Claire kissed Lily's clammy forehead and followed her out into the kitchen.

"It's snowing again," Emma said, staring out the window. "I can't believe it's dark already. So much for meeting back here at noon."

Claire sank into a chair, cradled her head in her hands. "You got lost?"

"I got lost." Emma shook a cigarette out from her dwindling pack and struck a match. "Was Lily at Evelyn's?"

"No, she was here when I got back. I found her in the bedroom."

"Are you okay?"

Claire lifted her head, surprised. Emma reached across the table and took her hand. "Whatever happened at Evelyn's…it must have been bad."

Claire couldn't put it into words. She shook her head.

Emma shrugged. "Well, if you decide you want to talk about it—"

"You're not mad I was drinking?"

"I'm giving you a chance to explain. If you want to."

Claire exhaled, felt all of her anxieties boiling to the surface. She looked at Emma through the curls of smoke, saw the concern written in the lines of her face, and realized there was no point in hiding anymore. She needed Emma. She had gone to so much effort to prove otherwise, driving a wedge between them for years—as if accepting Emma's help made her weaker somehow—but she'd never feel weaker than she had the moment she'd pushed Emma to her breaking point. When Emma had said she was leaving her.

If there was anything Claire could do to salvage their marriage, she owed it to them both to try. So, she told Emma everything, from the horror of discovering Evelyn's mutilated body, to her suspicions about Lily's involvement. And Emma listened; she did not interrupt or question Claire's intuition.

When Claire trailed off, massaging the headache throbbing at her temples, Emma stamped her cigarette out, pushed back from the table with a glass of water, and circled around to Claire's side. "Drink this. You're dehydrated."

Claire emptied the glass and grimaced. "Thanks."

"Sure. Mind if I sit?"

She patted her lap and Emma sank into it, wrapping her arms around Claire, as if by hugging her tightly enough, she could wring the bad memories from their minds. Something inside Claire's chest gave. Grief and fear and frustration spilled over. She was sobbing like a child. Emma held her.

The lights went out.

"The generator," Claire muttered, sniffling. "I forgot to put more gas in. I was hoping we wouldn't need it."

"Get more wood while you're out?" Emma managed a thin smile as she handed Claire a flashlight.

"Oh, so I'm the one going out?"

"You've seen me with the stove." Emma clicked a second flashlight on and directed the beam up at her face, like a child telling campfire tales. "You really want to trust me with our power?"

"Fair enough."

"I'll go check on Lily." Emma was already making her way down the hall. The beam of her flashlight played over the bathroom door, angling toward the bedroom.

Later, Claire would long for that fragile moment when Emma had held her close.

When Emma had been whole.

EMMA

EMMA PANNED THE beam of her flashlight over the bed. Lily's skeletal form lay outlined beneath the blankets like the fossilized remains of some prehistoric predator, long bones joined by prominent knobs—inert, yet vaguely menacing. Emma couldn't see her face. A tangled nest of hair rested on the pillow. She was facing the wall, not lying on her back the way Emma had left her. The thought of Lily moving when she wasn't around made her uneasy.

She's fine. She just rolled over in her sleep. You can go back to—

A glimmer of white caught the light, winking up at her from the floor. Emma crept closer to investigate. Her boot rolled over something hard, and it stuck in her tread, clicking with every step. Emma's light darted up to the bed—not being able to see Lily's eyes was making her nervous—then down to the sole of her boot. She pried the object loose with her thumbnail.

It was a tooth.

And there were others…many others, scattered around the bed in a ring.

A rustle of fabric.

Emma's light jerked up. Lily had turned toward her. But her eyes were closed. Her breathing was slow and deep. A thin string of drool hung from her slack mouth, clinging to the pillow.

Still asleep.

Careful to avoid shining the light on her eyelids, Emma peeled the blankets back from under Lily's chin. The combined reek of body odor and necrotic flesh was overpowering. Grimacing, Emma leaned in. She squinted into Lily's saliva-strung mouth, then parted her lips, running her fingers gently over Lily's gums. Empty sockets outnumbered her remaining teeth, three to one.

Not empty.

New teeth were already pushing through. Their needle-sharp tips scratched Emma's skin, drawing blood. Lily's tongue pushed between her fingers.

A cold blast of carrion breath.

A flash of eyeshine, electric green.

Lily's jaws clamped shut with an audible crunch. Her hands closed around Emma's right arm like bands of iron. Nails dug into Emma's wrist, her bicep. Lily hissed, spraying blood across the pillow.

The flashlight in Emma's free hand was the only weapon at her disposal, but she couldn't bring herself to use it. She couldn't force her eyes away from the shredded bandages stuffed between the wall and the bed, couldn't scream or collect her thoughts to reason with Lily, convince her to release her hold.

Can't-can't-I-can't

Shock had delayed the pain, but Emma could sense it building on the horizon, like lightning-heated storm clouds. Approaching fast. Crackling.

Her light jumped to Lily's face—the pursed, wet hole where her fingers had disappeared between her daughter's lips. A mad, hungry light burned like infection in Lily's eyes. Whipping her head, she yanked Emma over the mattress, teeth snapping, gnashing, climbing past Emma's knuckles to the meat of her palm. Another loud crunch, and Emma's knees buckled. The scream locked in her chest tore free. Black spots bloomed, blotting out the flashing green mirrors, the starved mouth ascending her arm.

And then a snarling shadow dove between them, driving Lily back against the wall. Agony raced white-hot through Emma's nerves. Her consciousness sputtered.

Warm light fell across the bed from the hall, illuminating bared teeth and churning limbs. Emma grabbed for Oscar's collar. He was trying to bite Lily; she had to separate them.

But Lily didn't need her help. With Emma's hand still pinned between her jaws, Lily knotted long fingers in Oscar's scruff and lifted him like a puppy. He thrashed, kicking. Emma ducked. She pulled on her trapped hand. And screamed.

A door slammed.

Claire was shouting her name.

Oscar yelped as Lily pitched him across the bedroom. He collided with Claire in the doorway, knocking her backwards into the hall.

Alone together once again, Lily fixed her manic eyes on Emma. The corners of her mouth twitched, spreading wide as she wedged herself between the bed and the wall. Grinning with blood-streaked fangs, Lily lifted her chin, reeling Emma in. She braced her blackened feet against the bed frame, kicked. The bed shot out from under Emma, clattering toward the door.

Emma couldn't pull any longer. Not with her arm contorted behind her back. The pain was too great. Tendons and muscle stretched like pulled taffy as Lily dragged her over the floorboards.

Swearing.

Barking.

A roar she could feel in her nerves.

"Don't hurt her," Emma mumbled. She didn't know who she was speaking to—Claire or Oscar or Lily—wasn't even sure she'd spoken aloud. She just wanted the noise to stop, so she could rest. So she could forget the pain burning like a fistful of magma below her wrist.

"Please...don't hurt—"

A blow to Emma's skull flicked the lights off.

The darkness rushed in to claim her.

CLAIRE

WITH HER BOOTHEELS braced against Lily's chest and forehead, Claire seized Emma's unconscious form by the shoulders and pulled. A low growl rumbled up from Lily's throat. Claire kicked. Bone crunched, tendons snapped. And then Emma's mutilated hand slid free—half a palm, gnawed past the knuckles between her pinky finger and thumb.

Claire dragged Emma into the hall. Lily did not follow. She lay on her back, limbs splayed across the floor. For the span of one tortured breath, Claire was certain she'd broken Lily's neck. She flipped the wall switch. Beneath the scarlet spray that painted Lily's cheeks and forehead, her skin was pale as a corpse.

You kicked your own daughter in the head.

You killed her.

The muscles in Lily's cheeks bunched, circling her jaw around.

Chewing. She's chewing Emma's fingers.

Claire pulled the door shut. The lock was on the outside; she flinched as it clicked into place, an echo from the past. She was just like her mother, locking her fears away instead of trying to understand. Overwhelmed by guilt, Claire reached for the knob.

The door shook in its frame. Claire jerked her hand back, uttering a startled shriek as Oscar bumped into her from behind. He sniffed at Emma, licked her cheek. Emma's head lolled sideways. Claire shook her. She needed Emma to wake up, tell her what to do.

You have to stop the bleeding.

They'd used the last of the bandages on Lily.

Stop. Breathe. Think.

You can do this.

Claire ripped open drawers in the kitchen, gathering hand-fuls of clean white cotton dishtowels, a roll of duct tape from under the sink. Steeled for the inevitable surge of nausea, she knelt beside Emma. Her eyes flicked down—*locate the wound, place the towel*—and then Emma's ruined hand was hidden from sight. Claire applied pressure, ignoring the sticky warmth kissing her palms.

"Well, look at you," Emma slurred. Her eyes were glassy, unfocused. "Where's...Lily?"

"I locked her in." Claire ducked as Lily rammed the door behind her. "Your hand, Em, I can't stop the bleeding."

"How bad is it?"

Claire added another towel, clamping down. Stains bloomed around her hands like roses. Wincing, Emma said, "Your bedside manner needs work."

"I'm conscious. I'd call that progress."

"Thank you," Emma whispered.

"I thought..." Claire bit her lip. "When I heard you scream, I thought...I never should have left you alone with her."

"You don't have a choice."

Claire frowned.

"Tomorrow, I mean." Emma reached up to stroke Claire's cheek. "You still have to go. She needs help."

"*You* need help."

Emma smiled. "I have you."

"And when I'm gone?" Lily slammed into the door. Wood splintered.

Emma said, "We have to sedate her somehow...before she hurts herself."

Claire thought of the prescription bottle hidden in her purse. She'd meant to tell Emma about the sleeping pills, but after months of procrastination, the subject had developed the unpleasant sensitivity of a shameful secret. Footsteps thundered. The door jumped in its frame.

"I might have something," Claire said, averting her eyes as she exchanged sopping towels for dry ones. "But I have no clue how we're going to get her to take it."

Lily collided with the door again. Abandoning her battering ram approach for a continuous assault, she hammered at the barrier between them, pounding and stomping. Tremors shook the floorboards. A split appeared above the doorknob.

"We need to hurry," Emma said. "If she gets out..."

The thought hung unfinished between them as Lily's footsteps thumped away from the door then slowly returned, accompanied by the weighted grinding sound of furniture being dragged across the floor.

Claire helped Emma into the kitchen. Oscar watched from the couch, nose tucked under his tail. She went to check him for injuries, running her hands through his fur, but he appeared unharmed. His tail thumped. Oscar licked her chin. Stroking his head, Claire retrieved her purse from the corner table. When she turned back toward the kitchen, Emma was bent over the counter, holding her mangled hand over a coffee mug.

"Don't look," Emma said.

"A little late for that. What the hell are you doing? We're trying to *stop* the bleeding, remember?"

With the iron-rich odor of Emma's blood hanging thick in the air, there was little chance of breathing through the nausea. But Claire couldn't risk stepping outside for air. She wouldn't leave Emma alone with Lily again—not unless she absolutely had to. She dropped into a dining chair, turning the pill bottle with her name printed on it in capital letters, like an accusation. Smeared prints covered the label. Grimacing, she wiped her hands on her pants.

Emma raised her eyebrows. "What's in there?"

"Sleeping pills. Ambien."

Emma whistled. Her hand dripped, filling the mug. She reached for the drawer with the clean dish towels and swaddled her hand. "You know the dangers of drinking with those?"

"I'm not drinking now, am I?" Claire snapped. It was comforting to seize upon the anger flaring in her chest, to feel the familiar shell hardening her defenses. "The last thing I need right now is a lecture."

"Yeah? And I don't need to come home one night to find you drowned in a lungful of vomit. If you took too many, if the kids found you—"

A loud crack issued from the end of the hall as something heavy crashed against the door. Clattering sounds followed.

"Never mind. We don't have time for this," Emma said. She snatched the bottle from Claire and scanned the label. The cap slipped, resisting her efforts. "Fucking...child safety..."

Claire twisted the cap off, handed the bottle back. Emma shook two pills out into her palm, paused, then added a third.

"I'm sorry," Claire said. "I should have told you. I just didn't...It seemed like..."

"One more thing to fight about?" Emma sighed.

The door cracked again. They were running out of time.

Emma crushed the sleeping pills between two spoons. As she poured the powder into the mug, stirring, Claire's eyes widened in horror. "You're not going to..."

"Can you think of a better way? She won't drink water—believe me, I've tried."

Claire raised her hands in surrender, disgusted. But Emma was right. They would never be able to force the pills down Lily's throat, and she'd rejected everything they'd offered her so far. Save for what she'd taken for herself, from the end of Emma's arm.

"I low-balled the dosage, to be safe," Emma said. The color was already returning to her cheeks.

Claire envied her ability to function calmly under pressure. Emma stayed focused and determined, while Claire just felt sick, uncertain. Using her wife's strength as a shield might have felt better if their daughter wasn't the threat.

"Lily?" Emma leaned her head against the bedroom door. The door shook on its hinges. Cracks widened.

Claire pulled Emma back a step, and blood sloshed over the rim of the mug, pattering onto the floor. Oscar growled from the opposite end of the hall. Lily mimicked the sound. The doorframe vibrated against Claire's palm. Lily's purple-black tongue writhed under the door, lapping up the spilled blood.

"We have more," Emma coaxed. "But we need to open the door. Lily, honey, can you move back?"

Floorboards creaked. Lily's moaning faded. Claire braced for impact as Emma unlocked the door, but Lily did not strike. When Emma pushed, the door eased open an inch before bumping to a stop. She pushed harder, but something was blocking it from within. Claire peeked through the gap and saw a drawer lying upside down near the door. Wood pieces littered the floor.

"She broke the dresser," Claire said. "Here, move for a second."

Emma stood aside as Claire rammed the door with her uninjured shoulder. She felt the dresser budge, tried again. The gap widened, exposing part of the dresser lying on its side. Lily was huddled in the far corner, hugging her knees.

She's still growing.

"That's wide enough," Emma whispered. She knelt with the cup, staring in at Lily.

"Leave it," Claire hissed. "Quick."

Emma deposited the mug on the floor. As the dark silhouette in the corner surged forward, Claire swung the door shut and turned the lock. Sickening feeding sounds filtered through—slurping, ecstatic moans. Oscar whined.

Pacing the length of the hall, Claire asked, "How long until the pills kick in?"

"You tell me," Emma replied. Then: "I'm sorry. That was uncalled for. I don't know. She's almost doubled in weight since she came back. Maybe I didn't give her enough."

"Mom?" Lily's voice, soft and lilting.

"I'm here, Lily." Claire pressed her cheek to the door. "We're both here. Memma, too."

"Memma?"

Emma uttered a watery gasp. "Yes, honey, I'm here. Oh, it's so good to finally hear your voice."

"I don't..." Lily groaned. "I don't feel good."

"I know, honey. You're going to feel a little sleepy." Emma rubbed the door in slow circles with her palm, the way she'd rubbed Lily's back through every childhood illness. As if her touch could turn time forward, make the misery pass. "You just need some rest. Lie down and close your eyes. You'll feel good as new soon."

The doorknob rattled.

"Let me out." The knob rattled again, harder. "Please? My stomach hurts. I need—"

A wet cough.

Lily's next words were thick, choked—too garbled to understand. But the heavy thud, the drumming noise that followed, filled Claire with dread. Emma unlocked the door and threw herself against it. The broken dresser scraped back as she forced her way inside. Claire grabbed for her sweater, missed.

Lily convulsed, jittery limbs beating the floorboards. A thin trail of pink-laced foam trickled down her cheek as Emma moved her head to her lap. Emma's lips were forming the same phrase on repeat. Claire stood in the doorway, immobilized.

And then Emma's words sank in.

"Not again?" Claire said. Emma jolted as if she'd been shocked. "What do you mean 'not again'?"

"I-it happened once before," Emma stammered, "when she came back after…when I tested her blood sugar. I thought—I mean, the monitor *had* to be broken. There was no way her diabetes could have just…And it was such a low dose."

"You gave her the insulin anyway."

"She had a reaction."

"This reaction?" Claire stabbed a finger at Lily's twitching form. The anger rushed in, filling the cold vacuum of fear in her chest with fire. "We did this? We fucking poisoned her, Em…and I let you. Oh god, I *gave* you the pills."

"Stop it," Emma screamed. "She can hear you!"

Forgetting her injured hand, Emma tried to cover her ears. Her pained cry cut through Claire's rage. Lashing out at Emma had provided a temporary respite from the fear, made her feel like she was taking action instead of cowering. But it was only an illusion. Her anger wasn't helping anyone.

As Lily's seizure subsided to isolated tremors, her spine went slack. Emma collapsed over her limp body, weeping.

"Is it over?" Claire asked. She couldn't bring herself to apologize. Emma had been wrong. They were stuck in the same old cycle: fucking up and saying sorry, learning nothing. Changing nothing. *Rinse and repeat.*

Emma checked Lily's pulse.

Lily shifted. Her jaw wiggled, then resumed its tireless grinding.

"She threw up the meds," Claire said, eyeing the inky puddle of vomit near the door. Lily's long black fingers flexed. She scratched at the floorboards with hooked, yellowed claws.

Claire's stomach dropped like an elevator with snapped cables, sparking panic all the way down. Lily's fingers had too many joints. "Em, she's going to wake up soon. We need a new plan."

"The basement," Emma whispered.

"No. No fucking way."

"There's a deadbolt. And we can move the table over the door if we need to."

Claire's view of the room changed by increments, time-worn walls rising up around her as she shrank into the frightened little girl from her childhood. Helpless. Pleading, "There has to be another way. The shed—"

"No heat."

"We'll board up the bedroom then."

"And if she throws herself through the window? What then? If she gets outside while you're gone? I'm sorry, but—"

"Don't be," Claire said, bitterly. "You're right."

"What your mother did you, locking you down there for weeks—"

"*Years.*"

"It was wrong. Horrible. But she did it out of fear."

"How is this any different? I'm *terrified*, Em."

Emma sighed. The lines creasing her face made her appear ancient, weary beyond her years. "Because we're doing it out of love. It's only temporary, to buy you enough time to reach the One Stop."

Claire raked fingers through her hair. Would the doctors even be able to help Lily now? Her nightmarish transformation was moving beyond the scope of modern medicine. Claire's mind conjured images of laboratories, test tubes, locked doors and key cards and classified charts. Restraints.

A cage.

"They'll be able to fix her," Emma said. "They're better equipped. We just have to keep her safe and secure until you can return with help."

"You'll stay with her while I'm gone? In the kitchen?"

"I'll talk to her the whole time. I'll put some music on."

"I think she'd like that." Claire nodded, pushing up from the floor. "I'll get the basement ready."

"I can help."

"It'll be faster if I do it. Let's get her into the kitchen first, though. I'm not leaving you back here with her."

As Claire moved the dresser away from the door to clear their path, something fell out onto the floor.

"What's that?" asked Emma.

Claire lifted the cracked leatherbound book. "Your guess is as good as mine."

Lily moaned. Claire tossed the book atop the broken dresser and hurried to help Emma move her. Grunting and panting, they rolled her onto a blanket. As they dragged her into the kitchen, Oscar shrank into the narrow space behind the couch. Claire hauled the twin mattress out. She gathered pillows, more blankets. It would be cold down in the basement.

The cabin was only a few degrees warmer than the freezing temperatures outside. Firewood lay scattered throughout the living room. She'd dropped everything when she heard Emma screaming. They would need to build another fire if they were going to survive the night. The wind had resumed its blustering. The snow was falling, fat white flakes adding minutes and hours to the long walk awaiting her in the morning.

"Claire?"

"Sorry, coming." Claire scrubbed her face with her hands. She closed her hands around the keys to keep them quiet—not because she was afraid of waking Lily, but because the sound of their jingling would change her mind. She was Lily's jailer now, no better than her own mother. The deadbolt slid back. Claire began carrying everything down.

Seated beside Lily on the floor of the kitchen, Emma took one look at the bucket swinging from Claire's hand and paled.

Claire took the bucket downstairs and left it in the far corner of the basement without comment, though the urge to alleviate her own complicity by sticking Emma with the blame was almost impossible to resist. The basement had been Emma's idea, after all. But it was the only idea they had left. She was still deciding whether she should remove the jars, to avoid the potential hazard of broken glass, when Emma shouted, "Claire, she's waking up."

They brought her down together, Claire's shoulder rubbing against the wall to their left as they carried the blanket between them down the stairs. Lily bumped over the steps. She stirred, groaning.

They lowered her onto the mattress positioned against the far wall, beneath the porch. Claire avoided looking to her right, where the dirt pushing through the crumbling concrete still bore the marks of her feeble attempts to dig her way out. Her mother had never seen her bloody fingertips, the missing nails. To see would have meant opening the basement door.

"Claire…" Emma was pulling on her arm. "We have to go."

Lily kicked the blanket off. Her new fangs emitted a percussive clicking sound, like stroking the fine teeth of a comb. A bass rumble loosened Claire's bladder.

She's growling at us.

Crouched like a feral animal, Lily crept toward Claire on all fours. Her eyes flashed green, two shiny-bright coins. But Claire remained locked in place. She was trying to commit Lily's face to memory. The next time she saw her, Lily would look even less like the daughter they'd raised. More like the thing that was scuttling forward, eagerly. Drooling between spiny teeth.

Claws grazed Claire's boot. If Lily hobbled her now, she would never make it to the One Stop; it was this thought that finally got Claire moving, sent her scrambling up the steps, shoving Emma ahead of her. The basement door fell into place.

Emma dropped down on top of it just as Lily struck from below. The door bounced beneath her. Claire joined Emma on the floor. Their combined weight held the door closed long enough for Claire to turn the key. The deadbolt rammed home.

While Emma's back was turned, Claire slipped the keys into her pocket. She would take them with her in the morning. If their roles were reversed, she wouldn't be able to resist opening the door in Emma's absence. One intelligible plea from Lily would disarm her, calling up more echoes from the past when she had been the helpless one, begging to be released.

Better if Emma didn't know.

"If you want to see her or talk to her," Claire said, tapping the slot set in the basement door, "you can open this. Just…keep your fingers out of there."

Emma snorted. "Yeah, no shit."

Oscar paced the kitchen floor, sniffing.

"He's probably hungry," Emma said.

"I'll feed him after we get you into bed."

Emma blinked, bleary eyed. "Let me build us another fire at least."

Claire kicked firewood out of their path. Irritation nibbled at her frayed nerves, but she held her tongue. Emma just wanted to be useful, to lighten her load. "I'll build the fire, Em."

"I should clean up." Emma shook her head at the stained floorboards. "The mess—"

"Just leave it." Claire steered Emma into her mother's bedroom, pulled back the blankets, and helped her into bed. Emma's eyelids fluttered. She forced them open again long enough to say, "You'll come back for him, won't you? For Silas?"

"Yes."

"Because he's still alive, Claire." Emma's hand drifted up to her heart, tugging at her bloodstained sweater. "I can feel it."

"Me too." She turned away so Emma wouldn't read the lie on her face. She wished she had Emma's faith. But Claire had begun to suspect that Emma's certainty was nothing more than a symptom of grief, like an aching phantom limb—a lost piece of *them*. Maybe time would heal their wounds, but their family would never be whole again.

Claire kissed Emma's forehead and closed the bedroom door. After lighting a fire in the woodstove, she cooked the remaining meat for Oscar's dinner, then filled Silas's backpack with bottled water, a few granola bars, a flashlight. The rifle was in the corner. She patted the pockets of Evelyn's coat; the box of ammunition was still inside.

Claire removed the knife and deposited it in one of the kitchen drawers. She'd packed everything she could think of, yet her mind was restless. She should be sleeping, conserving energy for the long walk ahead. But she was afraid to close her eyes. Her imagination toyed with alternate outcomes; in her nightmares, those possibilities would come alive.

If she hadn't made it back in time to hear Emma's screaming.

If she had grabbed the rifle before running down the hall.

If she had kicked too hard.

If Lily hadn't let go.

If.

Her eyes landed on her mother's Bible, lying askew on the coffee table.

"Yeah, right," she muttered as she turned and moved down the hall to the children's bedroom. The dusty old tome had reminded her of the leatherbound book that fell out of the dresser.

Keeping her eyes above the bloodstained floor, she grabbed the book and exited quickly.

"Claire?" Emma called from the master bedroom. "Is that you?"

"You're supposed to be sleeping."

"I can't...I had a nightmare." Her voice was thick, as if she'd been crying.

She crossed to the bedroom and flicked on the light. Emma winced.

"Sorry," Claire said, climbing into the bed beside her. "Feel like reading a creepy old book with me?"

"Another one?" Emma smiled weakly. "Your mother's journal was pretty creepy."

Claire recalled her mother's increasingly unhinged scrawled notes about "the Devil child." Was this the journal Deborah had found in the abandoned boarding school when she was searching for her dead husband?

Brittle pages whispered beneath Claire's fingers as she cracked it open. Someone had carefully written the name *Grace* on the first page.

Her mother had refused to finish reading the journal because she'd believed its contents were evil. She'd said she was going to put the journal "where it belongs, with the other one." Claire had assumed that meant she'd burned it, but its location in her childhood bedroom offered another interpretation: she'd put the journal where it belonged, tucked it away inside the room of *the other one*: the other Devil child who she'd locked in the basement and devoted years to reforming.

Claire's hands tightened on the journal, creasing the pages. In that moment, she wasn't just glad her mother was dead; she hoped the end had been painful. She hoped her mother had suffered.

Emma rubbed her arm. "Hey…you okay?"

Claire forced her hands to relax. "Yeah, just thinking about my mom."

"Aw…" She curled an arm around Claire's waist and leaned her head against her shoulder. "Want me to read?"

"Sure."

"Okay." Emma shifted closer and began reading from the journal. "Grace is not my name."

EMMA

EMMA PACED BETWEEN the kitchen and the living room windows, feeling too restless to sit but too exhausted from the night before to do anything more than check repeatedly for signs of Claire's return. They'd stayed awake into the small hours of morning reading the journal, and after they'd finished, neither of them could sleep.

Weak gray light stuttered through whirling snow, bleeding the rooms of color. The wind pried tortured groans from the cabin. Every pop and creak made Emma flinch, forcing her to return to the basement door to check the lock.

She still didn't know what to make of the journal's contents, and Claire had left so early they hadn't had a chance to discuss the many questions and possibilities aroused by Grace's stories. Emma's thoughts kept returning to the details surrounding Father's grisly appetite. But surely whatever had happened at the boarding school could not be as Grace imagined it. She was a young girl, enduring harsh living conditions in a strange and isolated place; it would be enough to give anyone nightmares. That she had coped with her trauma by inventing fantasies was no surprise.

But Emma did believe that Father had been cruel, that he had beaten the children and deprived them of nourishment. Starvation plays tricks with the mind, causing hallucinations in the end stages. Grace's journal was a frightened child's account of her last days, before...

The sounds coming from below were unbearable. Emma chewed her lip, staring down at the basement door. Her mutilated hand pulsed in agony, the bleeding unstaunched by her sloppy attempts to stitch the wounds closed left-handed. She needed a surgeon. And something stronger than aspirin.

As the dishtowel swaddling her hand dripped onto the open slot in the door, her thoughts turned to the simple tasks she usually took for granted. Writing her name would be a struggle. It was silly, sobbing over a signature when her handwriting should have been the least of her concerns. She shook her head. She was dizzy. The heat from the woodstove was making her feel sick. She needed to get away from the obscene panting coming through the slot, and from the tongue that kept snaking out, laboring over the blood leaking onto the door.

Lily continued licking until only stains remained. The dry rasp of taste buds gathering splinters was driving Emma steadily closer to madness. She needed space to catch her breath. Distance. Lily's eager snuffling followed her through the kitchen to the doorway, fading as Emma moved beyond the perimeter of the basement below. The ground beneath the living room was solid. Emma's chest loosened a little.

She shook out the contents of her purse, snatched the pack of cigarettes, and fled to the porch with the box of matches. Oscar squeezed out behind her. He paused to sniff at the snow accumulating on the porch, then ran down the narrow path Claire had carved with the shovel. Emma poked a cigarette between her lips, wondering if he would return. She had hoped Claire would take Oscar with her, but neither of them had wanted to consider what would become of him if something happened to her on her way to the One Stop, and entertaining the possibility aloud felt like tempting fate. And so Claire had left him with Emma—*for company*—as if she needed another life to feel responsible for. As if she could bear the anxiety of losing anyone else.

Emma squinted through the whiteout for any sign of the dog. Everything beyond the porch steps was a blur. It was so cold, it hurt to breathe. In her hurry to escape the cabin, she'd forgotten her coat. Snowflakes pecked at her exposed skin, stealing the heat from her body. Shivering, Emma struck a match. The wind extinguished the flame. The next match sprang free from her numb fingers. Emma scowled. She couldn't light a match and shield it from the wind one-handed. Where was the dog? She should have leashed him.

You should have gone after them.

Emma shouted for Oscar, but the wind carried her voice away. She shouted several more times, until her throat was raw, and then retreated inside. She could watch for him through the windows. Striking a match, she winced internally at the guilt that accompanied smoking indoors. The flame singed her fingertips. She let it drop. Pacing, she smoked her cigarette down to the filter, then lit another off the end.

A drawn-out cry trapped between a song and a howl warbled up through the cabin floorboards. Inhuman noises wormed into her ears, spiking to soprano keening, then plummeting to a bass rumble that vibrated the marrow in her bones. "Mm…ma?" She pictured a menagerie caged in the basement, animals teaching themselves to speak. It was easier to believe that than the truth. No person was capable of making those sounds—certainly not her beautiful daughter.

No. She'd imagined it. There were no words, only noise. Oscar scratched at the door.

Relieved, Emma stamped out her cigarette and let him in. Her cheeks were wet. She curled her fingers in Oscar's thick black coat, pulling him close. He was so warm, so very alive. Real. And so was she. Being alone in a place like this, it was easy to forget.

"You know what we need?" Emma said. "Music. Loud as it'll go."

Barking, Oscar bounded over to the record player in the corner as if he understood. Claire was right; the dog was something—some*one*—for Emma to talk to. She was so overwhelmed by gratitude for his companionship, she had to blink back tears to read the titles on the records. Emma cleared the lump from her throat. "Any suggestions?"

Oscar pawed at the record in her hand. It was an old one, the cover scuffed down to white, the names barely legible. But she recognized the voices swelling to fill the living room.

"You're a Peter, Paul, and Mary fan?" Oscar cocked his head. "Lily, too. She used to listen to 'Stewball' on repeat for hours."

She smiled, remembering how Claire had shuffled through their music collection, searching in vain for a new favorite song for Lily.

You're the one who got her hooked.

I was just listening to some of my dad's old music. I didn't think we'd be living with a racehorse for six months straight.

And I wish he were—

Don't. Don't you dare. What about this one? Paul Simon.

The needle traveled the grooves in the record, flooding the room with harmony. Emma turned up the volume. The couch rose up to greet her. As Oscar curled up beside her, Emma checked her watch. Four hours had passed since Claire's departure. Emma had helped to prepare her for the journey as best she could.

Leave your clothes on, even if you're burning up. Hat and gloves. Keep the scarf over your nose. And stay hydrated. Did you pack enough water?

But she didn't know how long to wait before she should start to worry. She snorted. *Start to worry.* As if her gut hadn't been twisting into knots ever since Claire stepped off the porch. Claire probably couldn't see past her outstretched arms, but Emma had let her go anyway, sent her off to stumble blindly through the cold.

Oscar pushed his nose under her fingers. Emma ran her hand down his back and tried to shut off the working part of her brain: the nurse that refused to quit, even though years of training insisted that Lily's transformation was irreversible, that medical science was woefully unprepared to cope with whatever was changing her daughter into...

She didn't know what.

Stop it. What kind of mother are you?

You should have gone after them.

"Hnn..."

Oscar stiffened.

Emma sat up, eyes sliding sideways to the kitchen.

"Hnnu...ng." Lily was trying to speak. Her blackened fingers curled through the slot, twitching like spider legs as they explored the edges. She sank her claws into the tired old wood. The door shook.

Emma got up and edged into the kitchen, waiting for a hole to open in the floor, for the kitchen to fall through and the rest of the cabin to follow, sucked down into the splintered throat that was calling out to her now in a voice that was not her daughter's.

"Mm—*ma*. Memm…ah. Hnn—garr…" Long fingers tapped the lock. Beseeching. "Hung…gry."

The thing that was not Lily tittered, a silvery giggle that prickled Emma's skin like glass slivers, raising gooseflesh on her arms. She hugged herself as Lily repeated the word: "Hungry."

"I can't," Emma whispered. "There's nothing—"

"*Hungry.*"

"I don't have anything to give you."

"Hungry!"

"I can't, Lily! I don't have anything!"

Laughter. The dishes in the cabinets shivered, clinking. Emma crushed her ears with both hands, ignoring the pain from her wounds. "Stop it!" she screamed. "Shut up! *Just shut up*, please!"

She grabbed the closest object—the knife block—and hurled it at the basement door. Knives clattered and spun. Emma pinned a butcher knife under her boot.

"Please?" Lily seized on the new word, repeating it, a madman's echo. "*Please.* Please-please-please."

Emma hefted the knife's weight. It felt good, like she was doing something. Oscar whined from the living room, a quivering shadow cowering in the half-light of the storm.

"*Shut up,*" Emma roared.

Oscar ran for the front door and pressed against it so tightly he might have been painted on. As Emma stomped toward him, he released a frightened snarl. Emma's rage faltered. *What were you planning to do?* She'd lost herself for a moment. Tears stung her eyes as she lowered the knife.

Emma returned to the kitchen, determined. Dragging a chair out, she slammed the knife down on the table and unbuckled her belt. Her pants fell around her ankles. She sat and unwound the towel from her hand. The bleeding had slowed to a steady ooze. She dried her hand as best she could.

Which side, right or left?

She pinched the skin of her left thigh between her thumb and pinky finger. The effort pulled on her stitches. Blood leaked down her wrist, slicking her palm. The knife slipped. Emma moaned through clenched teeth. Her hand was cramping. She couldn't keep the flesh pinched.

Just get it over with, quick.

Her left hand found the knife, touched cold steel to her thigh. The blade was sharp. Emma's fingers slipped again, but that was all right; with the skin peeled back, it was easier to hold. Her left hand worked, sawing the length of the blade back and forth, moving downward from hip to knee. A thick, glistening strip of flesh parted from her thigh.

Emma frowned. She'd expected it to hurt more; maybe she was going into shock. Barking laughter, she shook her head. *Going into shock.* As if she had ever left it. She'd reached her limit, that was all. Like a breaker tripped by circuit overload, her mind was shutting down.

It was a relief.

The knife sliced through the skin above her knee, and then the strip in Emma's hand was no longer *her.*

It was meat.

Emma dropped to her knees as the thing that was not Lily grunted and scraped its teeth against the slot. The strip of meat jerked taut. Emma let go. The meat slapped the door, flapping as the thing below slurped and swallowed it whole.

Limping into the bathroom, Emma climbed into the tub. She sloshed Betadine over her wounds, screaming through gritted teeth as the antiseptic burned. The faucet sputtered, spat lukewarm water, then nothing. Emma re-bandaged her orange-stained hand and wrapped a towel around her thigh, securing everything in place with long strips of duct tape.

It was over.

Claire would be back soon, and then they could go.

WHEN EMMA RETURNED from pumping water and gathering firewood, "Stewball" was playing. She stood, swaying in the open doorway.

Listening to Lily sing.

Though her daughter's voice was thin and strained, it was the most beautiful sound Emma had ever heard. As she limped into the kitchen, two voices drifted up through the slot …

Emma fell to the floor and pressed her ear to the cracks between the boards, hope surging inside her. Had they—? No, it wasn't possible. If their son was down there, they would have seen him when they carried Lily down. Still, she pressed her ear closer, straining to listen.

When the second voice spoke again, Emma uttered a breathless cry and struggled up from the floor. He was down there! Her boy. Somehow, they'd locked him in with his sister, and Lily wasn't herself. She might hurt him—almost certainly would, if left to go hungry for enough time. Emma's hand throbbed, evidence of the violence Lily was capable of.

She had to separate them. *Now.*

"Silas?" She wheeled, searching for the rabbit's foot keychain. "Hang on, baby, I'm coming."

Where are the fucking keys?

"Are you an animal?" Silas asked. He sounded so close, as if he was sitting on the steps just beneath the basement door—close enough to touch, if she worked her fingers through the slot. His voice was nasal, his breathing labored. He'd probably caught a cold from hiding down in the basement for weeks. Emma's heart cramped with longing. She needed to release him, to wrap him in blankets, and make him a cup of his favorite hot cocoa or soup or whatever he wanted. Anything.

"An animal?" Lily chuckled. "Not…quite."

Emma froze. She'd listened to them play this game countless times. And though Lily often helped Silas clarify his questions, she was a stickler for the rules.

Yes or no answers only.

Silas's laughter bubbled up between the floorboards, sticky and wet, like the dying breaths of an animal drowning in mud.

Emma backed away, rethinking.

"Are…you…a…person?" Silas was gasping between words. He was sick, exhausted, probably starving.

What kind of mother are you?

Break the lock! Your son needs you.

A long pause, and then Lily said, "Not exactly."

Oscar padded into the kitchen and lay atop the basement door near the slot. Lily's fingers whispered through the opening. Emma watched nervously as her daughter scratched under Oscar's chin, remembering how Silas and the dog had instantly formed a connection. Remembering the way Oscar had snarled as he tackled Lily.

When Lily wasn't herself.

And now?

Oscar's tail thumped. He rolled onto his side, squirming in delight as Lily's gnarled fingers moved to his chest. Emma waited for the claws to hook his exposed belly, to rake and disembowel him; for his own safety, she should tie him up, pull him away, at least. Instead, she knelt beside him, calling out, "Lily, honey…is Silas with you?"

"Yes." The voice was so close it might have come from inside her head. But Emma didn't pull back. Desperate to get closer, she pressed her ear to the slot and said, "He's down there with you? You're sure?"

The record stopped playing. The silence that followed stretched for an eternity.

"With me," Lily said. "Yes."

"Good." Emma swiped at the tears streaming down her cheeks and laughed. "Good. Thank you, Lily. Can you tell me…I know it's dark, but how does he look? Is he okay? I'm going to get you both out of there, I just need to—"

"Hmm…*more.*"

"What? Honey, I can't underst—"

"*You.*" An accusatory growl, followed by soft whimpering. As if Lily was dragging the words from deep within and tearing out pieces of herself in the process. "More. You care more…about him."

"*No.*" Mortified, Emma curled her fingers through the slot. "Lily, that's not true at all. I just—"

Lily struck the door from the underside, releasing a high wail that sent Oscar scuttling under the kitchen table. "Can't. Trying, but..." A cacophony of feral noises rose from the basement. "Won't...let me. Can't, Memma. I—"

"Okay, it's okay. Shh..." Emma clung to the door. She needed to touch her daughter, to let her know everything would be all right. She moved her left hand to the slot's edge. Frozen fingers pushed through, brushing the back of her hand before pressing in. "We'll talk about something else. Anything you want. Yosemite? You're going to love it there. I remember the first time Mom and I went, just before you were born. We'll need to get you a new tripod, of course, because Silas..."

Silas had used her old one to construct a flying machine. Emma tried to laugh at the memory, but the strangled sound that emerged from her lips was an expression of pain. Her heart ached. Instead of getting angry at Silas for breaking the tripod, Lily had helped him improve the design of his new machine. She'd also prevented him from launching himself off the roof with it by suggesting they test the contraption with a stuffed animal first. Emma rambled on, so tangled up in her memories she couldn't tell whether she was thinking or speaking aloud. She had begun to doubt she would ever hear her daughter's voice again. She had to keep Lily talking.

But the soft, musical voice Emma loved so much was slipping. She was losing Lily all over again. A growl issued from below. Lily moaned, "Sorry."

Emma jerked her hand back as mottled flesh filled the slot. She glimpsed fangs. A terrible rattling filled the kitchen, hollow and dry, like porcupine quills.

"Silas?" Emma listened, but her son did not speak again. Unfathomable darkness enveloped her heart. It had all been a trick. The thing in the basement was toying with her, using Silas like bait. Trying to get her to open the door.

"Memma?" a man's voice, pitched high to sound like a girl's. The blood drained from Emma's face. Carrion breath wafted through the slot, a breath of winter. Tainted.

"Hungry," the thing that was not Lily said. "Please?"

Not Lily...though it could be—*would be*, again.

Emma's eyes shifted to the knife on the table.

CLAIRE

THE ONE STOP was closed. Claire searched the growing darkness, found a cinder block under the eaves by the back door. No alarm sounded when she shattered the front window. Disappointed, she reached through to unlock the door. Bells jingled.

The phone was behind the counter. She pressed the handset to her ear: no dial tone. She'd come all this way for nothing.

Rage thudded in her temples as she eyed the liquor shelved behind the counter. The main road was unplowed; there would be no through-traffic to flag down for a ride—not tonight. Tomorrow, maybe.

Claire grabbed a bottle of vodka by the neck and pitched it. It bounced off the wall and rolled down the snack aisle, unbroken. Laughter welled up from deep inside her, breathless and without humor. The bottle was plastic. With her fingers frozen inside her gloves, she hadn't noticed. Her laughter subsided into quiet gasps.

The nearest town was an hour's drive from the One Stop. Claire slumped to the floor. The rifle clattered against tile as she lay down, curled up with Silas's backpack hugging her shoulders. In the back of her mind, Emma was nagging her to drink water. Eat something. But that would require her to move again. Right now, what she needed was rest and a new plan for evacuating her wife and daughter from the cabin. She would sleep for an hour or so, then take a map from the rack near the door, pick a direction, and start walking again.

She tried to relax and let herself slip away, but whenever she stopped thinking about the challenge of getting her family to safety, she began to obsess over the journal. And that line of thinking inevitably led to her punishing herself. She should have sent Emma home with the children the instant they found those strange tracks on her mother's property. Grace's monster might have been imagined, but Claire did not doubt the atrocities documented on the pages. Humans were capable of monstrous acts, and the taint left behind by Father's influence was still palpable—Berry had felt it, and so had Claire. Even the animals knew to stay away from the boarding school.

Had she known about the site's history, she never would have let her family near those ruins. Hell, she never would've come back at all. And now that she had, she might never...

Claire's eyes closed. Her feet twitched, trudging doggedly through the snow even in sleep, though her steps led her backward, not forward.

Back to the cabin, to the forest strewn with Lily's clothes. Everything Lily loves is there, strung among the trees, abandoned. Claire tries to gather her daughter's possessions, but there is too much to hold; she can't take it all.

No. She can't leave anything behind.

Lily's camera bubbles in her hands, disgorging a cloud of fat black flies. The trees shiver overhead. Photographs skewered on branches bleed color into the snow. Dissolving where she touches them, faces eaten away to holes. Sticky brown rot fills her nostrils. She's carrying an armload of decay—tattered flesh, a jumble of bones. Emma's fingers climb from the pile, scuttling up Claire's arm. Worming between her lips.

A distant rumble shakes the ground.

Claire sat up, disoriented. The rumbling had followed her out of the dream. It grew louder.

Approaching.

Headlights shone past the front windows of the One Stop. A splash of yellow followed like a bright ray of sunshine piercing the night. Angled blades parted the snow. Behind the snow-plow's fogged windows, the driver was an indistinct blur. Red taillights bid Claire farewell. She was going to miss it.

"Help," Claire cried out. She staggered outside, waving her arms. "Help! I need help!"

Her calf cramped. She swung the rifle around, thumbed the safety off, and pointed the barrel at the sky. *Click.*

Claire swore, trying to recall how her father had fixed her rifle when she was a girl. Something about the cold and the firing pin...and working—

The bolt.

As the snowplow's taillights faded to distant embers, Claire stripped off her gloves and unloaded the rifle. Mimicking the movements of her father's strong hands, she worked the bolt and pulled the trigger to loosen the firing pin.

Six clicks, eight.

Claire reloaded the rifle. When she pulled the trigger again, the rifle cracked like a whip. Taillights flared in the distance. She fired again. The door on the driver's side swung open. Claire ran.

The driver waved. His plaid snow hat glowed red in the taillights. He took in Claire's wild expression, the rifle, and said, "I don't want any trouble..."

"No—" Claire gasped. Her lungs were on fire. "No trouble, sorry. I just—I needed you to stop."

He scratched his wiry copper beard, nervously. Claire made a show of engaging the safety, then slung the rifle over her shoulder and raised her hands in supplication. "Please, my family is hurt. I need to call for help—an ambulance."

"There's a phone inside..." Glancing at the One Stop's shattered window, the driver said, "Guessing you tried it already."

"The line was dead."

The driver nodded, chewing the inside of his cheek. "Storm probably knocked a pole down somewhere. Cell service is real spotty until you get into town. I could give you a lift—"

"Do you have a radio?"

The driver shook his head. "Sorry, ma'am. Radio's been busted for over a year now. Was supposed to be fixed, end of summer. I keep telling them it's a hazard. Old Marge here's the only plow this part of the county. Not like I can catch a ride with just anybody if I break down."

"Look..."

"Andrew," the driver said, grinning sheepishly. His hand was hanging between them.

Claire shook it, saying, "Sorry, I'm Claire. Now—" Urgency gnawed at her; they were wasting time.

Andrew's smile wavered. "Wait. That's where I know you from. We went to school together." He pulled off his hat, revealing a curly thicket of ginger hair. "Drew Hill. Remember?"

"Drew..." Claire's eyes widened. "You broke your arm, falling out of that tree."

"Right, when we were racing."

"They thought I pushed you."

Drew laughed. "Didn't you?"

"I got suspended for a week. My mother—" Claire's mouth clapped shut. She'd almost mentioned the lashing she'd received from the leather strap: thirty solid whacks that welted her backside and thighs so she couldn't sit, had to lie on her stomach to sleep. "Drew, I'm sorry, but my wife and daughter are very badly hurt. They're back at my mother's cabin. We still haven't found our son."

Drew gaped. "Your kids, they were the ones went missing?"

"My daughter came back, but she's—something's wrong. We need to get her to a hospital. My wife, too."

"Shit, we'd better get moving then." He took the rifle, tugged on Claire's backpack. "Let me get these. Climb in."

As Drew reversed the plow, Claire pointed through the windshield. "Town's that way."

"Sure is." Drew braked and spun the wheel, then shifted into drive. "But the road isn't cleared yet—same as the road up to your place. I'd have to plow both roads for the ambulance to get through anyway. I figure we'll go get your family first, then drive out to Crane Lake. Call the ambulance from there."

"You think we'll all fit?" Claire was thinking of Lily's growth spurt. "We have a dog."

Drew grinned. "Might be a tight squeeze, but we'll make it work."

The engine growled. The plow lurched onto the dirt road. Claire's leg jittered as she watched the speedometer. Drew cleared his throat and said, "I'm real sorry about your kids.

I've been hearing about it around town for weeks now. Wish I could've taken the time off from work, but...my little girl has this auto-immune disease, and her mom ran out on us a couple years back. I've been working two jobs to cover the cost of meds. And a sitter. Still, I wish I could've helped."

"You're here now." Claire squeezed Drew's arm. His eyes glistened in the lights from the dashboard. "Wait...are you the Andrew who works as Evelyn's handyman?"

"Yeah, I do a lot of little side jobs in the area."

"She mentioned she'd ask you to help us haul some things from my mom's old cabin. Were we out when you stopped by?"

He frowned. "No, I haven't been by yet. I was waiting for a call from Evie. Never got one, though."

And you never will.

Claire fidgeted in her seat. So the footprints hadn't been Drew's, after all. She had suspected, but now she knew for sure. Not that the knowledge was worth a damn. She'd had enough of unsolved mysteries—enough to last her a lifetime—and yet, they just kept coming.

Squinting through the windshield, Drew said, "Lotta snow up this road. What happened to your mom, by the way? If you don't mind me asking..."

"She died."

"Shit, I'm sorry."

"I'm not." The words were out of her mouth before she'd had a chance to think. Claire surprised herself by laughing. Considering the circumstances, catching up with her old classmate felt surreal.

Drew shot her a look, and she wiped her eyes. "Sorry. I'm exhausted."

Drew chuckled. "Well...not to speak ill of the dead, but she was a scary fucking lady, your mom."

"Scary is accurate."

"We had some pretty crazy theories about what happened to you. After you stopped coming to school, Kristy started a bunch of rumors. So...what really happened? If you don't mind me asking."

Claire leaned back into the seat. She didn't want to explore the past, not while her present was unraveling, her future an unthinkable blur. But the alternative was silence, the agonizing wait as she willed the plow to move faster. "My mother was very...religious. After my father passed away, he left behind this gaping hole. She filled it with her faith. Everything was 'God's plan.' And I couldn't fit into His grand design. Not that she didn't try. Prayer, fasting, discipline..."

Devil child.

She laughed, bitterly. "I guess it didn't take. She couldn't love me for who I was, didn't want her only daughter to burn in hell for being...So, she pulled me out of school, to hide me away from all the evil in the world. Homeschooled me herself. But I still couldn't be who she wanted. And I knew she'd never stop...so I ran.

"I walked the main road, waited for a car with out-of-state plates, and begged for a ride. Once I made it out to California, I was homeless for a while. A few years later, I met my wife. We married, had two kids. I don't know why I came back here. I should have stayed away."

"Well..." Drew sniffed and sat up behind the wheel. "Fuck 'em, right? Our parents, I mean. Remember how I sported a black eye for most of middle school?"

"The neighbor kid used to jump you on the way to the bus stop. Kent-something."

"Brewer. And yeah, that's what I told everybody."

"I remember. He broke your nose."

"Yeah, well...*Kent Brewer*"—he lifted his hands from the steering wheel to form air quotes—"wasn't real. My dad laid into me a lot back then. He'd mostly hit me where it didn't show, keep the teachers and the church folks from asking questions. But every now and then, he'd tie on one too many and get careless. It was me or my mom. And after he put her in the hospital, I couldn't let him hurt her again. I was young. Figured I'd bounce back better."

Drew's gloved hands gripped the wheel, twisting. "So...I get it. The not fitting in. I still don't know who he wanted me to be, why everything I said or did was wrong. Hell, I doubt he even knew. He just kept hammering away at me until the day I got old enough, big enough, to hammer back."

Watching as they passed Evelyn's driveway, Claire said, "You're stronger than I was. You stayed and fought back. I just ran."

Drew laughed. "Yeah, I stayed—too long. Got stuck here. You were the smart one, taking off first chance you got."

"Drew, I should tell you…" Claire turned to look out the window so he wouldn't read the half-truths lurking in her worried expression. "My wife and daughter have been through a lot over the last few days. When we get to the cabin, I need you to stay in the truck. I have to go in alone."

"You got it."

With the distance closing between her and the cabin, Claire's anxiety returned in full force. Worst-case scenarios played through her mind, a parade of ugly outcomes.

"They're going to be okay," Drew said. "You'll be at the hospital drinking crappy coffee from the cafeteria before sunrise. I'll get you there. I promise."

The snowplow slowed around the final turn at the mailbox, then accelerated. The pines and cedars parted at the end of the driveway, opening into the clearing.

He parked and left the engine idling. Whistling through his teeth, he said, "Jee-*zus*. What the hell is that?"

"A moose," Claire said, unfastening her seatbelt. "Something chased it through the clearing, and it hit the truck. I couldn't get it out."

"No shit. Thing probably weighs a ton. Hey, no one's coming out. Should I honk?"

"No, they're probably asleep. Just…wait here, okay? Please? We'll try to be quick." Claire reached into the back seat and grabbed the rifle.

"You think you're gonna need that?"

She shrugged. "Probably not."

She slammed the door before Drew could question her further. Something was wrong. Emma was a light sleeper; the plow should have woken her. Claire thumbed the safety off.

The cabin's front windows stared back at her like flat empty eyes, reflecting the headlights and the clearing beyond. Yellow light shone from deeper within—the kitchen. No signs of movement.

Quit stalling.

The door was locked.

As Claire shuffled through the keys on the rabbit's foot keychain, Oscar struck the door from the opposite side, barking.

"Oscar, it's me! It's Claire." At the sound of her voice, Oscar's barking dissolved into frantic whimpering. "Emma? Can you hear me? I'm coming in…"

Armed.

She re-engaged the safety. Who was she planning to shoot? Lily?

Never.

Oscar forced his way out past Claire without acknowledging her, nails scrabbling over the porch as he ran for the clearing. She did not go after him. The smell struck her at the door: a musky animal odor mixed with the cloying reek of decay. She gagged. The scent of iron was a tangible presence, pushing up her nostrils, coating her tongue. She leaned back through the open door to inhale a lungful of clean, cold air.

You can do this—in and out.

Claire pulled her scarf over her nose and headed straight for the kitchen. She lowered her eyes slowly to the basement door, cringing in expectation, but the door was closed. The blood-splattered floorboards sucked at her consciousness like a sinkhole. Thick smears decorated the basement door, concentrated around the open slot. The dining chairs were dappled red. As her vision funneled down to a distant point of light, Claire groped behind her for something to slow her descent. She couldn't faint, not now.

The plow was waiting.

Emma was slumped on the floor beside the kitchen table in a pool of congealing blood, her injured hand cradled under the other arm. She wasn't wearing any pants. Duct tape trailed from the sagging corner of the towel wrapped around her left thigh, as if she'd grown too weak to finish bandaging her leg. A pile of blood-soaked dish towels lay discarded under the table. It looked as though Emma had changed her bandages several times while Claire was out. The amount of blood she must have lost in the meantime…

"What happened to your leg?" she asked. Was Lily responsible somehow? "Em? Emma, can you hear me?" Claire forced her feet to shuffle forward. Emma's face was porcelain white, her mouth and cheek striped with more blood. She pictured Emma wrestling with the tape and using her teeth to tear it.

She knelt beside her, shrugged off the rifle's strap, and dropped the keys as well. As they struck the floor, jingling, Emma inhaled a shuddering gasp. She shifted, and the loose tape on her leg gave way. The towel sloughed back to reveal a raw, weeping trench. Fresh blood leaked down her thigh.

Emma's bloodless lips spread into a wistful smile. "You're back." She unfolded her arms to touch Claire's face.

Claire recoiled. Layers of duct tape had transformed Emma's ruined right hand into a fist. A twelve-inch blade protruded from the silver stump.

"What?" Emma frowned. Her hand drifted up absently to tuck her hair behind her ear. Claire grabbed her wrist before she could sink the knife's point into her eye by accident.

With a bewildered laugh, Emma turned the knife as if seeing it for the first time. "Oh…this. I can explain…" She trailed off, head turning slowly toward the basement door.

Claire searched her stump for a corner of tape to peel back. If Drew saw Emma like this—

No. We're so close.

"Em, I need you to listen to me," Claire said. "There's a man outside with a plow. He's going to take us to—"

"Shh…" Emma pressed a red finger to Claire's lips. "Do you hear them?"

"Emma, we have to go. Please."

She shushed Claire again, then pointed at the basement door.

A low, irregular hum drifted up from below. It didn't resemble a tune Claire recognized, though there was a clear structure.

"It's 'Stewball,'" Emma said. She hummed several bars.

"Em, what happened? What did you do?"

"We've been talking…about our plans for the summer… about college…."

"And Silas? Did she mention him?"

"Huh?"

"*Silas*. Did she say anything: where he is, what happened?"

"Oh." Emma raised her right hand; the blade nicked her temple. Blood beaded. She stared at the flashing steel and said, "Yes."

Hope exploded in Claire's chest.

"She knows where he is…," Emma whispered. "We just have to feed her."

Grimacing, Claire wrestled Emma's hand down and tore away a strip of tape. "We have to get you and Lily into the plow."

But Emma continued as if Claire hadn't spoken. "She was hungry…not herself. I had to feed her. The feeding brings her back—the memories. It brings everything back."

Dread spilled through Claire's veins like ice water.

"Don't look at me like that." Emma sighed. "You should have heard her talking, Claire…then you'd understand. Here…let me show you."

Emma began undressing her thigh.

"No! Emma, *stop*." Claire grabbed her face between her hands and pressed their foreheads together. "I need you. Please, Em, do you hear me? *I need you* to help me get through this last bit, and then we can both fall apart."

But Emma was ignoring her, still pulling on the towels taped to her leg. Claire didn't want to see what her wife had been doing in her absence, what she had meant when she'd said, "I had to feed her." The knowledge would drive her to madness.

"We can't leave," Emma said.

"Please," Claire screamed. "I can't do this without you! We have to go!"

"Not without Silas. You promised." Tears carved tracks through the blood on her cheeks. Her lips moved soundlessly. She was staring at the basement door again, but at least she was leaving the towels alone. Claire added tape to the makeshift bandage on her thigh.

At the sound of heavy footsteps behind her, she tensed. *No. Please, no.*

"What…" Drew stood in the doorway to the kitchen with his hand looped through Oscar's collar. As he looked from Claire to Emma, his expression hardened. "What the hell is going on here?"

"You were supposed to wait in the truck."

"The dog got out. I heard screaming." The muscles in his jaw bunched. He released Oscar's collar, taking in the blood-slicked kitchen and the half-naked woman crumpled against the wall. His beard quivered.

"Drew…" Claire spoke softly. She needed to calm him, convince him that he had the situation all wrong. "Listen—"

"Help," Emma cried. "You have to help me, please. She's lost her mind!"

Claire reeled back, eyes widening in disbelief. "What? No—"

Bang. The basement door jumped in its frame as something struck it from below.

Not something—Lily.

"She drinks," Emma said. "It makes her do things. Please, you have to help us. Save us."

She shrank back from Claire, kicking her naked legs.

Drew's nostrils flared. His eyes shifted to the basement door. "Is that her down there—your little girl?"

Claire could see him piecing it together: Emma wounded and retreating, their daughter locked up below. He raised his hands against Claire's stammered excuses, warning her back. *Don't come any closer,* those hands said. *I see what you are.*

Emma pushed Claire, hard, away from her. Drew stepped between them. His hands found the rifle and swung it around. Claire stared up the barrel, frozen.

"Stay there," Drew said. "I'm taking them with me. But you— you can wait here for the deputy."

"Oh, thank you," Emma whispered. "Thank you. She didn't mean it. She just blacked out, like she always does."

After everything she'd gone through to bring back help, Claire was in shock, too gutted by Emma's accusations to even form a defense. When she opened her mouth to ask Emma how she could turn on her, Drew snapped, "Shut up!"

"But—"

"No, don't even start. You think I don't know what it looks like, a mean drunk tuning up on their fucking wife? And your kid, did you beat her too?" Drew edged toward the basement door. Knuckles rapped softly from below. Claire put out a hand to warn him, but he pointed the rifle at her. "Where's the key?"

"I..." Claire patted her coat pockets.

"*Where's the fucking key!*" The rifle jittered in his hands. He spat, "I bet your kids were never missing at all. What happened to your boy then? Is he down there too? You're sick, fucking *sick*—"

"Shut up," Claire screamed. Rage cut through her confusion, white-hot and laced with grief. "Emma, tell him the truth. Please!"

But Emma wouldn't even look at her. "I'm sorry, Claire. I can't lie for you anymore."

"Give me the key," Drew said.

Unable to look away from the rifle trained between her eyes, Claire searched her pockets.

The keys were gone.

"Hurry up, come on." The barrel of the rifle poked her in the forehead.

"Fuck, just give me a minute," she shrieked. "I'm looking!"

The keys jingled, pulling their attention toward the kitchen table. The lucky rabbit's foot danced below Emma's outstretched hand. As Drew bent, reaching for the keys, Emma pulled them back.

And buried the knife in Drew's throat.

The scream raced up from Claire's chest. Her eyes captured the grisly tableau in the kitchen, committing every painstaking detail to memory. A nightmare—she was having a nightmare, must be, because Emma would never...

Blood coursed over the silver tape swaddling Emma's fist. Drew licked his lips, then coughed. His eyebrows twitched into a puzzled frown. As if the knife in his throat was a misunderstanding, and he only needed a moment to collect his thoughts. His eyes drifted to Claire, seeking an explanation. His mouth opened. Emma's fist bobbed as Drew attempted to swallow, to dislodge the obstruction in his throat. Words welled up between his lips, drowning in a crimson flood.

Grimacing, Emma wadded up a dish towel. Claire pinned her lips shut with her teeth, screams leaking through her nose as Emma pressed the towel to Drew's throat. Emma could help. She was a nurse, a fixer. With the right amount of pressure, she could undo this. She could still save him.

Determination hardened Emma's features. She splayed the fingers of her left hand against Drew's chest and twisted the knife, wrenching the blade stuck in his neck. Drew moaned. The meaty *pop* of his severed windpipe broke Claire's paralysis. She crawled toward Emma—*too late, too late*—and clutched a handful of her sweater. Emma shook her off, struggling with the knife.

Drew rocked forward, dragging the knife down with him, and Emma cried out in pain. And then Claire was beside her—despite the dry-heaving, the terror pulsing red between her temples—and she was pushing Drew back against the wall and holding him there. Emma's lips formed a question.

"Don't," Claire whispered. "Just...hold him."

Claire turned her attention to Emma's hand. She was no longer in her body, but above it, watching from a distance, as she picked at the tape adhering the knife—*the murder weapon*—to her wife's fist. From somewhere close behind her, Oscar whined. The tape slipped from between Claire's fingers. "Out!" She shouted at the dog. "Now!"

But Oscar growled and circled around to the basement door. Claire threw a dish towel at him, but he refused to retreat. Fingers poked through the slot, and Oscar darted in low, snapping. He clamped his teeth shut on Lily's fingers and tugged, degloving blackened flesh from bone. Claire screamed at him to stop, scrambling to seize his collar, but he was frenzied, tearing at the necrotic skin.

"Lily!" Emma's voice joined the chaos. She lunged toward the basement door. "Stop him, Claire! He's hurting her!"

As Claire pulled at his collar, the fingers retracted into the basement. Oscar thrashed harder, breaking her hold, and pushed his muzzle against the slot in pursuit. His snarls were cut short as the fingers stabbed up, plucking his eye from his skull. He released an agonized yelp and retreated, slamming into Claire. She lost her balance, fell.

"Lily," she panted, staring at the skin hanging in tatters from her daughter's bones, "are you all right?"

Oscar pawed at his wounded eye. As Emma moved toward Lily's damaged fingers, Claire shouted at her, "Keep away from that fucking slot!"

Beneath the floorboards, Lily chortled. Her claws punctured the stolen eyeball, dribbling fluids onto the basement door. As her tongue protruded to lap up the mess, Clair rose shakily to her feet. She grabbed Oscar's collar and retreated from the kitchen, pulling him in her wake.

They collapsed into a heap in the living room. As Claire blinked through a deluge of tears, Oscar wiggled against her side, whining. He laid his head on her chest and nuzzled her chin. "I'm sorry, Oscar. You poor thing. I'm so sorry." She wiped the blood from his missing eye with her sleeve and hugged him to her, murmuring more apologies. Her injured shoulder throbbed. She'd tried so hard, yet both the dog and her daughter had hurt each other regardless.

She wished Evelyn was here to comfort him properly. Claire petted the trembling dog the way the old woman had, in her final moments, determined to sooth his nerves. She felt him relax into her, heard his whining cease. "Shh, you're okay. We're okay."

We are not. She buried her face in his coat and wept.

Emma was shouting, calling her back to reality. If Claire went back into the kitchen, she would have to act. She would be forced to make a decision about what to do with Drew's body— about the remains of the boy she'd once raced to the top of a tree.

He has a daughter.

Claire bit her lip. *Had. He* had *a daughter.*

The shouting from the kitchen ceased, replaced by the jingling of keys.

Then the creak of the basement door, opening.

EMMA

EMMA PEELED THE last of the tape away from her hand. The knife was still stuck in the meat lying on the floor, but the hardest part was over. The keys jingled. The deadbolt slid back. Hinges creaked as Emma struggled to lift the door. It thumped back into place; she couldn't raise it high enough, one-handed, to get her other arm underneath. She called out for Claire.

They had to get the meat into the basement, or this would all be for nothing.

Claire's long trek to the One Stop had given Emma plenty of time to think. To experiment. It was a simple matter of quantity. More meat would buy them more time for questions. Feeding Lily quieted the ravenous thing inside her, loosening its hold so she could come forward. But it only worked for a little while. And if the topic of conversation turned to Silas, that time was cut in half.

It was lucky Claire had arrived when she had, bringing the solution to their problems. After Lily fed, her memories would return. But Claire needed to be the one to question her. The children had always trusted Claire with their secrets. Where Emma had failed, Claire would succeed. Lily would tell her everything.

Emma smiled. The basement door was rising. Lily had sensed her need and was lending her strength. Icy fingers curled around Emma's ankle. A chill rushed up her leg, prickling her tattered skin with strips and patches of gooseflesh. Emma fell, heels jerked out from under her. She heard but did not feel her head striking the floor. She was numb, deliciously so.

Claire dove onto the basement door. She lifted it, slammed it down—hard—onto Lily's arm. Lily howled. Her hold on Emma's ankle loosened. As Claire brought the door down again, Emma pulled free. Lily's arm contorted, seeking. Hooked claws snicked closed a hair's breadth from Claire's eyes.

"Pull it back," Claire snarled. She rocked back, brought the door down harder. "Pull it back, or I'll break it off."

Emma frowned. If Claire continued treating their daughter like an animal, then Lily wouldn't tell them anything. Couldn't she hear the pain in Lily's cries?

No, Claire wouldn't even use Lily's name. She was hurting her. Emma's eyes narrowed. Perhaps the basement was working its evil on Claire, like it had with her mother. With Lily trapped below, where they couldn't see her, it was all too easy to believe their daughter was a monster, to pretend the isolation—the cruelty—was for her own good. Claire was right; they never should have locked her in the basement.

But if Lily ate, then Claire would recognize her again. There was plenty of meat. The thing driving Lily's impulses would be sated for hours.

"Lily!" Emma shouted over Oscar's barking, Claire's cursing, the pained grunts coming from the basement. "I have something here for you, but you have to—"

"Shut up, Emma," Claire snapped.

"Lily, you have to back down the stairs if you want to eat!" The arm jerked then stilled.

"Open the door," Emma whispered to Claire.

"Like fucking hell."

"She can't pull her arm back with you pinning it."

Claire relented and lifted the door slightly. After Lily retracted her arm, Claire slammed the door shut again.

"Good," Emma said. "Now help me."

"I'm not moving. Give me the keys, Em."

"She won't try to—Lily, tell her you won't try to get out."

Silence, followed by a cold burst of air through the slot. Emma nodded and turned toward the meat lying behind her on the floor. "Help me with this, please?"

"With *this*," Claire repeated. She was looking at Emma as if she didn't recognize her, as if they were on opposing sides. "He was a person, Em. He had a name—a daughter."

"We can't think about that right now."

"Maybe *you* can't."

"We need to focus on getting Silas back. Unless..." Anger stirred in Emma's chest. She had hoped Claire would understand, but it was clear that Emma was the only one who believed their son was still alive. "You think he's dead, don't you?"

Claire's lips worked soundlessly. She pressed her palms into her wet blue eyes, dragged them down her cheeks to cover her mouth.

"You're wrong," Emma said. She moved out of Claire's reach, refusing her touch. It hurt to look at her now that the truth was out.

Emma curled her good hand around the handle of the butcher knife and yanked the blade from Lily's next meal. Then she lifted one of its limbs and pulled, hauling it across the floor a few inches. "Get off the door, Claire."

"You can't," Claire moaned, hugging herself as Oscar whined from the living room. "We were *saved*, Emma. We had a way out. And now—"

"You promised we wouldn't leave without Silas." Ignoring the pulsing ache from her wounds, Emma leaned back, digging her heels in. The meat slid forward another inch. "I know how to find him. I have a plan; you just have to trust me. If you aren't going to help me, then get out of my way."

Claire stood aside. Muttering under her breath, she turned in slow mechanical circles, hands opening and closing on nothing.

Oscar edged into the kitchen. He lowered his head to sniff at the meat, his remaining eye watching the basement door warily. His eyelids twitched, exposing his weeping socket in flickers. When Emma moved to chase him off, he flinched.

"Don't! Claire snapped, "Don't you fucking touch him."

"I..." Emma looked from the dog to Claire. "I would never hurt Oscar. Silas loves him."

"You have to stop this, Em. We can't keep Lily here. She needs help—you both do. Please. We can still take the snowplow. And whatever happens after, I'll try to protect you. I'll tell them it wasn't your fault. It was stress, grief—you had a psychotic break. It could happen to anyone."

"Them?" Emma hesitated. She stared down at the work boot under her arm. *Oh.* Claire was thinking too far ahead, already planning to turn Emma in for...what? Taking necessary steps to restore their daughter's mind, to find their son? Emma tightened her hold on the meat and said, "Fine. But we wait until after she's eaten. She'll be sedated, more like herself. It'll be easier to get her into the plow. Safer."

"Em..."

"You know I'm right. Please...help me finish this."

Claire's shoulders slumped. She joined Emma, and together they dragged the meat the remaining distance. Claire cracked the door open. Lily's long-fingered hands scuttled through the gap like thin black arachnids. She sank her claws into the meat and jerked it toward her. The limp flesh shuddered and flopped through the gap, thumping down the stairs below.

As Claire bent to retrieve a plaid snow hat from the floor, Emma grabbed the cast-iron skillet from the stove—*sorry, I'm so sorry*—and swung it at the back of Claire's head. The skillet connected. Claire collapsed into a boneless puddle.

Emma felt for a pulse, then wrestled the door open. The stairs were vacant, striped with a swath of blood. The left-hand wall was speckled with dried gore from previous feedings, as was the railing, as if Lily had shaken her meals from side to side with her teeth as she consumed them. Dragging the meat to Lily had exhausted her, so lifting Claire was out of the question. Emma settled down on the floor, planted her feet in Claire's back, and pushed until her wife's slack torso was drooping just over the edge onto the top step. Then, she climbed in after her, hooked her arms around Claire's chest, and pulled her headfirst onto the stairs. She hauled her down two steps, three, four. Gasping for breath, she propped Claire against the wall and adjusted her limbs on the steps so she wouldn't tumble to the bottom.

Claire was half-conscious, already stirring. Her lips formed the same words, repeating: *No. Please, no.*

Emma kissed Claire's forehead and whispered, "Just talk to her, and you'll understand. She'll tell you where to find him."

Claire clung to her wrist, trying to keep her on the stairs, but the distant rumble of the plow's engine was calling to her. While Claire talked to Lily, Emma could drive it to Evelyn's, then walk back and clean up the mess, scrub the cabin top to bottom. If anyone came looking, she would tell them the driver had come and gone. He'd checked on them and moved on.

"I have to go now," Emma said.

Time, she needed time. She needed to move the plow.

She could fix this. She had to.

The dog was behind her, growling. Emma lunged, snagged Oscar's collar, and pulled him into the basement. At first, he struggled, but when he saw Claire lying on the steps, he ran down to her and curled around her protectively. He bared his teeth at the darkness below.

Emma lowered the door. A turn of the key, and the deadbolt thudded into place. Claire wailed. Her fingers poked through the open slot, reaching.

"Please forgive me," Emma said. "I'm doing this for Silas, for Lily...For us."

CLAIRE

CLAIRE POUNDED ON the basement door with her fists, hating the ease with which she backslid into the old frantic desperation—the nerve-humming, electric fear of a trapped animal. The years she'd spent locked in here returned with sudden force. As if her escape had never happened. As if the life she'd built with Emma had been invented as a coping mechanism—a dream born from isolation.

"Emma!" Claire craned her neck, but the slot yielded the same limited view of the kitchen it always had. "Let me out, please! You have to let me out!"

Pounding on the door sparked a riot in her throbbing head. Wincing, she explored her scalp with tentative fingers. When she encountered the sopping patch of hair at her crown, she withdrew. She didn't want to know how bad the damage was. Her neck was slicked with warmth. Between her shoulder blades, her sweater was soaked, already cooling in the frigid air. She shivered. Panic cinched her throat shut. She was going to bleed to death or freeze—maybe both.

Her fear turned to anger. She wasn't a powerless little girl anymore. She wasn't some piece to be forced into someone else's plan. By giving her mother's journal to Emma, Claire had revealed the darkest hours of her life, secrets from her past that she had never revealed to anyone. And still—*still*—Emma had locked her down here, knowing what it would do to her. Claire poured her fury into her fists, assaulting the door.

"Emma, let me out!" Rage pounded war drums in her skull. "Let me out, you fucking bitch! *Let me out!*"

A voice answered her, finally. Not from above but from below.

"Mom?"

Lily?

Claire turned away from the light of the slot, waiting for her eyes to adjust to the surrounding dark. The light switch was at the bottom of the stairs, too far to risk now when Lily could be anywhere, on the mattress in the far corner or under the stairs. They'd left the light on when they brought Lily down. Had she turned it off? Something pushed against Claire's thigh, and she shrieked. Her arms came up to shield her head, brushing against fur. A metallic jingle cut through her panic. She'd heard that sound plenty of times in the last few days: the jingle of dog tags.

"Oscar?" She reached out and felt something cold and wet bump her palm. Her heart surged with relief as her trembling fingers drifted down his neck, over his chest, molding the shape of a large black dog. Always before, she'd been locked in the basement alone. But Oscar was with her now, a friend in the dark.

"Where did you come from?" Claire whispered, as the dog squirmed into her lap. He was crushing her legs, pressing on her bladder. She didn't care. Hugging him around the neck, she let Oscar's warmth seep into her, felt the reassuring thump of his heartbeat. *Not alone, not alone down here.*

Oscar was trembling. Had Lily hurt him again? Claire combed through his fur and checked his limbs, whispering all the while, "I know. Shh, I know. I'm scared, too."

From the far left-hand corner of the basement where Claire had positioned the mattress, there came a loud moist *pop*. Wet pattering, like rainfall. Oscar's soft whining joined the grisly slick whisper of membranes and fat parting. The sounds of feeding. Tendons snapped. Muscle tore back from bone.

Lily's moaning echoed off the concrete walls, a song of starvation, of gluttony and hunger insatiable. They were not sounds of pleasure, Claire realized. It sounded like Lily was crying, choking as she struggled to draw breath between swallows.

Stop, please, Claire thought. *I can't—I—*

With a last wet hiccup, the feeding sounds ceased. But the silence that followed was worse. Distant shuffling. A rattling cough.

A barely discernable silhouette moved at the bottom of the steps, darker than the surrounding black. Claire stiffened.

Growling, Oscar uncoiled from Claire's lap. She held fast to his collar. She couldn't let them become separated, couldn't be alone with—

"Mom?"

That voice again—unmistakably Lily's.

Claire's tongue lay limp against the back of her teeth. Instinct demanded she keep quiet. But her heart...

Somewhere in there, she's still your daughter. Your Lily. And she's just as frightened as you are. If not more.

"This is my fault," Claire whispered into the darkness. "You don't deserve this. Lily...I'm sorry. I'm so sorry."

The steps creaked. Claire shuddered.

"You're cold?" asked the hunched shadow crouched halfway up the stairs.

Claire nodded.

"Me too," Lily sighed.

The stairs shook as Lily closed the distance between them. Claire shoved Oscar behind her, holding him back.

Icy breath stirred Claire's hair.

"You're scared of me?" Lily sobbed.

Oscar's growling tapered to a soft whine. Guilt rushed in, dispelling Claire's fear. Lily could see her mother recoiling. She could see Claire trying not to scream, her horrified expression.

"No, honey." Claire reached for Lily. "I love you—more than you could ever possibly imagine. It's the basement. I..."

The narrow rectangle of light from the open slot framed the ragged remains of Lily's lips, chewed back from pale gray gums. Her delicate nose had been reduced to a seeping cavern. Her sunken eyes flashed green above gaunt cheekbones. A whimper escaped Claire's throat; she couldn't help it. Lily's mirror-like eyes were palm-sized—round and bright and ravenous.

She needs you.

Claire forced her stiff arms to soften and fold around Lily's enlarged head. She hugged her daughter's mangled face to her chest, the way she had once cradled her as an infant, and tried not to picture Lily's jaws snapping shut on her breast like the metal teeth of a bear trap.

"It's the basement I'm afraid of," Claire said. If she could keep talking, then Lily would have to see her as a person, as a mother, not a meal. "My mother—your grandmother—used to lock me down here as a girl."

She stroked her daughter's tangled hair with one hand while the other moved lower, bumping over the ridge of Lily's spine. Frozen skin whispered under her palm. Lily's clothes were shredded, pulled apart at the seams by her accelerated growth. Barely hanging on.

"Come closer," Claire said. "We'll keep each other warm."

Oscar did not growl as Lily moved closer. Hunched like a gargoyle on the step above, the dog leaned over to sniff at Lily's forehead, then licked her cheek.

Lily giggled. And in a voice that could only be Silas's, she said, "Silly boy, that tickles."

Claire's blood turned cold. She must have misheard—some kind of stress-related auditory hallucination? Both she and Emma had been down here already, and there had been no sign that their son was hiding in the basement.

Was Lily somehow imitating his voice? Maybe it was her way of coping with whatever had happened to her brother. Tears spilled down Claire's cheeks.

Lily whispered, "Your mom put you down here?"

"When she found out I was gay..." Claire swallowed. "She didn't approve. She thought that if she—if *we*—just prayed hard enough, then I could change. The Devil would lose his hold on me."

Claire let her head fall back against the wall, bumping the forgotten wound and spiking agony through her skull. Fresh blood trickled down the back of her neck. Lily vibrated in her arms and then pulled back slightly. The space that opened between them felt warm in the absence of the perpetual chill emanating from her skin.

Lily groaned. "I think I'd better...go back...over..."

"Wait," Claire protested. But Lily was already retreating down the steps. Claire could just make out the passage of a form so massive, it reduced the scale of the stairs to dollhouse furnishings. She hid her face in her hands, bit down on her thumb. She would not shame Lily by screaming.

"There's someone over here," Lily whispered. "In the corner."

Oh, no. Can she see in the dark?

"A man. He's not moving. There's blood…"

No, no-no-no. She doesn't remember? How can she not remember?

Lily wailed.

"Lily?" No answer. "Lily, come here. Come to me, please?"

Claire heard a loud thud, followed by the crash and shatter of fallen objects. Had Lily backed into the shelf, or had she fallen, caught in the throes of another seizure? She could be lying in broken glass, thrashing, and Claire would have no idea. "Lily, answer me! Say something!"

Light—she needed light. Claire cursed her father's poor planning for putting the switch at the bottom of the stairs instead of the top. And then she cursed herself for sounding just like her mother. As she scooted down the steps, Oscar followed. She wondered how far the dog would go to protect her, to keep both of them from falling into Lily's clutches, but she didn't plan to find out; she kept a tight hold of his collar.

Claire found the switch, flipped it. The bare bulb flickered on. Lily spun, a nightmarish blur stuffed inside a matchbox of a basement, elbows racking the shelves as she covered her face.

"Turn it off," Lily howled. "I don't want you to see me like this."

"Lily—"

"NO LIGHT." The roar shook the cabin.

"Okay. *Okay.*" Claire switched the light off. "No more light, I promise. I'm sorry."

"Did I—Was this me? Did I do this?"

"It's complicated."

Lily's keening reverberated off the concrete walls.

Claire longed to comfort her daughter, but her heart was hammering in her chest like it was about to explode. She couldn't breathe. How was she still conscious? She couldn't do this—no parent could. It was too much.

She recalled Grace's harrowing account of the transformation that had turned Father into a monster: the appetite for human flesh, the shocking changes in height and appearance.

The aversion to light.

If Lily couldn't remember feeding, had her mind blocked the experience to spare her from the trauma of her actions, or was it possible that she hadn't been in control of her actions at all? And if not...who or what had been feasting on Drew's corpse? Claire shivered.

A series of pops and cracks echoed through the basement, and Lily screeched as if she was being skinned alive. "Something's wrong," she growled. "*Oh, fuck.* It hurts."

Laughter, throaty and harsh.

Not Lily.

"Lily, you need to eat," Claire said.

"It hurts," she whimpered. "Oh, it hurts."

"Please, Lily. You have to eat." Images of the carnage in Evelyn's bedroom flashed through Claire's mind. "I know it's hard, but try not to think about it. You'll feel better after. And then we can talk some more, okay?"

A hoarse giggle accompanied the scraping of flesh over concrete. The feeding sounds resumed. Oscar growled. Claire retreated up the steps, clinging to his collar.

Time passed—minutes, maybe hours—and then Lily said, "Mom?" Glass jars clinked together. Tin cans clattered to the floor, rolling. "Mom, say something. Please?"

Remembering why Emma had put her down in the basement, Claire said, "Lily, I need to ask you something...about your brother."

"Can't," Lily moaned. "It won't let me."

It? Claire thought again of the possibility that something else might be responsible for her daughter's violent behavior. But even if Lily was not always herself, she must remember something from the day she and Silas went missing. If Claire could only pry those last moments from her, she'd at least have a clue, somewhere to start piecing the rest together.

She needed something, because the alternative was that Silas had run out through the cabin's front door and simply vanished from their lives forever.

"I'm sorry," Claire said. "I know it's hard for you to talk about it, but Memma says you know where he is. She's convinced he's still…and if she's wrong, she won't believe it unless you—"

"Do you have my camera?" Lily asked.

Claire pulled at her hair, blinking back tears. "Lily, I need you to tell me about Silas."

"I need my camera."

"Is he—"

Jars crashed to the floor, spraying glass onto the stairs. The walls quaked. Lily was going to bring the cabin down on their heads.

"Lily, stop," Claire pleaded. "Try to calm down."

"Here," Lily roared. "With me—I told you!"

Wedged between Claire and the railing, Oscar barked furiously at the tantrum unfolding below. Something whizzed past Claire and shattered against the wall behind her. She cried out, "Okay! Yes, you told me. I believe you. Lily, I believe you!"

Lily paused, panting. Waves of cold raised gooseflesh on Claire's arms.

Lily repeated the words like a question: "With me?"

"Yes, I heard you. I'm listening."

An idea was forming in Claire's mind. No, not forming, but surfacing; it had been there all along, buried deep under layers of grief and denial. But she could only ignore the obvious for so long.

Lily had spent two weeks lost in the cold without her insulin. Perhaps the guilt of what she'd done—what she'd been forced to do to survive—had broken her mind, left her unable to face the truth. Against all odds, Lily had returned.

Alone.

She'd survived without insulin, yes. But without something to eat?

Without some*one*?

Lily sniffed. "Where's Memma?"

"She's—" Claire bit back a sob. "She's not here."

"She went back to California?"

"No, she had to…take care of something. But she'll be back soon."

A chorus of pops and cracks dragged another tortured shriek from Lily's lips.

"Lily, come here," Claire said, trying to be firm. To be strong. She couldn't let Lily suffer alone.

"Can't," Lily panted. "It comes back…faster…every time. I can feel it…in my bones…my teeth. What if—"

Noise, like animals fighting. And then Lily forced the question out: "What if Memma doesn't make it back in time?"

The lie came effortlessly. "She will. She promised. And you know your mother."

Impossibly—miraculously—Lily laughed. "You should've told her…it was none of her business. To stay out of it."

"She'd be letting us out right now." Claire wiped her eyes, inhaled a watery breath.

"Letting *you* out, maybe." Lily sighed. "I can't…I think I hurt her. She couldn't love me again, not after what I did."

"Lily, our love for you is all we have left."

"It wasn't supposed to be like this," she whispered. "I just wanted…to keep him safe."

"Silas?"

"It stepped out of its skin and into mine, but I couldn't let it…I had to keep us together. Bring us back. I promised him, but I didn't—" A guttural growl chewed Lily's words into fragments; the rest was incoherent.

More than anything, Claire needed to hear the truth. She needed closure.

But Lily needed her mother.

The noises being wrenched from Lily's vocal cords suggested the effort required to focus on Silas was excruciating. And yet she kept trying. Because it was important to her mothers. Sweet, selfless Lily would continue gutting herself for as long as they asked it of her.

To make them happy.

Claire couldn't let her do it any longer. "Lily, are you listening?"

"Yes."

"I don't want you to think about us anymore—not me, or Memma or your brother. I need you to think about yourself. I need you to eat. Eat as much as you possibly can."

"That's what *it* wants." Lily sounded tired, so very young and weak.

"And what do you want?" Claire asked.

"I want this to be over."

"It will be, just as soon as Memma gets back. But I need you to eat, to keep it away until then. Stay with me, okay?"

"Okay."

Claire knew what was coming. The darkness spared her from the sight, but it did not shelter her from the sounds, and where her eyes failed, her imagination leaped to the task with heartless vigor.

Sometime later, Lily started coughing, hacking and choking like she was trying to regurgitate something caught in her throat. And then:

"Are you a girl?" Silas's voice, clear and inquisitive.

Claire could almost see her son's impish smile curling at the corners, his freckled nose wrinkling to push up his glasses. Oscar's tail thumped the wall.

"Am I female, you mean?"

"Fee-male." Silas giggled. "Yeah."

"No," Lily replied.

A ponderous hum. "Are you somebody who's still alive today?"

Claire hugged the railing, breathing in the fruity watermelon scent of Silas's shampoo. She whispered at Oscar to stay, then descended the steps. Moving toward the light switch.

"Shh," Lily hissed.

Claire could hear the nervous tension in Silas's voice as he whispered, "What is it?"

"I thought I heard something."

With her finger on the switch, Claire hesitated. She had promised Lily she wouldn't turn the light on again. But…

Silas sniffled. "Lily, I'm cold."

"I know. Try not to think about it. How many questions do you have left?"

"I don't remember."

"Well, you started with twenty, and you've already asked three."

"I'm hungry."

Sighing, Lily said, "Me too."

"Yeah, but I'm so hungry I could eat a horse."

"Well, *I'm* so hungry I could eat an elephant."

"Lily?"

"Yeah?"

"I'm scared."

"Me too," she whispered.

"Are we ever going to get out of here?"

Lily did not answer. After a long pause, Silas said, "Seventeen questions left."

Lily's teeth were chattering. Shuffling in the darkness, she said, "Fire away."

"Are you famous?"

"No."

Silas hummed, then asked, "Are you good or evil?"

"Evil."

Oscar growled. Claire pressed closer to the wall, retreating up a step. Something wasn't right. Lily was a stickler for the rules. She would never answer an either-or question.

"Did you steal?" Silas asked.

"Yes."

"Were you...a bank robber?"

"No."

Stomach acid stung Claire's throat. All traces of Silas's shampoo had vanished, overwhelmed by the stench coming from the mattress in the corner.

"Did you kill people?"

"Oh, yes." Wheezing laughter. "And worse."

Claire's nails bit into her palms. Lily's voice had changed, sinking into a lower register, grating and unfamiliar. As if someone was speaking through her, using her like a puppet. This thought opened a new avenue of possibilities, none of which she wanted to consider, but in the dark, she was at the mercy of the worst thoughts imaginable.

"You're not supposed to elbowrate," Silas complained. "It ruins the game."

"El-a-bo-rate," Lily said. "Next question."

Silas huffed, ill-tempered. "Well, what's worse than killing people?"

"Now who's elbowrating," Lily growled. "Forget it—sorry. I'm just tired. I need to rest."

"But you told me to keep you awake."

"Leave me alone."

"But, Lily—"

"Fuck off, you little brat!"

The outburst made Claire jump. It confirmed her suspicion: Lily wasn't the one speaking. No matter how angry she was, Lily never swore at her brother.

She would never hurt an innocent, defenseless boy.

But Grace had known someone who had hurt many boys.

And worse.

Lily had claimed that something stepped out of its skin and into hers. What if she was telling the truth? What if White Hook had somehow survived Grace's attempt to kill it? Had it found Lily during her time in the forest and...

What? Taken over?

Claire shook her head, then winced at the pain. She'd been raised religious, but she'd always found the idea of possession ridiculous.

Until now.

She needed to see. She needed to be sure the voices were coming from Lily. Because if Silas was in the basement with them, then that meant the stranger was too.

Claire switched on the light.

Lily recoiled from the bare bulb overhead. Her blackened hands flew up to cage her face. "No light!" she shrieked. "You promised me!"

Oscar advanced, snarling, trying to get between Claire and the hulking giant huddled in the corner.

"Don't look at me," Lily wailed. As she pulled the mattress up like a shield, Drew's remains slid down into a grisly pile at her feet. "Turn it off. The light! Turn it off!"

Yanking on Oscar's collar, Claire fell backwards on the stairs. Lily unfolded from the corner, rose up toward the light, and seized the bulb in her fist, crushing it. The light went out, but not before Claire got what she wanted—not before she *saw*.

Silas was not in the basement. There was no stranger, outside of Lily's damaged mind.

Claire had broken her promise for nothing. The exchange had sounded so real, she'd believed the impossible, but Lily must have been mimicking her brother's voice, perhaps in an effort to comfort herself. The stranger's voice may have been a symptom of trauma. And now she had betrayed Lily's trust.

Or maybe there really is something inside her, and you're inventing excuses because you're too afraid to face the truth.

"I'm sorry I turned on the light," Claire whispered.

Silence yawned wide between them, and then Lily said, "You love him more than me. You and Memma both do."

"No, of course not. I—"

"You do. I trusted you, but all you care about is S—" Lily choked on her brother's name, unable to finish.

"That's not true, Lily. I would do anything for you."

"Memma couldn't stop talking about him either. It hurts my head, my stomach, and I want to…It hurts, but I try and…" Something clattered against the wall, breaking. "You don't *listen*," Lily snarled. "I need my camera. I need it."

"It's in the bedroom, Lily. I don't have it. We're locked—"

"I trusted you," Lily whimpered. She was growing again. Claire could hear the ripple-pop of her daughter's bones spreading, elongating. "I saw your face, when you saw me. You're disgusted. I'm disgusting." Then she screamed.

"Are you okay?" Claire cried out, gripping the railing with one hand while the other clenched Oscar's collar. "What can I do? Please, tell me how to help you!"

"I want to go home," Lily sobbed.

Oscar whined in response, as if he too would rather be anywhere else. "I know," Claire said. "Me too."

A brittle snap, and Lily cried out.

"What's happening?"

"Don't come near me!"

It took every ounce of self-control Claire possessed, but she'd already ignored her daughter's wishes once. She owed it to Lily to listen. The sounds coming from the far corner of the basement reminded her of the nights she'd lain awake in bed as a girl, listening to the cabin's beams shift and creak in the cold. Like it was a living thing, a monstrosity swelling around her, preparing to rise and disappear into the forest. *Growing pains*, that's what her mother had called it.

"Talk to me," Lily said, "Talking helps."

"Okay, um…" Claire was at a loss, shuffling through the fragments of her once-normal life in search of a harmless topic to occupy their minds. She'd spent the last year disappearing into herself and shutting her family out. How many dinners had she sat through, bleary on her second bottle of wine, pretending to listen while she pushed her food around?

"You mentioned a boy at school," she ventured. "Louie?"

"Liam." Lily's breathing was evening out.

Relieved, Claire said, "Tell me about him."

"He's…been tutoring me in math. He's always bringing me things…flowers…rocks."

"Rocks?"

Lily forced out a laugh. "He polishes them first. They're… pretty."

"Sounds like he likes you."

"Maybe. But it would never work. He'd get tired of having to explain things to me all the time. He wants to engineer rockets. The math we're doing is kiddie stuff, and I still can't get it. I'm too stupid for him."

"You're not stupid. Math is stupid." Claire rested her head on her knees. Oscar licked her ear, and she pushed his muzzle away. Her skull was throbbing. She wanted to sleep but was afraid to close her eyes. Weren't you supposed to stay awake after a concussion? Rubbing her hands over her face, she said, "You should ask him out if you like him."

Lily laughed, a raven's caw that made Claire jump. "With how red his neck gets when I'm joking around, I think he'd have an aneurysm. And anyway, he would never...not now."

"That's not—"

"Do you think Memma will make it back?" Lily asked. "Be honest."

Claire sighed. "I don't know. Her leg is pretty bad. You know how she is, though."

"Yeah," Lily said. "Do you remember our hike up Mount Lassen?"

The memory surprised a laugh from Claire. "A little altitude sickness wasn't going to stop her from summiting."

"You leashed me to your wrist with the lanyard from the car keys so I wouldn't wander off while you helped her down. You were practically carrying her. I'd never seen you so...strong."

"Your mother can handle just about anything on her own. When she actually needs my help, I try to be there. It doesn't happen much—hasn't for a long time."

"Maybe you haven't been paying attention." Lily was chewing again. *Feeding*. Her words were slurred, muffled by the red, wet contents of her mouth. "What if she doesn't make it? Mom...I'm afraid of what I'll do."

"What does it feel like? You don't have to answer if you don't want to. I'm just trying to understand."

"I start to forget...little things, at first. Like, I'll picture my camera, but I don't have the word for it anymore. And after a while, I don't know what it does. The picture is clear, but I don't know what it's for. And there's this gnawing in my stomach. Once I start forgetting the bigger things—faces, my name— then it's like the hunger's all I can hear. It's like a dog wearing its teeth down on the outside of my skull. I can stuff my stomach, but I never feel full." Her voice whispered like sandpaper. "The growing is worse. It's like my stomach grows with me. When it's over I'm hungry again. And everything I remember slips away. I forget, over and over, no matter how hard I try not to."

Worried that Lily might see her crying in the dark, Claire wiped her tears and tried to put some steel in her tone. "We're going to get out of here, get you help. You just have to hold on."

"Help? There's only one kind of treatment for what's happening to me and that's—"

"Lily."

"—to take me out back like Old Yeller—"

"That's *enough*," Claire shouted. "I won't listen to you talk like that. I can't. You're breaking my fucking heart, Lily. Do you understand?"

"Fine." Sullen. "Sorry."

Claire's thoughts were muddled. Despite her fear, she struggled to keep her eyes open. If she was concussed—and the blood leaking down the back of her neck, combined with the nausea, suggested that she was—then she needed to stay awake. "What about colleges?" she asked. "Have you thought about where you might like to apply?"

There was only silence, except for the scratching—a constant *scritch-scritch-scritch* coming from the right-hand corner of the basement where Lily sat.

"Lily?" She tried a new angle. "I'm thinking when we get back to California, we should take a vacation. Somewhere warm…Death Valley, maybe?"

But no matter how many times she tried to change the subject, Lily remained silent.

The scratching sound was lulling Claire to sleep. She rested her head against the wall to take the weight off her neck. Just for a minute. Oscar wriggled into her lap, smashing her legs, but he was warm, and no longer growling. His rhythmic panting was soothing.

Claire dozed. She woke to the same scratching, louder now. Relentless.

"Lily…" Unsure whether she was awake or dreaming, Claire asked, "What are you doing?"

"Call it a backup plan," Lily said. "Go back to sleep. Talking makes it hurghh—harder to think. It's okay. I promise not to hurt you. You're…"

Safe.

AN ENGINE RUMBLED in the distance.

Emma?

Claire's eyes were crusted shut, raw from crying. Her legs had fallen asleep under Oscar's weight. Blinking in the dark, she pushed him off. Pins and needles tingled as the blood flow to her feet resumed. The scent of damp earth filled her nostrils. Dirt and rust, an inhuman stench...

It came back to her then—the corpse, the feeding—and Claire pulled her knees up to her chest.

A car door slammed. Claire pressed the button on the side of her digital watch, illuminating its face with a bright green glow. She'd slept through the night.

"Lily?" She used the railing to drag herself upright. "Lily, say something."

Footsteps on the porch—boots stomping off snow.

A knock.

In the light from the open slot, Oscar's ears pricked up. Claire tensed, waiting for the barking to start. She didn't know whether to stay quiet or call out. If someone had noticed the missing plow driver, they might have called law enforcement. Whether there was an armed deputy at the door, or just a former volunteer from the search party stopping by with a casserole, she would not be able to explain the bloodbath in the kitchen or the carnage in the basement. If she kept quiet, then maybe the visitor would go away and give Emma time to return and clean up the evidence. And if she cried out for help, then what? Would they open the basement and see her in here with a frightened teenager...

Or a monster?

"Lily," Claire whispered. *Why wasn't she answering?*

More knocking. Claire felt it in her head, pounding.

"Hello? Mrs. Brooks?" A man's voice, deep. "It's Deputy Berry. Anyone home?"

Please, go away. Please.

"Claire Brooks?" the deputy called out. His footsteps thumped across the porch, fading in volume. Claire pictured him peeking through the living room windows. "Emma Brooks! If you can hear me, please respond."

The footsteps grew louder as Berry approached the kitchen window.

Oh, God.

Had they drawn the curtains in the kitchen? If not, then the slaughterhouse within would be on full display, and it was only a matter of time before—

"Jesus Christ," Berry said. "Jesus Christ...What the hell—"

"I'm here," Claire cried. She didn't know what else to do. "I'm inside!"

"There's blood everywhere. Are you hurt?"

How to answer? She was locked in the basement with a dead body and a daughter who was supposed to be missing. No matter what she said, Berry would not leave now, not until he'd laid eyes on her to be sure she was all right.

She could use his help to escape the basement, but how was she supposed to explain being locked in here without implicating Emma?

"Mrs. Brooks?" Berry shouted, "*Are you hurt?*"

Fuck it, give him the truth.

Emma had made her choices. Claire didn't want to betray her, but she had to get herself and Lily away from the cabin. She would just have to hope he would be understanding about Lily's condition.

"Yes, I'm hurt! I'm locked in the basement. I can't get out!"

"Ma'am, I'm coming in!" The door slammed back. Emma must have left it unlocked. Heavy footsteps thudded across the floorboards overhead. "Ma'am? Where are you?"

"The kitchen!"

The footsteps halted. Claire heard a metallic snap and pictured Berry unholstering his weapon. The deputy swore— above her now, boots scuffing as he turned. "Where in the kitchen?"

"Down here," she said. She poked her fingers through the slot. "I'm locked in."

Berry rattled the knob. A long pause, and then the keys jingled; Emma had left them behind. The deadbolt slid back.

Light spilled down into the basement. Oscar leaped out past the deputy, eager to be free. Claire went to follow, but a flash in the corner of her eye prompted her to look back down at the stairs.

Silas's glasses had been placed on the step below her, the frames neatly folded with the cord wound around them. Claire held them up to the light. The glasses were real: a piece of her son, returned to her from—

A hand closed around Claire's arm, pulling her into the kitchen. Distracted by a sudden metallic grinding noise from below, Berry pushed Claire behind him and released his hold.

"Who else is down there?" He moved toward the open door with his service pistol raised.

"My daughter. She came back to us. Please, don't hurt her."

Berry relaxed, lowering the pistol as he descended far enough down the steps to duck beneath the level of the kitchen floor.

"Lily?" he called. "Can you hear me?" He glanced back at Claire. "Why isn't she responding?"

"Lily," Claire said, "the deputy is here to drive us to the hospital."

Berry unhooked a flashlight from his belt and clicked it on, descending further down the stairs. His breath caught. "What the—" He fell back onto the steps as a loud crash shook the cabin.

Where he'd been standing moments before, a washing machine protruded from the concrete wall. It had obliterated the railing and missed him by a sliver. Claire shouted over the dog's frantic barking and the deputy's curses: "Stop, Lily! He's here to help us!"

Berry rose into a crouch, angling his flashlight into the depths of the basement. His face contorted into an expression of disbelief and he raised his pistol, taking aim.

Claire reached for him, screaming, "No! Stop."

"What is that?" he yelled. "What the fuck is that?"

"It's Lily! She's not—She's changed!"

Metal scraped across concrete.

Berry shouted a warning, then scrambled backward up the steps as the dryer smashed into the washing machine, blocking the stairs below him. The flashlight fell from his hand and rolled. In the stunned silence that followed, Claire heard a soft clink as it struck the basement floor.

And then the pistol came up again. Claire shrieked an incoherent cry for Lily to run, though there was nowhere for her to go. Claire knew that better than anyone. The basement was a box, a trap. Lily would be impossible to miss. She had to stop him. Berry swore, braced himself.

And fired into the darkness.

EMMA

EMMA WOKE TO the sound of her own labored breathing. Through the frost-webbed windshield, the first golden touches of dawn limned the boxy silhouette of Evelyn's cabin. Shivering, she turned the keys in the ignition. Cold air streamed through the vents. She bounced in the seat, trying to get her blood flowing.

She'd only meant to close her eyes for a moment, to rest in the heated cab, gather her strength for the walk back. The gas tank was low but not empty. She must have lost consciousness sometime after shutting off the engine. Emma frowned at the towel lying across the passenger seat. A sense of urgency stirred inside her. She remembered wiping the seat and bumping her leg against the steering wheel—a final spike of agony. Everything else was a blank.

But the towel. Something about evidence…

Emma sat up, panicked. She'd killed a man. The realization lifted her stomach into her chest. She was going to prison. Nausea bent her over the steering wheel. She'd murdered a man in cold blood, and now his little girl would grow up without a father.

She clamped a gloved hand over her mouth. What the fuck had she been thinking, driving the snowplow to Evelyn's? Claire was back at the cabin alone with Lily. Emma had locked her wife in the basement—the place Claire feared most—all because she was convinced that Lily would reveal Silas's whereabouts.

But their son was gone. She'd been so tangled in her own denial, so deluded by hope, she had…

She was going to be sick.

Evidence.

There was no time to wait for the heater to warm her. She had to leave now, get back to the cabin as fast as possible.

Emma held her gorge down as she killed the engine and hurriedly swabbed down the interior of the cab. She left the keys in the ignition, grabbed Silas's backpack from behind the seat, and fled.

The wind greeted her with a cold slap. Snowflakes pelted her from all sides. As she limped through the trees, her mind cycled through various alibis, determined to defuse the panic ticking in her chest. She couldn't afford to turn into a useless wreck. Claire and Lily needed her.

Stupid, stupid.

Back home, Emma could navigate the city blindfolded. But the forest? Covered in snow, everything looked the same. She slogged through ranks of identical trees, searching for a landmark. Was she moving toward the cabin? Emma turned a slow circle, but the forest wouldn't give up its secrets. She'd been walking for what felt like hours.

You should have followed the road.

Lost, you're fucking lost.

The wind froze tears to her cheeks. She put her head down and poured her remaining strength into her legs. Every step hurt more than the last. The ground passed beneath her, unseen. She was a ghost, an empty shell. Everything that mattered, everyone who made her whole, was back at the cabin—or gone, swallowed up by the same forest that would eagerly claim her, if she stopped moving.

You should have gone after them.

When Emma finally looked up again, she lurched to a halt. She had been so focused on her boots, she'd almost run into the back wall of the shed. The tarp covering the woodpile rippled in the wind like a flag. Beyond the shed, a squad car was parked in the clearing. Shouts came from inside the cabin.

No. She had needed more time—to clean up the cabin, to apologize, and to find out if Claire had learned anything from Lily. They needed to decide on a story to tell the authorities, a simple believable lie they could repeat a thousand times over without error.

As her numb feet carried her closer, she saw that the squad car was empty. Fresh prints led from the car to the porch. Her pulse quickened. A loud crash echoed out of the cabin followed by more shouting and barking. Someone—*Claire?*—screamed. Forgetting her injured leg, she began to run.

A gunshot rang out.

Emma flew up the steps and through the front door as a second shot cracked. Oscar skittered sideways toward the woodstove, surprised by her sudden entrance. His one eye bulged, fixed on the standoff unfolding in the kitchen.

Deputy Berry stood on the basement stairs, his lower half obscured by the floorboards. He swayed, clutching his chest, his face pale and drawn. Claire's back was to her, her head tilted as if she was trying to make sense of the red stain blooming across the deputy's uniform.

Berry turned and slowly climbed the steps into the kitchen. His service pistol fell and struck the floor. Scowling in confusion at his blood-coated palm, he struggled to catch a breath that wouldn't come.

Claire dropped the rifle.

A hand emerged from the basement and blackened fingers closed around Berry's ankle, yanking him off his feet. And then he vanished, like a rabbit pulled back into a hat—magic reversed with a greedy wet snap.

Emma limped toward Claire, kicked the rifle aside, and pulled her wife away from the open basement door into the living room.

"I had to," Claire said. "He shot at Lily." Her hands clamped around Emma's wrists like cold shackles. "I had to, Em. He was going to kill her."

Emma folded Claire into a tight embrace. Claire was shaking. They both were.

"The journal," Claire sobbed. "Grace's journal, it's real. Everything about White Hook, the feeding—"

"What? Calm down. What are you saying?"

"It's not Lily. I think there's something inside her." Wild-eyed, she seized Emma's face in her hands. "Grace thought she killed it, but she was wrong. And now it's got Lily. It's…inside her."

"You're saying, what? That she's possessed?"

Saying the word aloud seemed to lend it new weight. Emma thought of the man's voice she'd heard in the basement. She'd been so excited to hear Silas and Lily conversing that she hadn't dwelt on the source of the other voice. And she'd failed to consider what might be taking Lily's place when she wasn't acting like herself.

When she was behaving like a vicious animal.

Like a monster or a demon.

"It must've gotten to them while they were lost," Claire said. "Whatever she did to Silas"—she caved inward as if she'd been stabbed—"it wasn't her fault. We can't blame her. Do you understand?"

The cabin blurred around Emma, rolling underfoot. "Are you telling me that our daughter…killed our son? That she… ate his body?"

"Not Lily—Father. *White Hook*. I don't know how it survived down in that fucking well all this time, but it did, and now—"

"Oh my god." Emma pried Claire's hands away and looked past her into the kitchen, where the basement door stood open. "But…you can't know that for sure. It could be psychological or—"

"No, Em, I thought of that already, but it's not. She *told* me. I didn't want to believe it, but she said it climbed into her skin. She said it wouldn't let her talk about Silas, that it hurts her. And she's changed so much—all this time, she's kept growing."

Emma stared at the basement door, unable to move, as she waited for an unrecognizable figure to emerge from beneath the floor, a creature like the one Grace had described. Her thoughts were a senseless blur. She didn't know how to process this new information, if it was true. She was trained to deal with medical emergencies, could shut her emotions off to deal with any high-stress situation at the hospital, but if Claire was right, then Lily's condition went beyond the physical and psychological. Emma had always discounted the supernatural before, but, as she heard the strange man's voice in her memory, coming through the slot, she felt a grim certainty take hold of her. "How do we stop it?"

"We start by getting her the fuck away from this place," Claire said. The breathless note of fear was gone from her voice. She turned and stalked into the kitchen, then picked the rifle up from the floor. "If she's"—her bravado slipped for a second, and she looked as if she might retch—"eating the deputy, that should buy us some time to get her to the nearest town. We can take the squad car, if she'll fit in it—"

"If she'll fit?"

"I told you, Em. She's still growing." Claire went to the drawer beside the sink, removed a large leather sheath with a hunting knife tucked inside it, and snapped it to her belt. She pulled a flashlight from the kitchen cabinet, checked the rifle's ammunition, then shouted, "Lily?"

Silence from the basement.

"What do you need the rifle for?" Emma asked.

Claire glanced down at the weapon in her hands. "In case that thing inside her needs some convincing. It knows what a rifle is."

"White Hook," Emma said. She was still having difficulty coming to terms with the idea that a century-old nightmare had crossed the breach of time to invade their daughter's body. But Claire believed. She was more resolute than Emma had ever seen her. "You're not going to shoot her."

"Of course not."

"No matter what. Promise me."

Claire looked hurt. "I would never do that. But we need her—*it*—to cooperate. We won't have much time."

"Okay…" Emma's gaze moved to the front windows and the squad car parked outside. "Wait—shit. Did Berry have his keys with him? *On him*, I mean…" She trailed off, nodding at the basement door.

Claire swore. "I don't know."

"Let's check the squad car."

"Okay, yeah." Claire puffed her cheeks, blew the air out of her lungs in a rush. She looked at Emma's leg. "You stay here. I'll be right back."

"You should take Oscar with you and leave him outside. We don't want him getting hurt again."

"Good call." Claire coaxed a frightened Oscar off of the couch in the living room, then led him outside.

Emma limped into the kitchen, shut the basement door, and sank to the floor on top of it. She waited quietly, listening for signs of movement from below but heard nothing.

Time stretched, elastic. "Claire?" she shouted. "Are you okay?"

"Em…" The return call was faint, strangely distant. But it wasn't coming from outside.

"Emma! I'm in the basement…" The rest was too muffled to make out.

Emma gritted her teeth and used the windowsill to haul herself to her feet. It took her three tries to wrestle the basement door back open. She leaned against it, panting. "Claire?"

"Come down here. You have to see this." Her voice carried a tremor of fascination that piqued Emma's curiosity, despite the urgency of their situation.

She stared down at the wreckage of machines on the steps. "How?"

"Come down as far as you can. I'll help you from there." The sound of boot soles scuffing concrete approached. A beam of light stabbed at the stairs from below.

"What are you doing down there? Did you get the deputy's keys?"

"They weren't in the car."

"Damn it. I left the keys in the snowplow at Evelyn's. If we take Lily there…" Emma limped onto the step just above the ruined machines, feeling the stairs quake beneath her. "Is she okay?"

"I don't know."

"What do you mean you don't—Lily? Honey?"

"It's just me. Lily's not here. Wriggle over the edge and hang your legs over. I'll catch you."

Emma followed her instructions, grunting as her injured leg rubbed against the steps. "What do you mean she's not here?" As her boots dangled into emptiness, she imagined Lily rushing through the dark and locking onto her, dragging her down the way she'd taken the deputy. When Claire touched her leg, she yelped.

Claire hugged her legs to take her weight, and Emma released her hold on the step. Claire helped her land gently, then let go and turned to sweep the basement with her flashlight. Dented cans and shattered glass littered the floor. Several broken shelves hung at an angle. Save for a tangle of stained blankets, the mattress in the left-hand corner was bare.

The basement was empty.

A swath of glistening scarlet marked the deputy's passage across the floor, weaving between mounds of loose earth and concrete chunks toward the right-hand corner of the far wall. Emma's boots led her forward against her will. The flashlight's beam stabbed into a ragged hole.

Not a hole—a tunnel.

The streak of gore climbed the wall, disappearing into the earthen throat beyond. The distant sound of barking reached her, coming from somewhere beyond the wall and above.

"Oscar found it while we were outside." Claire whispered. "But he wouldn't come down with me."

The rough outline of a heart marked the wall beside the tunnel, painted in red, a shaky "S" drawn at its center. Emma stared at it in shock.

Claire braced her hands on the lip of the tunnel.

"No way," Emma said. "We are not crawling through there."

"Why not? This is the way Lily went. This was her backup plan, after you locked me in here with her."

Emma flinched. "So she wouldn't hurt you if I didn't make it back in time?"

"That's our Lily, always thinking of others first." Claire's smile was a sad, fragile thing.

"I'm sorry for locking you down here," Emma whispered. "I'm so fucking sorry. If I could go back—"

"I know." Claire's expression softened. "I'm sorry too. For everything."

In the clearing above, Oscar's barking intensified. Emma's focus returned to the hole burrowed through the earth.

"I can't crawl through there like this." She gestured helplessly at her leg with her bandaged hand. "But I can't get back up the stairs without you. I'm sorry, I know I'm holding you back—"

"No, you're right. I wasn't thinking. Let's go back up to the kitchen."

"How are we supposed to find her now?"

Claire's head tilted as the barking sounds seemed to circle the cabin. "I'm worried he already has. Come on, hurry."

They rushed through the dark to the damaged stairs. Claire boosted Emma up first. Despite having only one hand to brace herself, Emma managed to struggle back onto the steps. But when she turned to reach down for Claire, the flashlight's beam was moving away already, back toward the tunnel.

"Claire?" Emma shouted, panic taking hold.

"I'm going to follow her footprints, see if I can find her and convince her to follow us to Evelyn's. I'll be back in a few minutes."

Everything was happening too fast; her exhausted mind couldn't follow the moving pieces. If the deputy had called for backup, they could already be on their way. And if they arrived while the cabin was still drenched in evidence, they wouldn't wait while Emma tried to explain that their missing daughter was now on the loose in the forest. Hell, they might catch Lily *with* the deputy. What then? Would they try to reason with her, or just shoot her? "Claire, did the deputy call for backup? Did you hear him use the radio?"

Claire swore again. "I don't know. I can't remember."

"They could be on their way here. They'll find all that blood and—"

"Burn it down."

"What?"

"The cabin." Claire's voice echoed back from within the tunnel. "We don't need it anymore. We're leaving. Burn it down."

"How?" Emma tried to recall the documentaries they'd binge-watched together on television. Destroying evidence left more evidence. If she wasn't careful, they'd both end up in prison. But there wasn't time to plan. She was so tired.

She called out to Claire again, but there was no answer.

She limped into the living room and hesitated, waiting for Claire to appear in the clearing beyond the front windows. *No time, no time.* She needed to prepare for the walk to Evelyn's, and their clothes were covered in bloodstains. They would have to change before driving into town.

Emma grabbed a garbage bag from the kitchen and went down the hall to the master bedroom. She'd leave their suitcases to burn. The fire should look unexpected, like an accident—no time for suitcases. Stuffing clothes into the plastic bag, Emma carried it outside and left it beside the shed. She heard Oscar barking in the trees but couldn't get a fix on his location. She called his name, and then called for Claire and Lily, but no one responded.

She had to hurry. Dreading the sound of approaching sirens, she rushed back to the cabin and allowed herself only a few minutes to sweep through the wreckage in the children's bedroom. She grabbed Silas's favorite robot toy and stowed it in her coat pocket, then looked around for Lily's camera, but the room was a mess. Lily had destroyed everything when they'd locked her in.

Emma tossed aside twisted clothes, kicked through the flattened blanket fort. Where was the fucking camera? Broken dresser pieces tilted underfoot as she gave up and made her way back to the hall.

In the master bedroom, she snatched Grace's journal from the foot of the bed. Perhaps the key to saving Lily was hidden inside—something they'd missed on their first reading, back when they'd believed the monster was imaginary. She crammed it into another of her coat pockets. From her suitcase, she retrieved the scented candle she'd brought from home when she'd been picturing a romantic getaway. She shook her head, disgusted. To think she could have been so fucking naïve.

Back in the kitchen, she spun the knobs of the wretched antique stove. Gas hissed softly. Satisfied, she grabbed the box of matches and hurried to the front door, carrying the scented candle.

She knelt and placed it just inside the entryway. Taking one last look around, she struck a match, touched the flame to the wick, and closed the door behind her.

She scanned her surroundings from the porch but saw no sign of a hole. Claire and Oscar's footprints led from the squad car toward the eastern edge of the clearing.

Christ, how long is this tunnel?

She retrieved the bag of clothes from beside the shed, then followed the trail into the forest. Wending through the trees, she called out to Claire. When she found the tunnel's exit, she dropped the bag beside it and stared. Blood surrounded the ragged opening. A shallow footprint marred the snow. Emma swayed on her feet. The print was huge. She followed the pock-marks left by Claire's boots as they pursued a trail of red droplets. The next print of Lily's was spaced an impossible distance from the first. Fear coiled around Emma's heart, sickening her. She shouted again for Claire, Lily, and Oscar...

Nothing.

She pictured Claire out in the forest somewhere, hunting their possessed daughter. She wanted to believe Claire wouldn't shoot Lily, but people made stupid mistakes when they were afraid. Emma needed to find her, make sure she kept her promise.

As she limped alongside Claire's prints, she cast a glance back at the cabin. How long before the gas filled it enough to ignite?

Barking cut through the silence, drawing closer. Emma froze and waited. From deeper in the forest, Claire shouted something. A black shape shot between the trees to her left, headed toward the cabin.

Cursing, Emma changed directions and limped after the dog as fast as she could, calling his name. What if he was at the front door, expecting someone to let him in, when the gas ignited?

Her wounded leg was slowing her down. As she waded through the snow, a wave of dizziness twisted the surrounding tree trunks into a striped blur. She fell to her knees in the snow, crying out as pain spiked her thigh.

The knowledge of everything she'd done up until this moment held her there, crushing her. She'd fed Lily pieces of herself, murdered a man, hurt her wife, and her family was still trapped here, because of her. Because she had refused to accept the possibility that her son was...

You should have gone after them.

Sobbing, she forced herself to stand. She wasn't going to be responsible for getting the damned dog killed too. She didn't want that guilt on her conscience. As she limped back into the clearing, she was relieved to find the porch was vacant. Oscar bolted from behind the cabin toward the shed, then reversed direction with his head angled up at the treetops, as if he was chasing something. Emma looked up. The trees swayed in the wind, revealing nothing. She shouted for the dog, but he ignored her.

As she limped after him, a whooshing sound came from the cabin and an explosion of heat and glass knocked her sideways. She rolled over, saw flames licking from the windows, and all she could think was, *Good*.

Finally.

A tree separated from the surrounding forest, streaking toward the cabin in a blur. Emma blinked, puzzled. Trees didn't run.

Lily. Oh god, Lily, no.

She watched as her daughter collided with the cabin wall outside the children's bedroom. Lily snaked her long arms through the flaming window and tried to force her enlarged head through the opening. When that failed, she dug her claws into the wood, squeezing and rending and splintering. She tore logs from the wall as if the cabin had been built from toothpicks. Chunks of wood struck the trees at the edge of the clearing. She dove through the hole, into the fire.

Emma ran toward the burning cabin, screaming Lily's name. Over the roar of the flames, and the hiss and pop of burning logs, she heard barking. Smoke filled her nostrils. She choked, coughed, retched as heat seared her skin. From her right, Claire broke from the tree line, gasping for air, with Oscar following behind her.

"Em? Where is she? I lost her..." She followed Emma's gaze to the fiery hole in the cabin's wall. "Lily? Lily!"

"Why would she go in there?" Emma moved toward the flames, but Claire held her back. "What's in there? I don't understand." "Oh fuck," Claire whispered. "The camera. Did you leave it in there?" Her fingers gouged deep into Emma's arms. "She kept saying she needed it when we were in the basement. Where is it?"

"I—I tried to find it. I couldn't." Emma gasped as the splintered bedroom wall birthed a massive, burning shape.

Lily unfolded to her full height, flaming hair brushing the roof as she rose above it. Her camera dangled on its strap, swinging from her blackened fist. Naked, marred by a network of livid burns and charred flesh, Lily cradled the camera between her damaged breasts. And then she looked at Emma, eyes like saucers radiating feral intensity—trying to communicate. Emma felt it in her mind, like an impulse:

Follow.

Lily crossed to the tree line in a blink. Barking, Oscar shot after her.

"Come on," Claire shouted, taking Emma's hand.

Inside the cabin, something crashed to the floor. Emma flinched. It was all falling apart, coming down. She couldn't stop it now.

Your fault, your fault.

You should have…

There was nothing left to do but follow.

CLAIRE

CLAIRE CHASED LILY through the forest, dragging Emma behind her. Treetops bent in the distance, then sprang upright, launching Lily's soot-streaked form toward the lake.

When Emma collapsed for the third time, Claire tried to help her up, but she shook her off and gasped, "Go." The snow where she'd fallen was stained red, her pant leg soaked through.

"I'm not leaving you," Claire said.

Emma was shivering violently. Her teeth chattered a *tak-a-tak-tak* rhythm as she said, "You'll nev-ver ca-catch her w-with m-me hold—ding you b-b-ba—back."

"Get up, come on. I've got you." She ducked under Emma's arm and hauled her upright, sliding an arm around her waist for support. She would carry her to the lake if she had to. "I need you with me, Em. I can't do this alone."

Claire pulled Silas's glasses from her coat pocket, and the haze cleared from Emma's eyes; she stared at the glasses, rapt. A question plumed like smoke from her blue-tinged lips: "Wh-where?"

"Lily left them for me," Claire said, towing Emma along beside her. "When I was in the basement, I think she... coughed them up."

A faint yelp from Oscar somewhere ahead of them quickened Claire's pace. Emma was silent for several minutes. Claire listened to the harsh whistle of her breath, wondering if she'd made a mistake by sharing her suspicions about Lily. And then, Emma's shoulders shook. Racking sobs caved her chest in. But she did not stop walking; she picked up her pace until she was the one pulling Claire forward. Emma's determination bled into her, fueling them both, driving them toward the ruins of the boarding school.

Claire craned her neck to look up, but Lily's progress was obscured by the branches above. When they passed a towering pine, denuded of snow, Claire began counting her steps. She counted to one hundred, two-twenty, three hundred. Another bare pine came into view. Oscar's paw prints formed hectic loops around the trunk. A splash of blood colored the bark. A shape lay nearby in the snow.

Braced for the sight of torn black fur, Claire approached. Fabric clung to the shape. A knob of flesh poked from the end of the ripped sleeve where the arm had been wrenched off at the shoulder.

"Berry," Emma said, her face ashen. "She's carrying him with her. Feeding as she goes."

They pressed on.

The trees opened into the clearing beside the lake. The ruins of the boarding school lurked beneath layers of fresh snow, hunkered low like a camouflaged predator. Oscar rocketed out from the trees near the lakeshore, kicking up snow as he ran along the water. He jumped up at Claire, bowling her over. She dropped the rifle as he stomped on her stomach. Sputtering under the affections of his wet tongue, she seized him by his shaggy scruff and embraced him.

Oscar stiffened and pricked his ears, snapping his muzzle shut. His shiny dark eye was fixed over her shoulder. Gooseflesh prickled her skin as his ears flattened. He bared his teeth and growled.

Claire turned. Beyond the patch of snow disrupted by their reunion, Emma's boot prints angled toward the nearest tree, but then—where was she?

Claire stood, using Oscar's back for support as she willed her legs to turn solid. Perhaps Emma had intended to lean against the trunk, catch her breath, but there were no tracks beyond the tree; its branches were stripped of snow. Everything—the forest, the clearing, the frozen lake beyond—was deathly still, like a winter scene encased in a snow globe. Trapped under glass. No movement at all, except for the static dance of snowflakes.

"Emma?" It was as if she'd been plucked straight up from the ground. "Emma, where are you? Emma!"

Oscar ran from the tree where Emma had disappeared to the tree line on the opposite side of the clearing, headed in the direction of the pit. His black tail flickered between the trees as he too vanished from sight.

Raucous barking followed. Claire retrieved the rifle from the snow, careful not to dwell on whether she would be capable of firing it at Lily if the need arose. That kind of thinking would destroy her. Leaning into the wind, she waded through the snow. The barking was coming from the forest beyond the clearing.

As she moved through the trees toward the pit, she brought the rifle up. She no longer felt the cold. Between the gusts of wind rustling the branches, a heavy silence stretched. As if the land was holding its breath. Waiting.

At the center of the pit, Lily's hunched back rose like a pale gray mountain. Patches of blisters formed boiled continents across marred her flesh, charred strips cracked like cooling lava to reveal weeping crevasses. Seared pink whorls twisted and seeped. The trees quivered as she shifted her weight. Bones cracked beneath her bare feet. Even crouched over, Lily's burned scalp was level with the lowest branches of the pines. When she stood, how tall would she be?

The strength ran out from Claire's legs. The rifle was a child's toy, a toothpick, compared to the colossus in the pit. *Lily. It's Lily—your daughter.*

Claire shook her head, aghast.

Maybe before. But now?

Lily would never try to kill her mother, not if she had a choice.

This was White Hook, revealed in all its vicious, ravenous brutality. It was devouring Emma, swallowing her headfirst. Oscar, a snarling black speck, hovered like a gnat at the bottom of the pit, darting in to snap at White Hook's ankles. It swatted him away so hard that Oscar sailed up through the air and landed on his side with a yelp behind Claire. And then he was up again, bolting back down into the pit before she could even call his name. Oscar latched onto the back of White Hook's arm, but the creature was otherwise occupied with Emma.

Feeding.

Blackened fingers entwined around Emma's thighs like enormous sickly roots. Pinned between rows of bristling teeth, Emma's torso bucked and relaxed, convulsing. Her chest and shoulders were locked inside White Hook's mouth, her forearms thrashing weakly. Her legs jittered.

Struggling.

She's still alive.

Oscar leaped and wrested a chunk of meat from White Hook's triceps, then darted back in, scaling ribs to lock onto White Hook's ear. The lobe tore. Oscar burrowed into the crook between neck and collarbone, seeking the throat, but White Hook threw him off with a powerful shake of its head.

Its splinter teeth lifted from the fabric of Emma's coat, arching like snake fangs. The creature extended its neck, flexed its jaw, and settled its teeth even lower into Emma's stomach, pulling her deeper. Swallowing her whole.

"Lily!" Claire rounded the pit and planted the rifle's stock beside her shoulder, angling the barrel up, up...

White Hook rose, looming over her.

Claire's boot kicked something lying in the snow: Lily's camera. She lifted it by its fraying strap and held it out like a talisman, hoping the sight of Lily's most prized possession would bring her daughter's consciousness back. "Lily," she shouted, "if you're in there—if you can hear me—you have to let her go!"

Emma's legs kicked, feebly. Bumps stretched White Hook's throat from the inside—the contours of an elbow, a hint of a face pressing against the skin, concave mouth opened wide. Emma was alive, and slowly suffocating. Claire could still save her if she didn't hesitate. She looped the camera's strap around her neck, pleading as she brought the rifle up again. "Lily, she's your mother—your Memma! You have to let her go! Please, Lily. Now, goddamnit, *now!*"

White Hook cocked its head, lips chewed back in a permanent grin. The grin spread wider with Emma pinned at its center. Rancid air hissed, rattling quill teeth. White Hook chuffed through the hollows of its nasal cavity.

It was laughing at her.

Claire aimed the rifle at the sky and pulled the trigger. It fired with a deafening crack. The thing that was not Lily flinched. And then it flexed its jaws again, reeling Emma in deeper.

Claire didn't know where to aim. White Hook's distended gut sloped above her like a scorched moon eclipsing the leaden sky. The rifle's barrel drifted over ribs like concrete pilings, shoulders like cathedral domes. She only wanted to hurt the creature enough to force it to regurgitate Emma—not to kill it.

Lily, Lily.

She couldn't do it. Her hands were shaking too hard.

But if she didn't act, she would lose Emma forever. There was no one else to call to for help, no one else to take control and rescue Emma from White Hook's jaws. She was alone.

It had to be her.

She took aim. Fired. The rifle bucked. Blood erupted from White Hook's throat, descending in a steaming arc.

Claire dropped the rifle, knotted her hands in her hair, and wailed.

You missed.

You fucking missed.

White Hook fell to its knees. The tremor knocked Claire off her feet. Something snapped inside her, but the pain didn't register. She stared at the pool of blood filling the bottom of the pit, unable to pull her eyes from the wounded creature sinking at its center. Gushing its lifeblood in a crimson waterfall, White Hook slumped.

As Oscar bounded up the slope, leaving a trail of red prints in his wake, Claire struggled upright.

She skidded down into the pit, vision narrowing to a pinprick focused on the boots dangling from White Hook's mouth. The creature's head sagged lower, past its chest, overhanging its bent legs. Blood painted its thighs.

Emma's legs weren't moving. As Claire waded into the blood still flowing from White Hook, she took care not to look down at the fluid sloshing around her ankles. She couldn't afford to lose consciousness now. Heat rose off the pool as she approached the creature's drooping head.

Lily's head—Lily's.

Look what you've done to your little girl.

Hanging from its strap, Lily's camera bumped against Claire's chest, beating where her heart could not. She scrabbled at White Hook's slippery thigh, scaled its bulging gut, and jumped. Her fingers snagged Emma's boots; gravity did the rest.

As Emma slid from White Hook's throat, Claire caught her. White Hook toppled backwards with a wet sigh, gurgling as blood filled the space Emma had vacated. Claire dragged her wife backwards through the rising tide to the unblemished snow above.

She felt for a pulse—it was there, throbbing faintly—and sobbed with relief. She rolled Emma onto her side, hooked two fingers between her lips, and scooped out a sticky mass of fluids. When her airway was clear, she laid Emma on her back, positioning her hands to administer chest compressions. After the first series of pumps, Emma drew in a shuddering gasp and coughed. Stringy mucous flew from her lips. When she caught sight of Lily lying prone in the pit below, she tried to wrestle free from Claire's hold but winced, grabbing at her side. She peeled her coat up and stared at the bleeding trench beneath her ribs where the rifle's bullet had grazed her. "What…Did you shoot me?"

"No, I—" Confused, Claire paled. "I didn't mean to. I shot *it*—White Hook. I had to."

No, you missed.

You shot your daughter *through the throat. Shot your* wife, *in the process.*

There was no accusation in Emma's eyes, no anger. Only sadness. "Is she…?"

The answer came from the pit. Lily's voice was faint, but it was hers alone. "Mm…ma?"

She coughed, tried again. "Mom?"

Claire forced herself to look. This was her handiwork, after all—her fault. There was no one else to blame. Whatever happened next, she would not shy away. She would drink up every detail, let the memory haunt her for the rest of her days.

Lily's arm was extended, her claws groping. Her hazel eyes were glazed. She stared up at the overcast sky, unblinking. The snow melting beneath her head was so dark it was almost black.

Emma held her side as Claire helped her stand. Then she started limping down the slope into the pit. Claire caught up and slipped an arm around her shoulder, lending support as they waded into the blood pooled at the bottom. Submerged bones shifted under their boots. Oscar watched their progress from the rim of the pit, whining softly.

As her mothers approached, Lily's eye rolled sideways to greet them. She reached for Claire with one hooked claw. The camera's weight lifted from her chest then thumped back down between her breasts. Claire ducked out of the strap and held the camera out in a daze.

Lily's brow furrowed. A groan shook the trees.

She coughed a fine red mist, uttering an atavistic litany as she fought the sickness that had driven her to madness. She was trying to speak again. Trying to make Claire understand. Claire laid her hand on Lily's cheek. As Lily turned toward her mother's touch, blood spilled between her teeth, clearing her airway. Claire moved closer, desperate to hear her voice again before it became a part of their past, something to be distantly remembered with sorrow and longing.

"With…me," Lily coughed. Her hand closed around Claire's arms. Grazing the camera with her thumb, she frowned. Pleading. "With me."

"Turn the camera on," Emma murmured, hugging Lily's wrist. "She wants to see it."

Claire switched the camera on. The pain was cleaving her in two, grief and regret spreading her ribs, tearing her to pieces. Sobbing, she turned the camera so Lily could see the screen.

"I'm sorry I hurt you," Claire whispered. "I didn't mean to. I was just trying to—I didn't know what to do. I'm so sorry."

Lily nudged the camera again, closing her eyes. "With…me."

"We're with you, honey." Emma tucked a lank scrap of singed hair behind Lily's ear and pushed up on tiptoes, grimacing at the pain from her many wounds as she kissed their daughter's temple. "We're here."

Lily scowled and shook her head. She bumped the camera again.

Claire turned the camera around. The digital screen showed a closeup of Lily's face: bushy hair, frostbitten features. She remembered finding Lily in the bedroom after her return, recalled the way Lily had angled the camera as if she was taking a picture of her tongue. Swiping at her eyes to clear her vision, Claire scrolled through the photographs. Most were out of focus: over a dozen shots of Lily's teeth and tongue. Blurry.

And then—

Claire dropped the camera with a soft, injured cry.

"What?" Emma bent to retrieve it, hissing through her teeth as she clutched her side. She frowned at the screen, puzzled. Her lower lip began to quiver. "Oh…oh, fuck."

Lily had turned on the flash to illuminate the inside of her mouth, the depths of her throat. To capture what was hiding just behind her tongue.

Fingers.

Small fingers, reaching up.

With me.

She'd been trying to tell them. All this time, she'd been trying to tell them, to make them understand.

"Had to," Lily whispered. She stroked her bulging stomach. "With me…I promised."

Lily's hand drifted to Claire's hip and flicked the leather sheath snapped to her belt.

"Have to…help him," Lily groaned. "Please. Running… out…"

Understanding dawned, flooding Claire's mind with sorrow and senseless rage. It wasn't fair, any of this. Despite everything they'd been through, Lily was bleeding out in the snow. They were losing her.

It was too much.

No mother could be expected to cope with this level of suffering. Huddled beside their daughter while Lily used the last of her strength to pluck at the knife, begging them to—to—

"D-did she…" Emma was staring at Claire, eyes shivering in their sockets. "Did she e-eat…" She couldn't finish.

Tears burned down Claire's frozen cheeks as she watched Lily fumble the knife out of the sheath. Claire grabbed the handle, resisting Lily's efforts.

"Losing…him," Lily murmured. Her long fingers moved from the handle to the blade, angling it at her stomach and tugging at it. "Losing…"

Emma pressed her ear to Lily's side. Her eyes widened. "Claire, I hear something."

As Lily pulled the knife closer, the blade nicked her flesh below the ribs. Blood beaded. Claire swallowed back a surge of nausea and pulled the knife away. She couldn't do it. Lily was asking her to do the unthinkable. The impossible.

"Ticking," Emma said. Her voice was so small, Claire could barely make out the words. "Claire, something's ticking inside her."

Lily exhaled. A fine red mist descended over their upturned faces. She was trying to form a word, but her sluggish tongue refused to cooperate. She spat blood, eyes rolling blindly in her head. Her lipless mouth worked in agony. She managed a whisper:

"*Hurry*."

Emma and Claire locked eyes, fear and bewilderment passing between them with the question they didn't need to speak aloud.

They already knew the answer.

Lily's intent was as clear as she forced the blade toward her swollen stomach. Claire wrestled for control, but the knife's handle slipped in her grasp. She looked to Emma, trying to pass the burden to her, but Emma shook her head and held up the bloody rags swaddling her right hand. "I can't do it, Claire. Not like this. I can't. I won't be able to."

"It has to be you, Em. The blood—I'll pass out. Please. I need you to—"

"I can't!" Emma screamed, hiding her face behind Lily's shoulder.

"Okay…Okay, I'll—" Claire choked as grief crushed her chest. She spoke the words long after she'd made up her mind, knowing she would have to live with the consequences for the rest of her life, to bear the burden Emma could not. Her heart was breaking into shards, cutting her apart from the inside out. "I'll do it. Just…close your eyes, Lily. I'll do it."

"How can I help?" Emma's eyes darted over Lily's body, unfocused. "I don't know what to do. I—Tell me what to do, Claire."

"Hold her. Talk to her, until…"

The end.

As Claire climbed atop Lily's stomach, Emma began to sing their daughter's favorite song.

Claire gripped the knife handle. Lily's hand floated, sketching a line from sternum to navel.

"I love you, Lily," Claire said. "I'm so sorry."

As the blade bit through Lily's skin, Claire whispered a stream of words—a song without music—breath fogging the air in the shape of her love. Lily did not struggle or cry out. Below, Emma cradled as much of their daughter's head as she could hold, singing into Lily's ear as Claire drew the knife down. Smiling, Lily nodded, urging Claire on.

"I'm sorry," Claire whispered. And:

"I love you, I love you, I love you."

She couldn't bring herself to say goodbye.

From a pocket behind Lily's ribs, a membranous sac slid down, spilling out through her opened belly. Stunned, Claire pulled the sac into her arms. The figure nestled inside shifted. A fleshy cord anchored the sac inside Lily's deflated chest, connecting it to…

Her heart.

Claire thought of the heart Lily had drawn on the basement wall, and the "S" at its center. As she severed the cord with the knife, she lost her balance, but Emma caught her. They fell in a tangle of limbs. Claire reached for the sac, but her hands were shaking. The knife spun from her grasp. Emma picked it up. She knelt beside Claire and said, "Pinch it for me. Hold it up."

Claire did as she asked, and Emma sliced through the membrane, rupturing the sac. Fluid burst out into Claire's lap. The membrane sloughed away. Claire parted wet blond hair, wiping it back to reveal a face: closed eyes, pursed lips.

Silas.

Emma touched his cheek, tentatively, as if to prove he was really there. Claire hefted his weight to be sure.

But he was naked, cold. His lips and eyelids were tinged purple. And he was so very still, an ice sculpture of a child. The pocket watch clenched in his fist was ticking.

"He's alive," Emma whispered. "He's *still alive.* Claire, how…?"

Silas's expression was serene. The slow rise and fall of his chest beneath Claire's hand—she had to be dreaming.

As Oscar licked the fluids from Silas's face, Claire said, "I don't know. But…he's breathing. He's—"

Silas opened his eyes with a gasp.

"Are we home?" he asked. And then:

"Where's Lily?"

SILAS

IT CLINGS TO the wall of the well above, hanging upside down. Breath like roadkill stuffed with rotten fruit. Its voice is the papery whisper of wasps crawling from a nest, the soft crackling rustle of pages burning to ash. The words thrum deep in Silas's bones.

Behind him, Lily stiffens. She does not scream. Silas feels her arms wrap around him, drawing him close. Squeezing, as though she means to fuse them together, make them inseparable.

It tells them they are dying.

It offers Lily a trade.

The darkness grows fingers, charcoal strokes with needle tips. It caresses Silas's cheek.

Never, *Lily hisses, beating back the shadow with her hands.*

Never? *Laughter shakes the well.*

You will die, *it says.* And then *he will die.*

Lily's chin is digging into the top of Silas's head. It hurts. She's holding him so tight he can't breathe.

Her consent is a vibration in his ear.

Me. Take me, instead.

Silas remembers the lighter. His frozen fingertips fumble with the flint. He's shivering, almost drops it. A rasping click.

The flame springs to life.

A face hovers inches from his own: the woman from the window, the one who lured them into the forest. Their grandmother. But her skin is all wrong. Dangling in loose folds, it sags like an ill-fitting costume. And what lies beneath is too thin to be a skeleton. It's a charred, splintered thing. Not flesh and blood but ash and teeth. Eyes like green mirrors peek out from behind torn sockets. A second mouth moves behind their grandmother's lips, rippling the skin like a silken mask.

You are hungry.
Like static, that voice.
You are cold.
Weak.

Deafening white noise rushes through Silas's mind like an avalanche, blurring his thoughts, driving them under. Burying him. He screams, but the sound is muffled by ice, clamping down on his head from both sides. Pressing in.

Not ice—Lily's hands. She's covering his ears, trying to shut out the noise. The ground, the well around them, Lily: everything is shaking.

Lips against Silas's ear. Blizzard's breath.
Lily's shouting: Do you trust me?
And before the lighter burns his thumb
Close your eyes.
before the darkness swallows the flame
I'll keep you safe.
the image of the thing climbing into his sister's skin
I'll take us home.
Silas sees Lily's mouth yawn open wide.
We'll be together, always.
He feels her heart, pounding between them. Warmth, swelling outward to envelop him.
I promise.
As Lily whispers, both around him and through him:
I love you.

EMMA

THEY HAD TO drag Silas from the pit. He fought them like a rabid animal, kicking and scratching. Wailing for his sister. Now that Lily's body was bled of the malevolent force that had held her hostage, it was shrinking, curling inward like a shred of paper kissed by flames.

Emma clung to Silas, forgetting the pain of her wounds as she wrapped him in her coat. And when he struggled, screaming Lily's name, she folded her limbs around him to anchor him in place and pressed his face into her chest to prevent him from looking back. They couldn't let him see her, not like this.

Claire descended into the pit. Kneeling beside Lily's body, she rocked back on her heels, tilted her tear-streaked face skyward.

And screamed.

Emma wept as Claire laid their daughter to rest at the foot of the tallest pine bordering the pit, digging through the snow with bare hands to claw at the frozen earth beneath. A layer of crumbling dirt, a blanket of snow, and Lily was gone. There wasn't time for a proper burial. Just an apology, whispered into the cold. A grave marked not with a headstone but with a camera tied to a nearby sapling, because the branches of the pine were too high for Claire to reach.

She deserved so much better, their Lily. There were still so many things left to say, a lifetime of conversations and arguments and celebrations stripped down to a lonely farewell.

Goodbye, drifting from blue-tinted lips like the ghost of a future lost.

Emma was losing her grip on Silas; she couldn't hold him any longer. Claire scooped him up, threw him over her shoulder, and reached out a hand. Emma took it, felt Claire hoist her up— her wife, stronger than she ever could have believed possible.

Claire was leading them out.

Home.

Oscar darted ahead, nose lowered to the snow. He doubled back to leap at Claire's back, trying to lick Silas's face. To quiet his screaming, perhaps.

"You promised!" Silas pounded Claire's back with his fists, howling Lily's name into the wind. He kicked. He bit. "Lily, you promised!"

Claire bore his fury, the burden of his infinite sorrow, without complaint. Whatever promise Lily had made was broken. Silas, in his grief, was only trying to make sense of the pieces she'd left behind.

When Emma stumbled and fell, Claire lowered Silas to the ground. She put her boots on his feet, laced them up tight. Taking his face between her hands, she said, "Listen to me. Your mother is hurt. She needs us—*both* of us—to be strong. Lily would want—she would have wanted us to get Memma to safety. Can you do that for her? For us?"

Silas chewed his trembling lip. "Lily's not coming with us."

It was not a question.

Claire stroked his cheek with her thumb, then shook her head.

Silas nodded. He wiped his eyes and shuffled past Claire to where Emma had fallen. Oscar was circling, whining. Silas laid a hand on the dog's shaggy black head. Solemnly, he whispered, "It's okay. We're going home now."

And Oscar fell silent.

Emma gazed up through the whirling snow, through the black spots dancing in her vision, at the look of grim determination on her son's face. She took the small hand he offered, dimly aware that Silas was ducking beneath her arm to shoulder it like a yoke. As if he were prepared to bear her full weight, carry her to safety—alone, if he had to. The simple purity of the gesture gave Emma the strength she needed to stand. But Silas wasn't alone, and neither was she.

They had each other still, after everything.

Oscar wove through the pines, carving a path back toward the stream and the wavering pillar of smoke beyond. Supporting

Emma between them, Claire and Silas followed. They trudged through the snow with the wind at their backs, pushing them forward.

Across the stream and through the forest, they carried Lily with them the only way they could, the only way anyone can ever truly hold a loved one lost to the ravages of time.

In their hearts and minds.

Their memories.

And so they reached the clearing.

Together.

EPILOGUE

SILAS

SILAS PULLED THE rental truck into the parking lot of the One Stop and killed the engine, squinting through the glare of the afternoon sun at the wooden letters perched atop the slanted roof. Compared to the lush greenery of the surrounding forest and the piercing blue summer sky, the building appeared faded, as though the One Stop hadn't seen a fresh coat of paint since he'd last visited, fifteen years before.

A string of bells jingled against glass as he entered. He paused to touch the sign on the counter: *Bathroom for Customers ONLY!!!*

A thin snapping sound drew his attention to the woman behind the register. She smirked, then blew another bubble, popping it between her teeth. He tried to picture her without the graying hair, the lined lips that suggested she spent more time outside smoking than minding the counter. She could be the same cashier from all those years ago, when he'd first come here with Lily and Memma.

"What do you want?" the woman asked, mouth quirking as if she'd tasted something bitter. "Bathroom's for *paying* customers only."

"Yeah, I remember."

The woman cocked her head. Her eyes flicked over him, like she was cutting him down to parts. "You look kinda familiar."

"My family stayed up the road one winter." He shifted, running a hand through his hair. "But that was a long time ago."

Snap. The cashier—*Maisie*, read the name tag pinned to her chest—leaned over the counter, narrowing her eyes. "You used to have glasses?"

Silas pinched the bridge of his nose. "Yeah. Can I use your phone, please? I don't get service out here." He waved his useless cellphone as evidence.

But she was still examining him, tilting her head like a crow eyeing a shiny piece of trash. "Never any service way out here. Those blank spots on the map when they're talking about coverage—you know, the commercials?—that's where we're at." She spread her hands, momentarily distracted by the flashy lacquer on her fingernails. "You wanna use the phone, you gotta buy something."

"Yeah, okay. Fair enough." Silas wandered down the snack aisle. Memories flickered at the edges of his mind. He could almost hear Lily's footsteps behind him—but, no, that was just another customer. The back hall was as dim as he remembered, the door to the bathroom shut. The second *Customers ONLY!!!* sign taped at eye level was new, perhaps intended as a stern reminder to those foolish enough to try wiggling the knob.

He turned, half-expecting to find Lily waiting patiently for him to finish. Instead, he saw only Maisie leaning against the register, apparently suspicious that he might break into the bathroom without providing the requisite compensation. She waggled a bright yellow rubber ducky at him, shaking the key tied around the toy's neck as she called out, "Bathroom's locked. Too many folks try to sneak in when I'm not looking."

Silas shook his head, then blindly selected a bottle and carried it over to the counter. Heads turned as he slammed it down harder than he'd intended.

Maisie raised her penciled-on eyebrows. "Needa see some ID."

Sighing, he handed his driver's license over. He hadn't meant to grab a beer. He didn't even drink, and he wasn't about to start, not with the return drive waiting for him at the end of day. He'd promised to be back on the road before dark.

Snap. "California boy, huh?"

"Born and raised." The grin felt uncomfortable on his face, as if any expression of joy so close to the site of his family's greatest tragedy was a slight to Lily's memory. He laid a crumpled twenty-dollar bill on the counter. "So, can I use your phone now?"

"Brooks," Maisie muttered. Her eyes widened. "I know you. You're that miracle kid."

Silas gripped his wallet in both hands and said nothing.

"You *are*. You were in all the papers. You know, they never did find the animal that tore up that deputy and poor Evelyn. She was a nice lady."

Silas considered leaving, but he'd sworn to Memma that he would call from the One Stop before driving up to the cabin, and again later on his way back to the highway. Knowing his mother, she'd been sitting by the phone for several hours with a full itinerary, so she would know the precise moment to start worrying. The thought was strangely comforting.

"And that other guy, Drew? The one who ran the plow your... *moms* drove into town?" The smile slid from Silas's face. There was a hint of accusation in Maisie's tone as she said, "His kid's all grown up now, just like you. She's teaching my kid at the elementary school. Kinda sad, her not knowing what became of her daddy and all—a real shame. Don't suppose you might remember anything? Anything new?"

"I was just a kid." Silas was surprised he could get the words out around the lump in his throat. If Lily was here—

But she wasn't. All these years later, the reminder still felt like a metal sliver twisting in his heart.

But that was going to change. It was why he'd come here, driven cross-country despite his mothers' protests: to bring his sister home.

"Yeah." *Snap.* "It *was* a long time ago, I guess."

Silas tipped his head toward the phone.

Maisie reached for the handset, holding it hostage. "You ever watch that show—what's it called...*Cryptid Seekers*?"

The title had a familiar ring to it. And then he remembered: countless messages left on their answering machine, a barrage of emails, the unwanted visitors with cameras, knocking.

Maisie continued as if he'd answered her question through facial tics alone. "They came around asking about all kinds of crazy shit, like you wouldn't believe."

"You might be surprised," Silas said, and winced internally as Maisie perked up.

"Oh?"

"I just meant...I believe they came around here asking. But the case has been closed for years."

"Yeah, limited resources, cutbacks, blah-blah." Maisie flapped a hand. Her eyes glittered. "Still, quite the unsolved mystery. They said the same thing that killed the deputy might'a been what got your sister when you two went missing. Said they never found her, either. Is that why you're here?"

Silas's breath rushed out. For the first time, Maisie seemed taken aback. She stammered, "Oh, I'm—I'm sorry. I didn't— Me and my big dumb mouth."

"It's fine." A line had formed behind Silas during Maisie's interrogation. She jerked her chin, signaling for him to come around the counter as the next customer stepped forward.

"I didn't mean nothing by it," she said, muttering out the corner of her mouth. "It just gets so fucking boring around here. Sorry."

Silas turned his back and dialed their old home number in.

Emma answered on the first ring. "Hello? Si?"

"Hey, Memma. I can't talk long. Just wanted to let you know I made it. I'll call back a few hours from now."

"What time?" The tension in her voice was palpable, humming like a live wire stretched from California to Minnesota.

"I don't know yet. Depends on..." *How long it takes me to find her. If I can find her.* "I'll call as soon as I'm done."

"Hang on, your mom wants to talk to you." Emma called out, "Claire? *Claire!*"

Silas flinched. The distance between them did nothing to dampen the shrillness in her tone. He pictured his mothers seated together on the couch for the remainder of the day, hands knotted into a nervous ball of fingers. Waiting for him to call.

Fearing that he wouldn't.

A voice spoke into his ear, soft and hesitant. "Silas?"

"I'm here, Mom. Just checking in." Longing to embrace his mothers, unable to offer physical reassurance, he hugged himself instead, pressing the handset to his ear. "Miss you."

"We miss you too." Claire sniffed. Was she crying? Silas swallowed back tears, conscious of Maisie, eavesdropping behind him. "You'll be careful?"

"I will."

"Out before dark?"

"Yes."

"And you remember how to find her?"

Silas ducked his head, whispering into the receiver. "The camera, yeah."

A gasp, barely audible. "I love you."

In the background, Emma shouted, "We both do!"

Claire laughed. The sound warmed Silas inside. Smiling, he said, "I love you too. Both of you."

"Si?"

"Yeah?"

"Thank you. For…" A watery sigh. "I'm sorry we never—We always meant to…"

"It's okay." Silas checked his watch, blinking his vision clear. "I'd better get going. I love you. We'll talk soon."

"You come back to us."

"I will. I promise."

Silas ended the call and rounded the counter, murmuring an apology as he shouldered through the line of customers.

Maisie called after him, "Hey, man! You forgot your beer!"

Silas rolled down the truck windows, breathing in the clean summer air as the One Stop receded in his rearview mirror. The cashier was standing in the parking lot, waving her arms. Silas surprised himself by laughing aloud. What a fucking head-trip that had been.

In an effort to dispel his anxiety, he turned the radio on. The stations hissed static. An unpleasant memory uncoiled in the back of his mind.

He switched to the CD player, relaxing as a stream of oldies poured through the speakers. Despite his teasing about antiquated technology, he was grateful for the CD Memma had made for his road trip.

Paul Simon was singing about dogs—it was their song, his mothers'. Beyond the nicknames he'd heard them use affectionately on many occasions, plucked from the song's lyrics, Silas had never understood the song's sentimental value. He'd always assumed it was an inside joke between them. So much of their history was a mystery to him. As if the terrible events at the cabin had cleaved his family's timeline in two: before, when they were whole; and after.

Now.

Silas guided the truck up the dirt road. The trees formed a vibrant green corridor, shot through with warm rays of sunlight. Nothing looked familiar. The scenery was foreign without its blanket of monotonous white snow. He drove slowly, tires bumping through ruts and potholes, as he scanned the surrounding forest. He shut off the radio and listened to the silence hovering beyond the rumble of the truck's engine. The absence of wildlife was nothing new.

The gate, however, was. It barred the road just before Evelyn's driveway: a metal monstrosity painted yellow and fixed with a heavy-duty padlock.

Silas got out and spun the dials to the year his mothers had met. The lock clicked open. He pushed back the thick bar, swinging it clear of the road. It squalled, jiggling under his hands. The gate didn't get much use, he supposed; its job was to keep people out.

He hesitated. He was tempted to drive up to Evelyn's first, but he couldn't afford any added delays. And besides, going there would be purely to satisfy the curiosity tugging at his gut. He'd never actually been to Evelyn's cabin as a boy. There were no hidden memories there, waiting to be recovered.

As soon as they'd been able to scrape the funds together—selling the gallery, taking out a second mortgage on their home—his mothers had purchased Evelyn's property. They'd put a gate across the road. A barbed wire fence extended outward to either side and was festooned with *No Trespassing* signs to discourage those who might be tempted to invade on foot. His mothers had poured their life savings into cutting this place off from the rest of the world—an expensive tourniquet cinched tight to prevent the poison from spreading.

They had always been honest with him, not holding anything back. From the time he was a boy recovering in a hospital bed right up until he'd revealed his plans to return, Emma and Claire had answered every question that could be answered. The rest was speculation.

Doubt.

Worry.

Because they couldn't be certain that whatever had possessed Lily had died with her. According to his mothers, it had already survived once, had been transformed.

They had begged him not to come.

But Lily's death had taken a piece of Silas's soul and left him with a promise, unfulfilled. His mothers had seen that—how could they not? It was present in every canvas Silas painted, every mural. Tragedy haunted his brushstrokes. He buried his sorrow beneath layers of paint, but every line and shadow spoke his loss aloud to those close enough to read the firm press of his mouth, the way his eyes drifted out of focus, back to the past.

Without Lily, he could never move forward.

Silas closed the gate behind him and continued on. Pulling into the overgrown clearing at the end of the driveway, he stared at the hole in the ground where the cabin had once stood, now reduced to a few crumbling concrete walls the earth had yet to claim. He squeezed his eyes shut, took a deep breath. His heart was pounding.

You can do this.

Before he could change his mind, he retrieved a shovel, a sledgehammer, and a black duffel bag from the toolbox in the bed of his truck.

Time had not been kind to the stream; it was little more than a trickle now, hardly the rushing torrent that had swept him toward the lake as a child. He stepped across it, secretly hoping the lake would also be diminished, dried into a hardened patch of cracked mud, devoid of life.

But when he emerged into the overgrown clearing, White Hook Lake was waiting for him, curved around the site of the boarding school. Sunlight sparkled on the surface of the water. Gentle waves lapped at the shore. A warm breeze ruffled the branches of the pines.

The buildings had deteriorated into rough suggestions of their former shape, reclaimed by the encroaching greenery. But Silas found the well easily enough.

He still dreamed of it, every night.

The well's stone-rimmed mouth gaped up at him. Silas wasted no time at all. He poured all of his rage and frustration, his tireless grief—the nights he woke, drenched in sweat, screaming; the moments he felt too paralyzed by fear to move or breathe— into the swing of his arms.

He swung the sledgehammer at the well's rim, knocking the stones from around its yawning black maw until it was a toothless thing. Nothing to be feared. He shoved the stone slab and watched it tumble into the enlarged hole, blocking the throat. Choking it.

Good. Let it starve.

The sun was sinking lower in the sky. Silas turned toward the trees. The anger had rushed out of him, leaving him feeling hollow. Drained. The black bag dragged at the end of his arm like a lead weight. But he'd come for a reason, crossed hundreds of miles and ignored his mothers' warnings. He couldn't stop now.

Lily was waiting for him.

The pit was a barren patch of earth. The animal bones within had been layered over with detritus, the exposed ones sunbleached but otherwise undisturbed.

Silas crouched at the edge of the pit where he'd once struggled against Emma's unbreakable grasp, where he'd looked back and glimpsed Claire shoveling snow with her hands.

There.

He could just make out the irregular shape of a camera, dangling from its fraying strap.

The authorities had never recovered Lily's body. They hadn't known to go looking again. His mothers had never mentioned her return.

Silas knelt beneath the tallest pine ringing the pit and brushed at the loose earth. He uncovered Lily in pieces, dusting the dirt from each bone with reverence before placing it carefully inside the duffel bag. He worked slowly, patiently. This wasn't a task to be rushed, tarnished by fear and regrets.

It was a reunion.

The only one they would ever have.

"We're going home, Lily," Silas whispered as he drew the zipper closed, resting his forehead against his sister's remains. He could feel the press of her skull through the bag, the warmth of her rising up to greet him.

The returning whisper was soft and clear.

Music to his ears.

"Together. Just like I promised."

ACKNOWLEDGMENTS

WHEN I SET out to write this story, I wanted to explore the depth and meaning of love in the face of difficult circumstances. So first, I must thank those who taught me to love and be loved. To Dre, my husband and best friend, thank you for all of the times you've anchored me during this journey and for always believing in my dreams. And thank you for listening to the early draft of this novel and for helping me talk through some of the wilder scenarios in this story, as you do with everything I write. Without you, none of this would have been possible. To my grandmother, Leota Grady, thank you for your love and unfailing support. You were the first to set me on this journey all those years ago, when you handed me a paperback copy of Stephen King's *IT* in a used bookstore. I will forever treasure the scary movies and books we've shared together. To David Weist, your love has always been something I can count on no matter what, and I am lucky to call you my father. Thank you for providing assistance with the medical details contained within this novel. Any errors are one hundred percent the fault of the English major. To Toni Weist, thank you for being my shark-loving cheerleader. Your enthusiasm never fails to make me smile. To Heidi Andrews, my wonderful friend and fellow horror lover, I owe my heartfelt thanks for reading the early draft of this novel and for providing feedback. Having you to talk to over these last few years has kept me sane. I am so grateful to have you in my life. And finally, I want to thank my mother, Kathi Grady, who was the first to listen to my story ideas when I was a girl and the first to believe I would succeed at writing. Were she still with us, I know she would be proud.

Thank you to my editor, Marissa van Uden, for crawling inside my head for this journey. Your hard work and invaluable insight helped transform this novel into the lovely, twisted piece of work it is today. To Rob Carroll and the team at Dark Matter INK, thank you for your tireless efforts. This debut novelist feels so fortunate to have found a home with you for her story.

And to you, readers…Without you, we writers would be echoes in the void. Thank you for turning pages to keep the nightmare alive.

ABOUT THE AUTHOR

R. L. MEZA is an author of horror and dark science fiction. She lives in a century-old Victorian house on the coast of northern California, with her husband and the collection of strange animals they call family.

Also Available or Coming Soon from Dark Matter INK

Human Monsters: A Horror Anthology
Edited by Sadie Hartmann & Ashley Saywers
ISBN 978-1-958598-00-9

Zero Dark Thirty: The 30 Darkest Stories from Dark Matter Magazine, 2021–'22
Edited by Rob Carroll
ISBN 978-1-958598-16-0

Linghun by Ai Jiang
ISBN 978-1-958598-02-3

Monstrous Futures: A Sci-Fi Horror Anthology
Edited by Alex Woodroe
ISBN 978-1-958598-07-8

Haunted Reels: Stories from the Minds of Professional Filmmakers curated by David Lawson
ISBN 978-1-958598-13-9

The Vein by Stephanie Nelson
ISBN 978-1-958598-15-3

Other Minds by Eliane Boey
ISBN 978-1-958598-19-1

Frost Bite by Angela Sylvaine
ISBN 978-1-958598-03-0

Monster Lairs: A Dark Fantasy Horror Anthology
Edited by Anna Madden
ISBN 978-1-958598-08-5

Chopping Spree by Angela Sylvaine
ISBN 978-1-958598-31-3

The Bleed by Stephen S. Schreffler
ISBN 978-1-958598-11-5

Free Burn by Drew Huff
ISBN 978-1-958598-26-9

The House at the End of Lacelean Street
by Catherine McCarthy
ISBN 978-1-958598-23-8

The Off-Season: An Anthology of Coastal New Weird
Edited by Marissa van Uden
ISBN 978-1-958598-24-5

The Dead Spot: Stories of Lost Girls
by Angela Sylvaine
ISBN 978-1-958598-27-6

Grim Root by Bonnie Jo Stufflebeam
ISBN 978-1-958598-36-8

Voracious by Belicia Rhea
ISBN 978-1-958598-25-2

Abducted by Patrick Barb
ISBN 978-1-958598-37-5

Available or Coming Soon from Dark Hart Books

All These Subtle Deceits by C. S. Humble
ISBN 978-1-958598-04-7

All the Prospect Around Us by C. S. Humble
ISBN 978-1-958598-05-4

Rootwork by Tracy Cross
ISBN 978-1-958598-01-6

Mosaic by Catherine McCarthy
ISBN 978-1-958598-06-1

Apparitions by Adam Pottle
ISBN 978-1-958598-18-4

I Can See Your Lies by Izzy Lee
ISBN 978-1-958598-28-3

A Gathering of Weapons by Tracy Cross
ISBN 978-1-958598-38-2